Praise for *The Chaos of Standing Still*

A Winter 2017-18 Indie Next Pick

★ "Absorbing from first page to last, Brody's novel
gradually unveils Ryn's complicated history and
celebrates her most profound moments of truth."
—*Publishers Weekly*, starred review

"Jessica Brody has made me believe that getting
stuck in an airport overnight would be the most
fantastic thing in the world. I fell hard for this story
of love, loss, friendship, and bad airport food."
—MORGAN MATSON,
New York Times bestselling author of
The Unexpected Everything

"A beautiful and deftly told story of letting go
and starting over. *The Chaos of Standing Still* is
laugh-out-loud funny, deeply stirring, and of
course wonderfully swoony. You'll love it."
—JULIE BUXBAUM,
New York Times bestselling author of
Tell Me Three Things

"Even those who haven't experienced a devastating
loss like Ryn's will relate to her struggle: feeling stuck
between moving on and holding on. Ryn's one-year/
one-night journey to find her new normal is funny,
insightful, empowering, and filled with heart."
—TAMARA IRELAND STONE,
New York Times bestselling author of
Every Last Word

Also by Jessica Brody

The Chaos of Standing Still

Jessica Brody

Simon Pulse

New York London Toronto Sydney New Delhi

SIMON PULSE

An imprint of Simon & Schuster Children's Publishing Division

1230 Avenue of the Americas, New York, New York 10020

First Simon Pulse paperback edition May 2019

Text copyright © 2017 by Jessica Brody Entertainment, LLC

Cover illustration copyright © 2019 by Karina Granda

Also available in a Simon Pulse hardcover edition.

"Eternal Flame"

Words and Music by Billy Steinberg, Tom Kelly, and Susanna Hoffs

Copyright © 1988 Sony/ATV Music Publishing LLC and Bangophile Music

All Rights on behalf of Sony/ATV Music Publishing LLC

Administered by Sony/ATV Music Publishing LLC,

424 Church Street, Suite 1200, Nashville, TN 37219

All Rights on behalf of Bangophile Music Controlled and

Administered by Songs Of Universal, Inc.

International Copyright Secured All Rights Reserved

Reprinted by Permission of Hal Leonard LLC

Cover design and illustration by Karina Granda copyright © 2019 by Simon and Schuster, Inc.

Background paper texture copyright © 2019 by Shutterstock

Back cover snow pattern copyright © 2019 by iStock

All rights reserved, including the right of reproduction in whole or in part in any form.

SIMON PULSE and colophon are registered trademarks of Simon & Schuster, Inc.

For information about special discounts for bulk purchases, please contact Simon & Schuster Special Sales at 1-866-506-1949 or business@simonandschuster.com.

The Simon & Schuster Speakers Bureau can bring authors to your live event.

For more information or to book an event contact the Simon & Schuster Speakers Bureau at 1-866-248-3049 or visit our website at www.simonspeakers.com.

Interior designed by Mike Rosamilia

The text of this book was set in Weiss Std.

Manufactured in the United States of America

2 4 6 8 10 9 7 5 3 1

The Library of Congress has cataloged the hardcover edition as follows:

Names: Brody, Jessica, author.

Title: The chaos of standing still / by Jessica Brody.

Description: First Simon Pulse hardcover edition. | New York : Simon Pulse, 2017. |

Summary: Ryn, eighteen, trapped by a massive blizzard in the Denver airport, meets some unique characters who help her cope with survivor's guilt on the first anniversary of her best friend's death.

Identifiers: LCCN 2017007753 | ISBN 9781481499187 (hardcover) | ISBN 9781481499200 (eBook)

Subjects: | CYAC: Interpersonal relations—Fiction. | Best friends—Fiction. | Friendship—Fiction. | Guilt—Fiction. | Airports—Fiction. | Blizzards—Fiction. | Death—Fiction.

Classification: LCC PZ7.B786157 Ch 2017 | DDC [Fic]—dc23

LC record available at https://lccn.loc.gov/2017007753

ISBN 9781481499194 (pbk)

To Nicole Ellul,
for always being a safe place
to land in a snowstorm

* Contents *

Descending Through Weather

The view from the window of seat 27F is like trying to look through a snow globe after you've shaken it so hard the artificial white flakes don't know which way is down.

"Restless" is the word that comes to mind.

Is it safe to land a plane in a snowstorm?

I stroke my fingertip against the screen of my phone, leaving behind a sweaty streak of mysterious residue.

Is it normal for fingertips to sweat?

My heart pounds in anticipation of our landing. In the battle between solid ground and thirty thousand feet in the sky, solid ground wins every time. Hands down.

We've been circling for almost forty-five minutes, waiting for our turn on the *one* plowed runway.

I glance around to make sure no one is looking, unlock the screen of my phone, and swipe the little green Airplane Mode toggle to Off.

My phone searches for a signal. I silently will it to connect. But it won't. We're not close enough to humanity yet.

I toggle the switch back to On.

The flight attendants were all asked to take their seats fifteen minutes ago. "We're expecting a little turbulence as we descend through some weather in Denver," the pilot said.

Why do they call it "weather"? Why not use a less innocuous word? A more accurate word? "We're expecting you to be bounced around like the last few Tic Tacs in the box while we descend through this shitstorm that we probably shouldn't be flying through to begin with."

"Weather" could mean anything. It could mean sunshine and fucking rainbows. It could mean warm rain and cool breezes. But they never use it to describe anything good, do they? When it comes to the airline industry, "weather" is unequivocally bad.

Maybe that's how I should start referring to my life.

As in, "Don't worry about Ryn. She's just descending through some weather. It'll be choppy for a bit."

At least then it implies transience. Weather always changes. It eventually morphs into something else. It never stays for long.

It sure as hell beats the term supplied by the therapist my mother has been making me see for the past ten months. "Survivor's guilt."

There's nothing short-term about that.

I will always be a survivor. I will always be the girl who didn't get in the car that day. That will be my identity until the day I die.

After that, no one can call me a survivor anymore.

∞

Miraculously, through the chaos of white, I finally spot the ground below. It's dark down there, even though it's only two o'clock in the afternoon. Spotting the ground makes me feel how I imagine old-time sailors felt when they spotted land after months in treacherous seas. It's a beacon of hope. I am that much closer to not perishing in this storm. I am that much closer to continuing my legacy as a survivor.

The plane shudders, dropping what feels like a thousand feet in a heartbeat.

A few passengers yelp.

What causes turbulence?

Do pilots ever get scared when they fly?

I peer down at my screen and try the toggle again. This time, my phone starts to connect. We are close enough to make contact with the rest of the world.

I know I'm not supposed to use my portable electronic device in transmission mode until after we've landed. As a girl who's never so much as stolen a cookie from a cookie jar, this little act of defiance makes me feel strangely alive. Is this what it's like to be a criminal?

What do kleptomaniacs feel when they steal something?

Fortunately for me, my crimes will most likely go unpunished, because no one is around to witness them. The flight attendants are still fastened into their double-duty restraints.

Why do flight attendants have different seat belts than the rest of the passengers?

The guy sitting in the aisle seat next to me has been completely absorbed in his e-reader since we took off. The fear in this cabin is palpable. I'm surprised the oxygen masks weren't released after the collective breath everyone stole when we started to toss around the sky like a balloon that someone let the helium out of. But this guy has barely looked up. Maybe he knows something the rest of us don't. Maybe his book is just that good.

The middle seat between us is empty.

I wonder if that person was running late and missed the flight.

If we crash in the next five minutes, two months from now, he'll be sitting in a stuffy therapist's office getting outfitted with the shiny new label of "Survivor's guilt." It will fit him as awkwardly as a suit made for a one armed, three-legged man. No matter how you put it on, there will always be an extra limb dangling out. An extra hole that will never be filled.

As soon as I have bars, I race to open an Internet search page and type in my first query.

Is it safe to land a plane in a snowstorm?

The answer surprises me, It's not the storm in the air that's the problem. It's what it's doing to the ground. Ice, slickness, snow-clogged runways. Nothing that makes me want to choose pilot as a career path.

The rush of finding the answer eases my anxiety. The answer itself does not.

My fingers move fast, one by one resolving the remainder of my backlogged inquiries. In the next few minutes, I learn the following:

1. It's not particularly normal to get sweaty
   fingers, but it's not *abnormal*, either.
2. Turbulence is the random, chaotic motion of
   air, caused by changes in air currents.
3. Yes, sometimes pilots *do* get scared.
4. Kleptomaniacs feel a fancy cocktail of emotions
   when they steal something: fear, anxiety,
   sometimes even relief.
5. Flight attendant seat belts are actually safer
   than ours. They need to physically be able to
   help us in the event of an emergency.

The adrenaline of the search distracts me from the fact that we are landing on what could be a runway made of slippery glass, and I highly doubt this plane has been equipped with snow tires.

We touch down hard, and the plane seems to tilt too far to the left, like the pilot's attempting to do an impressive "wheelie." I clutch my phone in my hand as the brakes screech and complain, and I wonder if sparks are flying out behind us. I suck in a breath along with the rest of the passengers. I bet they're all really wishing they'd stayed in Atlanta right about now.

We finally slow to a safe, controlled crawl, and the plane erupts in applause.

I skip the ovation and type another question into my awaiting search box.

Why do some people live while others die?

Although the search results are numerous, there is still no conclusive answer.

I'm not sure why this time I expected there to be one.

∞

Terminal A of the Denver International Airport is a hornet's nest that some idiot eight-year-old boy has smacked with a baseball bat. The crankiness in the air hits me like a brick wall as soon as I step off the plane.

Every chair is taken. Tired passengers are sitting (and lying) on the floor. Small children are running through a maze of bodies. Gate agents are fighting for airtime on the overhead speaker system. People are grumbling to each other about flight delays and their ill-fated decision to fly through this particular airport.

I check the clock on my phone, which has recently synced to the new time zone. It's now 2:58 p.m. Mountain Standard Time. Even after our in-flight game of Ring Around the Denver Airport, I still have more than thirty minutes to make my connection.

Plenty of time.

I grip my phone tighter in my hand, feeling the sharp corners of my *Doctor Who* Tardis case biting my skin. Gate A16. All I have to do is get to gate A16. That's where I'll find a plane waiting to take me home to San Francisco.

Home.

It's been eleven months, and the word still doesn't sound right in my head. San Francisco isn't Home. It's a city on a postcard. A pin on my mother's vision board. A destination on a boarding pass.

Then again, Atlanta isn't Home either.

And Portland?

No. Portland is a just a dark spot in a rearview mirror that gets farther away with each passing day. All the things I once loved about the Portland house—drawing in my sketch pad on the back porch, Mom and Dad sharing a love seat in front of the TV, Lottie sleeping on the pullout trundle bed in my room—is gone.

That's the thing about Homes. After you lose the things that make them worthy of a capital *H*, all you're left with is an empty, lowercase house.

My phone buzzes in my hand and I swipe on the screen.

The tiny red number above the message app has changed from 1 to 9. I tap it and read seven texts from my mom and one from my dad. Pretty typical. Mom's texts usually outnumber Dad's by at least three to one. She's a big fan of texting. She says it's the least intrusive means of communication. Then she sends eight stream of consciousness messages in a row.

Mom: Hey . . . have you landed yet?

Mom: The news says there's a huge storm in Denver!

Mom: I hope your pilot is properly trained.

Mom: Do they practice landing in snow?

Mom: I mean like real snow. Not simulated snow.

Mom: Simulated snow is NOT the same as real snow.

Mom: Ryn?

Mom: Text me as soon as you land!

Dad: Hope you made it safely to Denver! I hear there's a big storm.

I delete the texts without responding and return to the home screen, holding my breath as I watch the little red counter above the app return safely to 1.

One unread message.

I release the breath and shut off the screen.

Hiking my bag farther up on my shoulder, I step into the crowd. Bodies press against me from all sides. There's a distinct smell in the air. The kind that results from staying in one place for too long.

I glance up and take note of my current gate number. A4. I bow my head and push on, reminding myself that I only need to get to gate A16.

The plane waiting there may not take me Home, but it can certainly take me far away from this.

∞

The only reason I have a layover in Denver is because Dad wanted to save money. So he booked me a flight from Atlanta to San Francisco on one of those cheap-o airlines that makes you zigzag across the country to get anywhere and charges you for every little thing.

Do you want a sip of water?

That'll be two dollars.

Do you want your stuff to fly with you?

It's twenty-five dollars to check a bag or thirty-five to carry one on.

I'm surprised they haven't outfitted the bathroom doors with coin-operated locks. You have to pay to preselect your seat, but if you want to sit on the toilet, that's totally free. Something to be grateful for, I suppose.

I think about writing this one down. Dr. Judy, my therapist, says there are silver linings everywhere—hidden in plain sight. It's our job to look for them and identify them. She wants me to keep a list in my phone of all the ones I find. But somehow, I don't think she'd appreciate my literal toilet humor here. Plus, if I added this one, I'd have to show her the rest of the list, which consists of approximately zero items.

I guess there was no way for Dad to know that this New Year's Eve Denver would experience one of the worst blizzards in its history.

That's a pretty bold statement given, you know, how long Denver has been around.

When was the city of Denver founded?

I try not to run into anyone as I walk through the sea of people and tap the question into my phone.

1858.

So I suppose I shouldn't exactly blame Dad when I arrive at gate A16 and spot the big fat DELAYED sign posted behind the counter, dooming me to spend God knows how long in this over-crowded airport full of cranky travelers.

It would be so easy to, though. Blame him, that is.

But Dr. Judy says that's a trap you don't want to fall into. It only feels safe for a minute. Every minute after that is just paving a road to eternal misery.

I've never actually told her (or anyone, for that matter) that I'm already on that road. That I've been on that road for the past eleven months and thirty-one days. That I'm not sure life will ever be anything else but that road.

And since I'm already there, I guess there's no harm in laying a few more bricks.

I swipe at the screen of my phone, tap on the Productivity folder, and open my note-taking app. I click on my *other* list—the one Dr. Judy doesn't know about—and add three lines.

72. I blame Dad for being too stingy to spring for a nonstop flight home.
73. I blame Cheap-O Airlines for placing their "hub" in a city where it snows.
74. I blame Shannon for marrying my father and making him move to Atlanta.

When I finish typing, I do what I always do. I scroll up, skimming my long list of grievances, until I find the first three stones in my path to eternal misery. The ones that started it all.

1. I blame the cook at Pop's for serving me a beef hot dog that was way past its expiration date.

2. I blame Lottie for being a health-nut
   vegetarian and ordering salad.

3. I blame the universe for giving me food
   poisoning that day when I should have been in
   that car too. When I should be dead.

I stand in the long line of people ready to grumble to the poor, overworked gate agent about the delayed flight. As if she, herself, placed an online weather order directly from God.com. I overhear her saying the same things she probably told the last ten grumblers and will repeat to the next ten.

"No, we don't know when the flight to San Francisco will take off."

"No, we can't reroute you through another city. All flights out of Denver are currently on a weather delay."

"No, I don't know how long this storm will last."

"If you want more information, please see a representative at our customer service counter at gate A44."

Okay, so now I just have to get to gate A44.

As I pass by the food court and step onto one of the many long, moving walkways that appear to define the Denver airport, I hear my stomach protest my decision to skip breakfast this morning. It sounds a lot like the grumblers waiting at gate A16.

I lean against the railing of the walkway and type furiously into my phone.

Why do stomachs make noise when you're hungry?

I press Search, but before I can read any of the results, my foot snags on something and I go tumbling forward. My phone flies into the air, and I, in a failed effort to catch it, crash into something hard before landing ungracefully—facedown—on the dirty airport floor.

My stomach, always with the one-track mind, lets out another growl.

My chin feels like it's on fire. I try to stand up but a wave of dizziness overtakes me, and I settle for kneeling. That's when I see what I tripped on. The end of the moving walkway. I was so focused on my typing, I didn't realize I had reached stationary ground again. That's also when I see what I crashed into.

A person.

A guy.

He's on his butt a few yards away. Dazedly, I watch him jump to his feet and rush over to me.

"Are you okay?" His hand reaches down to help me. Embarrassed, I bypass it and push myself up.

"Yeah," I mumble. "Just great."

Once standing, I have a better view of my would-be rescuer. He looks about my age. He's dressed in jeans and a navy blue T-shirt with Animal, the Muppet, on the front. The strap of his messenger bag is pinching the shirt so that Animal's overly bushy eyebrows look like they're knitted together in confusion. Despite the snow globe outside, I don't see a coat anywhere on or near his person.

A connector, like me. Probably flying from one warm climate to another.

His hair is short and dark, his skin is light brown, but his eyes are iridescent blue. It's a startling contrast.

If I were anyone else in the world, I'd say he was cute.

But I'm not anyone else in the world. I'm me. So he's just a guy.

"That's the thing about moving walkways," he teases. "They kind of stop."

And, apparently, also a comedian.

"Thanks." I force a smile and bend down to pick up my fallen phone. I'm about to swipe it on to check the message app, when he says, "Where you heading to?"

He really wants to do this? Right here in the middle of the moving walkway junction between gates A32 and A34?

I can hear Dr. Judy's voice in my head, reminding me that my actions affect people. Even if I don't want them to. Strangers don't know what happened to Lottie. They won't understand my desperate need to avoid human interaction (her words). So my best bet is to just be polite.

I clear my throat. "San Francisco. You?"

"Miami. Well, at least, trying to. Or *not* trying to. I haven't figured that part out yet."

I'm not following. But I don't want to get involved. I have my own ambiguity to deal with. "Well, good luck with that," I say, forcing a smile that Dr. Judy would be proud of.

I count the seconds that social propriety requires me to wait before I can turn and leave, but I must miscalculate because he's staring at me like I'm supposed to say something else. Then, to my surprise, he's suddenly reaching for me, finger outstretched toward my face, and I fight the instinct to swat his hand away like a hovering fly.

He points to—but doesn't touch—my chin. "I think the carpet might have taken a little bit of your skin as a souvenir."

I rub at the raw flesh. It screams in response.

"Does it hurt?" he asks.

I adjust my backpack on my shoulders and stand up straighter. "I'll be fine . . . thanks."

Then, without bothering to count another second, I stride off in the direction of the customer service counter, wisely opting to skip the next moving walkway.

Politely exchanging destinations is one thing. Comparing pain thresholds with a complete stranger is a whole other ball game.

Besides, he'd definitely lose.

The Reinvention of Lottie

Lottie Valentine was always reinventing herself. She went by Charlotte for most of her life, until one day, in the middle of eighth grade, she announced that she wanted to go by Lottie instead. Apparently, she'd read the nickname in a book or something and decided she liked it much better. She made an official proclamation to the entire class. *"From this day forth, everyone shall call me Lottie."*

And everyone did.

That was Lottie. She made a decision and it was so.

It wasn't just her name, though. She was constantly changing her hair, her clothes, her favorite shade of lipstick, her signature scent, even her aspirations. She'd come to school dressed like a punk rocker, claiming that she was going to be a rock star when she grew up, and then the next week, she'd come to school dressed in overalls claiming she was going to be a potato farmer so she could eat all the french fries she wanted.

After that it was a psychologist, a personal shopper, a

veterinarian, an astronaut (until she realized how much math was involved), and a little over a year ago, she told me she was going to be a flight attendant. I told her I'd heard that before but she swore to me this one would stick.

"A flight attendant's life is so glamorous!" she waxed poetic. "And free! Nothing to tie you down to one place. Think of all the exotic places you get to go. And the people you meet. You could have a boy in every port!"

It's anyone's guess what might have come after that. Librarian? Beekeeper? Bus driver? Or, who knows, maybe flight attendant really would have stuck.

I'll never know, because two weeks later a fuckbrain with faulty brakes decided to get behind the wheel with more alcohol in his blood than blood.

That was the final reinvention of Lottie.

"Are you gonna move up?" a voice snaps from behind me. It's only then I notice that the line has moved and I'm still standing in the same spot. I turn around to mumble a less than heartfelt "sorry" to the impatient man behind me and then step up, immediately returning my gaze to the young, female flight attendant I've been staring at for the past five minutes. She's leaning against the wall of gate A44, whispering into her phone, her hand covering the mouthpiece. Her whole body seems to be hunched toward the conversation. I watch her eyes dance as she lets out a playful laugh.

I marvel at how much she looks like Lottie. The same crimson gold hair and button nose, the same pole-shaped body and wide-set eyes, even the same flirtatious laugh.

"See," I hear a voice say. "A boy in every port."

I don't turn around at the sound of this voice. I know it's not coming from behind me. It's coming from my own head.

"Why are you even waiting in this line?" the voice whines. "You already checked the information screens like four times. The flight is delayed. What more can they tell you? Let's go find that cute boy with the Muppet shirt."

I glance at the twenty or so people who stand between me and the two overworked employees at the customer service counter. She's probably right. I'm probably wasting my time. The screens gave me no estimated departure time, which probably means there isn't one. But I can't bring myself to step out of line. I need some kind of answer. And right now, those two harried employees are my only hope of getting one.

When I turn back to the redheaded flight attendant, I see that she's no longer on her call. She's now biting her lip as she taps something into the phone.

"I bet she's sexting him," says the voice excitedly. "I bet he's a pilot. Flight attendant–pilot relationships are soooo cliché yet soooo hot. But what's the deal with that awful pantsuit? What happened to the heyday of airline travel when stewardesses wore sexy dresses and cute hats?"

The flight attendant looks up, as if she too can hear the voice, and her eyes land right on me. I quickly avert my gaze, searching for anywhere else to look. I spot a dark haired boy, who looks to be about ten years old, sitting in a nearby chair. He's slouched forward with his chin resting against his chest. For a moment, I think he might be sleeping, but then his head snaps up, and I notice the small handwritten sign hanging around his neck by a thin cord.

UNACCOMPANIED MINER

The sign looks like it was scribbled out in a hurry, hence the misspelling. I attempt to stifle a laugh, but I must not do a very good job because he too looks straight at me. We share a look of commiseration before he drops his head back down.

That poor kid. He looks about as miserable as I feel. If there's anything worse than getting delayed in an airport during a snowstorm, it's getting delayed in an airport during a snowstorm as an unaccompanied minor.

"Forget about him," the voice interrupts. "What's the flight attendant doing?"

I sweep my gaze across the gate to the wall, but it's now occupied by an agitated-looking family with four kids. My flirty flight attendant is gone.

The impatient man behind me clears his throat, and I realize there's another huge gap in front of me. This guy must think that I've never waited in a line before. That I don't know how it works. I mumble another "sorry" and move up.

"When I become a flight attendant, I'm going to work for one of those international airlines where the flight attendants still wear cute minidresses. None of this pantsuit garbage. I mean, really, what is that?"

I think it's called feminism, I silently tell the voice.

"Pshaw. Feminism is a woman's right to dress sexy if she wants to. Pantsuits deprive us of the innate sexiness that is our God-given right."

I know there's no use in arguing. Lottie always wins. Even in death.

∞

I realize you're supposed to tell your therapist everything. That's kind of the point of having the therapist. Otherwise, it's just money down the drain. It'd be like going to the dentist but never opening your mouth to show him your teeth.

But there are a lot of things I haven't told Dr. Judy. For instance, I've never told her about the blame list I keep on my phone. I've never told her about the one unread text message.

And I've certainly never told her that I still talk to my dead best friend.

Because, c'mon, I'm not crazy.

∞

"Wanna hear something crazy?" was how Lottie started pretty much every conversation.

"Always," was always my response.

"Emmett totally just asked to touch my boob." She nodded across the crowded party at a tall, slender guy currently engaged in what looked like a very heated conversation with a Disney princess. I couldn't tell which princess. They all kind of blended together in my mind.

It was my seventeenth birthday, and since I was born the day before Halloween, Lottie decided to throw a birthday/ Halloween bash in my honor. I was convinced that the wall-to-wall people currently standing in Lottie's backyard had come for the Halloween half of the event. Not my birthday. If the invitation had simply read *Ryn's Birthday Bash*, I don't think we would have gotten quite this large a turnout. I didn't know that many people.

But Lottie knew everyone. Or at least, everyone knew Lottie.

I didn't mind getting upstaged by a pagan holiday though. I was used to it by now.

Everyone had dressed up. Per usual, Lottie's costume was the most creative. Mine was the most unoriginal—a hippie. I had already vowed that next year I was going to let Lottie dress me.

"He did *not* ask to touch your boob," I countered her bold accusation.

She nodded emphatically, taking a gulp from her red plastic cup. "He did. I swear to God. He said, 'Hey, Lottie! I just spun the wheel and I got Right Hand on Red!'"

I burst out laughing and stared down at Lottie's costume. She was dressed as a Twister board. She'd taken a skintight white minidress (which, of course, she looked amazing in) and taped rows of red, blue, yellow, and green circles on it. The red dots were unmistakably positioned across her chest, while the blue, yellow, and green dots were stacked respectively underneath.

"Can you believe the nerve of that guy?" she said, shooting an evil look in his direction. But I knew she secretly loved it.

Lottie was the most flirtatious person I'd ever met. She flirted with everyone. Guys, girls, teens, adults, babies, even old ladies in the park. It wasn't weird. It wasn't inappropriate. It was Lottie. She was just shiny. And it's a known fact that people are attracted to shiny things.

"So," I asked, "are you going to let him put Right Hand on Red?"

Lottie bumped me playfully with her shoulder. "Of course not. What kind of girl do you think I am?"

"The kind that tapes large red targets to her boobs."

Lottie giggled. I could tell she had already passed tipsy and was rounding the bases toward full-on drunk. "Besides, I have my eye on a new mystery man tonight."

I laughed as I took in the colorful grid of dots on the front of her dress. "Let's just hope this mystery man doesn't spin Left Hand on Green."

The Denver airport feels like a bargain bin of different kinds of people. Every age, gender, ethnicity, race, religious affiliation, and fashion sense seems to be represented. As I continue to wait in line at the customer service counter, I distract myself by watching people. I spot a young woman dressed in full-on hippie garb (complete with flower headband) glide by on the moving walkway, and it makes me think of that last Halloween party Lottie threw. I wonder what happened to Lottie's Twister dress. It's probably packed in a box in her parents' basement along with the rest of her stuff. The thought of anything belonging to Lottie winding up in a boring cardboard box reminds me of just how disorderly the universe really is.

There're only five people in line in front of me now. I'm not sure how long I've been waiting here, but I figure I'm at least using up time. My fingers itch to swipe on my phone. To check the clock. To ask Google the myriad of questions that have been piling up in my head. Things like:

How much do flight attendants make?

What are the age restrictions for flying as an unaccompanied minor?

When was the game Twister invented?

But I refrain because, last I checked, my battery was at 21 percent. I never let it go below 20. That's when the little battery icon turns red, and I can't deal with the battery icon turning red. All of that toggling On and Off Airplane Mode during our choppy descent must have sucked up a bunch of juice.

I have a charger cable in my backpack but I'd have to get out of line to use it. And I'm too close to quit now.

So I clutch the phone in my hand, rubbing my thumb back and forth against the sharp edges of my Tardis case.

A woman at the counter starts yelling at one of the airline employees, ranting something about how they can't call it customer service if they refuse to actually *serve* you. I watch her take out her phone and press a button on the screen. She holds it up like she's taking a photo.

"I'm filming you right now," she warns. "And I'll send this video to your supervisor. I'll do it. So tell me again what you just said."

"Ma'am," the employee replies, desperately clinging to what little patience she has left. "Please put that away."

"Why?" the woman shrieks, panning the phone this way and that like a crazed documentary filmmaker. "Afraid of what your supervisor will think? Afraid the corporate office will see how you *really* treat people?"

The frazzled energy in this small, confined space is starting to make my breathing erratic. If my phone battery weren't so dangerously close to the red zone, I'd blast some music in my ears.

"Fine!" the woman yells, stuffing her phone back into her purse. "But I'm calling my lawyer. I've had about enough of this bullshit." Then she stomps away from the desk.

Four people.

I hear another commotion to my right, and turn to see the Unaccompanied Minor boy getting ushered away by an airport employee in a dark suit.

"Oh, come on!" the boy yells. "This is preposterous!"

"Sorry," the employee says without looking sorry at all. "Airline policy."

"This is the perfect example of common sense tripping over the frivolity of bureaucratic red tape," the boy argues. "I am fully capable of using the lavatory myself."

The employee ignores his protests and proceeds to escort him toward the men's room. I feel horrible for that kid.

There's another throat cleared behind me, and I instinctively take a step forward.

Three people.

"I really need to get to Detroit *tonight*," the next passenger is saying. "Is there any other flight you can get me on? I don't care if I have to go through Honolulu—I just have to get there tonight."

My stomach seizes in panic.

Tonight?

Why wouldn't he get there tonight? It's barely three o'clock. Is there a chance the flights might not leave until *tomorrow?*

No. That's not possible. I can't stay here. I'll get out there and shovel that runway myself if I have to.

The thought of staying the night in Denver makes my head buzz.

The thought of having to spend tomorrow—New Year's Day—around this many people is simply unbearable.

The thought of watching the clock strike 10:05 a.m. in any other time zone is—

The gate agent sighs. "I will check, but as of now, there are no flights leaving Denver. Can I have your confirmation number?"

Confirmation number. Right. I'm going to need that.

Which means I'm going to have to turn my phone back on.

My pulse instantly kicks up a notch. I try to steady my breathing, warning myself not to get too excited. I'm only going to pull up my confirmation number. Then the phone is going off again.

I click the button and swipe my finger across the lock. But the sight of the screen suddenly makes me dizzy.

Oh God. This is all wrong.

The home screen. It's a mess! Everything is in the wrong

place. All my folders are gone. The apps are scattered haphazardly in no particular order. The weather app is fraternizing with the calendar and the clock. The camera is comingling with the notes app and the music app. The camera is not supposed to be next to the notes app *or* the music app! It's supposed to be safely tucked away in the Photography folder with the photos app and the photo editing apps.

I desperately swipe right three times, my throat tightening with every jumbled, disorganized page.

What is happening?

Did my phone reset somehow?

Do I have a virus?

Do phones get viruses?

I would ask Google, but I can't even find the Web browser!

Then my gaze falls on the messaging app and my heart sputters to a dead halt.

The little red badge with the number 1 is gone.

No unread messages.

I feel my knees get wobbly. I've never fainted before, but this must be how it starts.

I jump out of the customer service line. The impatient man behind me must be rejoicing. I stumble over to a rare empty chair and collapse into it, staring blankly at my phone. At the mess of icons. At the sad, empty message app.

I can't breathe.

Oh my God, I can't *breathe!*

Hot moisture stings my eyes, blurring my view of the anarchy.

Then the phone vibrates, and I let out a yelp, blinking the incoming tears away.

Incoming Call flashes across the screen.

And the number displayed on the caller ID is *my* phone number.

The Reinvention of Ryn

Lottie tried to reinvent me once. It didn't go over well. She took me to the mall and bought me all kinds of clothes on her father's credit card. He was an investment banker who made up for hardly ever being home by paying the Visa bill and never asking questions.

Standing in that dressing room, surrounded by the carnage of Lottie's discerning taste, I looked good. The dresses were all the right length. The colors all coordinated. The stripes weren't too stripy. But that was with Lottie sitting in the corner offering commentary like a sports announcer. Once I got home and stood alone in the context of my real life—my room, my mirror, my music on the speakers—all the clothes looked off somehow. Out of place. Like I had raided someone else's closet. A girl much more adventurous and daring and interesting than me. A girl who wore *stripes*.

An hour later I drove myself back to the mall and returned everything.

"Would you like store credit?" the saleslady asked. It was the same woman who had happily swiped Lottie's shiny black Visa only a few hours ago. She didn't seem too thrilled about erasing the commission right off her paycheck with every return tag she scanned.

"No," I said politely. "Just put it back on the same card."

The next morning at school Lottie frowned at my customary jeans, hoodie, and sneakers. The same old, same old Kathryn Gilbert.

"What happened?" she asked with a pout. "We picked out such cute stuff for you!"

I racked my brain trying to think of how to explain it in a way that someone like Lottie would understand. Someone who reinvented herself daily. Like it was nothing.

"When I got home, none of it seemed to fit anymore."

Lottie scowled. "How is that even possible? It all fit in the dressing room."

I shrugged again. "I guess it was just a trick of the light."

A crying baby wails over my left shoulder as I stare at the vibrating phone in my hand.

One time Lottie made me watch some old show called *The Twilight Zone*. Every episode was a weird story about something unexplainable. Watching my own phone number appear on the screen, I feel like maybe I'm trapped in one of those episodes.

If I answer it, will my own voice be on the other line?

Like from the past?

Or the future?

I take my chances. "Hello?"

"Hey," a somewhat familiar, lighthearted male voice says. "Is Danny Ocean there?"

Curiouser and curiouser.

"Um . . . who?"

"Danny Ocean." A long, expectant pause. "You know, from *Ocean's Eleven*."

I frown. "Ocean's what?"

"*Eleven*. The movie. George Clooney plays a thief. And you're a phone thief. Because you stole my phone."

I balk, unsure which of these randomly strung together sentences I should address first. "I've never seen *Ocean's Eleven*."

There's a peculiar gurgling sound on the other end. "What? How could you never have seen *Ocean's Eleven*? It's a classic! I mean, the original was good, but the remake was *soooo* much better."

Somewhere over my shoulder, the sobbing baby lets out burp, followed by a giggle.

"You know what?" the caller says after an awkward silence. "Never mind. I think you have my phone and I have yours."

Suddenly, like a plane connecting with the icy ground, everything shudders into place. The moving walkway, my award winning clumsiness, his chest, my face, the airport carpet, my chin.

The guy. The Muppet shirt guy. He must have also dropped his phone in the collision. I must have picked his up by mistake.

But how could I have not noticed?

I pull the phone away from my ear and study the case. It's

exactly the same as mine. Shaped like the blue police box from the British TV show *Doctor Who.*

What are the odds of two people having the same phone case?

Maybe higher than you'd think, given how many people watch the show.

Then again, I *don't* watch the show.

Then again *again*, I'm an anomaly.

In more ways than one.

"Hello?" The voice sounds distant, like it's calling from the bottom of a well. I quickly return the phone to my ear.

"I'm here."

"So, should I just keep your phone or—"

"No!" I answer so urgently a few people sitting nearby turn and stare. The baby begins to wail again. I take it down a notch. "No."

He laughs. "Good. 'Cause that was a joke."

I laugh too. The difference is, mine sounds like a monkey being strangled. "I knew that."

Even without knowing the exact probability that two people stuck in the same airport would have the exact same phone with the exact same phone case, I decide I don't like the odds.

"So," he says after a long pause. "Where should we meet?"

$$\infty$$

It was Lottie's idea to get summer jobs. She certainly didn't need the money. She was doing it for the boys. Lottie was always very calculating when it came to boys. It was about the only calculating she did.

"Just think about it, Kathryn," she said as she drove her BMW convertible to the mall. "If we work at a place that sells *girls'* clothing, the odds that we'll meet any cute boys are like a million to one. The only guys who come into places like that are ones shopping for their *girlfriends*. But if we work at a place where *boys* shop, our odds increase by like infinity."

Her logic was sound, even if her computations sounded a bit off. But I didn't correct her. She was on a roll, and when Lottie was on a roll, the rule was, you just let Lottie roll.

We took applications from five different stores, all specializing in men's apparel. Or, as Lottie distinguished it, *Hot Guy* apparel.

"I'm not going to spend my summer helping Grandpa pick out a new pair of suspenders," she explained as we found seats in the food court and Lottie produced two sparkly purple pens from her bag and handed one to me.

We proceeded to fill out our information in quintuplicate. When I was finished, Lottie took my applications and examined them. The way she bit the tip of her pen as she reviewed my efforts—it reminded me of my mother scanning her carefully made grocery lists for missing items.

"Did I get all the answers right?" I teased.

She tapped her teeth with the pen. "I was just thinking . . ."

I felt my toes squeeze in my shoes. It was never a good thing when Lottie was thinking. It meant that a plot was brewing.

"Wanna hear something crazy?" she asked.

"Always," I responded instinctively, even though, this time, I wasn't really sure I meant it.

Truth be told, *most* of the time, I wasn't sure I meant it.

"What if we changed your name?"

I rolled my eyes and tried to grab the stack of applications from her. Lottie quickly moved her hands away, avoiding my reach. "I'm serious! You've been Kathryn for sixteen years. Aren't you tired of it? Don't you want to be someone else for a while?"

"I'm not changing my name."

"Not like a total makeover," Lottie explained. "Just a touch-up."

"A touch-up? On a name?"

"Yeah. Everyone named Kathryn always goes with something boring like Kathy or Kate or Kitty."

"I've never gone by any of those."

"Exactly. Because you're *not* boring. You need something more unique!"

I was pretty sure I *was* boring, but I kept that to myself.

"How about just *Ryn*?"

"Ryn?" I repeated doubtfully.

Her eyes lit up as the sound of her own idea echoed back at her. "Yes!"

"It sounds like a species of sparrow that my mom looks for on one of her birding trips."

Lottie punched the top of the pen with a decisive *click*, and then proceeded to scratch out every iterance of "Kath" on all five of my applications.

She tilted her head back to admire her handiwork and smiled. "I like it. It's fitting. It's a conversation starter."

I was still bordering on skeptical. "A conversation starter?"

"Yeah, you know, like, 'What's your name?' 'Ryn.' 'Ryn? That's an interesting name. Is it short for something?' 'Actually, it is.' And, voilà! Instant conversation."

I wasn't sure I wanted a name that was a conversation starter. I usually avoided unnecessary small talk whenever possible. But it was too late. Lottie had made up her mind, and I didn't really feel like getting five new applications and starting over.

A few days later we both started jobs at A-Frame, a store that specialized in surf and skate apparel. When the manager handed me a name tag with my newly minted moniker printed on it, I stared at it for a good thirty seconds, marveling at how with just a simple stroke of her purple pen, Lottie had effectively turned me into an entirely different person.

It was the only reinvention that stuck.

∞

"Ryn Gilbert," I carefully pronounce my name to the customer service representative before remembering that my airline ticket was issued under my full, legal name. "Sorry, I mean, *Kathryn Gilbert.*"

By the time I got back in line at the customer service counter, the impatient man was already gone, but a kind woman in a business suit seemed to recognize me and took pity, letting me cut in front of her. Muppet Guy offered to meet me in the Terminal A food court in twenty minutes to swap phones, so I decided to at least try to get some information about my flight in the meantime.

I listen to the *pitter pat pitter pat* of the woman's long, manicured fingernails tapping against the keys as she pulls up my confirmation.

"Compliment her," Lottie whispers. "That's how you get what you want in these situations."

I don't think complimenting her will stop a blizzard, I whisper back in my mind.

"It can't hurt."

"I like your nails," I blurt out, bending forward to try to make out the design painted on each one. "Are those snowflakes?"

The woman stops typing and looks up at me. For a brief moment I see her entire demeanor shift, like she's shedding a layer of clothing. The layer labeled BITCHY CUSTOMER SERVICE REP.

"Yes," she says brightly. "I do them myself."

My reaction is organic. "Wow. Really? How long does that take you?"

She smiles and curls her nails under to look at them. "A few hours. But it's a labor of love."

"I'm impressed."

"Thank you." With an entirely new personality she goes back to typing.

"See?" Lottie says. "Can't hurt." Although she's only a voice in my head, I can picture her looking smug.

The woman frowns at her screen. "Well, I have your confirmation here, and I see you're booked on a flight to San Francisco, but I'm afraid there are no flights leaving Denver right now because of the storm."

I feel myself deflate.

"I suggest you keep checking the monitors for updates. We'll post them as soon as they come."

"So, there are no other answers you can give me?" I confirm.

She shakes her head, looking genuinely apologetic. "I'm sorry. Not at this time. I'm afraid we all just have to wait out this storm."

I turn and gaze longingly out the window behind the customer service desk. The snow doesn't seem to be falling so much as uninhibitedly dancing. Like it's just been released from prison. If it weren't so crazy loud in here, I bet you could hear it beating against the window, begging to be let in.

I sigh and repeat the word that I have a feeling is about to become my least favorite entry in the English dictionary. "Wait."

∞

Each of the three terminals of the Denver airport is designed as a long, vertical strip of gates with a round shopping center in the middle. I know this only because I used Muppet Guy's phone to pull up a map. It felt weird to use his Internet, his connection, his keyboard. Like I was jogging in somebody else's running gear.

Not that I jog.

Or own running gear.

Come to think of it, I don't really do much of anything anymore. Besides type questions into Google.

The food court where Muppet Guy suggested we meet is in the middle of the A terminal. Getting there is another story. The corridors seem to have shrunk in size since I've been standing in that line. Either that, or the number of people lingering in them has quadrupled.

It reminds me of a highway in one of those disaster movies where everyone's trying to get out of town but eventually they all just give up and park in the middle of the road to watch the asteroid/tidal wave/larger-than-life lizard monster destroy the city they left behind.

Stranded travelers are parked all up and down the row of gates. They're sitting, lying, sleeping, watching movies on iPads. They've made impromptu pillows out of coats, backpacks, computers, laps. A group of parents have created a makeshift playpen out of roller bags, and their babies are crawling around inside it. A bunch of older children are trying to figure out what to do with a deck of cards.

I, once again, decided to bypass the moving walkway. A decision I'm now starting to regret as I attempt to weave and climb through the hordes of stationary people. As I pass gate A32, I can see the food court in the distance. It feels like an oasis at the end of a long desert journey. But I stop when I notice that everyone at gate A32 is staring up at the television screen mounted on the wall. A local newscast is on, and the headline plastered in the lower third makes me skid to a halt.

WINTER STORM UPDATE

This has got to be the quietest section of the entire airport. No one is making a peep. All ears are trained on the weatherman's voice.

"Nine News is tracking this massive winter storm that has been deemed the biggest blizzard in over a century. We're issuing a severe blizzard warning to all parts of the Denver metro area. There are already reports of up to seventeen inches of accumulation in the south. Road conditions are icy and visibility is poor. Current road closures include I-25 from Monument to Lone Tree and I-70 from the Vail pass through the Eisenhower Tunnel, but we're expecting more closures to be announced imminently. We strongly advise residents not to leave home or attempt to travel anywhere."

I scoff.

Too late for that.

The scene shifts from the suited weatherman sitting pretty in the studio to a poor newbie who has been thrust into the middle of the blizzard. She's dressed in a hooded down jacket that looks more like a sleeping bag with arms than a coat. The furry hood is pulled up around her face, and her gloved hands are clutching the microphone as if it's the last of her life force. Behind her is a solid wall of agitated snow. Her eyes are tearing up as she attempts to describe to the camera exactly what she's experiencing.

But she doesn't really need to say anything. This is one of those prime examples of a picture being worth a thousand words. Maybe two thousand, in her case. I pull my eyes from the TV and glance outside, suddenly very grateful that I'm in *here* and not out there.

The weatherman returns and tells us that they'll be continuing to interrupt the regularly scheduled programming with updates as they come. Then the screen changes to one of those daytime talk shows where four women sit around and argue over which celebrity is more likely to be bulimic.

One of the hosts—an older lady with a colossal plastic

surgery bill—is interviewing a man and a woman named Dr. Max Hale and Dr. Marcia Livingston-Hale, the famous biracial couple who write those popular parenting psychology books called *Kids Come First*. My mom began reading the series religiously when she divorced my father six years ago. The day after they sat me down and explained that they weren't going to be married anymore, the *Kids Come First* books started appearing on my mother's nightstand. Titles like *Kids Come First: Set Them Free*, *Kids Come First: A Guide to Divorce*, and *Kids Come First: Discipline Without Anger*.

The cover of the latest title in the series suddenly fills the TV screen.

KIDS COME FIRST: 101 ANSWERS TO YOUR MOST COMMON PARENTING QUESTIONS

"Dr. Hale and Dr. Livingston-Hale," the host of the show begins, "this is now your tenth installment in the *Kids Come First* series, which released just this week. Can you tell us what makes *this* particular book stand apart from the rest of your titles?"

"Of course," Dr. Marcia replies breezily, brushing a lock of shiny blond hair from her forehead. "This is a very special install-ment. It's more of a dialogue with our readers than a how-to guide. We wanted to write a book dedicated entirely to our fans."

"Yes," Dr. Max continues seamlessly, like a football handoff. He's a handsome African American man with thick dark hair that's been trimmed short. "We receive so many letters from parents with questions about the *Kids Come First* method. So we selected the most frequently asked questions that we receive and answered them in this book."

"Well, your publisher tells me that it's on track to be your bestselling yet," the host says with a cheesy thumbs-up.

Dr. Marcia laughs heartily, her blue eyes brightening. "Numbers don't really matter to us anymore. Unless it's the number of people we're helping."

Dr. Max takes his wife's hand in his and gives her a tender look. Something about that look makes my stomach flip, yet I can't seem to pull my gaze away from the screen.

My mom stopped reading the *Kids Come First* books about a year ago. That's when the other books started appearing on her nightstand. Books with titles like *Grief Is a Raindrop, Guiding Your Child Through Loss,* and *Bringing Your Survivor Back from the Dead.*

It was like she'd graduated from a basic bachelor's degree in parenting and moved on to a Ph.D.

I wonder what the most frequently asked questions about parenting actually are.

What do normal parents ask about?

What do normal teenage girls deal with?

The phone in my hand vibrates, and I peer down at the screen. There's a text message from my number.

Just arrived. Are you here?

It's then I realize that most of my fellow TV viewers have walked away or have redirected their attention to other activities. I'm the only idiot still staring up at the ceiling.

I start to tap out a response but a horrifying progression of thoughts drags my fingers to a stop.

He sent me a text message.

He's in my messaging app.

He could read something.

He could erase something.

I'm suddenly kicking myself for not getting to the food court faster. For allowing myself to be pulled into a stupid weather report that offered absolutely nothing that I couldn't get from just looking out the fucking window. For giving a stranger unlimited access to my phone for longer than absolutely necessary.

For being too damn stubborn to lock my phone with a passcode because it would hinder my access to the Web browser.

I switch off the screen and take off at a run toward the food court. I'm no longer being polite as I climb through people. They are just tall weeds and annoying vines in the jungle now. And my elbows and oversize backpack are my machetes.

Circular References

"Do you want to talk about your parents' divorce?" Dr. Judy asked on my very first visit. I sat on the couch fiddling with a rubber snakelike gizmo that Dr. Judy called a "busy toy."

Do all shrinks have busy toys?

My "busy" hands itched for my phone. For the sweet relief of swiping my fingertip against the cool, smooth surface of the screen. For typing and typing and typing until there were no more questions left in my brain. But Dr. Judy had a no-phone policy in her office. There was a sign right on the door. I wondered how strict a policy that was. What would she do to me if I reached into the front pocket of my backpack and just touched it?

Just a little feel.

A quick squeeze.

Would she kick me out? Would she fire me as a client? Would she tell my mother?

Do all shrinks have no-phone policies?

I almost laughed as the question popped into my head. We'd just learned about circular references in my computer programming class at school. Basically, it says that you can't create a formula that references itself. It results in an error.

My request to ask my phone about a no-phone policy felt like that. A circular reference. A closed loop.

I wondered if my brain would error out. Shut down.

ZAP.

At least then I wouldn't have to be here anymore, talking to a stranger about my life. How can a stranger possibly give advice about something she knows nothing about?

My mom insisted that it would be good for me, even though she'd never been to a shrink either. She doesn't like talking about things. At least not things that matter. Neither does my father. I suppose that's what made them such a good couple.

Until they weren't anymore.

"No," I finally responded to the question. For me, it felt like an eternity since she'd asked me if I wanted to talk about my parents' divorce, but Dr. Judy didn't seem fazed by the time lapse.

"No?" she repeated.

"Not really."

"Not *really*?"

If this was how this conversation was going to go, then my mom was wasting her money. I could sit around all day in a dimly lit room and repeat everything back in the form of a question. Would someone pay *me* two hundred dollars an hour?

Maybe this was just how therapists worked. Maybe this is

what all those textbooks on her shelf taught her to do. To add question marks to the end of sentences.

How should I know? I'd never been to a shrink before.

My best friend had never died before.

I fidgeted with the snake in my hand. I wasn't sure what the point of it was. Twist it. Untwist it. These seemed to be its only two features.

I placed it on the table to my left.

"You don't like the busy toy?" she asked.

"I'd feel better if I could hold my phone," I told her.

She tilted her head. "Why?"

"I just would."

She nodded. "Okay."

I dove for my bag on the floor, feeling my pulse race as I touched it. Grasped it. The plastic case digging satisfyingly into my palm. When I sat back up, Dr. Judy was writing something on her notepad.

Suddenly, the phone didn't feel so comforting anymore.

For a moment I feared she was going to ask me about the phone. About the case. About the text message. But she seemed to be satisfied with her note and moved on.

"How long ago was the divorce?"

When I didn't reply, she tried something else. "Was it a messy separation?"

Take three: "Do your parents still get along?"

"I didn't think I was here to talk about the divorce." My response was like a boomerang. It shot out of my mouth so fast, I didn't even realize how agitated I sounded until it came flying back and slapped me across the face.

"What do you think you're here to talk about?"

I clutched my phone with both hands and tucked them between my thighs. I squeezed until my fingers went numb.

Dr. Judy's eyes tracked down, studying me with a relaxed interest.

"What do you do with the phone?" she asked.

"What does anyone do with a phone?" I asked back. I didn't recognize my own voice. It wasn't mine. It wasn't me. Dr. Judy's office was a magic portal that turned you into someone else. Some ugly, irritable version of yourself.

She shrugged. "I don't know. I suppose different people use their phones for different purposes."

"I make phone calls."

She nods. "Is that all?"

"I search the Web."

"What do you search the Web for?"

How does she do that? How does she know exactly which questions to ask?

I glanced over at her bookshelf once more, searching for a thick tome about mind reading.

I swallowed and kept my gaze on the books. "I ask questions."

"What kind of questions?"

"Any kind."

"Can you give me an example of a question you might ask?"

No.

"They're just random questions. They don't matter."

"They matter to you," she pointed out.

My head swung back toward her, and I pressed my lips together. "I don't like unanswered questions."

She watched me for a very long time. For some reason it felt like a challenge. For some reason I didn't feel like backing down.

"What about Lottie?" she asked. "Is she an unanswered question?"

I looked at my lap, forfeiting the challenge.

"Lottie is dead. You don't get a more finite answer than that."

∞

The food court is a buzzing swarm of hangry people struggling to be civil to one another. As civil as a thousand lobsters swimming in a seafood restaurant tank can be.

The word "zoo" immediately comes to mind, and I picture all the people in line for the McDonald's as hyenas waiting for their daily servings of meat. The longest line by far though, is the one for the Caribou Coffee. This is where the gang of slouchy meer-kats queue up to get their pep juice.

There are only so many tables to sit at, so several small tribes of diners have set up camp on the ground, just outside the food court barrier. It's like someone tore a seam in a giant grain sack of people and they're spilling out onto the floor.

How am I supposed to find him in all of this anarchy?

Just then I feel a tap on my shoulder. I spin around and there he is. The same light brown skin, the same dark brown hair, the same striking blue eyes. Animal, wild-eyed and midscream, stares back at me from his T-shirt. If I were to choose a Muppet to put on my clothes, I wouldn't choose the craziest, most schizo one of them all. I'd probably choose Kermit. He's always so calm and composed, even when his psycho pig girlfriend is running around screaming.

Muppet Guy is brandishing my phone toward me like a game show hostess would. It takes all the strength I have left not to reach out and snatch it right from his hand.

If the hangry mob can be relatively civil, then so can I.

"Thanks," I say, offering his phone to him.

Do we just swap?

Is it like one of those scenes in a spy movie where neither of us trusts the other, and we have to do it at lightning speed?

He casually hands me my phone, and I do the same with his. It would be the most uneventful exchange ever, if it weren't for the fact that, for just a moment, his fingers brush against mine and I flinch. Partly because I wasn't expecting to touch him, but mostly because I'm surprised by how warm his hands are. It's hard to believe anyone's hands could be that warm during the middle of a history-making blizzard. Somehow it feels unnatural.

He clears his throat. "I must say, you have excellent taste in phone cases."

"Thank you," I mumble.

He laughs.

Was that funny?

I didn't intend for it to be funny.

But he's still grinning, and I can't help but notice how straight his teeth are. Definitely the result of some very expensive ortho-dontic work. No one is *born* with teeth like that.

"By the way," he says, slipping his phone into a phone-size pocket on the strap of his messenger bag. "I think you have an unread text message."

My stomach clenches like it's trying to protect my kidneys and liver from a black-market organ thief.

"Did you read it?" The question explodes out of me. It's not civil. It's not polite. It's not the least bit restrained. It's a full-on ambush attack.

If he read it, then that's it. That's the end.

There's no way to mark a text message unread once you've read it.

I've Googled it hundreds of time.

He blinks rapidly, obviously startled by the sudden hostility in my voice. I ignore his reaction and swipe on the phone, my eyes darting to the messaging app on the bottom of the home screen.

A red number 1 hovers over it like a heavenly halo.

One unread message.

I breathe out the dragon fire–tinged air that's trapped in my lungs.

"Of course not," he finally answers. "I just used the phone to call you. And send you that text a minute ago. I realized it wasn't mine as soon as I turned it on." He snickers like we share an inside joke that I don't remember. "The folders were my first clue. That's one organized phone you got there. How long did it take you to do all of that?"

His cheeks begin to twitch like little chipmunk cheeks. It would be endearing if he weren't clearly making fun of me.

"I like knowing where everything is, okay?"

He holds up his hands in a defensive gesture. "Hey, I'm not knocking it. I'm just . . . impressed."

But he doesn't sound impressed. He sounds like he's talking to a patient in a mental hospital after entering the kitchen to discover the patient has organized all the spices by country of origin.

"Look," he says, hooking a thumb into the strap of his messenger bag. "I think we may have gotten off on the wrong foot." He chuckles again. He just can't help himself. "Actually, you got off on two wrong feet."

He pauses, like he's waiting for me to get it.

I get it. I'm the one who tripped on the moving walkway. I just don't laugh. We haven't known each other long enough to have inside jokes.

He clears his throat again. "Anyway, do you want to maybe get a bite to eat with me?"

Instinctively, I look back at the zoo. A zebra and a lion are arguing over who gets to sit at a table that just opened up. I think I know who will win.

Muppet Guy laughs. Does he do anything else *but* laugh? Maybe he should be standing in line at McDonald's with the rest of the hyenas.

"Not here," he says quickly. "A buddy of mine told me about some secret, hidden burger place in Terminal B. It's just one stop on the train. He says they have amazing burgers. You know, as amazing as airport burgers can be."

"I'm a vegetarian."

He nods. "That's cool. I'm sure they have veggie burgers. And it's probably much quieter than this place." He unhooks his thumb and jerks it toward the food court.

For the briefest moment in the history of brief moments, I consider going. But only because my stomach is still complaining about my unplanned fast, and I'm dying to go somewhere—anywhere—quieter than this.

But then he says, "C'mon. We can talk about *Doctor Who*."

The unnaturally straight teeth. And the warm hands. And the Muppet shirt.

And I can't.

"Actually, I have to go."

Another laugh. "Do you have somewhere to *be?*"

This is funny. I know this is funny. Because none of us has anywhere to be but stuck in the middle of this mayhem.

I stroke the phone case in my hand.

My phone case.

My phone.

The questions from the last twenty minutes have been piling up and they won't answer themselves.

"I just have to go."

His smile fades. The curtain is drawn over the sideshow of perfect teeth. "Okay. No worries. But hey, if you change your mind, the secret burger place is at B89. But don't like tell a whole bunch of people. Then it won't be a secret anymore."

"B89," I repeat with a nod. Not because I need to remember it. But because I need him to let me go.

Because I need to go.

"Thanks," I mumble, staring down at my phone. "I guess I'll see you around."

I turn and leave the zoo.

I know he hasn't moved yet. I know he's watching me walk away. Even through the buzzing swarm, I can sense it. Like he's standing alone.

Like he's the only human in the room.

∞

75. I blame the Denver airport for making moving
    walkways that stop too abruptly.
76. I blame boys with Muppet shirts for not
    recognizing their own phones on the ground.
77. I blame the factory in Taiwan for manufacturing
    too many *Doctor Who* phone cases.

∞

After that first visit, Dr. Judy stopped asking about Lottie. I tried to psychoanalyze what that meant, but I found myself trapped in another frustrating loop—the circular reference of a patient trying to analyze her therapist trying to analyze her—and eventually gave up.

Besides, what's that saying about looking a gift horse in the mouth?

I figured I probably shouldn't question her decision to omit my dead best friend from the conversation. I had no interest in talking about Lottie.

"How are you fitting in at your new school?" she asked me on my second visit.

My thumb absentmindedly stroked my phone as I shrugged. "Fine, I guess."

"Fine, you guess?"

I was starting to learn that open-ended statements were dangerous inside these walls. They usually required follow-ups. And follow-ups led down dark rabbit holes. It was best to end things with decisive periods.

"Fine."

"Are you taking any art classes?"

I gave her a quizzical look. It seemed like such a random question.

"I assume you like to draw," she clarified.

"Did my mother tell you that?" I asked, feeling defensive. Feeling betrayed. I didn't like the idea of Dr. Judy talking to my mother about me behind my back. It seemed like cheating. Insider trading.

Dr. Judy nodded toward my left hand, the one holding the phone. "I noticed the ink stains."

I surreptitiously tried to wipe away the evidence. I hadn't realized there was any left. It had been two days since I'd last tried to draw something. Safe, innocuous things like trees and buildings and blades of grass. Two days since I stared at those crooked lines and distorted shapes and then angrily tossed them in the trash, where they belonged.

"So," she prompted. "*Do* you like to draw?"

"I used to," I admitted, intentionally omitting all the variations of the second half of that sentence.

I used to be good.

I used to impress people.

I used to be able to draw a straight fucking line.

"What happened?" Dr. Judy asked.

I remained quiet. Eventually, she got the hint and changed topics.

"Have you made any new friends at school?"

I studied the lampshade. It wasn't a particularly interesting lampshade. But it felt safe. "It's still early."

"Does that mean you *want* to make new friends?"

"Doesn't everyone?"

Dr. Judy smiled tenderly. "I'm not asking about everyone. I'm asking about you."

"Yes."

"Yes, you want to make new friends?"

I didn't like where this conversation was heading. It felt slippery. Like I could lose control of it at any moment. One minute you're talking about new friends, the next minute you're talking about old ones.

I dug deep down and conjured up the bubbliest, most enthusiastic smile I could conjure. "Yes. I would like very much to make new friends."

Dr. Judy didn't look convinced. She scribbled something down on her yellow notepad. I was starting to despise that yellow notepad. I was starting to despise her scratchy black pen and the cryptic hieroglyphics she scrawled with it.

The whole concept of a psychologist taking notes about you felt counterintuitive. It was like *inviting* a group of gossipy girls to whisper behind your back. To judge you when you're feeling the most vulnerable.

"Let's talk about that smile."

My face fell. "What smile?"

"The one you just gave me."

"I'm not allowed to smile?"

Dr. Judy put her pen down. I felt my muscles relax a bit. "I just think if you're going to fake a smile, it needs to look real."

The surprise must have registered on my face, because Dr. Judy chuckled. "Ryn." She said my name delicately, like I was a glass ballerina figurine whose broken leg had recently been glued back on. "I don't expect you to walk around grinning like life is some amazing gift. I don't expect you to be okay with this. You still have a lot of healing to do. But I'll be honest with you. There are going to be times when you're going to have to fake it. And you're going to have to do a better job than that if you want to convince people."

"You're encouraging me to lie?"

"I'm encouraging you to survive. Out *there*. In here, I don't care what you do. You can act tough, you can fall to pieces, you can pretend like you don't feel completely betrayed by the world. This is a safe space. But out there is very different. People won't understand. Strangers won't automatically know what you're dealing with. If you don't want people to ask questions, then you're going to have to do a better job convincing them there's nothing to know. You have to *sell* yourself."

"So, in other words, *pretend* to be normal so people leave me alone."

"Well, I suppose that depends."

"On what?"

She rested her hands atop her pen. "On whether or not you want to be left alone."

∞

Desperate to get away from all the people, I decide to wander. I take a random escalator up from the shopping rotunda and find myself in some kind of hidden balcony that overlooks the A gates. It's surprisingly empty. I'm the only one here.

I find an outlet nearby, under a bench of seats, and plug in my phone. The first thing I do after I see the little charging icon is set up a passcode. I definitely learned my lesson with that one. Sure, it will create one more step between question and answer, but it's worth it. I never want to feel that vulnerable and exposed again.

I lean on the railing and stare down at the two long rivers of people flowing on each side of the moving walkway below. Most of the people seem resigned to their fate and are sitting on the floor. Some are still trying to get to places. Imaginary destinations with imaginary deadlines.

I breathe in the emptiness of my little hideaway, and for the first time in several hours my shoulders part ways from my ears.

How long before other people discover this place?

How long before the river down there floods and pushes the excess up here?

Being this high, watching over everything, I'm reminded of the tree house that Lottie used to have in her yard. Back when she was Charlotte and I was Kathryn and neither of us could drive and the world was a safe place.

It wasn't really *her* tree house. It came with the house that Lottie's parents had bought from a family with two boys. Apparently, they had built the tree house with their father. Lottie used to joke that the only thing her father could build was hedge funds.

I never understood what that meant.

I don't think Lottie did either.

We used to have slumber parties up there when we were kids. I would draw and Lottie would gossip or try on makeup or dance around to whatever pop song was popular at the time

Lottie always had contraband in the tree house. Stolen Double Stuf Oreos and bags of Doritos and bubble gum with sugar in it. Over the years, it continued to be Lottie's hiding spot. Except the smuggled goods became less innocuous. Tiny airplane liquor bottles swiped from her father's carry-on after he got home from a business trip. Adult DVDs acquired from some guy in the mall parking lot. Lipsticks shoplifted from the drugstore down the street. Lottie insisted that because they were all cheap lipsticks in shades no one should ever wear, it was okay.

When Lottie's mother found the stash a month after the accident, I told her it was mine. The gaudy makeup. The liquor bottles. The DVDs. All of it.

Two weeks later my mother decided to move us to San Francisco.

A week after that my sessions with Dr. Judy started.

I should probably tell my mother the truth one of these days. So she doesn't continue to think I'm an alcoholic pervert with horrible taste in lipstick.

I tear my attention away from the people below and stare at the bank of information screens on the wall to my right. I run my eyes down the long list of (allegedly) departing flights.

Boston, MA	1240	4:45 p.m.	DELAYED
Detroit, MI	541	3:50 p.m.	DELAYED
Ft. Lauderdale, FL	3672	4:02 p.m.	DELAYED
Miami, FL	211	3:32 p.m.	DELAYED
San Francisco, CA	112	3:31 p.m.	DELAYED

No estimated departure time for any of them. It's like the whole world has been put on an indefinite pause.

I check the clock on my phone. 3:56 pm. God, I'm hungry. When was the last time I ate? I was still in Eastern Standard Time.

I sit down and riffle through my backpack until I find a crushed granola bar at the bottom. It's less of a bar now and more just granola. I search the crumpled wrapping for an expiration date, but I can't find one.

Do granola bars expire?

I type the search into my phone but find inconclusive results. Apparently, there's a differing of opinion out there about the safety of consuming expired granola bars.

Normally, I wouldn't chance it, but I'm that hungry.

I rip open the package with my teeth, shake a few trampled

morsels onto my hand, and toss them into my mouth.

"Eew. You're really going to eat that?" Lottie chimes in with her culinary expertise.

It's not like I have a lot of options here, Lottie.

"And to think, you could have been eating a burger right now."

Veggie burger.

"Yeah, about that. Since when are you a vegetarian?"

Since I got food poisoning from a hot dog.

She sighs, and I can almost feel her hot breath on my ear. "Yeah, that sucked big-time."

I pop another handful of granola into my mouth. It's crunchier than it probably should be.

"I can't believe you didn't go with that guy," she continues to gripe. "Do you know what the odds are of finding a *Doctor Who* fan who is also cute?"

One billion to one? I guess.

"Exactly! And you let him walk away!"

Technically, I did the walking away.

"Even worse! Have I taught you nothing, Ryn?"

"No, Lottie," I whisper aloud to the empty balcony. "You taught me everything."

"Then what are we still doing here? Let's GO!"

I shake my head. *I need to stay here and watch the screens. There could be an update about my flight.*

Lottie huffs. "Yeah, 'cause there are no other information screens in the entire Denver airport. It's just these. Hidden way up here where no one can find them."

And I have to charge my phone.

I pour another helping of granola into my hand and shovel it in, grimacing as I chew. Something tastes off about this mouthful. That definitely didn't taste like granola. Oh God. It might be mold. What if it's mold?

"So you'd eat mold just to get out of spending time with a cute guy?"

I drop the granola bar onto the seat next to me and start typing into my phone again.

Can granola grow mold?

The answer, disturbingly enough, is yes. Apparently, pretty much anything can grow mold.

Even mold.

"*Doctor Who*, Ryn! He likes *Doctor Who*!"

Yeah, and I don't, I remind her.

"Your biggest flaw, in my opinion."

Well, I didn't ask your opinion, did I?

I didn't mean for that to come out as harsh as it did, and I instantly regret it because Lottie falls quiet. You would think being that she's a figment of my imagination I could control when and where she makes her appearances.

You would think.

I tip my head back and pour the remaining questionably moldy granola into my mouth, trying to warrant a reaction, but the chatterbox in my head is still chatterless.

I crumple the wrapper and toss it toward the nearest trash can. It misses by about two feet.

Resting my phone on my chest, I kick my feet out in front of me and lean back in my chair, trying to get comfy. It would be nice if these stupid armrests weren't between each seat, so I could lie down, but other than that, it's not so bad. I could stay up here until my flight takes off. No problem. I think I even saw a restroom on the other side of the escalator.

I let my heavy eyelids sag. But just before they close, my phone starts to vibrate. I know immediately—from the string of seven notifications in a row—that it's my mother texting.

I unlock the screen and read through them one by one.

Mom: The weather channel says the storm is getting worse.

Mom: Why aren't you texting me back?

Mom: Before I forget, do you want me to pick up anything from the supermarket?

Mom: Have you eaten anything today?

Mom: You need to eat.

Mom: The Denver airport website says there's a bagel place in Terminal C.

Mom: But you'll have to get on a train to get there.

I'm about to tap out a response when I notice a flicker of activity to my right. I whip my gaze toward the screens, and that's when I notice the change.

Flight 112 to San Francisco no longer has a big fat DELAYED stamp next to it. It now says:

AT 7:41 P.M.

I look at my phone. That's less than four hours from now.

I'm going to be getting out of here in less than four hours!
Thank God.

My stomach, obviously not satisfied with my meager offerings, lets out another low rumble, as if to say, "What else you got up there?"

I glance at the screens again, just to make sure I wasn't imagining it.

Nope. We have liftoff at 7:41 p.m.

Which means I have nothing else to do between now and then except kill time.

Fine, I think with a huff, standing up, yanking my charger from the outlet, and flinging my backpack over my shoulder. *But I'm not doing this for me, Lottie. I'm doing it for you.*

I expect this to bring her back. It's just the kind of incendiary remark that she loves to respond to. But as I ride the escalator back down into the chaos, in search of a route to gate B89, Lottie remains suspiciously silent.

Stranded Passenger Bingo

"Open it! Open it!" Lottie bounced up and down, which I didn't think was the brightest idea, given that we were in the tree house and who knew how stable this construction was. I doubted the previous owners of Lottie's house had gotten all the proper permits and inspections.

I carefully peeled back the wrapping paper of the small rectangular gift. I'd never been a ripper. I'd always been a peeler. It drove Lottie crazy.

"C'mon!" Bounce. Bounce. Bounce. "Molasses melts faster than this."

"I don't think that's the phrase."

"The phrase is, 'Rip it already!'"

The Halloween/Ryn's Birthday Bash was over. All of the guests had gone home, and Lottie had dragged me up to the tree house. I was worried she wanted to drink more and that I would have to restrain her, because she was already pretty intoxicated. But as soon as we made it up the ladder, she didn't lunge for the tiny liquor bottles like she usually did. She lunged for something else.

My birthday gift.

I peeled off the last strip of shiny silver paper and stared down at the object in my hand.

"Um . . ." I hesitated. "It's . . ." I looked up at her. "You shouldn't have?"

Lottie burst into uncontrollable fits of drunken laughter. It lasted a good twenty seconds. At one point she actually hooted. "You should have seen your face! Oh my God. You would have thought I'd given you a dead horse head."

"I don't think you have to specify that the horse head is dead. Once they disconnect it from the body, the dead is implied."

This made her laugh more and stagger backward a bit. I reached out and grabbed her by the arm to steady her.

She half sat/half fell onto the ground and crawled over to her stash. She selected a miniature bottle of Grey Goose, unscrewed the top, and tipped her head back. Most of the vodka went into her mouth. The rest dribbled down the front of her white Twister dress.

I never knew how Lottie's father acquired so many of those tiny bottles. And I never asked. He always just came home from his business trips with loads of them, and Lottie always just lifted them from his bag.

She grimaced at the taste of the alcohol, then tossed the empty bottle haphazardly over her shoulder, and settled into a cross-legged position.

"So," I began again, shaking my gift. "Why did you get me a *Doctor Who* phone case?"

"It's a joke! Because I know how much you *loooove Doctor Who*."

I lowered down next to her, setting the Tardis phone case on the floor. "Yeah," I responded dryly. "Totally love it. It's a grown man who travels through time in a big blue box."

She leaned forward to swat at my leg but missed by about a foot. "Ryn Ryn. You have *no* imagination."

Ryn Ryn. She called me that only when she was drunk. Sometimes she added a cheesy effect to make it sound like an old-fashioned ringing phone.

Her failed swatting effort caused her to tip forward, and I caught her just in time. "And you have *no* tolerance."

She gave up trying to stay upright and collapsed with her head in my lap. I pulled her long red hair from her face, tucking it behind her ear. I always loved that hair. Envied that hair. It was the most vibrant shade of red I'd ever seen. Like a brilliant sunset. Most people thought it was straight from a bottle. Lottie never corrected them. She just let them go on thinking whatever they wanted.

But I knew the truth.

Lottie would never let any chemicals near her perfect hair.

"Ryn Ryn?"

"Mmm?" I murmured.

Her voice changed then. Grew more sober. "I have a serious question to ask you."

I stared down at her grave expression. "What?"

"Why don't you like *Doctor Who?*"

Now it was my turn to laugh. Lottie tried to act offended. "I'm dead serious! This is a very important matter. I'm not sure we can continue to be friends. It's just too big of an issue."

"You only started watching it because of your crush on Mr. Bowman in the eighth grade."

"What does that matter?" she asked. "I still loved it once I started watching it."

Of course, the crush was totally inappropriate, being that Lottie was thirteen and Mr. Bowman was twenty-seven, but propriety had never been Lottie's strong suit. When Mr. Bowman referenced the show in science class, Lottie immediately went home and added it to her Netflix queue. It was the most interest she'd ever shown in science in her entire life. By the time the semester ended, Lottie had moved on to her next crush, but she was still hooked on the show.

"Why, Ryn?" Lottie pestered. "Why don't you love it like I love it?"

"There was an entire episode about farting politicians," I reminded her.

She tried to push herself up, but it didn't work out too well. Her head plonked back down into my lap, and I continued to stroke her hair. "It was a metaphor!" she slurred. "About politicians being full of hot air."

"Ahhhh!" I said, faking an epiphany.

"You get it now?"

"I get it now."

Her eyes started to sink closed. "Now you like the show?"

"Now I like the show."

She giggled hot air into my paisley hippie skirt. "You're such a bad liar."

"I guess I don't have as much practice as you."

That made her giggle harder. "Wanna hear something crazy?"

"Always."

"I totally let Emmett put Right Hand on Red."

I gasped in mock outrage. "You did not!"

"I did. And I might have let him explore some other colors too."

"His Disney princess must have *loved* that."

Lottie frowned. "Huh?"

"Never mind. What about the mystery man you said you had your eye on tonight?"

She pulled her legs up to her chest and snuggled tighter against me. "He turned out to be a wanker."

"A wanker?"

She nodded. "A big wanker."

"So where's Emmett now? Why didn't you bring him up here?"

"It's *your* birthday. I wanted to spend it with *you*."

I smiled in the darkness of the tree house.

"And besides," she went on, "I had to give you your big present."

I glanced at the phone case next to my leg. "Thanks," I deadpanned. "I'll cherish it always."

"Ryn Ryn?" she asked after I was sure she'd fallen asleep.

"Mmm?"

"The phone case was a joke, you know?"

"I know, Lottie."

"You don't have to use it."

I chuckled. "Thanks for the permission."

"I know you probably won't use it anyway."

I leaned back on my hands. "Nope. Probably not."

∞

I clutch the phone case tightly in my hand and step off the escalator onto the main floor of the A terminal.

"There you are!" a voice shouts. I look around, even though I'm positive the voice is not talking to me. Who would be talking to me? I don't know anyone here.

"Over here!" it calls out. "I've been looking *everywhere* for you."

I stop a few feet from the second escalator that will take me down to the train platform and look left and right. My gaze finally lands on a pair of long, scrawny arms waving wildly in the air. I turn around, certain whomever the voice is summoning has to be standing right behind me, but the only person there is a harried-looking businessman pushing past me to board the escalator.

"This is my sister. We're traveling together."

The voice is now directly in front of me, and I can see it belongs to a young boy in jeans and an oversize sweater. I recognize him from gate A44. He was slouching in a chair with a misspelled sign around his neck. I peer down to see the sign is still there. And it's still misspelled.

UNACCOMPANIED MINER

He's standing next to an airline employee in a dark blue suit with a name tag that reads SIMON.

"Sis, where have you *been?*" The boy sounds annoyed now.

I'm still confused as hell, convinced a guy with a camera is going to jump out at any minute and tell me I'm going to be on YouTube.

"What?" I ask.

The boy shoots me a look. "I was just telling Simon here that he doesn't need to accompany me anymore because I'm traveling with my sister who's older than sixteen and, according to the airline's company policy as stated on their website FAQ page, as long as I'm traveling with someone older than sixteen, I'm not considered an unaccompanied minor." He glares back at Simon. "*Minor.* M-I-N-O-R. Not M-I-N-E-R. I don't work in a coal quarry." He turns back to me and lets out a huff. "Amateurs."

I can tell Simon is fighting off the eye roll of the century. He somehow manages to keep his composure as he asks me, "Is this true? Are you traveling with Troy Benson?"

The boy's eyes narrow in a disconcerting mix of supplication and warning.

I don't want to get involved. This is exactly the kind of awkward encounter that I tend to avoid. And yet, there's something in the boy's eyes—the same misery I saw back at the gate that I see every time I look in the mirror. And before I know it, I hear myself saying, "Yes. He's with me."

And I instantly regret it. I know nothing about this kid. Or the airline's policies. What if they ask to see my ID? What if they want some sort of proof that we're related? What if I get in trouble?

Troy's pink cheeks deflate like two balloons. He wheels on Simon. "See! So now, shoo! Skedaddle. Scram. Go back to being pointless."

Simon looks like he's going to clock this kid in the face, but he also looks completely relieved to have the opportunity to ditch him.

Whether or not he actually believes this little charade becomes irrelevant when he turns to me and says, "He's your responsibility now. Just make sure he gets on his flight." Then he spins on his heels and stalks away.

The boy—Troy Benson—sighs dramatically and rips the cord from his neck. "Thank you. You saved my life." He dumps the paper sign ceremoniously into a nearby trash can. "Metaphorically speaking, of course. Do you *know* how humiliating that was? Having to be chaperoned to and from the lavatory?"

I smile politely. "I can imagine."

"Such imbeciles!" he rants, still riled up from the incident. "I have a college degree from Stanford. I'm currently getting my master's at Harvard. And I was walking around with an 'Unaccompanied Minor' sign around my neck. *And* it was misspelled!"

I blink in surprise at him. "You're getting your master's? How old are you?"

He hooks his thumbs cockily into the straps of his backpack. "Fourteen."

"Fourteen?" I spit back. I could have sworn he was ten.

The cocky expression on his face vanishes. "Well, don't sound so flabbergasted about it."

I school my face. "Sorry. I just—"

"Okay, so technically I'm still thirteen. I turn fourteen next week." His bitter scowl is back. "But those idiots at the airlines have some inane policy that you can't travel by yourself unless you're fourteen. I mean, seriously. It's six days, people!" He's yelling now, shouting into the crowd, as if they're all to blame for the inane airline policy. I cringe and take a small step away from him. "Sorry," he offers. "I can get a little agitated. You should see me in class when we discuss condensed matter."

My head is swimming. "So you're some kind of child genius?"

"We prefer the term 'prodigy.' 'Genius' was tainted when those morons at the Apple Store started using it. Ooh! Look at me! I can do a hard reset on your phone! I'm a genius!" His voice gets all high and squeaky. Then it cracks. He clears his throat, looking embarrassed. "Anyway. Thanks for your help. I'm off to observe the second law of thermodynamics as proven in an isolated airport environment."

I squint, hoping it will make this boy less confusing. It doesn't. "The what?"

"The second law of thermodynamics," Troy repeats, then motions to the masses of people swarming around us, as if this simple gesture will help clarify the garble coming out of his mouth. "The entropy of an isolated system not in equilibrium will tend to increase over time?"

I shake my head, still not following.

Troy sighs. My ignorance is obviously a complete inconvenience to him. "Basically, it says that any system, if left unattended or isolated, will eventually result in entropy. Or chaos." He makes a sweeping gesture with his hands. "Take this airport, for example. We're all trapped here in this snowstorm—hence, *isolated*—with nowhere to go and left to the whim of the worthless blockheads running the place. And what do you get?" He points to the food court where the zoo animals are still fighting for control of the limited resources. "Chaos."

I follow the direction of his finger, my gaze lingering a beat too long on two parents trying to distract one screaming child while keeping the other from running away in a fit of giggles.

When I turn back around, Troy is gone. Panicked, I scan the busy shopping rotunda, finally spotting his dark hair bobbing up and down as he makes his way through the crowd. I run to catch up to him. "Wait!" I say. "You can't just leave. I'm kind of responsible for you now. Simon says."

He chuckles at the pun. "Simon also says, 'Touch your nose!' 'Touch your ears!' 'Touch your head!'" Then he walks off again. I jog to keep pace with him. He stops and faces me. "Look. You're nice and all, but I'm kind of on a mission here."

"A mission?" I ask dubiously.

"No offense, but you wouldn't understand."

"I—" I stammer, unsure how to respond to that. I've never had my intelligence blatantly insulted by an almost-fourteen-year-old before. "I—" I repeat lamely.

"Yeah, you keep thinking about that. I'll catch ya later. Thanks for helping spring me from the pokey."

Then once again, he's off, disappearing into the chaos. And I'm left too dumbfounded to follow.

∞

Lottie and I would often spend the night in the tree house. Half the time it was because she was drunk and didn't want her parents to know, the other half it was because she just didn't want to go inside. I never understood this. Her house was gorgeous. It had everything you could ever want in a house. And yet, every so often, Lottie would just refuse to go in.

The morning after my birthday party, I woke up with the sun. Lottie was still passed out on her sleeping bag. I didn't want to wake her, so I quietly reached for the sketch pad I kept in the tree house, flipped to the first blank page, and started to draw.

I wasn't picky about my subjects. I drew whatever I felt I could do justice to. Whatever I could realistically bring to life. That morning it was the view from the window. Lottie's stunning Mediterranean-style garden lit up by the sun.

"It looks like a photograph," Lottie said, startling me. I hadn't realized she was awake. I also hadn't realized how long I'd been drawing.

This happened a lot. I would often get lost in my sketches. Minutes and hours would disappear right into the page, blending in with the shadows and smooth lines.

"Thanks," I said, putting the finishing touches on the big leaf maple that stood in the center of the garden, next to the gazebo. The real tree outside was already scorched with the fiery shades of fall, but I never drew in color. I preferred the simplicity of my black sketch pen. It turned everything into black and white. Right and wrong. Truth and lie.

It uncomplicated a complicated world.

"How do you do it?" Lottie asked, sitting cross-legged beside me so she could peer over my shoulder. "How do you make it look it so real?"

I shook my head. "I don't know. I guess I just draw what I see."

She leaned back on her hands, quietly pensive for a moment. Then she mumbled, "You're lucky, then."

My pen came to a stop as I turned to look at her. Even with the hangover that I knew was swirling around her like a storm cloud, she still glowed. "Lucky how?"

She turned and glanced out the same window I'd been staring out for I don't know how long. At the same beautiful house surrounded by the same beautiful garden. I watched two lines appear between her eyebrows—a barely visible crack in her otherwise flawless façade.

Then she sighed and said, "That the world looks real to you."

∞

I have to take the train to get to the B gates. It reminds me of a much cleaner version of the BART. And much emptier. I'm the only person in my car. I imagine during a normal airport day, these trains are packed full with passengers arriving, departing, connecting, but today is not a normal day. No one needs to get anywhere within the airport. Everyone's waiting upstairs to *leave* the airport.

I disembark onto another deserted platform and ride the escalator up. The B terminal is even worse than the A terminal. There are so many people, I can barely see the other side of the shopping rotunda.

It's clear, from my limited view, that *this* is the nicer terminal. Every airport has one. An updated, fancy terminal that all the money goes into. The restaurant selections here are better. The shopping is more diverse. Even the modern art sculpture in the center of the rotunda is more impressive.

According to the signs, gate B89 is all the way at the end of the terminal. I feel like I'm walking for miles. I must be halfway to Kansas by now. I glance out the nearest window just to make sure the storm is still out there, and I haven't walked clear into another climate.

It would be faster if I just took the moving walkways, but I think I've proven I can't be trusted on those.

I hit a literal dead end at gate B60 and, for a moment, wonder if I've been going the wrong way this entire time. Then I notice a narrow corridor leading off to the right, like a back alley. Do airports have bad neighborhoods? Because I feel like I'm walking over to the wrong side of the tracks.

The corridor opens into a smaller extension terminal. Less crowded. Brighter. Definitely a well kept secret.

The burger place Muppet Guy was talking about is called

New Belgium Hub. There's a menu just outside of the seating area, and I'm pleased to see that it does, in fact, have a veggie burger, among many other selections.

"Hey! Ocean! Danny Ocean!" I hear the familiar voice and look up to see Muppet Guy standing at the back of the line, waiting to place his order at the counter.

I blow out a breath—*here goes nothing*—and sidle up to him.

"You came," he states the obvious and, admittedly, I get a tiny surge of delight watching those perfect teeth flash as he smiles. Only because they're so damn straight. They should be in a museum or something.

"I came," I restate the obvious, feeling incredibly stupid.

I don't talk to guys. Lottie always did the talking. I just did the standing around and nodding. But I have a feeling that tactic won't work so well here.

"I was hungry," I add.

There's that chuckle again. "I'll try not to take offense by that."

My face warms. "It wasn't . . . I mean, I wasn't . . ."

"Relax. I'm kidding." And then he touches me. It's the simplest, most innocent of touches. On my arm. A graze. It's nothing.

It's nothing.

"So," he says, changing the subject. "How long have you been a vegetarian?"

Eleven months, thirty days, and eighteen hours.

I swallow. "About a year."

He nods. "That's cool. I was a vegetarian for about a week."

"Only a week?"

He runs his fingers through his hair. "Yeah, it was really just to piss off my parents. They took me to some expensive steak restaurant to celebrate this big career accomplishment, and I told them I was a vegetarian."

"Did it work?" I ask, genuinely interested.

"Better than expected. My dad was all sorts of ticked off. He accused me of lying to purposefully try to spoil their big day. So, to prove him wrong, I had to keep the act up. But it only lasted for a week. I was so freaking hungry all the time."

I let out a small laugh, surprised by how it sounds coming out of my mouth. Like a foreign language. Like a *Martian* language.

Sell yourself.

That's all I'm doing. I'm going door-to-door selling normalcy like a sweaty bald guy selling vacuums.

This one comes with the giggling girl attachment. For all your hard-to-reach places.

"What about you?" he asks. "Why are you a vegetarian? Health reasons? Animal rights? To piss off your parents?"

"Personal reasons," I reply vaguely, hoping this will suffice and he won't expect me to elaborate.

No such luck.

"Let me guess," he says, tapping his chin. "You had a pet cow as a kid?"

I shake my head. "No."

"You *were* a cow in a previous life."

Despite myself, I laugh again. "No."

"Your best friend died from mad cow disease?"

I fall quiet and stare at the floor, forcing myself to take deep breaths.

Oh God. This was a huge mistake.

How am I supposed to have a conversation with this person—with any person—when every single topic is a land mine? At the time I made the decision to come here, all I could think about was the food, the promise of a brief reprieve from the anarchy of the shopping rotunda. I didn't consider the fact that I was about to have a meal with a stranger. Someone who would ultimately ask me questions. Someone who would expect answers longer than two words.

Thankfully, just then, the customer ahead of us finishes ordering, and we find ourselves face-to-face with the girl running the cash register. I've never been so happy to see another human being in all my life.

I can feel Muppet Guy looking at me. I keep my gaze trained on the menu posted behind the cashier's head and try to pass off my silence as indecisiveness.

"Do you know what you want?" he asks, and I hear the tinge of confusion in his voice. He's trying to figure out what he did wrong. He's trying to ascertain if I really did have a best friend who died from mad cow disease.

"Um . . ." I stammer, frowning at the menu.

"Ooh! Ooh! BINGO!" the girl cashier yells, startling me out of my deliberation process.

Confused, I glance behind me, then back at her. "Excuse me?"

She turns to a large, plump young man in a white chef's jacket who's filling up a cup from the soda fountain behind her. "Bingo! I win!"

The man turns and studies me, hand on hip, mouth twisting to the side. "Hmm. I don't know. She doesn't look mopey *enough*."

The cashier lets out a huff and gestures theatrically to me. "Are you serious? Look at her! She's the poster child for mopey. She's the eighth dwarf, Dopey's long-lost cousin . . . *Mopey*!"

"Uh," I falter, glancing down to make sure I hadn't accidentally spilled something on the front of my shirt. "What are you talking about?"

The cashier turns back to me. She looks to be about my age, tall and slender with rich, toffee-colored skin and a dark brown bob. Her eyes are heavily lined with inky black makeup, and she has a diamond stud in her nose.

"Sorry," she says with a tilt of her head. "We get bored sometimes. We make up games. It helps pass the time. Today we're playing Stranded Passenger Bingo."

Muppet Guy takes a step closer to the counter, suddenly intrigued. "What's Stranded Passenger Bingo?"

The girl lights up at his interest. "Oh! It's so much fun. We create bingo cards for each other with different types of passengers that we have to find. If you get five in a row, you call 'Bingo!' and you win."

"I still need a Couple on the Verge of a Breakup," the guy at the soda fountain says. "So if you see one, be sure to let me know, mkay?"

Cashier Girl nods to me. "You were my top left corner."

"Me?" I say, feeling the walls of the restaurant closing in. "Me specifically?"

She laughs. "No. Not you, *specifically*. That would be creepy. See, Jimmy back there"—she jerks her thumb over her shoulder at the guy who's placing a plastic lid on his cup—"he put Mopey Girl on my card." She pulls a folded up piece of paper out of her apron pocket and smoothes it out on the counter. It's a grid made up of twenty-five boxes. Inside each one, someone has scribbled things like, *Gay and Doesn't Know It, Dresses Like It's Still 1995*, and *Unhealthily Obsessed with Hair Gel*.

Several of the boxes have large X's scratched through them. Then, in the top left corner, where the cashier's long, black-painted fingernail is tapping, are the words "Mopey Girl."

"I'm not mopey," I say dryly.

Muppet Guy laughs beside me. "You're a *little* mopey. But that's okay. I like mopey. I seek *out* mopey. It's kind of my thing."

I'm not sure who I'm currently more infuriated with. This random girl who just insulted me, or the guy standing next to me, who agreed with her assessment.

"Sorry," Jimmy says, punching a straw into the top of the drink he just filled and taking a sip. "I created the card. I get final veto power. She's not mopey enough."

I don't like this spotlight on my face. I don't like all of these strangers assessing me and my level of mopiness like students huddled around a microscope. I can't even handle when Dr. Judy stares at me for more than five seconds.

I consider screaming at all of them. I consider yelling

something dramatic like, "You know what? You can't walk around labeling people you know nothing about!" and then storming off to find something else to eat. I consider *reacting*.

But when I open my mouth, all that comes out is, "I'll have the veggie burger, please."

Cashier Girl snatches up the bingo card and stuffs it back into her apron pocket. "You're mad. I'm sorry. That was totally inappropriate. I shouldn't have shown you that. It's just that you two looked cool, and, let's face it, you're like the only people here who are our age, and I've been in a foul mood today—"

"She's in a foul mood *every* day," Jimmy says, passing behind her with his drink.

"Get back into the kitchen and make some burgers!" she growls.

He winks at her and disappears behind a door.

"I'm in an *especially* foul mood today," she clarifies. "You see, I was supposed to go to this killer New Year's Eve party in like"— she squints at the cash register screen—"five hours, but it doesn't look like anyone is getting out of here tonight, so—"

"That's not true," I blurt before I even realize what I'm doing. "My flight is leaving at 7:41 p.m. The board said." The desperation tastes salty in my mouth.

"Um." Cashier Girl gives me a blank stare. "I can't even dig my car out of the parking lot. You think they're going to be able to get a 737 off the ground in this shit?"

My throat catches fire.

No. I have to get out of here.

I can't stay here.

I can't be here tomorrow.

"Don't they have special tools and trucks and stuff for clearing the runway?" I ask, glancing frantically between Muppet Guy and the cashier. Neither one looks particularly helpful. "Why would the board say we're leaving if we're not leaving?"

"Sweetie," the cashier says, her voice taking on an odd syrupy cadence that makes my skin crawl. "I'm sorry to be the one to tell you this, but you're stuck here. We all are." She pulls the crumpled sheet of paper from her apron pocket again. "May I interest you in a game of bingo?"

∞

I collapse into a chair at one of the tables and numbly sip my soda. Muppet Guy lowers into the seat across from me, holding on to the plastic number eleven we received for our order.

Eleven used to be my lucky number.

Back when I used to have things like lucky numbers.

Back when I believed in luck.

"Look," he says, trying to be helpful. "What does she know? She's just an employee at a restaurant. She doesn't work for air traffic control. If the board says your flight is leaving at 7:45—"

"7:41," I correct.

"Right. If the board says that, then it's true."

I appreciate his efforts, even if they're not making me feel any better.

"So," he says, sipping his drink. "Are you coming or going?"

I blink and look up at him. "Huh?"

"San Francisco? Is it home?"

"Oh," I say, feeling stupid. "Yeah. Home, I guess."

"Home, you guess?"

"It's where my stuff is."

He chuckles. "Okay."

"And you? You said you were going to Miami? Is that home?"

"Noooo." He elongates the word, lowering the tone of his voice to the point where it could almost pass for the voice of the Muppet on his shirt. "Not home. Los Angeles is home. My parents are in Miami. I'm flying out to meet them."

"That's nice."

He releases a strange noise from the back of his throat. It's the first sound I've heard from him that can't be described as "jovial." "Nice. Sure. I guess that's one way to put it."

"You don't want to go to Miami?"

"I don't have a problem with Miami. I just don't want to be anywhere near my parents."

"Oh." I fall quiet, sensing that I've inadvertently crossed some sort of line. The kind of line you don't cross until you've known someone for at least a full day.

I'm incredibly grateful when he changes the subject. "I should probably ask your name, huh? So I don't have to keep thinking of you as Phone Girl."

A ghost of a smile cracks the concrete surface of my face.

"Is that funny?"

I take another sip of soda. "I've been thinking of you as Muppet Guy," I admit softly.

He peers down at his shirt, as if he forgot what he was wearing. "Ah. Right. Well, as creative as those names are, I have another idea."

"What's that?"

He opens his mouth to answer, but just then the cashier arrives with two trays. "Here we are!" She sets down a monster double bacon cheeseburger in front of my dining companion and a much daintier-looking veggie burger in front of me.

It's only then that I notice the cashier has a name tag pinned to the front of her red apron.

I stare up at her in disbelief "Your name is Siri?"

She gives me a hard stare. "Yeah. So?"

"Nothing," I say hastily, "It's just—"

"The name was fine until those douchebuckets at Apple decided to make it synonymous with information," she snaps, indicating I've hit a sore spot.

She and Troy should really get together. They could commiserate for hours over their beefs against Apple.

Siri goes on. "Now everyone thinks it's so funny to 'Ask Siri,' 'Ask Siri,' 'Ask Siri.'" She groans. "You don't know how many customers I get every day asking me stupid shit like, 'Hey, Siri, what's the weather in Palm Springs?' or 'Hey, Siri, what's the Broncos score?' They think they're *sooooo* clever. My parents joke that they should have just named me 411." She tucks the tray under her arm and scowls. "I still don't understand what that means."

"You could always ask Siri what it means," Muppet Guy suggests, and I hide another hint of a smile behind my cup.

"Oh, you two are *hilarious*," she says. "You should have a Web series on YouTube." She stalks away, and I bite my lip to keep from laughing.

"Hey, Siri!" Muppet Guy calls after her. "Can we get some napkins over here?"

"Get 'em yourself!" she calls back.

He stands. "I suppose I deserved that."

"I suppose you did." But my amusement fades the moment he leaves and I'm left alone with our food. I eye his giant double patty burger a mere foot away and try to swallow back the bile that rises in my stomach. The dark, grilled meat is hanging off the side of the bun. A small pool of red-tinted juice has formed on the plate next to it.

I hold my breath, but it's too late. I catch a whiff of the cooked beef and suddenly a slew of images are flickering across my vision.

Regurgitated hot dog pieces floating in the toilet.

Lottie's brain splattered against the dashboard.

10:05 a.m.

10:05 a.m.

10:05 a.m.

Forever and ever and ever . . .

"I hope it doesn't bother you if I eat meat," Muppet Guy says, returning with a pile of napkins. He slides back into his seat. "If so, I can order something else."

I shake my head. "No. It's fine."

It's so not fine.

What are you doing here?

You shouldn't be here.

"Relax," Lottie whispers seductively, and I almost sink in relief at the sound of her voice. "It's just meat. It's not like he's consuming a live cow in front of you."

Where have you been? I hiss silently back to her. *You convinced me to come meet this guy and then you totally abandoned me.*

"Awww," she coos, the sarcasm thick in her tone. "Did you miss me?"

I can't do this alone.

"I hate to break it to you, Ryn Ryn. But you *are* alone."

Are you drunk? I ask her.

"Are you?" she asks with a gasp.

You only call me Ryn Ryn when you're drunk.

"That was when I was alive. Now that I'm dead I can call you Ryn Ryn whenever I want."

I watch Muppet Guy take a big messy bite of his burger, ketchup oozing out the side and meat juice running down his chin. He grabs for a napkin and lazily wipes the juice away. I avert my eyes and focus on my veggie burger. I'm still starving, but my appetite seems to have evaporated in this mile-high climate. I set my phone down next to my tray, grab the plastic knife that came with my food, and start cutting my burger into perfect quarters.

"Anyway," he says, chewing and swallowing, "I was about to tell you my brilliant idea."

"God, he's so cute," Lottie pipes in. "Look at those blue eyes. With his skin tone, that's very rare. You should totally find some janitor's closet to make out in. There's probably even beds in one of the first-class lounges . . ."

I clear my throat. "Yes, you were."

He takes another bite, chews, swallows. "I was thinking instead of introducing ourselves, which is so totally normal and boring, let's make up new people to be."

"Oh, I *really* like him," Lottie approves.

"New people?" I ask dubiously.

"Yeah. You know, we're mysterious strangers, stuck in an airport on New Year's Eve. We're never going to see each other again. We could be anyone we want."

I finish cutting my burger and pick up one of the pieces. "I guess so, but why?"

"I don't really feel like being myself today," he says by way of explanation. I wait for him to elaborate, but he just takes another bite of his burger.

His suggestion instantly makes me suspicious. What is he hiding? Why doesn't he want to be himself? Is he a serial killer on the run? Is he wanted in forty-nine out of fifty states?

Then again, if he doesn't have to be himself, that means I don't have to be *myself*, either. It gives me a free pass to lie. To forget about busted dashboards and unread text messages and *Doctor Who* phone cases.

I'm not sure why I didn't think about it before. Lottie used to reinvent herself all the time. Why can't I?

It's the ultimate sales strategy

Be someone else entirely.

And let's face it. It's probably the *only* way I'm going to get through this meal.

"Okay," I tell him. "I'm in."

Deflating the Universe

By my tenth visit to Dr. Judy's office, I had played with all the busy toys and deemed the expanding ball my favorite. It was constructed out of hundreds of interlocking plastic pieces in various colors that collapsed in on themselves. You could squeeze it into the size of a tennis ball or expand it to the size of a basketball. I liked it because it felt like I was holding the whole universe in my hands. The ever expanding and contracting universe. It was about the only thing I felt I had control over. Because the real universe didn't seem to want to cooperate anymore.

Dr. Judy still let me keep my phone on me, but I usually just placed it in my lap, leaving my hands free to fidget with the toy.

Ten sessions, and I still hadn't talked about Lottie. Dr. Judy hadn't asked about her since my first visit. And that was fine by me. She kept to safer topics. My parents' divorce. The move from Portland to San Francisco. How I was liking my new school. It felt like the world's most expensive small talk.

My mom, who was footing the exorbitant bill, didn't know much about it. When she picked me up, she would simply ask, "How was your session?" and I would say, "Good," and then she'd switch to talking about paint samples or flooring or a new lamp she had her eye on.

Both my parents are good at that. Filling entire car rides with conversations that don't matter. That you won't even remember in the morning.

I kept waiting for Dr. Judy to broach the subject again. To mention Lottie's name. But she never did. It was like some unspoken rule between us. A silent agreement. I'll keep coming to these stupid things if you promise never to talk about the real reason I'm here.

I couldn't decide who was getting the better end of the deal.

"How did *you* handle the divorce?" she asked me as I contracted the universe back into a single dense atom.

I shrugged. "How anyone handles a divorce, I guess."

"How does anyone handle a divorce?" She sounded genuinely interested. I'd learned that about her. She was really good at making your statements sound like groundbreaking discoveries in the field of mental health.

"I was upset."

"You were upset."

"Yeah. I didn't want them to split up. That's only natural. But I guess it was better than some of the other divorces I've seen."

"What other divorces have you seen?"

I inflated the universe back to its massive, immeasurable size. "You know, people at school. People on TV."

"How were those divorces different?"

I yawned. "They were dramatic. Lots of yelling. Lots of fighting. Battles in court. The works."

"And your parents' divorce wasn't like that?"

I shook my head. "In truth, it was kind of anticlimactic. I kept expecting there to be more of . . . you know, more of that other stuff. But they barely even raised their voices. They used a mediator instead of lawyers. They both signed the papers willingly. They pretty much agreed on everything."

"Sounds very civil," she remarked.

Universe contracted. "I guess."

"Is that how everything is done in your family?" she asked.

Universe expanded. "Define 'everything.'"

She smiled. "Are your parents usually very civil about things? Do they not show emotions often? Do they not grieve outwardly?"

Universe contracted. Secret agenda uncovered. "Is that what you're getting at? That I don't know how to grieve? Because my parents never taught me?"

She feigned innocence. She was really good at that, too. Acting like everything that surfaced in this room was purely accidental. A fluke. "Children do learn coping mechanisms from their parents."

I set the universe down on the coffee table with a clunk and picked up my phone. "What coping mechanisms did they not teach me?" My voice was laced with irritation.

"Let me ask you this," she said, derailing my question. "Did you cry when Lottie died?"

The room cooled to an inhabitable temperature. A whole ice age confined to this small space.

She broke the agreement.

She said her name.

Aloud.

She conned me.

I stared at the abandoned universe on the table. It was in a sad state of in-between. Not quite an atom, not quite a vast, infinite cosmos. Like God had simply run out of air.

I swiped my phone screen on and stared down at my messaging app.

One unread message.

One unanswered question.

One piece of her still left. Still alive. Still existing in the world.

"Not everyone cries," I muttered.

∞

"You go first," Muppet Guy says, popping a fry into his mouth.

I shake my head adamantly. "Nuh-uh. No way. This was your idea. You go first."

He sighs. "Fine. My name is . . . uh . . . Reginald."

"Reginald?" I repeat dubiously.

"What? You don't believe me? You think someone wearing a Muppet shirt can't be called Reginald?"

"Okay," I allow. "Reginald what?"

"Oh, right, last names. I need a last name. Reginald . . . Schwarzenegger." And then, upon seeing my expression, he adds, "And no, there's no relation. But I get that a *lot*."

I can't help but chuckle. The new me is already way better at acting normal, and I haven't even invented her yet.

"Your turn," he says.

I take a deep breath. "Nice to meet you, Reginald Schwarzenegger. My name is . . ." I rack my brain for something good. For something creative. Something that won't make me feel like the uninspired dud that I always feel like.

"Jezebel Jeweltupple! Lacey Leroux! Vivica Van Derzendanzen!" Lottie throws her suggestions into the hat.

"Lottie," I say quickly.

"Lottie?" he echoes, and I immediately regret choosing that. The sound of her name on his lips . . . it's wrong. It's so very *wrong*.

"Lottie?" Lottie screeches in disgust. "Why would you use my name? That's so morbid. Jeez, Ryn."

She's right. It is morbid. I had the chance to reinvent myself. I had a Get Out of Jail Free card and I chose to rip it up. I chose to lock myself in my cell and throw away the key. What is the matter with me?

Muppet Guy opens his mouth to say something else, but I hastily interrupt him.

"You know what? I just forgot. That's not my name."

He cocks an eyebrow. "You forgot your own name?"

I let out a nervous laugh. "It happens. I'm a little insane like that."

"Okaaay," he says, taking a sip of his soda. "What *is* your name?"

"It's . . ."

C'mon, think.

Anything is better than Lottie.

I glance down at my burger for help. "Vege . . . Vege . . ."

Spit it out!

"Veg . . . ina."

Okay, maybe not anything.

Soda shoots out of Muppet Guy's mouth like a geyser. He coughs. "Your name is Vegina?"

My face warms to roughly the temperature of the sun.

"Wow," Lottie muses in my head. "You are *really* bad at this."

I laugh too in an attempt to cover up my stupid, stupid answer. I consider trying to change it again, but Muppet Guy looks far too amused. Maybe this is the new me. Maybe the new me doesn't get embarrassed by words that sound like body parts. Maybe the new me is bold and sassy and *likes* making boys laugh.

Maybe the new me is more like Lottie.

"Yup," I say confidently. "Vegina. Do you have a problem with that?"

He schools his expression, and is actually brave enough to take another sip from his straw. "Okay . . . Veg . . . ina. Do I even dare ask your last name?"

I shrug. "That's up to you."

He grins. "I'll take my chances. What is it?"

I glance around the small restaurant, searching for another piece of inspiration. I catch sight of a Starbucks across the small extension terminal.

Muppet Guy follows my gaze. "Yes?" he prompts.

"Starbucks," I say, satisfied.

He looks skeptical. "Your name is Vegina Starbucks?"

I nod. "Yes. I'm heir to the Starbucks fortune. I'm worth like a gazillion dollars."

He lets out a low whistle. "Wow. I should have let *you* pay for lunch."

I nod. "You should have."

He leans back in his chair, clearly enjoying his game. And I admit, I'm kind of enjoying it too.

Or, at least, *Vegina* is.

"So," he says, "if we were to walk over there right now and ask for a latte, they would *have* to give it to you for free."

"Yes, but Daddy really doesn't like me doing that."

Reginald Schwarzenegger bursts into another fit of laughter. "You're funny, you know that?"

His words puncture me, letting all the air seep out. Any confidence I've built up over the past two minutes is deflated like a popped tire. Lottie was always the funny one. Not me. I was only funny in relation to her. She started the joke and I piggybacked on it like a comedy freeloader. She set the ball and I spiked it. Without the setter, the spiker is a pretty pointless position.

"I'm not that funny," I tell him, glancing down at my half-eaten veggie burger.

But he ignores this. "Tell me more about life at the Starbucks mansion. How many ponies do you have? And servants! Do you have someone to brush your hair for you, like in Victorian times?

Do you have a personal mozzarella stick chef? I've always wanted one of those. I'd take him with me wherever I go. Just in case I get the sudden craving for mozzarella sticks."

"I do," I tell him, attempting to reinflate myself. "And a personal jalapeño popper chef."

His mouth drops open. "Shut the front door, Vegina!"

A few other diners look over at us, and I bow my head in total humiliation. Muppet Guy gives them a what-are-you-going-to-do? gesture and says, "That's her name. Unfortunate, I know."

I pick the burnt end off of one of my fries and pop it in my mouth. "What about you, Mr. Schwarzenegger? You mentioned you live in Los Angeles?"

"Yes," he says in all seriousness. "But we have a vacation house on Uranus."

I nearly choke on my fry. "Really?" I try to sound genuinely interested. "What's that like?"

"Cold," he says matter-of-factly.

"I can imagine. Not an ideal spot for a vacation home."

He shakes his head somberly. "It was one of those time-share scams. You know, they show you the brochure with pictures of a tropical island and white sand beaches, and then after you sign on the dotted line, they tell you that *your* time-share is actually on Uranus. Apparently, it was all in the fine print."

"But who reads the fine print?" I ask.

"Exactly. So, me and the fam, we pack it up every summer and spend some time on Uranus. You should come, Vegina. You'd like it there."

I press my lips together in an effort to keep the charade of a serious conversation going. "You know, I would. But I already have plans this summer."

He snaps his fingers. "Bummer. Being a caffeine heiress and all, your social calendar has got to be pretty full." He sighs dramatically. "But I took a shot."

"Yes. Very busy."

"So, what brings you to the airport today, Vegina?"

"On my way to a coffee convention in Bangkok, actually."

I watch his lips tremble as he tries to hold on to his slipping composure. I now realize this has morphed into an entirely new game. Who can get the other to break character first. I've had a lot of practice not smiling over the past year, so I imagine this should be a piece of cake for me. He clears his throat. "Where was that convention?"

"*Bang. Kok.*" I enunciate the two syllables with purpose, the new me keeping an effortlessly straight face.

He nods pensively, like he's trying to place it on a map in his mind. "I've heard of it. Don't they have like a famous track and field star there? A javelin thrower, I think."

I have no idea where he's going with this, but I play along. "Hmm. I'm not sure."

"Yeah, they do. I forget his name but he jaculates like a pro."

And I've lost.

I bury my head in my hands and giggle uncontrollably.

Muppet Guy is still playing along flawlessly. "Is everything alright, Vegina? Your face is turning red. Are you getting enough oxygen? I have a very high threshold for that sort of thing. Summering on Uranus, and all. The atmosphere there is quite thin."

I laugh harder.

"Okay, you two," comes a voice behind me. I pick my head up and wipe at my eyes. Siri is standing there with her hands on her hips, glaring at us. "You are having way too much fun over here. And *you*"—she jabs a finger in my face—"just negated my claim to bingo."

"All right, all right," Muppet Guy says. "No need to get crotchety."

I start giggling again.

Siri throws her hands in the air. "See! There's no way I can claim you as Mopey Girl now. Look at you! You're grinning and giggling like a sorority girl."

"She's right," Lottie says, sounding slightly annoyed. "Why weren't you ever this fun when I was alive?"

This sobers me up fast. I clear my throat and mumble, "Sorry."

"You should be," Siri says. "Jimmy only has one space left before he beats me. And the stakes are really high."

"What *are* the stakes?" Muppet Guy asks.

"Whoever loses has to clean the ketchup dispensers for a week. And do you *know* how gross a job that is?"

Muppet Guy points to me. "She has no idea. She's an heiress. She's never had to work a day in her life."

I give him a swift kick under the table.

Siri crosses her arms. "Really?"

I avert my gaze and shake my head. "No. Not really. He's just making that up." For some reason this girl completely intimidates me.

"Well, Your Highness, if you two are done eating, can you give up the table? There's about a thousand other stranded passengers who want to sit down."

I glance behind me and notice a long line has formed at the counter, where another employee in a red apron is taking orders. "Sorry. We'll leave."

I stand up and start to pick up my tray. "Don't touch that," Siri snaps. "I'll get it, Your Majesty. It's my job."

"I'm really not—" I start to say.

"Yeah, yeah, whatever. Get out of here. Go fly off to Saint Bart's or wherever it is you people go."

Muppet Guy stands and pulls his messenger bag over his head, crumpling Animal's face once again. I start to put on my backpack but can't manage to reach the second strap. Then, suddenly, Muppet Guy is behind me, holding the strap out for me. The gesture makes my stomach flip.

"Thanks," I mumble as I loop my arm through. He smiles at me, and I, like a coward, look away.

Siri finishes cleaning up our table and carries the trays back to the counter. As she goes, she calls over her shoulder, "You still owe me a Mopey Girl!"

I pull out the hair that's caught under my backpack straps. "I'll let you know if I see one," I say quietly, but I'm not sure she hears.

I glance back at the now empty table, and the breath catches in my chest when I see my phone lying there. I can't believe I nearly left it behind. I snatch it up and tap in the passcode, my eyes automatically veering toward the bottom of the home screen.

One unread message.

I check the clock, suddenly desperate to know how much time I've killed during this meal. It's almost five. A whole hour has passed.

Which means I have less than three hours to go.

I click the Web browser and hover my fingers over the keyboard, ready to ask Google all of the unanswered questions that have piled up in the past hour, but suddenly I can't think of a single one.

The thought unnerves me. I make one up fast.

How cold is it on Uranus?

Negative 371 degrees Fahrenheit.

"Everything all right?" Muppet Guy interrupts, nodding to my phone.

I shut off the screen. "Yeah. Fine."

"Wanna grab a Starbucks?" he asks with a wink.

"Sure."

On the twelfth visit, Dr. Judy asked to see my phone. It was a casual request that came after I'd already been sitting on her couch for a good twenty minutes. But it took me by surprise. She hadn't brought up my phone since the first session, when she gave me permission to hold it. There was no lead-up, no segue.

One minute we were talking about a book I was assigned to read in English and the next she was pointing at the device clutched in my hands.

"Are you allowed to ask that?" I replied, stalling for time. "Are you allowed to look at a patient's phone?"

"I'm allowed to ask," she stated neutrally. "And you're allowed to say no."

I hesitated, making a mental list of the pros and cons in my head. As it turned out, there weren't many.

Pro: If I hand it over willingly, like it doesn't even faze me, there's a higher chance she won't make a big deal about it.

Con: If she sees the text message, she might ask about it. She might read it.

The decision was made.

"Why?" I asked, trying to sound more curious than defensive.

"You said holding it makes you feel better. I'd just like to get a bit more insight into that."

With the screen off, I held up the phone, turning it around once. She reached for it. I returned it to my lap, flashing her what we both knew was an artificial smile. "Okay?"

She leaned back in her chair, chuckling softly. "Okay."

I let out an inaudible breath. I'd learned that breathing too hard was a giveaway. A sign of distress.

"It's an interesting phone case," she remarked, writing something down on her yellow pad. I watched her pen move, carefully observing the messy loops and scrawls. I'd found there was a direct correlation between my behavior and her scribbles. I was the earthquake and she was the Richter scale. The crazier I acted, the higher the magnitude.

My unwillingness to give up my phone: A 6.2.

A few broken dishes in your kitchen but not enough to bring down a house.

"Are you a *Doctor Who* fan?" she continued.

"Why would I have the case if I wasn't a fan?"

"I just never heard you mention the show before."

"We never talked about television before."

She smiled, her lips never parting. "True. Do you want to talk about television?"

"Do you?" I challenged.

She lowered her notepad, but kept the pen poised between her fingers. "Yes," she decided, and I felt conned once again. She'd called my bluff. "Tell me about *Doctor Who.*"

How does she just know? I wondered with a simmering fascination.

I grabbed for the expanding universe ball on the coffee table and cupped it in my hands. "What's to tell? It's about a guy who travels through space and time in a stupid blue box."

"*Stupid* blue box?" she echoed.

Stupid, careless girl, I scolded in my head.

I should have known better by now. In only a few short months, I'd become a master of concealment. But Dr. Judy had a tendency to bring out the worst in me.

The truth.

"That doesn't sound like a fan to me," she mused.

"What do you want me to say?" I snapped.

She glided effortlessly into her appeasement voice. "I'm just saying that a phone case is a very personal choice. A statement. Almost like a tattoo. Usually it means something to the person who chose it."

"Well, I didn't choose it. It was a gift."

She nodded and bent her head toward her notepad. Her Richter scale scribbles were getting more intense, building to the big one. The kind they make disaster movies about.

I knew what question was coming next. I knew I couldn't avoid it. I could hide under a table and strap down all my precious, breakable belongings, but it wouldn't do any good.

"Who gave it to you?" she asked, her eyes still downcast. The tip of her seismographic pen poised like a needle waiting for movement. Waiting for signs of a looming catastrophe.

I thought about asking Lottie for help, but I knew that was pointless. Lottie never spoke to me in here. It was like she was afraid of these walls.

I was alone.

I stretched the universe as far as it would go, threatening to break the whole damn thing apart. The plastic interlocking pieces dug into my skin. I heard them creak under the pressure.

The floor rumbled beneath my feet. The bookshelves started to shake.

"Did Lottie give you that phone case?" she guessed.

The toy ball snapped in my hands, the pieces scattering like ash into my lap.

"Yes," I whispered, my voice burnt and charred.

Dr. Judy studied me for five long seconds before scribbling furiously on her notepad.

Meanwhile, I plunged straight into the fiery depths of the earth's core.

∞

"Two grande lattes please," Muppet Guy says when we reach the front of the ridiculously long Starbucks line. So much for this wing of the airport being a well kept secret.

"Nonfat for me," I say.

"I'll have her fat," he says without missing a beat.

The male barista doesn't look amused by the comment. Apparently no airport employee is happy about being here today. He grabs two large paper cups from his dwindling stack and starts to scribble on them with a blue Sharpie. "Names?" he mutters.

Reginald looks expectantly to me. "Go ahead. Tell him your name."

I feel my face color again. "You can just write *V*."

Muppet Guy lets out a snort. "Cop-out."

"For his, you can write Mr. Schwarzenegger."

The barista glares up at me from behind the cup.

"And in case you're wondering," I add, "there's no relation. But he gets that a lot."

Muppet Guy snickers beside me as the barista passes the labeled cups to the one girl who's been tasked with making all the drinks. There appears to be about ten orders ahead of ours. It's going to be a while.

I steal a peek at the clock on my phone.

Two hours, thirty-seven minutes remaining.

"Nine dollars and eight-four cents," the barista announces from the cash register.

"Oh," Muppet Guy says knowingly. "Clearly you don't recognize her."

I slap his arm. "Don't," I warn through gritted teeth.

"Excuse me?" Grumpy Barista says, and I immediately wonder if *that* is on Siri's bingo card.

"You see," Muppet Guy begins haughtily, gesturing to me. "She is actually the daughter of . . ."

I kick his shin and he lets out a yelp. "Nothing," I say hastily, handing the clerk my mother's credit card. "He's just fooling around."

The barista swipes the card, and Muppet Guy and I wander over to the small mob of people ready to storm the joint if their caffeinated beverages don't appear in the next two minutes.

"I can't believe you paid for that." Muppet Guy shakes his head in disappointment. "All those perks. Down the drain." He makes a *whoosh* sound, which I assume is supposed to resemble the flushing of a toilet.

"I didn't want to cause a scene. There's a long line."

My phone vibrates quietly in my hand, and I glance down at the screen. It's my mother.

She's calling.

She never calls.

She always texts.

That's when I realize I haven't responded to any of her previous messages. She's probably worried sick.

"Sorry, hold on," I murmur to Muppet Guy, and swipe to answer the call. "Hi, Mom."

"Ryn! Thank God! Are you okay?" My mom's frantic energy vibrates right through the speaker.

Muppet Guy's eyes light up. "Mrs. Starbucks???" he mouths in awe.

I stifle a smile and turn away from him.

"I'm fine, Mom."

"The news says all the flights out of Denver are canceled."

"*Delayed*," I correct her. "My flight to San Francisco is leaving in less than three hours."

"Really? That's not what the news is saying."

"That's what the board is saying," I tell her. Although I feel confident that I have the more accurate information, I still feel a small solar flare of panic burst inside my chest.

"Well, maybe you should just *stay* in Denver. I don't know how I feel about you flying in that weather. It looks horrible."

I peer out the nearest window. It does look pretty horrible. But I assume whoever updates those information screens knows what they're doing. They probably have some super high-tech advanced weather system that's telling them the storm is on the way out.

"It'll be fine," I assure her. "If the airlines say it's safe to fly, then it's safe to fly."

My mom has become infinitely more paranoid in the last

eleven months and thirty-one days. I guess that's what happens when your only child just manages to outwit death on a technicality. You start to believe that death might try again.

"I'm going to start looking for hotel rooms just in case. You can stay the night and catch a flight first thing in the morning."

My throat starts to constrict.

The clock on the car's dashboard flashes wildly in my vision.

10:05 a.m.

10:05 a.m.

10:05 a.m.

"No, Mom," I rush to say. "Don't do that. I'm coming home *tonight*. I'm sleeping in my own bed tonight. Get off the Internet."

She hesitates. "Fine. But I don't like thinking about you stuck there all by yourself."

"You were just about to book me a hotel room all by myself," I remind her.

"I know. I just—"

"Besides," I tell her, "I'm not by myself, so you don't have to worry."

Silence. Then, "Oh?"

I turn back and share a look with Muppet Guy. "I made a new friend."

He flashes a wide, toothy grin.

"Who?" my mom demands. "Who is this new friend?"

"His name is . . ." I struggle to even say it. "Reginald."

"*His* name?" she echoes in alarm.

"Yes. Reginald is a he," I say, rolling my eyes.

"How old is he?"

I look Muppet Guy up and down. He stands up taller and straightens an imaginary suit jacket. "Uh. How old is he?" I repeat the question.

Reginald holds up ten fingers.

"Ten," I say automatically.

Reginald sighs and shakes his head, flashing eight more fingers.

"Ten?" my mother echoes in surprise.

"I mean, eighteen. He's eighteen. Same as me."

"Oh?" she says again, and I catch the dread in her voice. If she was still thinking about booking that hotel room, I've certainly put an end to that. "And where does this Reginald person live?"

"He lives in Los Angeles," I say, remembering our conversation in the restaurant. "But his family vacations"—I bite back the giggle that threatens to give me away—"elsewhere."

My mom is not amused. "What do his parents do?"

"What do his parents do?" I repeat, looking to Reginald for another prompt. But instead, his body stiffens and he seems to suddenly notice the small condiment counter behind him. He turns and makes his way over, avidly gathering up napkins and packets of sugar like he's stocking up for the apocalypse.

"I don't know, Mom," I snap, irritated that her question appeared to have made him uncomfortable. "I don't interrogate every single person I meet."

"Well, be sure to stay in a public, visible place."

"As opposed to all those dark, dangerous alleys in the airport?"

"Ryn," she scolds.

"Mom. I gotta go. Our coffee is almost ready. Shut off the news. I'll see you in a few hours."

I hang up the phone before she can say anything else. A moment later, a string of text messages vibrate my phone.

I click through each one without really reading any of them until there's only one unread message left.

"Sorry about that," I say when Muppet Guy returns with his supplies. "My mom is a little overprotective. She thinks that I'm going to go all crazy super slut on her. Or worse, that I already have."

He raises a single eyebrow. "Well, with a name like Vegina, who can blame her?"

I chuckle. "Right? She brought it on herself."

He looks me up and down, causing my cheeks to glow with heat again. "No offense," he says, clearly coming to some kind of conclusion. "But you don't strike me as the crazy super slut type."

"Know a lot of crazy super sluts?"

"Actually"—he slaps the sugar packets against his palm as though he thinks the action will make him look tough—"no."

I nod. "Didn't think so."

Muppet Guy glances down at my phone. It's then I notice that I've been incessantly rubbing the surface of the screen. I force my thumb to freeze. To act like a normal thumb.

"So," he says, looking back at me, "any particular *reason* she thinks you're going to go all crazy super slut?"

My thumb twitches again, searching for a way out of the mental force field I've built around it.

Yes. Because she read it in a book about grief.

Because she still thinks Lottie's hidden contraband was mine.

Because that's what good girls like me do when they lose their anchor. They get lost at sea.

"Grande nonfat latte for V and a regular grande latte for Mr. Schwarzenegger!" the overworked female barista calls out. She's so hassled, she doesn't even flinch at the name. The rest of the awaiting mob, however, all turn to look at Muppet Guy.

"No relation!" he calls out as he pushes his way to the front and grabs the two cups.

By the time we've both sweetened our lattes, he seems to have forgotten all about his question. And I'm grateful that I don't have to come up with another lie.

It Never Ends Well

My parents got divorced in the summer between sixth and seventh grade. Everything about the separation was clean and tidy. Like they'd been planning it since their wedding day.

Summer meant no missed school or carpools or homework to worry about. And since I was already moving from elementary school to middle school, it felt like a natural transition period. New school. New life. Easy. Peasy.

I spent the entire summer at my grandparents' house in Phoenix while my mom and dad ironed out the details at home. They assured me it was simpler this way. Neater. Less mess. My mother was a big fan of the Less Mess Method. Whatever path left the least amount of debris was the path for her.

When I flew back from Phoenix at the end of the summer, my parents were divorced. Just like that. Done. Finito.

It was strange. Like stepping through a wormhole and coming home to a parallel dimension of your life. When I boarded the plane in June, my mom and dad were husband and wife. When I disembarked the plane in August, I was another statistic. Another trapeze artist perpetually caught on a razor thin wire between two parents, two houses, two lives.

"What's it feel like?" Lottie asked me in the tree house later that night after I'd come home to a half-empty house. Not only had the divorce been finalized in my absence, but my father had moved out the remainder of his things.

I shrugged. "I don't know. It feels the same, I guess. Except my dad doesn't live with us anymore."

I was surprised by how true that was. Since I wasn't around to witness any of the proceedings or moving boxes or scheduled mediations, it simply felt like my dad was on a work trip. Except he'd taken all of his stuff with him.

"Are you okay?" Lottie asked, those perfect two lines forming between her eyes. Lottie hardly worried about anything. It just wasn't in her nature. So whenever I saw those matching wrinkles appear, I knew she was genuinely concerned about me.

I swallowed and tried to answer her question truthfully.

Was I okay?

I felt okay. Even though, somehow I knew I wasn't supposed to.

"I think so," I told her.

"I wish my parents would get divorced," Lottie said, collapsing onto her back, her shiny red locks spreading out around her head like a fiery halo.

"No, you don't," I told her.

"At least then they'd be forced to talk to each other." She stared at the rafters in the ceiling for a long time, like she was an architect studying their structural integrity, calculating out just how long they'd hold up before everything collapsed.

Then, after a silence that seemed to stretch on forever, she whispered, "I don't ever want to get married."

I lay down next to her and gazed upward, trying to figure out what was so interesting up there. "Never?"

"Never," she affirmed.

"Why?" I didn't understand her logic. If anyone should be anti-marriage it was me. I was the one who had just (sort of) been through a divorce.

"It never ends well."

"It *could* end well."

I heard her hair swishing against the wooden floor as she shook her head. "No."

The finality in her voice sent chills down my spine. I wanted to tell her she was wrong. That I wasn't the rule. I was the exception. We both were. But I was too cold to argue.

∞

"I should probably get back to my gate," I tell Muppet Guy. "You know, in case they decide to leave early." I hoist my sweetened latte in the air, like a really lame toast. "Thanks for lunch."

As distracting as the last hour has been, I'm anxious to peel off this strange girl's skin and go back to being myself. The girl who doesn't giggle uncontrollably and make lewd jokes with boys. The girl who sits quietly by herself, tapping questions into her phone, and having conversations with her imaginary dead best friend.

"Okay," Muppet Guy says. "I'll walk with you. I should get to my gate too."

"Okay."

As we walk, I silently berate myself for not devising a better escape plan. One that didn't come with some unintentional invitation to join me.

I should probably go help the baggage handlers unload luggage in the blizzard.

I should probably go change my tampon in the bathroom.

I should probably go jump in front of an airport train.

How fast do airport trains go?

Has anyone ever committed suicide by leaping in front of an airport train?

"Not that I'm in any hurry to get to Miami," Muppet Guy goes on.

"Don't you mean Uranus?"

He chuckles through a sip of coffee. "Nah. That's just in the summer. Trust me, you do *not* want to be on Uranus in the winter." He pretends to shiver.

I fake a smile. The new me is already wearing off. I can feel her slipping away the longer we walk through the B terminal. The closer we get to the train. The closer I get to reliving January 1st, 10:05 a.m., all over again.

The problem is, once that layer has been shed, once that protective coating has worn off, all that's waiting underneath is the old me. Ryn Gilbert.

And I really don't want him to be around when that happens.

We reach the shopping rotunda in the center of the B terminal.

It's shaped identically to the one in the A terminal, but the stores and restaurants are different. The food court is still stuffed with grumpy, frustrated people who would clearly rather be anywhere but here.

A female voice over the intercom system is paging passengers. The list seems endless. She actually has to pause and catch her breath at some point before continuing with what I swear is a sigh.

Diving back into the anarchy of the terminal's main hub instantly reminds me of Troy, the unaccompanied minor, off somewhere on some secret child prodigy mission that I wouldn't understand.

"Any system, if left unattended or isolated, will eventually result in entropy. Or chaos."

Well, he certainly seems to be right about that.

A moment later, as if in an effort to prove the boy's theory, I'm nearly steamrolled by a twentysomething woman storming out of a Brookstone store like a tornado escaping a bottle. I have to jump back to avoid the collision.

"If you love the damn back massager so much," she's ranting as she walks, "why don't you just *sleep* with it?"

Suddenly, a man comes running after her. "Miranda, will you calm down? I was just asking about its features!"

She stops and spins around to face the man. "Oh! Oh *really?* Because you're *so* interested in buying a back massager?"

"Maybe," he replies, but even *I'm* not convinced, and I don't even know what the fight is about.

"First you abandon me in line at the gift shop while I'm buying *your* stupid Altoids—that *have* to be cinnamon or else the world will implode—and then I walk all over this crazy place looking for you, only to find you flirting with a Brookstone employee!"

Muppet Guy and I continue walking, but I can tell this conversation is holding his attention too, because he keeps watching the couple long after we've passed them.

I think back to Jimmy, the plump cook at the New Belgium Hub, and his Stranded Passenger Bingo card. He needed only one space to win: Couple on the Verge of a Breakup. I fight the sudden urge to run all the way back to Gate B89 to tell him I found one. Anything to keep Siri from claiming me—the Mopey Girl—as her winning space.

I swing by the bank of information screens in the center of the rotunda and check my flight again. It's still leaving at 7:41 p.m.

Satisfied, I slip back into the human sea to make my way to the escalators. I can feel Muppet Guy behind me, pushing his way through the swells of people. I don't dare glance back for fear that I might lose my way. Or get crushed to death. When we're almost to the escalator, I spot a bookstore called the Tattered Cover a few feet away. I have every intention of just swimming on by, but something catches my eye. My gaze zeros in on a table of books positioned right inside the entrance of the store, focusing on one in particular. It's the most recent release by Dr. Max Hale and Dr. Marcia Livingston-Hale, those child psychologists I saw on TV earlier.

Kids Come First: 101 Answers to Your Most Common Parenting Questions.

I drop my empty latte cup in a nearby trash can and divert my course toward the bookstore. I want to see what these 101 most common questions are. If I can find just one that applies to me, then maybe there's hope for me after all. Then maybe I still have an ounce of normalcy left.

"What are you doing?" Muppet Guy asks, and I can't help remark on the elevated level of his voice. It sounds almost like panic.

Does he have some bizarre fear of bookstores?

Is he crazy and abnormal too?

The thought brings me a wave of comfort. Maybe I'm not the only one of us who sits in a therapist's office once a week playing with "busy toys." Maybe he has a Dr. Judy of his own. Maybe he likes expanding and contracting the universe just as much as I do.

What would a fear of bookstores be called? Libraphobia?

"I just want to see something," I tell him, making my way to the table and picking up a copy of Dr. Max and Dr. Marcia's book. I can feel Muppet Guy hovering next to me, fidgeting with the strap of his messenger bag.

"Are you okay?" I ask, glancing at him over my shoulder.

He runs his fingers anxiously through his hair and then strangely reaches for the book, ripping it from my hands and putting it back on the table. It sits slightly crooked atop the other copies.

"What are you doing reading that garbage?" He lets out a strange laugh that comes out more like a snort. "I mean, self-help books? Seriously? What are you? A forty-year-old spinster?"

I squint at him, completely thrown by his shift in behavior.

His voice. It's all high and squeaky. He can't possibly be going through puberty *now?* Look at him. He's at least six feet tall, and his body is—

I derail that thought and pick up the book again. "I just saw these people on TV earlier, and I was curious about something."

"Wouldn't you rather check out the young adult section? I'm sure there's some new end-of-the-world-catastrophe-and-we're-the-last-two-humans-so-we-better-start-repopulating-the-earth book out. Isn't that what all you hormonal teenage girls are reading these days?"

I shoot him another curious look and open the cover, flipping to the table of contents. "Hormonal?"

"You said so yourself!" he defends. "Your mom thinks you're turning into a crazy super slut!"

My eyes widen and I glance around the store. At least four other customers heard that and are now eyeing me with suspicion. As if Crazy Super Slut is actually code for Airport Terrorist.

"Sorry." He lowers his voice.

I peer up from the page and study his body language. He's shifting nervously from foot to foot, scratching at his hairline. I'm pretty sure he's considering grabbing the book from me again, so I take a step back and angle my body away from him.

I run my fingers down the table of contents, skimming each of the hundred and one questions listed.

My hope sinks to the floor like a dead body with cement shoes. I can't find one question that seems to apply to *me.* To *my* life. No wonder my mother switched to those other books. I'm no longer a commonly asked question. Now I'm a special circumstance.

When I look up again, Muppet Guy is watching me like a creepy stalker. His head is bent slightly, his teeth are going to town on his poor, defenseless thumbnail.

What is the matter with him?

And then I get another thought. If he really is a closeted libraphobic, maybe he'll have no choice but to leave and I'll finally be alone again.

"Is that really what you want?" Lottie asks, coming out of one of her sporadic hibernations. "To be alone?"

I'm not alone, I remind her, returning my attention to the book. *I have you.*

"And how long do you think that will last?"

I freeze. It's the first time either one of us has directly mentioned the elephant in the room. Or the elephant in my head, as it were. That she is a figment of my imagination. That she is a coping mechanism. That coping mechanisms are temporary.

That one day I won't need her anymore.

I grapple for a response. Something provoking. Something that will get her riled up enough to change the subject.

Besides, I tell her, *you're the one who said you never wanted to get married. You're the one who said that relationships never end well.*

It works. Lottie screeches back into my mind like an express train barreling through a local station. "I said *marriages* never end well. There are plenty of kinds of relationships that can be fun. Affairs. Casual flings. One-night stands in airports. Now, where is that first-class lounge . . . ?"

"Didn't you say you wanted to get to your gate?" Muppet Guy has shown some mercy on his thumbnail and is now back to fidgeting with his bag strap. "What if your flight leaves early? Do you really want to be stuck in this airport any longer than necessary?"

As weird as he's acting, he has a point. I set the book back down on the table. But as I turn to leave, I notice that I've accidentally placed the book upside down, with the back cover facing up. I tilt my head to get a look at the full-size author photograph printed on the jacket.

Muppet Guy lunges toward the table, knocking over several other books in the process. He grabs the *Kids Come First* book and hurriedly flips it over, doing his best to tidy up the mess he's made.

I bend to pick up some of the fallen books, but he waves me away. "I've got it," he snaps, crouching down and scooping hardcovers into his arms. "Why don't you wait outside?"

I ignore him and pick up the parenting book again, turning it over to get a better look at the photograph. Then I let out a gasp.

There, on the back of *Kids Come First: 101 Answers to Your Most Common Parenting Questions*, are Dr. Max and Dr. Marcia, posing with their teenage son. A boy with dark hair, light brown skin, and expressive blue eyes.

The same blue eyes that are now staring up at me in defeat from the floor of the airport bookstore.

∞

On the two-year anniversary of my parents' divorce, Lottie decided she needed to distract me. I insisted I was fine—I didn't need any distraction—but she insisted I was just really good at hiding it.

Lottie asked her Nanny of the Moment to drive us into the city for some sort of surprise that Lottie wouldn't divulge to me. Even though Lottie was fourteen and didn't really need a nanny, her parents consistently kept one on hand until Lottie got her driver's license. Mostly to drive Lottie around or run errands, or do random tasks around the house. She was kind of a catchall employee of the Valentine family.

The nanny dropped us off at what looked like an art studio in downtown Portland. As soon as I saw the sign in the door that read, DRAWING CLASS TODAY 1–3 P.M., I immediately backed away from the building.

"What are we doing here?" I asked in a panicked voice.

Lottie looped her arm through mine. "We're taking a drawing class."

"But I don't *need* a class."

I'd been successfully avoiding art classes of any kind since the day I first picked up a drawing utensil. My parents had offered to pay for art classes when I was younger, but I always refused. Drawing was my escape. My passion. My *thing*. It felt wrong for someone to tell me *how* to do it. Like taking a class on breathing.

"Yes, but *I* do," Lottie said. "You've seen my drawings. They look like stick figures drawn *by* stick figures."

She gave my hand a tug. "It'll be fun. I'll learn something, and you'll just impress everyone."

I reluctantly went inside. Lottie gave her name, and we were shown seats at small, white desks that were arranged in a circle.

Each desk was equipped with a stack of sketch paper and an assortment of pens.

After all the seats had been filled with students, a beautiful young woman wearing a pink silk robe waltzed into the room. She sat on a stool in the center of the sketch tables and casually untied her robe, letting it drape around her waist. I stifled a gasp while Lottie straight up giggled.

"This is *legit*," Lottie whispered to me. "I bet you've never drawn *that* before."

I dazedly shook my head, unable to tear my eyes away from the young woman. She was so comfortable up there. So relaxed. There were a dozen people circled around her who could see almost *everything*, and she was acting like she was alone in her room watching TV. My fourteen-year-old mind struggled to comprehend such confidence. I could barely bring myself to take a bath behind a closed door, convinced that someone would *accidentally* unlock it and walk in.

I stared down at the blank sheet of paper in front of me. For the first time in my life I felt daunted by the thought of turning it into something. Of doing justice to my subject. That had always been my criteria. Draw only what I could make real. If I couldn't transfer exactly what I saw onto the paper, I didn't even bother. Because I knew I'd only look at it and remember what it *should* look like.

For the next hour a middle-aged woman with wild curls and gentle eyes walked around the room, doling out advice to each student as we attempted to sketch the naked girl on the stool.

I chose to focus on her face. I couldn't bring myself to even look lower. And I was good at faces. Especially beautiful ones. I had been sketching Lottie for years, each drawing more realistic than the last. Lottie used to joke that it was better than looking into a mirror. That she preferred my drawings to her own reflection, because I mercifully chose to leave out all her flaws. I never told her that I just didn't see any.

But the longer I tried to capture this young woman's face, the more times I failed. I went through page after page, crumpling up my efforts and tossing them into the trash can under my table. Her eyes were too difficult. There was something in them I just couldn't capture. Something I couldn't understand. Confidence? Fear? Loneliness?

When the teacher finally reached my table, I had just started over on yet another attempt, my hand once again sketching the shape of the woman's now familiar widow's peak. The teacher paused and silently watched me sketch for what felt like hours. I grew more and more anxious with each passing second, convinced she would tell me it was horrible. That I should never pick up a pen again.

Then, just as I thought she was going to leave without a single word, she bent down, scooped up one of my discarded attempts from the trash can, and smoothed out the crumpled paper.

"Those are mess-ups," I hurriedly explained. "Mistakes."

She nodded like she understood. Like she could relate. But her eyes never left the page in her hand. "You know," she began pensively, "some artists believe there's no such thing as a mistake. That we draw what we see. What we feel."

I gaped at her, unsure what to say to that. But it soon became obvious that she wasn't expecting a response, because she placed the once-crumpled paper onto my table and gave it a final smoothing with her palm before continuing to the next artist.

I stared at the page for a long time. At the warped eyes and shaky cheekbones. The wrinkles in the paper made the mistakes even more pronounced. A deformation of a deformation. Those misshapen eyes glared back at me. Taunting me. Until I couldn't take it anymore. Until I grabbed the paper, crumpled it even tighter than the first time, and returned it to the trash.

I gripped the pen and refocused on my current attempt, trying desperately to keep my hand steady as I traced the woman's hairline. But it was no use. Everything was shaking. My vision. My hands. My lines. I finally dropped the pen and walked out of the studio.

∞

"Wait," I say, glancing between the boy in the photograph and the one on the floor of the airport bookstore. The boy on the back of the book is dressed in pressed khakis, a collared shirt, and a conservative navy blue sweater. The one rising up from a crouch opted for the more casual Muppet look. But there's no denying it. They're the same person. "You . . ." I point hesitantly at the book. "You're . . ."

Body slouched, head bowed, Muppet Guy places the armful of spilled books onto the table in a chaotic heap, no longer caring about their order. "Xander Hale," he says with a sigh. "Nice to meet you."

My mind struggles to keep up. I mean, his appearance makes sense—he has the same bright blue eyes as his mother, and the same dark hair as his father—but other than that, I'm at a loss. I mentally scroll back through all the conversations we've had in the past two hours, searching for a clue that I could have missed. But of course, there are none. We spent the past two hours pretending to be other people.

"I don't really feel like being myself today . . ."

"Okay," he says, looking jumpy. "You can say something now."

I clear my throat, glancing once again between the boy on the book and the boy in front of me. "I . . ." I stammer again. "Wow. What's that like?"

He laughs darkly. "What do you think it's like?"

Obviously, this is a rhetorical question, because he shuffles out of the store before I can formulate an answer. I place the book on the table and dart after him, but he's already halfway to the escalator. Apparently, we've swapped places. Now he's the one desperate to get away and I'm the one chasing after.

I simply have too many questions to walk away now. I'm the girl who—with one set of faulty brakes—jumped right off the page of his parents' book. But he's the boy who inspired the books. Who *lived* the books. He doesn't just have a Dr. Judy back home. He was raised by one. Or *two*, rather! On the spectrum of teenage psychological health, we're about as far apart as two people can get.

I picture long family dinners where everyone shares their feelings and asks insightful questions. I picture productive car rides full of scintillating conversation about anything but wallpaper samples and paint. If Dr. Max and Dr. Marcia got divorced, I bet their son wouldn't be shipped off like an inconvenient distraction for the summer. I bet he'd be invited to the mediation meetings, maybe even asked to give his opinion on the proceedings. Not that Dr. Max and Dr. Marcia would *ever* get divorced.

I catch up to Muppet Guy—*Xander*—by the escalator that leads down to the train. He stops and turns around. I nearly flinch at the sight of him. Everything about him—his face, his body language, his eyes—has changed. He's transformed into someone else. The happy-go-lucky, lewd-joke-cracking, messy-burger-eating guy from the restaurant is gone.

"I don't—" he starts to say, but tapers off, pressing fingertips into his eye sockets. "I don't want to talk about my parents, okay?"

"Okay," I say automatically, but inside, I'm screaming for answers.

How could he not want to talk? He's the son of two of the most famous child psychologists in the country! He's the poster child for raising happy kids. My mom pays all-the-money per hour for me to have someone to talk to, and I just sit there and fidget with plastic universes, trying to make sure Dr. Judy doesn't stumble upon any of my secret, locked doors. If anyone should be comfortable talking, it's him.

"Can we just forget you saw that?" he asks.

"Okay," I repeat, even though I know it's a promise I can't

keep. Especially now that his reaction to all of this is confusing me more than anything. "Do I have to go back to calling you Reginald?"

The tiniest hint of a smile cracks his newly hardened exterior. He pushes his hands so deep into his pockets, I worry he might tear right through the fabric. "No," he says. "But I think it's only fair that I know your real name too."

I wince, feeling like he just kicked me in the stomach.

I can't. I can't do it. If he knows my real name then there's nowhere left to hide.

Lottie huffs impatiently in my mind. "Just tell him, already. Stop being a baby. He's just asking for your name. He's not running a fucking background check. Why are you so terrified?"

Because . . . I hesitate. I want to answer her question honestly. I want to be truthful for one goddamn time in the past goddamn year. *Because it never ends well, remember?*

Lottie is quiet for a moment. If I could see her right now—if she wasn't just an imaginary coping mechanism in my head—then I know she'd be twirling a strand of ruby red hair around her finger. It's what she does when she's stumped. Or, seducing someone.

Or rather, what she *did*.

"I suppose it *could* end well," she finally admits, and I can hear it in her voice. The capitulation. The surrender.

Step right up, ladies and gents, and witness the world's first ever defeat of Lottie Valentine!

Despite the bedlam of the B concourse, there's a tense silence around me. Xander waits for me to answer his fairly simple and straightforward question while Lottie waits for me to claim my victory. For me to wave my arms and whoop and parade around her in a ridiculous chicken dance.

But I won't do that. Because I can feel the blood oozing from the wound in her pride. And because it's not nice to gloat to a dead girl.

I stand up a little straighter. My old skin feels tight and awkward as I roll it back on. Like a pair of jeans you haven't worn since you were in better shape. Since you were a better person.

"Ryn Gilbert," I announce like I'm standing up in court, pleading guilty in the hopes of reducing my prison sentence.

That's what life has become for me. A constant plea bargain. Forced, for eternity, to cop to a crime I didn't commit. To choose between two evils.

Xander reaches out and takes my hand in his. The warmth of his skin startles me again. I'm about to ask what he's doing— why he's suddenly touching me—but then he starts to pump my hand like an overeager salesman. "Pleasure to meet you, Ryn Gilbert."

The sound of my real name on his lips sends shivers through me, and I'm suddenly reminded of that very first day in the mall food court. When I ceased to be Kathryn. When Lottie crossed out half my name on those job applications and turned me into a whole different person.

"Ryn," Xander repeats curiously, stepping onto the escalator and glancing back at me. "That's an interesting name. Is it short for something?"

As I follow him down to the train platform, I can't help but smile.

"Voilà! Instant conversation."

Where the Train
Turns Around

Even after we got our driver's licenses, Lottie and I sometimes liked to take light rail into downtown. It was easier than trying to park.

One sticky summer day between junior and senior year, Lottie and I took the train into the city to get ice cream. She'd claimed to have a desperate, unyielding craving for Salt & Straw, a Portland staple. But after we'd been walking for a good five minutes, I realized I'd been duped.

I didn't recognize my surroundings but I knew we were nowhere near any of the Salt & Straw locations.

"Um, where are we going?" I asked as she led me through a dark alley that made the hair on the back of my neck stand up. I pulled out my phone and checked our location on the map. It was an area of Portland I'd never been to before, and definitely didn't want to return to anytime soon.

"Wanna hear something crazy?" she asked in response, and I knew I wasn't going to like whatever came next.

"Always," I said, my usual confidence in the word nowhere to be found.

"I found an amazing poker tutor on Craigslist."

I immediately turned around and started walking back toward the train station. Lottie jogged to catch up to me and grabbed me by the shirtsleeve. "C'mon, Ryn. Don't be a baby."

"On Craigslist?" I screeched. "You realize this guy could be a rapist! Or a serial killer!"

"Well, that's just sexist," was Lottie's comeback.

"Excuse me?"

She paused in front of an unmarked door. "The poker tutor happens to be a *woman*."

Recently Lottie had gotten it into her head that she wanted to play poker. No, not just *play* it. Master it. She wanted to be the first female to ever win the World Series of Poker main event in Las Vegas. It was a random dream that, like all of Lottie's dreams, seemed to have come out of nowhere.

In an effort to familiarize herself with the game, she'd started watching televised poker tournaments twenty-four/seven. When there wasn't one on TV, she'd turn to the Internet, where there was an archive of recorded games.

I knew this was just another seat in Lottie's constant game of identity musical chairs, so I'd gone along with it. The way I always went along with her reinventions. Humoring her until the music started again and she set off to find another chair.

"Ryn," she whined, stomping her foot a little. "Where is your sense of adventure?"

"Where is your sense of *survival?*"

"Will you relax? This woman is apparently a poker genius. She's going to teach us everything we need to know."

"Couldn't we just download an app or something?"

Lottie pouted. "If you want to be the best at something, you have to learn from the best."

She knocked on the door. It sounded like gunshots in my ears.

"You told me we were going for ice cream," I complained in a whisper, glancing anxiously over my shoulder for signs of danger. The alley was eerily quiet and deserted.

"Well, then, there's your first poker lesson," Lottie said smugly. "Know when your opponent is bluffing."

"Please stand clear of the doors. This train is departing."

Xander and I run through the deserted platform as the doors of the train start to close. He barely manages to slide through, and I quickly realize I'm not going to make it. Xander sticks his arm out, risking amputation. I close my eyes. I can't watch. The doors are going to crush him.

Lottie's brain splattered on the dashboard.

Lottie's slender, mangled body buried in the ground.

Lottie's blood sprayed across a clock forever stuck at 10:05 a.m.

I hear a whoosh and brave a look. The doors are opening again. Xander's arm is intact.

I dash inside to find the train completely empty.

"Please stand clear of the doors," the pleasant female voice says again. "*You* are delaying the departure of this train."

We both look up at the ceiling in unison.

"Wow. Talk about a guilt trip," he says.

The doors attempt to close again. This time, there are no body parts to stop them. The train pulls away from the platform, and I take a seat on the small bench in the front, next to a window that looks out at the darkened track.

"Nuh-uh," Xander says. "You can't sit. That's cheating."

I look blankly between him and the bench. "Cheating?"

He takes off his messenger bag and sets it on the floor. Then he positions himself between two of the metal poles, spreading his feet apart and extending his arms like he's on a surfboard.

"What are you doing?"

"Train surfing!" he says gleefully.

"Train surfing?"

"I've always wanted to do this, but it's usually so crowded on these things." The train speeds up, and he adjusts his weight, leaning forward. "The goal is to never grab the handrail."

"For your safety and the safety of others, please hold on to the handrails," the computerized train voice says, as though it can hear him.

I point at the ceiling. "She thinks you're crazy."

He beckons me toward him. "C'mon. Try it."

"Train surfing is really more of a spectator sport. I think I'll just watch."

The train lurches to the left and he goes stumbling forward. His arm instinctively reaches for the handrail, but he stops himself just in time, regaining his balance on his own.

"Phew." He wipes invisible sweat from his brow. "That was a close one."

He resumes his stance, legs apart, one in front of the other, arms out. He looks ridiculous. I watch him navigate the subtle turns and bumps of the track. I still can't believe he's the son of Dr. Max Hale and Dr. Marcia Livingston-Hale. I've heard them talk about their son during interviews. Mostly about how amazing and well-adjusted he is. "Because he comes first," I can picture Dr. Marcia saying. "Kids *should* come first."

I want so desperately to ask him more questions about his parents. About his life. About growing up in a house where people talk about things.

"Seriously, Ryn," he says without breaking his concentration. "You have to try this."

"I'm fine."

"Suit yourse—whoa!" The train abruptly slows, almost knocking him over again. He bends his knees until he's nearly in a crouch.

The woman's voice comes back over the speaker. "Please hold on. This train is approaching the . . . C gates."

I look to Xander. He stares blankly back at me. Then we both crack up.

After all of that—a mad dash across the platform, a near amputation, a guilt trip from the train—we got on going the wrong way.

The train pulls to a stop and the doors open. "This is the C gates. All passengers please exit."

Across the platform, I can see the sign for the train going back to the B and A gates. I stand up.

"Wait," Xander says, and I notice he's made no move to grab his bag from the floor. "Let's stay."

I'm not following his messed up logic. "The train to the A gates is across the way."

"But where does *this* train go? C is the last terminal."

Who cares where this train goes? I need to get back to the A gates. It's quarter to six. My flight leaves in two hours.

"The guilt-trip train lady told us to exit," I remind him.

"She also told us to hold on to the handrails."

"Which I did!"

The train still hasn't moved. I hear another voice come from just outside the still-open doors. This one is male. "No boarding from this position. All trains depart from the other side of platform."

"See?" I point in the general direction of the voice.

"Do you always do everything the automated voices say?" he asks, smirking.

"No," I reply defensively while at the same time realizing that the truthful answer is a resounding *yes*. They obviously programmed those instructions for a reason. Even if I don't know the reason, I'm still inclined to follow them.

"This train has to turn around eventually, right?"

I consider his argument. I suppose he's right. If C is the last terminal, the train must turn around. But what if it doesn't? What if *this* particular train is scheduled for maintenance and disappears into some dark garage and we can't get out?

"I've always wanted to know where the train turns around," Xander says, and I'm starting to comprehend his choice in Muppet paraphernalia. Animal is the crazy one. The chaotic one who runs around screaming. Who doesn't follow the rules.

"Haven't you ever wondered where the train turns around?" he asks with a roguish raise of his eyebrows.

"No," I say automatically. "I want to get to my gate."

"Relax," he tells me, and it strikes a nerve.

"I am relaxed," I snap even though I feel further from relaxed than I've felt all day.

"You still have"—he pulls his phone from his pocket and glances at the screen—"two hours until your flight leaves."

"What if they push it up?"

He shoos this away like a bothersome fly. "They're not going to push it up. If anything, they're going to push it *back*. Have you looked outside recently? This storm isn't getting any better. It's getting worse."

My heart hammers at the thought. It can't get worse. It *has* to get better. I *have* to get home.

"So really, you have no place to be but right here," he reasons.

I swipe on my phone to check the weather. To prove him wrong. He has to be wrong. But my chest tightens when I see the tiny little Searching sign where the bars are supposed to be.

There's no signal down here.

Even more reason to get out of this train. I'll just ride the escalator up to the C gates, connect to the network, and check the weather. And the information boards, while I'm at it.

"Will you chill out?" Lottie scolds. "You're acting crazy."

Because I want answers? I snap. *That makes me crazy?*

"Because you're starting to sound obsessive."

And you're starting to sound like Dr. Judy.

Lottie laughs her buoyant, infectious laugh.

What's so funny? I ask.

"You're a smart girl. You figure it out."

I need to check those information screens.

"You just checked them five minutes ago."

I'm beginning to lose patience with her. *A lot can change in five minutes, okay?*

"Like what?" she challenges.

"I'm sorry," I say to Xander, who must notice I've disappeared into my own head, because he's looking at me a little strangely. "But I have to—"

Just then, the doors glide swiftly closed, sealing us inside, ripping the choice right out from under me. The train rumbles into motion again. With a giddy "whoop!" Xander resumes his surfing stance. I gaze out the front window. There's nothing but darkness ahead of us.

Haven't you ever wondered where the train turns around?

Right now all I can do is hope that the train *does* turn around.

That this journey comes with a return trip back. That I didn't just surrender my fate to a dark tunnel with no visible light at the end.

At 10:00 you were alive, I say meekly to the voice in my head. *At 10:05 you weren't.*

Then, instinctively, I grab on to the handrail.

∞

What Lottie didn't know—but we soon discovered—was that the Craigslist ad she found for a poker tutor was actually a notice for an underground traveling poker game. Apparently, the name of the poker tutor in the listing—Madeline Meroni—is some secret code directing Portland poker players to the location of the next game.

I would have run the other way, but Lottie, being the girl that she is, didn't miss a beat.

"Of course we're here for the game," she said confidently when the large bouncer at the door peered down on us as if we were ants cowering below a skyscraper. He was as pale as a zombie and twice as frightening.

"What are you doing?" I hissed as the bouncer led us through a dimly lit hallway with a pungent odor that I couldn't quite identify. "We should leave. Like now."

"If you want to be the best at something," she replied, "you have to just jump right in."

"I thought you said if you want to be the best at something, you have to *learn* from the best."

"Exactly. And these guys are the best."

"At what? Murdering girls and burying their bodies in Vancouver? Lottie, I do not want to be buried in the 'Couve!"

The bouncer turned around and shot us both a glare. It was enough to shut even Lottie up.

We turned left down another hallway, descended a set of dusty stone stairs, and entered a large, smoky basement with a single overheard lamp. A table for ten had been set up in the center of the room, and nine of the chairs were already full. It was a motley assortment of players, ranging from full-on Portland hipster—skinny jeans, flannel shirt, fluffy beard and everything—to a massive bald dude with white eyebrows and a neck tattoo.

Regardless, they all looked like criminals to me. And in a way they were. This wasn't exactly a *legal* gambling establishment.

"I think this basement was part of the Shanghai Tunnels," I whispered into Lottie's ear. "Where they used to kidnap women and force them into prostitution."

She shook her head. "That legend has never been proven."

"Cashier's over there," the bouncer grunted. "We don't take anything smaller than hundies."

Lottie nodded like she'd done this a thousand times. "Gotcha." Then she grabbed my arm and pulled me over to the "cashier," who was really just a blond guy wearing sunglasses and a backward cap, guarding a dinged up metal cash box with a gun placed on top.

I felt my left lung give out. "Lottie," I screeched, grabbing hold of her coat sleeve and clenching my teeth. "He. Has. A. Gun."

But she waved this off as if I'd said something as harmless as "He has a dust ruffle."

"They never use it," she whispered. "It's just there to keep people from trying anything. It's probably not even loaded." Then she flashed her most perfect Lottie smile at the cashier and produced five hundred-dollar bills from her bra. She pushed them across the table with the tip of her finger. "Buy in for five hundred, please."

I didn't need to ask where Lottie got the money. Her father kept a stash of hundreds hidden in a safe in his office. Lottie had cracked the combination years ago. She claimed that he was never around enough to keep accurate count.

"Maybe if he came home more than three times a month, he'd notice when money went missing," she'd said to me once after swiping a hundred for a food court binge at the mall. "Until then, his loss, our gain."

"There's only one seat left," the cashier said, holding each bill up to a small lamp on the table. "Which of you is going to take it?"

"I am," Lottie said immediately, and some tiny, infinitesimal part of me felt the snub. Sure, I had no intention of actually playing. Sure, I was about the last person in the solar system equipped to play in an illegal, underground poker game. But the fact that Lottie came to the same conclusion about me stung. Just a little.

The cashier handed her a rack of green-and-white-striped chips and deposited her bills into the cash box.

Lottie hugged the rack to her chest and started toward the empty chair. I stepped in front of her. "Lottie, this is crazy!" I whisper-yelled. "I really think this is a very bad idea."

"Relax," Lottie said. "Portland was founded on this kind of debauchery. It's in our blood."

"You were born in Chicago!"

"Even better."

"You don't know how to play," I murmured, glancing over my shoulder to make sure none of the other players could hear me.

"I know the basics from watching TV. I'll just fake it until I make it. That's what I do best."

I wanted to scream at the top of my lungs. I wanted to grab her by her gorgeous cherry red locks and drag her out of there. Or, at the very least, I wanted to come up with another pointless argument for her to breezily negate. But as I watched her sashay to the table and slide into the last empty seat with a confidence that managed to fool even me, all I could think was, *Yes, Lottie. That is exactly what you do best.*

∞

I watch out the back window as the train rumbles slowly down the track, eventually reaching a fork and veering left to enter another seemingly endless tunnel that leads God knows where.

"This is so cool!" Xander says as he bounces a few times, readying his muscles for whatever comes next.

Death. That's what comes next. I'm almost sure of it.

The train continues down the tunnel of doom. I still have no idea where it leads, but I know it's not turning around. And it's not heading in the direction of the A gates. Where I need to be right now. Where I *should* be right now. Where I *would* have been if it weren't for stupid Lottie and her stupid obsession with *Doctor Who*.

"Hey!" Lottie screeches in my ear. "*Doctor Who* is not stupid!"

You can shut up now, I hiss. *You and your phone case got us into this mess.*

"Wanna hear something crazy?" she asks immediately.

No!

This shuts her up.

"Huh," Xander muses, bending down to get a better look out the window I'm practically plastered to. "It's not turning around."

No shit, Sherlock! I want to shout. But I stay silent, my eyes peeled to the empty track ahead of us. Because I'm a coward. A coward who can't make her own decisions. Who doesn't listen to her instincts when her instincts are clearly telling her—no, *shouting* at her—to get off the goddamn train!

"I wonder where it's going," Xander muses.

I grip my phone tighter, threatening to shatter the poor device in my hand. Not that it matters though. I won't need a phone after I'm dead.

Then, without warning, without ceremony, the train just stops.

Right in the middle of the track.

This is it. This is where we die.

This is where some robot monster sears off the top of the car with its laser claws, reaches down, and rips us right from the train.

This is where . . .

"Please continue to hold on," the female voice says. "The train will be moving momentarily."

I exhale the universe out of my lungs. I've never been so excited to hear an automated voice in my entire life.

"Aha!" Xander exclaims. "I get it. It doesn't actually turn around. It backs up onto the other track and then moves forward. So now we're going to be in the back of the train, instead of the front."

I nod, like I've been coming to the exact same conclusion.

Three seconds later the train starts up again, heading in the opposite direction. The *right* direction. I wilt in relief.

"All right, old lady," Xander says, walking unsteadily over to me. The way he has to zigzag across the car to keep his balance makes him look like one of the drunk hobos who wander the streets in downtown Portland. "No sitting this time around."

He can't possibly be serious.

"I'm not surfing in a train car," I vow.

"You are totally surfing in a train car."

I scoot farther back onto the bench, until I'm pressed against the window. He reaches out and grabs hold of my arm, giving it a tug. "C'mon, cheater. Get up. Use those perfectly good legs of yours."

I glance down at his hand on my arm. "Oh, look. You grabbed on to something. You lose. Game over."

He gives me a fake har har laugh. "Very funny, Vegina. But it has to be a real handrail."

He tugs on my arm again. I don't like the sensation of his hand on me. It's too close. Too personal. Too much. But apparently, the only way he's going to let go is if I play his little game.

"Fine," I say, scooting forward. He releases his grip.

I stand, feeling the rumble of the track beneath my feet.

"Backpack off," he orders. "It'll hinder your balance."

With a sigh I stuff my phone into the back pocket of my jeans, then reluctantly shimmy out of my backpack and set it by my feet, careful to keep one hand on the pole the entire time.

"Now," Xander says, returning to his ridiculous surfer stance. "Just let go."

I swallow and let my grip on the pole loosen. My fingers tingle in protest, wanting to squeeze tighter. I spread my legs to steady myself and release my hands, testing out my balance. It's more stable than I thought it would be.

Well, this is easy.

Of course at that very moment the train decides to lurch, and I go tumbling forward, halfway across the car. I crash right into Xander. For the *second* time today.

"Please hold on. This train is approaching the C gates."

She couldn't have warned me a second earlier?

Xander catches me with a laugh. And suddenly, the only thing I can feel is his hands on my shoulders. His mouth near my mouth. His eyes close enough to see inside. See all my secrets.

I jump back, grasping for my pole again.

The train pulls to a stop and the doors open.

"Exit here for all C gates."

I consider darting out right this second. There's got to be a walkway back to the A terminal. Hell, I'll walk outside in the snow if I have to.

"Don't give up," Xander encourages, as if my thoughts are

encapsulated in a tiny cartoon bubble above my head.

A melodic little five-note song plays. It sounds like something you'd hear between scenes of a laugh-track sitcom. "The doors are closing. Please keep clear and hold on for departure to all B gates."

I look hopefully toward the empty platform. If someone gets on, maybe we can stop this ridiculous game. But no one does. The doors glide shut again. The train starts to pick up speed.

"I don't think I'm coordinated enough for train surfing," I tell Xander from my pole. "It's probably safer if I just stick to the handrail."

"Safer, maybe," Xander agrees. "But not nearly as much fun."

A boisterous cackling laugh vibrates in my brain. "Wow," Lottie muses. "This guy is good. He's only known you for what? Two hours? And he's already got you pegged."

I'm not pegged.

So much for ignoring her.

"You are sooo pegged. You are like the most peggable person I know."

"Peggable" is not a word, Lottie.

"It is now. I just invented it."

You can't just invent words.

"I can do whatever I want. I'm dead."

"Everything all right over there?" That was Xander. Although, thankfully, I'm sane enough to tell the difference, I still flinch slightly at the sound of a real voice interrupting my conversation with an imaginary one.

"Yes," I say quickly.

"You looked like you were somewhere else," Xander says.

I was, I think at the same time Lottie says, "She was."

The train slows dramatically. Xander almost loses his balance. He takes two large, stumbling steps to realign himself. The doors open again. No one gets on.

"The doors are closing. Please keep clear and hold for departure to all A gates."

The voice is music to my ears.

You're almost there.

One more stop.

The doors close. The train wrenches into motion again. I let go of the handrail and step into the center of the train. If for no other reason than to prove Lottie wrong.

"Good!" Xander encourages, as if I'm a five-year-old afraid to dive off the diving board.

Fake it until you make it, I remind myself.

I spread my legs slightly and stretch my arms out to the side just like Xander's doing. I've never actually surfed before. Lottie wanted to take lessons after she fell in love with one of our coworkers at A-Frame, but by the time she got around to finding a local surf school, she'd already moved on to the guy who worked at the mobile phone kiosk.

"Try to put all your weight in your feet," Xander instructs.

"Where else would my weight be?"

The train banks slightly to the left. This time I'm ready. I shift to compensate, sticking my butt way out. It's not graceful but it works. I stay upright.

"Well, that's attractive," Lottie criticizes.

May I remind you, this was your idea.

"Actually, I think it was his idea."

"You're a natural!" Xander encourages.

We both anticipate the next dip, bending our knees and leaning to the left in an effort to right ourselves.

"Nice!" he says.

My lips curve into a grin. The expression feels foreign. Like a language I spoke as a small child but lost over the years, because I never had a chance to practice it.

"See? It's fun, right?"

Actually, it is. As stupid as it sounds, it might be the most fun I've had in eleven months and thirty-one days.

I feel a pull in my stomach as the train starts to slow. I brace myself for the change, rooting my feet firmly into the floor.

"Exit here for all A gates."

The doors open and I scoop up my backpack.

"No!" Xander protests. "Just one more stop."

"But the next stop is baggage claim."

"The train has to turn around again, right? We'll just ride it back to the A gates. Plus, you still have two hours before your flight."

"The doors are closing. Please keep clear and hold on for departure to terminal, ground transportation, and baggage claim."

With a sigh I set my bag down at my feet. "Okay, one more stop."

∞

Lottie ended up winning over six hundred dollars that night. It turned out she was a natural at poker. Not that I was surprised. Lottie was a natural at most things. It also probably didn't hurt that she blatantly flirted with every guy she was in a hand with. I watched her convince a six-foot-four dude with multiple piercings that her crappy two-seven offsuit was something to be afraid of simply by the way she pursed her lips as she bluffed up the pot.

It seemed like regardless of which cards she was dealt—rags, pocket aces, high kickers, low kickers—it never mattered. She always won.

Just like in life.

I sat behind her for three hours while she robbed every single person at that table of their hard earned cash, including a CEO type in an expensive-looking suit. Some of them griped and complained, some of them were just too enamored to be upset.

When she finally decided she'd had her fill, she scooted ceremoniously back from the table and announced, "Well, boys. This was fun. Next time bring more money, okay?"

I cringed at the jab. Even though I had come to relax somewhat since we'd arrived—convincing myself that no one was actually going to *die* here—I still didn't think it was a good idea to outwardly insult this lot.

But I was also overjoyed to be leaving.

Her departure was met by a chorus of protests and grumbles. I couldn't quite figure out if they wanted her to stay so they'd have a chance to win their money back, or because Lottie was infinitely nicer to look at than the rest of the players.

Probably a little of both.

"Sorry," she offered with a playful cock of her head. "But I have to get up really early tomorrow." She faked a yawn. "And I need my beauty sleep if I'm going to look this good for you next time."

Their grumbles quickly morphed into appreciative chuckles.

The single rack of chips she'd sat down with had multiplied by three. She could barely even carry them all. She handed one to me and we took them to the cashier.

"You did good, princess," he said, counting out Lottie's chips. "Beginner's luck?"

Lottie just winked at him. He laughed and counted out eleven crisp hundred dollar bills, sliding them across the table in the same way Lottie had done just hours ago.

Lottie smiled, folded the stack twice, and stuffed it into her bra.

"See you boys next time!" she called out as we headed for the door. But before we could reach it, one of the players—an early-twentysomething guy with light brown hair and matching facial scruff—gently caught Lottie by the hand.

"Hey," he said as he pushed his dark sunglasses onto his head. Underneath, his small green eyes sparkled the way only Lottie could make eyes do. "That was impressive."

She raised her eyebrows cockily. "Thanks."

"I was thinking you could probably teach me a few things."

Lottie didn't miss a beat. "I probably could."

"Do you offer private lessons?"

She twirled a lock of hair around her finger. That was her move.

Her signature move. The flirting, the eye batting, the winking, the lip biting, those were just everyday Lottie. She used those on everyone. But this. This she reserved for only the boys she was interested in.

My gaze darted suspiciously back to the boy. I took in his short hair with the tiny gelled spikes in the front, his thick eyebrows, his black-and-white-checkered shirt with black skinny tie. He was certainly more innocuous-looking than the rest of these guys, but that didn't make me distrust him any less. Don't all the best wolves know to dress in sheep's clothing?

"I might have time to give you a private lesson," Lottie replied suggestively.

The boy smiled. A devilishly handsome grin. Even with the dim lighting of the room, I could see his incisors flash.

"Give me your phone," she commanded.

He reached into the pocket of his skinny jeans and produced an oversize, top-of-the-line, latest-model device. Lottie grabbed it, swiped it on, and began typing furiously. She handed it back to him. "There you go."

Then she turned to leave. And I went with her.

"Wait," the guy said, running to catch up with us in the hallway. "What's your name?"

"Where's the fun in telling you that?" Lottie said.

"But how will I know which number is yours?"

She continued walking. Without turning around, she called over her shoulder, "I'm the only girl in your phone that you *haven't* slept with yet."

I didn't miss her addition of the word "yet." And I doubt he did either. It filled me with a sense of dread as I followed my best friend past the towering bouncer and into the street.

"Wanna hear something crazy?" Lottie asked giddily as she danced and twirled down the alley toward the train station.

"Always," I muttered with a sigh.

"I just won six hundred dollars playing poker!"

"Lottie," I said, nervously clenching and unclenching my fists. She stopped dancing and looped her arm through mine. "Yeah?"

"Promise me you won't see that guy."

She played innocent. "What guy?"

"The one you just gave your number to. I have a really bad feeling about him."

It was the truth. I *did* have a bad feeling about the guy. But I had a worse feeling about Lottie. And the kind of trouble she was capable of getting into. Especially with a guy who hangs out in seedy underground poker clubs.

"He was harmless," Lottie said with a giggle. "You just don't understand how these things work. Police officers and lawyers play in these kinds of games. None of those guys were dangerous."

But I wasn't comforted. "Just promise me you won't see him."

She rested her head on my shoulder as we walked. "Oh, Ryn. You know I never make promises I can't keep."

∞

Thirty minutes later Xander and I have surfed the Denver International Airport train route—from baggage claim to C gates—four times. We've started to memorize every twist and turn, every piece of uneven track, every programmed acceleration and deceleration, shifting our bodies to compensate for them as easily as a real surfer reads the waves. Neither of us has touched a handrail in two complete loops, despite our mutual efforts to throw the other person off-balance.

My legs are beginning to ache from all the crouching. My back is sore from all the leaning. But I'm having too much fun to stop. Plus, if I give up now, I lose.

As we approach the B gates for the fifth time that day, through the windows, I can see two people waiting on the platform outside. The doors open, and I nudge Xander, motioning toward them. He turns, and I immediately see the recognition on his face.

It's the same couple we saw earlier in the shopping rotunda. The one that was in the middle of that huge fight over a back massager. Or maybe it was over the girl *selling* the back massager. Regardless, the fight seems to be just about the last thing on the couple's mind now.

The doors open and they stumble inside, kissing and groping each other with the eagerness of two teenagers whose parents just left for the weekend. They seem to be completely oblivious to the fact that there are other passengers on this train. The man slams the woman up against the far window, pushing his whole body into her and running his hand up and down her side.

So much for Jimmy's bingo card.

Xander and I exchange a flabbergasted look. Both of us completely unsure what to do. Should we change cars to give them some privacy? What if they start having full-on sex right here? I guess that's one way to pass the time.

How many babies are born nine and a half months after historic snow-storms?

The musical interlude plays over the speaker, pulling both of our focuses toward the ceiling. "The doors are closing. This train is departing. Please keep clear and hold on for departure to all A gates."

The woman lets out a gasp in response. When I look over, her head is tipped back and the man has his face buried in her neck.

Xander covers his mouth, trying not to laugh aloud for fear of interrupting them. But seeing him fight so hard is making it even harder for me. I bite my lip, but it's not working. The uncontrollable giggles are building up. Xander shoots me a warning look.

Don't do it, his eyes plead. *If you lose it, I'll lose it.*

The first snicker erupts, pushing its way out of my clenched jaw in the form of a ridiculous-sounding snort. Xander lunges at me, pressing his hand against my mouth, trapping the laughter inside.

Meanwhile, on the other side of the train, the couple is kissing again, moaning so loudly, it's echoing in my ears.

Xander and I are both so focused on *not* breaking into fits of uncontrollable laughter, that neither one of us is prepared for the train's next shift. The one we both know so well by now.

The automated brakes kick in, lurching the train back, and both of us forward. Then suddenly, we're flying, out of control, foot over useless stumbling foot, heading right toward the kissing couple.

"Please hold on. This train is approaching the A gates."

The woman lets out another ridiculously loud gasp.

At the exact same moment, Xander and I both reach for the nearest handrail, admitting mutual defeat, but stopping ourselves just short of a very awkward collision.

We breathe out a synchronized sigh of relief just as the doors open and two uniformed police officers step inside.

We Go Down Together

The officers who board the train look more like a comedy duo than authority figures. One of them is tall and skinny with a slight comb-over, and the other is short and stout with unidentified crumbs on the front of his shirt. Their uniforms say AIRPORT POLICE over the breast pocket.

What's the difference between airport police and regular police?

I run my fingertips over the outline of the phone in my back pocket, vowing to wait until the police have arrested the gyrating couple before I get an answer to my question.

"All right, you two," the tall, skinny officer says. "You've had your fun. Time to come with us."

I watch the couple for a reaction. They've thankfully stopped molesting each other and are now standing side by side, hands clasped tightly like they're holding on to each other for support. I fully expect to see shame reflected all over their faces and remorse in their eyes. Being busted for getting it on in an airport train must be embarrassing.

I'm surprised, however, to see their heads are not bent in disgrace. They're not resigning to their fate. They're actually looking at *me*. But I can't, for the life of me, figure out why.

The tall officer takes another step into the almost empty train. Then another. I watch dumbfounded as he walks right *past* the couple and heads in our direction.

"Run!" Xander yells before scooping up his bag from the floor and darting out of the still-open train doors. One of the officers—the pudgy one—takes off after him.

Run?

What is he talking about?

What is happening?

"I think you're getting arrested," Lottie says unhelpfully.

Just then a cold hand wraps around my arm. The tall officer roughly grabs both of my wrists and secures them together in front of me with a plastic zip tie.

"Oh, don't worry. I know how to get out of those," Lottie says.

"I think there's been some kind of mistake!" I blurt out to the officer, my first words since he boarded the train. "I didn't do anything wrong, I swear!"

The officer points to a tiny black ball affixed to the ceiling of the train. "Cameras don't make mistakes. You've been riding this train for almost an hour. That's what the boss calls 'suspicious activity.'"

My eyes dart to the couple. They've fled the scene. Were they out of the camera's range? Did the police not get a good look at what was happening? I simply can't bring myself to believe that *I* am the bigger criminal in this scenario.

I look to the place where Xander once stood. Or rather, surfed. He's, of course, gone too. A current of rage streams through me. I can't believe he just left me! I can't believe he just abandoned me to take the rap for his stupid game. It wasn't even my idea. I didn't even want to do it! I was peer-pressured into it.

"I don't think you can consider it peer pressure if I'm dead," Lottie argues.

It's the third remark of hers that I've refused to answer. Because the truth is, I'm pissed at her, too.

Lottie and her fucking bravery. Lottie and her fucking sense of adventure.

She was always trying to get me to do things I didn't want to do. She was always trying to convince me to join her crazy schemes. And this is the very reason I always refused.

Rules are made for a reason. Automated recordings telling you to get off trains are recorded for a reason!

Xander and Lottie are exactly the same. They both tried to push me out of my comfort zone. And then, once I was standing on the other size of that line, freezing and scared to death, they both abandoned me.

Well, fuck them.

"Ryn Ryn," Lottie tries gently, but I slam a mental door on her face.

The officer gives me a tug and beckons for me to follow him out of the train.

"That's my bag," I say quietly, remarking at how tiny my voice sounds. It's a wonder he can even hear it at all, but he bends down and grabs my backpack from the floor before nudging me in the back.

I walk out of the train with my head bent low. Ironically, the very same look I searched for on the faces of that couple is now plastered on my own features.

Shame.

We ride the escalator up to the A terminal. I almost have to laugh. I finally made it back to the A gates. I just didn't expect to be in chains when I got here.

When we reach the concourse level, the second officer appears next to us, huffing and puffing. "Couldn't catch the other one," he wheezes. I scan the crowd for Xander, but it's like trying to find a single snowflake in a drift.

The officers escort me up another escalator until we're on that upper level that overlooks the concourse. They walk me to an awaiting golf cart and seat me on the backward-facing bench. As we drive, the human river miraculously parts to make room for us. The two pseudocops and their teenage delinquent. The world passes by me in reverse, making me feel like my life is playing on rewind. Journeying back to the beginning of this day.

Oh, how many things I would do differently.

I wonder where they're taking me. Are they kicking me out into the snow? Are they tossing me into airport jail and throwing away the key?

Do airports have jails?

I've never craved the touch of my phone as badly as I do right now. If my hands weren't zip tied I would reach into my back pocket and rip it out. I would type and type and type until this nasty, sick feeling in my stomach subsides.

I would answer every question in the universe until there were no questions left.

Until I reached the end of the Internet.

Until I had all the answers.

Until I could finally understand why everyone abandons me. Why, no matter what happens, in the end it's always me left alone to fend for myself.

∞

"I'm not going to abandon you," Lottie said to me for the fifth time. "I'm going to be here the whole time."

"What if I get caught?" I asked, eyeing the tube of lip gloss in my hands. It wasn't even a shade I would wear. What was the point of stealing something if you were never actually going to use it?

"Then we go down together," Lottie vowed. "You're my best friend. I would never leave you high and dry."

I rolled the tube back and forth between my fingers, feeling every groove, every curve of its surface. "I don't understand," I told her. "It's only five dollars. If you want me to have it so badly, I'll just buy it."

Lottie sighed. "That's not the point, Ryn."

"What is the point, then?" I was really hoping she would tell me. I was really hoping she could finally make me understand why I was standing in the middle of a drugstore aisle, preparing to stuff a tube of lip gloss down my pants.

"The point is, it's exhilarating! The point is, it makes you feel alive!"

"I already feel alive."

Lottie shook her head definitively. "No, you don't."

"How do you know how I feel?"

"Because I know you, Ryn. You've never done anything exciting in your entire life."

"I hang out with you."

She gave her scarlet hair a playful toss. "Well, that's true."

For a moment I forgot why we were here, what I was about to do. For a moment I got sucked into Lottie's sparkling atmosphere. Where everything glows. Where no one gets in trouble. Where the world is tinted pink.

I felt my face break into a smile.

"So," she said, regaining her seriousness. "Let's go over the plan again."

"I know the plan."

She crossed her arms like she didn't believe me. "Tell me, then."

"You're going to distract the cashier—"

"The *cute* cashier," she corrected.

I shot her a look. "You're going to distract the cashier. When I hear you say the magic words, I'm going to stuff the lip gloss down my pants, go to the register to purchase a pack of gum, and then meet you outside."

I waited for her approval. She appeared satisfied with my account of her Great Lip Gloss Heist. "Good."

She started to walk away. "Lottie, wait," I blurted out.

"What?"

"I really don't want to do this."

I expected her to look disappointed. I expected her to lecture me about being boring. About stepping out of my comfort zone for once. About how lame it is to go through life always playing by the rules. Always being me. But she actually looked sympathetic. She reached out and gently tucked a loose strand of hair behind my ear. "Are you sure?"

I nodded. "I'm sure."

She shrugged. "Okay." Then she plucked the lip gloss from my hand and started to tuck it into the waistband of her jeans. "I'll do it, then."

"Wait!" I grabbed for her hand. She extended it in a fist and then unfurled her fingers, revealing the pink tube lying on her palm. It looked so small. So insignificant. It was just lip gloss. It was only five dollars.

Would anyone *really* miss it?

Would stealing it really make me feel alive? Lottie was the most alive person I knew, and she stole stuff all the time. Maybe there was something to her crazy theory. It was a small price to pay—five dollars' worth of stolen merchandise—in exchange for whatever infectious, effervescent life force coursed through Lottie's veins.

I snatched the tube from her palm and motioned toward the registers in the front of the store. "Go," I said. "I can do this."

∞

I can do this, I repeat silently to myself as the golf cart ambles along the long corridor. *I can do this.*

We finally come to a stop in front of a pair of glass door marked by the words AIRPORT OFFICE, and I'm escorted inside. The plastic zip ties are starting to dig into my flesh and leave unsightly marks on my skin.

My guards escort me through a set of security doors that require a key card and into an office in the back. On the door is a gold-plated sign that reads CLAUDIA BEECHER. OPERATIONS MANAGER.

Inside the office a scrawny woman in a navy skirt suit— Claudia Beecher, I presume—is staring out a window at the rioting snow. I can't see her face. I can see only her stringy, dark hair, which looks like it hasn't been washed or brushed in days. I can also see puffs of smoke rising up above her head, making her look like she's actually on fire.

I peer around the small office. The desk is so cluttered with papers and empty cups and all sorts of other junk, I can barely see the surface. The mess makes me jittery, and I fight the urge to start tidying up.

When the woman turns, I see how haggard and tired she looks. Lines where there shouldn't be lines. A scowl that reaches places I didn't know scowls could even reach.

"This her?" she asks the officer behind me. It's the pudgy one. The other one is nowhere to be found. I hope he's out looking for Xander.

The traitor.

The officer must nod, because the woman transfers her glare from him to me.

"On the radio, you said there were two of them."

"There were," the officer says. "The other fled. We couldn't catch him."

I notice the subtle shift of the woman's gaze as she takes in the shape of my captor. I'm assuming she's thinking the same thing I am: *There's no way in hell you could catch him.*

She lets out a sigh and takes another drag of her cigarette, then instantly follows it with a spritz from a can of air freshener on her desk, dousing the office and herself in a fine mist. The fake citrusy potpourri scent does nothing to mask the odor of the smoke. Now the room just smells like *burnt* citrusy potpourri.

"Sit down," she tells me, gesturing to a chair across from her desk.

I do.

Then, for good measure, the officer presses down on my shoulders, as if to make certain that I'm really sitting.

Claudia Beecher dismisses him with a wave of her hand, and I hear the door close somewhere behind me.

She takes one last look out the window. You can barely see anything through the flurry of white. I can tell the storm is getting worse by the minute. I feel the muscles in my shoulders clench.

The woman yanks open a desk drawer and snubs out her

half-smoked cigarette in an ashtray overflowing with more half-smoked cigarettes. She spritzes the room and the inside of the desk drawer, closes the drawer, and sits down.

"Look," she says hastily, "I really don't have time to deal with this right now. But we're required, by law, to bring you in. When someone rides the train loop more than three times, it's considered suspicious activity by the Department of Homeland Security."

Suspicious activity?

Homeland Security?

If I ever see that Xander guy again, I swear I'm going to kill him.

They probably think I'm a terrorist. They're probably going to hold me for questioning in some dingy cell in the basement. They're going to use some kind of ambiguously legal torture methods to get me to talk.

Claudia closes her eyes for a brief moment before opening them again. "Listen up. The trains are for getting from one place to another. It's not a goddamn amusement park ride, okay?"

"Okay!" I agree quickly. "I'm really, truly sorry. We didn't mean anything. We were just wasting time while our flights were delayed. I swear. I—"

She shushes me again with a raise of her hand. "I believe you."

I sag against the back of the chair in relief.

"But it's my job to follow protocol, and protocol says I'm supposed to turn you over to TSA."

A lump the size of Cincinnati grows inside my throat.

TSA?

"Oh shit, Ryn, that's bad," Lottie offers her not-so-helpful commentary.

"Oh God," I plead. "Please don't do that. I will never do it again. Isn't there something you can do? Someone else you can talk to? Please! I've never done anything wrong in my entire life."

"Well, technically—" Lottie starts to correct. But I cut her off.

You shut the hell up! I'm not speaking to you. This is all your fault.

"Ryn Ryn," she tries, her voice softening, but I slam the door on her again.

Claudia opens her desk drawer and pulls out a pack of cigarettes. She stuffs one in her mouth and lights the end with a shaky hand. She looks contemplative as she takes a long drag. I can see her chest expanding as her lungs make room for the dark, nicotine laced air.

I wait for her next words with the anticipation of a death row inmate waiting on the results of her final appeal.

She turns her head and exhales the smoke to the side. It seems to snake out of her mouth and make a ninety-degree turn in my direction. I watch it slither toward me. I feel it wrap around my neck, squeeze all the good air out of me, replace it with nasty, burnt tar.

She grabs the air freshener and chases after the smoke with a long, continuous spray. I let out a small cough as the charred citrus odor hits me.

Claudia opens her mouth to speak, and I can immediately see from the way her haggard face somehow grows even more haggard that the news she's about to deliver isn't good.

But before she can get a single word out, the phone on her desk rings. She looks about as relieved as I feel to have a distraction. "What?" she snaps into the receiver.

I can't make out what's being said on the other end. I hear only soft, muffled murmuring. But Claudia's eyes dart accusingly at me as she listens.

"Really?" she asks, sounding genuinely intrigued. "I'll be right out."

She hangs up the phone and stands. The barely touched cigarette clutched between her fingers suffers the same snubbed fate as the rest in her drawer. She starts toward the door, then hastily turns back, grabs the can from her desk, and sprays it hurriedly around the entire office in a messy scribble, as if she's graffitiing the air.

"You wait here," she barks, and then disappears out the door, leaving me alone with the bitter taste of regret and fake fruit coating the inside of my mouth.

∞

I stood in the makeup aisle, listening to Lottie's melodic voice loft through the store as she flirted shamelessly with the *cute* cashier. I could no longer feel my feet. Or legs. I suspected my hands would soon go too.

I stared down at the lip gloss tube pinched between my fingers. I rolled it back and forth three times, willing the blood to keep flowing.

It was so small.

Just a tiny pink tube.

How could something so small cause me so much grief? How could something so tiny and insignificant make the blood stop pumping to half of my body?

"You simply *have* to let me come over and see that sometime!" Lottie exclaimed, raising up her voice a few decibels so I could hear. "I would *looove* that."

That was my signal. The magic words. It was go time.

I took one final look at the lip gloss in my hand.

So tiny.

So insignificant.

I bet they lose a thousand of these a year by sheer human error. Products disappear. Things fall off trucks. Someone records the wrong number in an inventory log.

They won't miss it.

It's nothing, I told myself. It costs five dollars. Probably only fifty cents to actually make. Maybe even less.

Lottie had stolen a dozen of these. And a dozen other more expensive things.

But you're not Lottie.

My own thoughts echoed back at me in stereo surround sound. And they were right. I wasn't Lottie. I'd never been Lottie. Lottie was already too much Lottie to leave even a tiny sliver for anyone else.

I angled my body toward the shelf to block the view of the security cameras, just like Lottie taught me. I pretended to sneeze, giving me a reason to double over slightly. As I bent forward, I swiftly lifted up the hem of my shirt and stuffed the lip gloss into the waistband of my pants.

It was over so fast.

One second I was an innocent shopper, the next I had a bulging lump in the front of my pants that I was convinced could be seen from outer space.

I surreptitiously glanced down, searching for any sign of the bump. But my waistline looked perfectly smooth.

So tiny.

So insignificant.

Then, why did it feel like I'd just stuffed a fifty-pound dumbbell down my pants?

"Here," I heard Lottie say, "I'll give you my number."

I knew what came next. It was all part of the plan. She would punch a fake number into his phone with a fake name to go with it. Then she would leave, and I would purchase my decoy pack of gum with the confiscated merchandise weighing down my pants like a toddler carrying around a huge load in her diaper.

"Cool. I'll totally call you." That was the cashier. His voice was low and kind of husky. Like he'd been chain-smoking since he was five.

No doubt he would call.

They always called.

I took a deep breath and started toward the front of the store. I could feel a million pairs of eyes on me, even though the store was mostly empty. When I reached the cashier, I perused the impulse shelf, plucking a pack of gum and placing it on the counter next to the register.

"Just this, please," I said, and I swore my voice shook like I was riding a lawn mower.

The cashier studied me for just a beat too long. I could feel cold sweat starting to pool on my lower back. Could he smell the perspiration? If I turned and ran, would he see the stain on the back of my shirt? Would he chase after me?

Or is a five-dollar lip gloss just not worth the effort?

I peered out the window and saw Lottie standing on the sidewalk, tapping casually into her phone.

The cashier ran the pack of gum across his scanner. "Eighty-five cents," he said, staring at me. His eyes morphed into X-rays. A humming sound filled the air, growing louder by the second, until I couldn't even hear my own thoughts.

I produced a dollar bill from my purse and thrust it at him. I was so eager to get out of there, to run and never stop, I almost said, "Keep the change," but I knew that would only make me look suspicious. No one says "keep the change" at a drugstore. Especially not a teenager.

His cash drawer opened with a bang, shattering the humming in my ears. He scooped his finger into one of the change slots. I could tell from his expression that he didn't have enough.

"One second," he said, and retrieved a roll of coins from under the cash tray. He banged it against the side of the drawer. Nickels came raining down, a few dropping to the ground.

"Shit," he mumbled, bending to gather them.

My heart pounded harder. Was this some kind of stalling technique? What if he'd already called the cops and was keeping me distracted until they got here? My eyes darted to the window again. I swore I could hear sirens, but I couldn't tell if they were actual sirens or some imaginary noise I was making up in my head.

I rubbed my sweaty palms on my jeans, feeling the lip gloss shift inside the waistband.

I froze.

Oh God.

It was slipping.

I could feel it inching its way out of the waistband grip. Any minute now it was going to slip right down my pant leg and tumble to the ground.

While the cashier was still scooping up fallen coins, I wiggled slightly, trying to shimmy the tube back into place. But my movement was all wrong. *I* was all wrong. And the lip gloss slipped farther.

I could feel the cold, hard surface of the plastic tube against my upper thigh now. If I took one step, I was certain it would fall. And it would all be over. I went to put my hand in my pocket to try to hold the tube in place, but then I remembered these pants didn't have pockets. Lottie picked them out, claiming that the pocketless design would make me look slimmer.

Damn you, Lottie, and your keen fashion sense!

I settled for placing my hand on my hip instead, pressing tightly against the slipping tube. I knew it probably looked like the most unnatural pose in the world, but it was better than hearing the echoey *plink* of the lip gloss hitting the tile floor.

"You know what?" I said shakily to the cashier. "It's fine. You can just keep the change."

"No, no," he said, standing up with a handful of nickels. "I got it. Besides, if you don't take your change, then my count will be all messed up, and I'll get in trouble." He dumped the coins into the tray and handed me my change and receipt.

I kept one hand firmly pressed to my hip while trying to stuff everything into my bag with the other. The cashier gave me another strange look, and I attempted to cover the whole thing with a smile.

This was a disaster.

But it was almost over.

"Thank you," I said.

Then I ran. I didn't care that it made me look suspicious. I didn't care about anything anymore except getting out of this store. Getting this thousand-pound lip gloss out of my pants and then burning them.

"Wait!" the cashier called after me. "You forgot your gum!"

I turned back just long enough to see him holding up my purchase. My decoy. The one thing that was supposed to make me look innocent. And I'd left it behind. Typical. I was dreadful at this. I don't know why I even agreed to do it in the first place.

"Keep it!" I yelled over my shoulder and kept running.

When I reached the automatic glass doors, I skidded to a halt, staring down at the threshold that divided the inside of the store from the outside world. The tile floor from the cement sidewalk. My innocence from my corruption.

I gulped in lungfuls of air, never seeming to get enough.

Then, before I could change my mind, I dug my hand ungraciously down the front of my pants, grabbed the lip gloss, and threw it on the tile floor behind me. I'm quite certain that it must have landed with the very same *plink* that I'd been dreading, but I'll never know for sure because I didn't wait around to hear it. I sprinted from the store without looking back.

Lottie saw me coming at her with the determination of a bull, and her eyes widened.

"What happened?" she asked, but I didn't slow. I ran right past her and jumped into the passenger seat of her car.

She got in behind the wheel and, sensing my urgency, started the engine and backed out, tires squealing. Once we were three intersections away, she asked again.

"What happened? Did you do it?"

I fought to catch my breath, to calm my pounding heart.

And then I tilted my head in a nearly imperceptible nod.

So tiny.

So insignificant.

Yet, my whole body shivered with the shame of deceit.

Lottie giggled in delight. "Oh my God! How do you feel?"

I swallowed. My throat was dry. My lungs burned. My heart hammered. "Alive," I told her, and it was the truth.

∞

78. **I blame the company that installed the cameras in the airport trains.**

79. I blame the useless snowplowers for not plowing the runways fast enough.
80. I blame cute guys in Muppet shirts for luring me into bullshit time-wasting games.
81. I blame my overly chatty dead best friend for talking me into it.
82. I blame myself. For listening.

∞

When the door to Claudia Beecher's office opens again, the pudgy guard saunters in and gently removes my plastic cuffs. "You're free to go."

What? Just like that?

I want to ask what happened. Why the sudden change of heart . . . and policy? But I'm smart enough to keep my mouth shut and just go with it. Probably the smartest thing I've done all day.

I grab for my phone and clutch it in my hands. My skin sings with the relief of touching the phone again. The familiarity of the hard plastic case and cool glass screen. The closeness of answers. Of truth.

But I make myself wait to search for anything until I'm far, far away from this place.

I walk outside into the main airport office and immediately lurch to a stop when I see who's standing there. Casually laughing and joking around with the tall, skinny guard.

Xander.

"What are you doing here?" I snarl.

He looks surprised by my question, placing a hand to his heart. "I came to set the record straight and spring you from this place. I'm your knight in shining armor." Then he actually bows. "M'lady."

The tall airport cop lets out a chuckle. "You crazy kids. You get out of here."

Baffled, I look between Xander and the officer. What just happened here? Did Xander put some kind of mind-bending spell on the authorities? Ten minutes ago these guys wanted my head.

"Well, that's just fucking perfect!"

"Don't worry," Xander whispers conspiratorially to me, as if reading my mind. "I took care of it."

I'm about to ask how when someone yells behind me. I spin to find Claudia, a phone pressed to her ear, pacing the length of the office lobby. She ends the call and throws the phone across the room. The pudgy officer catches it expertly with one hand. He barely even flinches, giving me the impression that this is a normal occurrence.

"There's a fight over a power outlet at C22," Claudia barks, waving dismissively at the two guards. "Go deal with it."

They nod and sprint out of the office, hopping onto their little golf cart and zooming off.

"And you two"—Claudia turns her tired, blue-gray eyes on me and Xander, who I notice has sidled up to me, standing beside me like some kind of unified front against an insurgent army—"promise me I won't see you in this office ever again. I don't have time for this shit. The airport is about to shut down, and I'm about to have three thousand angry passengers pointing pitchforks at me. As if the storm is *my* fault. I don't have room in my schedule for rowdy teenagers."

"I promise!" I rush to agree without thinking. But then something she said stops me cold. "Wait. What do you mean the airport is about to shut down?"

She tosses a hand impatiently toward the window. "I mean shut down. No one leaves. All flights canceled. One big fucking slumber party. La-di-DA."

In a panic my head whips in the direction of her office. I gaze past all the shambles of debris on her desk and toward the window. Toward the storm.

"No," I argue foolishly. "It's just delayed. The flights are just delayed. The board says so."

She gives me an odd look, and it's then I realize that I haven't actually *seen* a board in quite a while. Xander and I were in those train tunnels without phone reception for nearly an hour.

Suddenly, the white tempest on the other side of the window starts to infiltrate my vision. Cloud my mind until I can't see. I dig my fingertips into my temples, trying to stop the room from spinning. Trying to stop my brain from screaming.

Lottie's blood.

Everywhere.

Blood everywhere.

Staining everything.

Cracked skull.

Cracked glass.

Clock flashing 10:05 a.m.

10:05 a.m.

10:05 a.m.

"I can't!" I blurt out. "I can't stay here. I can't be here tomorrow. I have to get home."

I'm not sure what I expect my pleas to do. Change her mind? Stop the storm dead in its tracks? Turn back time so I can insist Dad buy me a nonstop flight?

"What do you want me to say?" Claudia asks with just the faintest hint of genuine remorse. "Sometimes Mother Nature wins."

Tackled in the End Zone

As soon as the large bank of information screens are in sight, I race toward them. Xander is close behind me, trying to keep up. "I'm so sorry about what happened," he's calling after me. "I swear I thought you were right behind me when I ran out of the train." I don't respond. I haven't spoken a word to him since we left the airport office, and I don't intend to start now.

My eyes drink in the data like a thirsty desert traveler, swallowing each flight number and then plunging back in for more.

Boston, MA	1240	4:45 p.m.	CANCELED
Detroit, MI	541	3:50 p.m.	CANCELED
Ft. Lauderdale, FL	3672	4:02 p.m.	CANCELED
Miami	211	3:32 p.m.	CANCELED
San Francisco, CA	112	3:31 p.m.	CANCELED

My heart climbs into the metal vise that's been waiting patiently in my chest and straps itself in, surrendering to its fate.

Canceled.

How can they just *cancel* a flight? I bought a ticket. I paid them money—or rather my father did—and that creates a binding agreement. I give you money, you take me somewhere. Somewhere far away from here. Somewhere that feels as safe as one could possibly feel on the first anniversary of her best friend's death.

"Death!?" Lottie screeches into my ear. "I'm DEAD?"

I ignore her. I don't have time for her comedy routine right now. I have to find a place to hide. To retreat inside myself. To disappear. But how do you disappear in a place like this?

Of all the locations I ever imagined spending New Year's Day, a busy, crowded airport full of people, like spectators at a gladiator match just waiting to watch me break apart, was *not* one of them.

Who gets hit by a drunk driver on New Year's *Day?* That's supposed to be the safe day! The end zone at the end of a long stretch of dangerous, enemy infested territory, where no one can tackle you anymore.

They all tell us. They drill it into our heads. They demand promises from us. No driving on New Year's *Eve*. That's when the dangerous monsters are out. That's when people get hurt. That's when teenagers lose their lives.

No one warns you about the morning after, though. No one thinks the danger is still lurking then.

But Lottie was always different. She was always an exception to the rule. I guess it's fitting that her death be an exception too.

I glance desperately around me, looking for a private corner or an empty space, but they've all been filled. These people—these stranded passengers—they're like a plague. A virus. They keep multiplying and spreading and filling in all the little gaps and crevices, consuming every available space until there's nothing left. Until this entire airport is just one giant red blob of disease.

Any system, if left unattended or isolated, will eventually result in chaos.

And I'm here trapped in the middle of it.

Three intrusive beeps blast over the intercom system, catching everyone's attention. Everyone around me stops whatever they're doing and stares up at the ceiling. As if they're waiting their next directive from a higher power.

"Attention, all passengers. Attention, all passengers. This is Claudia Beecher, operations manager of the airport."

I grimace. Not her again.

"This is an important announcement for all passengers and airline and airport employees. The FAA has ordered that, due to severe weather conditions, all flights out of Denver be grounded. As soon as it is safe to fly again, airlines will be rebooking passengers on alternate flights. While we realize this is not ideal, it is our job to make sure you are as comfortable as possible. The airlines are doing everything they can to issue hotel vouchers to passengers. Please check with your airline's customer service desk to obtain one. For those of you who remain in the terminal, blankets, pillows, and water will be distributed in all gate lounges. Meal vouchers will be provided by your airline for use at any participating airport restaurant. Restaurants will remain open late to accommodate everyone. We ask that you kindly remain calm and courteous to one another. As soon as we have additional information about the weather conditions, we will make a subsequent announcement. Thank you for your attention."

I can't feel my fingers. I can't feel my toes. Has the blizzard broken through the windows? Am I already frozen?

"Looks like we're both trapped here for a while," Xander says, and I startle. I forgot he was behind me. But the sudden reminder sends a hot lava river of anger coursing through me.

"And whose fault is that?" I snap, whipping around to face him.

He flinches. "Um, what?"

"This is *your* fault. This is *all* your fault!"

Xander looks like I've just slapped him. "Wait. WHAT? How could a snowstorm possibly be my fault?"

"Because you—" I hesitate, feeling frustrated. My rational side is a muffled, kidnapped prisoner in the back of my mind, screaming through a gag, trying to tell me that the flight cancelation has nothing to do with him. But my irrational side—the one that landed me in a weekly session with Dr. Judy, the one I didn't even know I had until my best friend's brains got splattered across a flashing clock—rules me with an iron fist. It pilots me. And it knows if I just search hard enough, I'll find a way for the pieces to interlock. I'll find a way to blame him for everything.

"Because the train!" I try again. "And your stupid game! I don't even like surfing! She wanted me to go surfing, and I said no! I said NO! But then you had to pressure me into it. You and Lottie! You both think you're so damn clever. And then you just left. You just left me! And the police! Airport police! And handcuffs! And fake citrus chain-smoking! And it's all your fault."

I realize I'm no longer making sense. I'm like a slot machine that never pays out. My reels keep spinning, trying to match up three pictures in a row, trying to find words that string together into a coherent sentence, but I just keep losing.

Always losing.

Xander blinks rapidly, undoubtedly thinking I'm crazy.

Well, good, it's about time he knew the real me. It's about time I stopped pretending to be someone else. Because, look where that got me. Arrested by the airport police.

"Hold on," Xander says, raising his hands in the air. "Back up. Who's *Lottie?*"

My hand flies to my mouth. The movement is instinctual. A knee-jerk reaction. I want to take it all back, suck it back in, press rewind. But it's too late. It's out there. *She's* out there, hanging between us like an acid-filled water balloon that no one can catch. It's about to explode everywhere. Burn through our skin. Singe a hole right through the floor beneath our feet.

I quickly weigh my options. There aren't many. I choose the obvious one.

I run.

∞

"Tell me about January first, 10:05 a.m.," Dr. Judy said at our last session before I left to visit my father in Atlanta. It had been a little over nine months since my sessions with her had started, and by now we'd adopted a relaxed rhythm. A functional coexistence. She was like a tennis pro, serving up easy shots, and I was the student, recognizing the balls' trajectory and speed and lobbing them back without much effort.

I'd learned just how much I had to say to appease her and just how little I could get away with.

I shrugged and fingered my phone case. "It's when Lottie died."

She nodded, tapping her pen against her bottom lip. "It's coming up soon."

"Yes."

"And how do you feel about that?"

"Sad," I tell her, confident it's the right answer. Then, for good measure, I add, "Angry."

"At Lottie?"

"At the guy who killed her."

"What about Lottie?"

"What *about* Lottie?"

"Are you angry at her, too?" Dr. Judy asked, planting her shovel in to the dirt and giving it a firm stomp with her foot.

"It's not Lottie's fault the guy was plastered at ten in the morning and got behind the wheel of a car with faulty brakes," I said.

Dr. Judy's sessions were the only time my rational side was allowed to come out. Ungagged, released from the closet, paraded around for the world to see. Like the well kept prisoner in a ransom video. See? Alive and well. We're even feeding her.

Dr. Judy teetered her head from side to side, reminding me of one of those bobble head dolls. I was afraid she was going to challenge me. She did that sometimes. She poked and prodded at Rational Ryn, making certain that she was real. That she wasn't just a blow-up doll full of hot air. But, to my relief, instead she asked, "Do you have any plans for the day?"

"Yeah," I replied snarkily. "I'm going to drive to the mall and wait in the middle of the intersection for a drunk driver to hit me, too."

Dr. Judy gave me a blank stare, waiting for me to take the joke back. I bowed my head apologetically. "No, I don't have any plans."

I didn't tell her about my intention to sit in my room with the lights off and the shades drawn, counting the seconds until the day was over. That wasn't Rational Ryn behavior. Rational Ryn would visit Lottie's grave site, bring flowers, dab at her eyes with a white hankie. Rational Ryn would erect a marble bench in the park with Lottie's name inscribed into the stone.

Rational Ryn would cry.

"What I meant was, how do you intend to manage that day?"

"Manage?" I repeated skeptically. It sounded so cold and clinical. A word that belonged in a corporate board meeting. A word Lottie would have hated. Especially if she knew it was being used in reference to her.

"Yes," Dr. Judy replied. "I think we should talk about your management plans. If you come up with a coping strategy ahead of time, you're much more likely to avoid unwanted . . . *episodes.*"

She let that word hang in the air. Knowing it needed no other explanation. We both knew what she meant. We both knew the *episode* she was talking about. It had happened a few months ago. At school. If it had happened anywhere else, I might have been able to avoid telling her. But teachers talk to principals and principals talk to parents and parents talk to therapists.

Then therapists ask why you locked yourself in a supply closet for two hours because of a number of a clock.

"I'm not going to have another episode," I assured her, even though the words felt swollen and misshapen in my mouth. It was amazing how good at lying I'd become in the past eleven months. How accustomed I'd grown to those misshapen words.

"So seeing 10:05 on the clock doesn't bother you anymore?"

I felt my throat start to sting. I swallowed incessantly until the heat cooled. And when I was certain that my voice wouldn't break, I said, "No. It doesn't bother me."

∞

I can hear footsteps behind me but I don't slow. I can't be sure those footsteps aren't just my imagination. Lottie's ghost chasing after me through this crowded, claustrophobic airport.

"Don't be ridiculous." Lottie slides into my head. "I don't have to *chase* you. I go where you go."

Don't remind me, I think, and she responds with a gasp followed by offended silence.

"Ryn!" a voice calls from somewhere in my wake. It's Xander.

He's following me. But I still don't slow or turn around. I need air. I need space. I. Need. To. Get. Out.

I pass the airport office and avert my gaze, praying that Chain-Smoking Burnt Citrus Claudia won't exit the doors just as I run by.

She doesn't.

I do, however, pass the kissing couple from the train. They're riding one of the moving walkways, and they're back to yelling at each other. I don't linger long enough to catch what the fight is about this time.

I sail by a lone TSA agent sitting at a desk, practically falling asleep into his hand. On my left is a sheet of glass that separates me from a security checkpoint, which means I'm leaving the supposed "secure" part of the airport and entering the wild frontier. Where no one is safe.

I keep running. Down a long sloping walkway until I'm in the main terminal. It's big and open and bright. The ceilings are so high, I have to crane my neck to see the top. They rise into tall peaks, giving me the illusion of being trapped inside a snow-capped mountain.

I have the option to go left or right. I pause and swing my gaze in both directions. There are people out here, too. So many people. Always people.

Where are they all coming from?

Don't they realize I need to be alone?

"So *now* you run," Xander says, coming to a stop next to me. He rests his hands on his knees, panting. "And here I thought I was in shape." He pivots his head and looks up at me. "Where was all this running when I told you to run?"

Ignoring him, I turn my head to the right and stand on my tiptoes in an attempt to peer over the sea of heads. I can just barely make out a door in the distance. It appears to be leading to the outside. Away from one storm and into another. I sprint toward it. Somewhere behind me Xander groans.

I dodge people and bags and children. I nearly slip on a slick spot on the tile floor. Before long, I reach a small, heated vestibule.

That's when I screech to a halt.

The only thing that stands between me and the outside now is a clear glass door marked with the numbers 612. It glides open with a *whoosh*, as if to say, "Go ahead, Ryn. No one is holding you back. No one is keeping you here like the prisoner you think you are."

Everything hits me at once. The cold, the snow, the wind. They slap me violently in the face, like I'm an unruly, fainting damsel in an old black-and-white movie. Smack, smack, smack!

My skin burns. My eyes try to adjust. I can't even see five feet in front of me. The blizzard is too thick. It's a wall. A wall of moving, breathing snow. The wind is so loud, it boxes my ears.

A second later the door slides shut, like it's given up on me. I can hear it laughing in my face. "And you thought you were so brave."

Then someone is beside me. I don't have to look over to know it's Xander. I've started to recognize his energy. The way it affects me. Riling me up and calming me down at the same time.

His presence triggers the door again, and it opens majestically, giving me a second shot.

Go, I urge myself. *You can do it. It's just a little snow.*

But that's the thing. It's not just a little snow. It's never just a little snow. It's never a small storm. It's always a fucking tempest. A total whiteout. Where you can't see your hand in front of your face. Where every step might be the one that takes you right over the edge of a cliff.

Another gust of wind rises up, blowing a bucket of frozen flurries into my face. I instinctively jump back and then glance down to see my shoes are covered in a fine, white powder.

The door closes again.

"Uh," Xander says, taking two giant steps away. "What are we doing?"

"*We're* not doing anything," I say impatiently. "*I'm* going out there."

I'm not sure whom I'm trying to convince more. Me or him. But it appears both of us need convincing.

"Uh," he says again. "*Why?*"

"Because it's just something I have to do."

"Freeze to death?"

I shake my head. "You wouldn't understand."

And he wouldn't. How could he? He grew up in a perfect life. With perfect parents who knew exactly what to do when something went wrong. Although I highly doubt anything ever went wrong for him.

I take another step forward. The doors respond, yawning open for a third time. I swear this time, I hear them asking with a sigh, "You again? Look, are you going to leave or not?"

I take a deep breath, puffing up my chest like armor. I hold up my hand to cover my face from the barrage of snow that lashes out at me.

"I'd just like to say for the record that this is a terrible idea."

I shut my eyes and try to block Xander's voice from my mind.

"I'd have to agree," Lottie chimes in. "This isn't your brightest moment, Ryn."

"Stop!" I mean this for Lottie, but fortunately Xander falls quiet too.

I shiver and zip my measly sweatshirt up to my chin, pulling the hood around my ears and tugging on the cord. My phone is still clutched in my hand. I glance down at the time: 7:49 p.m.

Less than fifteen hours to go.

I'm doing this.

I'm doing this.

I'm doing this.

I shove my phone into the pocket of my sweatshirt and take one step closer to the eye of the storm.

∞

Dr. Judy stared at me in silence, waiting for me to speak. I swiped on my phone and checked the messaging app.

One unread message.

Satisfied, I looked at the clock. We had only six minutes left. Six minutes and then I wouldn't have to do this again for two whole weeks. Even though I'd gotten used to the idea of being in therapy, it still didn't mean I liked going.

On the other hand I knew I was spending the next two weeks with my father and his new wife, and for a brief moment I couldn't decide which was worse.

"What about drawing?" Dr. Judy asked, shattering our mutually agreed upon silence.

I squinted at her. "What about it?"

"Art can be very therapeutic. Some people find that it helps them with the grieving process. Helps them pay homage to what they lost. Musicians write songs, authors write books, poets write poetry—"

"I don't draw anymore." I cut her off before she had a chance to finish. I knew exactly where this conversation was heading, and I wasn't going with it. There were vague answers I was willing to give to appease her. There were topics I was willing to skirt around for the sake of pretenses, but this wasn't one of them.

"And why is that?" she asked.

"I don't know. I guess I just grew out of it." I tried to convey an air of nonchalance in hopes that she would see this as a nonissue and move on.

But in this room, nothing was a nonissue. Everything was worth talking about. "And when do you think you 'grew out of it'?" she challenged, putting a strange emphasis on my words. Like she was testing their validity.

I didn't want to think about this. I *hadn't* thought about this in nearly nine months. But her questions were drilling holes in the brick wall I'd built up around those dark memories. Those first few nights at the very beginning. When I drove myself crazy.

When I sat in my bedroom until daybreak trying to capture her. Trying to draw her the way I remembered her. Trying, and trying, and trying, and failing.

Until I was surrounded by images of Lottie's disfigured face.

Until I was drowning in a pool of black ink.

I shrugged, careful to keep my expression neutral. "I don't remember, really. My passion for it just sort of fizzled out. It happens."

Dr. Judy watched me with vigilant eyes. I'd learned she had two kinds of stares. The pitying one and the one that called "bullshit!" This was the latter.

"Why do you think that is?" she asked.

I swallowed.

Because she's not deformed.

Because her eyes don't droop like that.

Because there's no point in drawing something that doesn't look real.

"I just don't enjoy it anymore," I said, looking down at the phone clasped between my cold, talentless fingers.

Because she's beautiful.

And I used to be able to draw beautiful things.

But my hands stopped working.

"Okay," Dr. Judy said, surprising me somewhat. I didn't think she was going to let the subject go so easily. But she clicked her pen with an air of finality. "Since I'm not going to see you for the next two weeks, I have a little experiment I'd like you to try while you're away."

"What's that?" I mumbled, disinterested.

"Do you know what a silver lining is?"

"I know what a *Silver Linings Playbook* is."

She didn't look amused. She rarely did.

I sighed. "Yes."

"What is it?"

I shrugged and checked my messaging app again. "It's like something good that can be found in something bad."

I didn't have to be an astrophysicist to know where she was going with this.

She opened her mouth to speak, but I cut her off. "There are no silver linings to Lottie's death."

She seemed to rethink her previous statement. "What if you're wrong?"

"If you think I'm going to try to come up with reasons why Lottie's death is a *good* thing, then *you're* the crazy one." I wasn't even trying to mask the irritation in my tone. I expected to see something flash on her face—some kind of judgment or displeasure or that subtle fascination she'd mastered so well—but her face was as placid as a lake.

"I want you to write down every silver lining that you find," she instructed.

I started to protest, but she held up a hand to stop me. "It doesn't have to be about Lottie. It can be about anything. Whenever you find yourself lamenting about something that you perceive to be 'bad,' I want you to try and find a silver lining within it and write it down."

"Is this like homework?"

She ticked her head to the side. "Kind of."

"Are you going to be checking it when I get back?" I mocked.

"Only if you want to show it to me."

Which meant I didn't have to do it.

Which meant I *wouldn't* do it.

"Let me ask you something, Ryn," Dr. Judy began, and for a second I almost feared that I had said that last part aloud. "What have you done to grieve Lottie?"

I didn't understand the question.

Dr. Judy rephrased. "What steps have you taken to grieve the loss of your best friend?"

"I didn't realize grief was an active emotion," I said without thinking. Without properly weighing the consequences. And I immediately regretted it.

Dr. Judy put her pen down. That was never a good sign. It meant whatever I had just said was so groundbreaking, so earth-shattering, that even her little ballpoint seismograph couldn't accurately capture its epicness.

"What exactly do you mean by that?" she asked.

I glanced at the clock. Two minutes remaining. Dr. Judy was usually very punctual. When that digital clock in the corner hit the hour mark, that was it. Session over. Next patient. But she had, in the past nine months, been known to make exceptions when the subject matter was deemed important enough. And by the way she was looking at me now, her body bent forward, her eyes searching, this felt like it was shaping up to be one of those exceptions.

I knew I had to defuse the situation. Steer her to another track. A track that got me out of here on time.

One minute remaining.

"I just mean," I began confidently, "I grieve Lottie every day. I don't really plan out how I'm going to do it, I just do it."

Dr. Judy sat back in her chair, picked up her pen again, clicked it, and started scribbling. The clock in the corner ticked over. A new hour had begun.

I stood up quickly. The room spun. I clutched my phone to steady myself.

"Well," I began breezily, "I guess I'll see you next year."

Next year.

A debilitating chill racked my entire body.

The next time I'm in this office, Lottie will have been dead for an entire year.

The next time I'm here, I will have made one full rotation around the sun without her.

I gripped my phone tighter, but for some reason, this time, it offered me no stabilization.

I wanted to turn around and scream at Dr. Judy. I wanted to tell her that she was wrong. Always, always *wrong*.

Grief isn't an active emotion. It's not something you *do*. It's something that happens to you. It's 100 percent passive. It's a tornado that rips your house from the ground, right off its foundation, twisting it around and around, before dropping it haphazardly back down to the earth. Sure, you're still in the same place, but everything has been destroyed. The windows face the wrong way. The china has fallen from the cabinets and smashed to the floor. The furniture is upside down. And you're standing in the middle of it all, wondering what happened. Wondering how you're ever going to put it all back together again.

And now she wants me to be an active part of that? She wants me to open the doors and the windows, too, and welcome the tornado inside with open arms?

I want to say all of this. The words are pounding at my lips. But I don't want to stay here another second. I don't want to give her any excuse to prolong this session.

I reach for the door handle, my hand shaking from the storm brewing inside of me.

"Ryn," Dr. Judy says, just as my fingers wrap around the cool brass.

I take a deep breath and spin around, fighting to keep the emotion from taking over my face. "Yeah?"

"You have to do *something*," she says, her voice full of compassion. Her searching eyes no longer searching. "If you don't control the grief, it will eventually control you."

I nodded vehemently, like this was the best wisdom I'd ever received in my life.

But really, I was just counting the seconds until I could close the door behind me and lock Rational Ryn on the other side for the next two weeks.

∞

My feet hover at the threshold, my toes just barely behind the invisible line that marks the inside of this airport from the scary, unknown world beyond. My body is blocking the door from closing again. The cold hits me like a million samurai swords slicing at my skin. The snow swirls around me, biting at my ears, my nose, my lips.

How could you just leave me?! I shout into the chaotic, meaningless white void of my mind. *How could you do that?*

But there is no response. The snow is too loud. Or I'm too small. Either way, my silent words get lost somewhere in the storm.

I stare into the frenzy of white. I can't take the pressure. I can't handle the cold.

I'm a coward.

I'm just as weak and pathetic and inept as Dr. Judy thinks I am.

I'm not cut out for this.

Lottie should have been the one left behind.

I'm the one who should have died.

You got the wrong person!

You took the wrong person!

"How long are we gonna stand here?" Xander asks. "'Cause I'm kind of freezing my ass off."

I wilt, stumbling backward in defeat. The doors close behind me, securing me inside, guarding me from the storm once again.

I collapse into one of the black leather seats in the vestibule and try to breathe. But the snow is still blocking my lungs. It's frozen inside of me. Keeping the chill in and the air out. I close my eyes tight.

Xander sits beside me. A moment later I feel his hand on my back. His touch sends warm tingles down my spine. I don't want him to move. And yet he has to.

I can't feel this warm when it's that cold outside.

It's not fair. It's not allowed.

Nothing can feel good if she's still gone. How would that ever make sense?

"Is this . . . ?" Xander begins tentatively, as if he's not sure how to talk to someone like me. A crazy person who runs into snowstorms. Or at least *tries* to. "Does this have something to do with the unread text message on your phone?"

I jump up, sending Xander's hand flying into the back of the chair with a smack.

"What are you talking about?"

He looks instantly regretful of the question. "Nothing. I just . . . I saw it when I texted you from your phone. It was from someone named Lottie. And then you used that name at the restaurant before you switched to . . ." He lets that hang. "And then when you were yelling at me a minute ago and I just thought . . . I don't know."

I can feel Irrational Ryn whipping herself into a frenzy. Only to be rivaled by the frenzy still banging against the glass door outside. I know once she's out, she'll be hard to put back in.

But I'm finding it hard to care anymore.

I suddenly want to let her out. I want to set her free. I'm tired of keeping her in chains.

"You just thought that because your parents are super famous, international bestselling shrinks that you can psychoanalyze everyone you meet?"

Xander falls very quiet. I notice his jaw clench. "You don't know what you're talking about."

I open my mouth again, the bitter, angry words burning the tip of my tongue. But just then, door 612 slides open and a gust of snow and wind comes barreling through the vestibule, stinging my eyes. Two people dressed as giant red marshmallows stomp inside, shaking snow off their massive jackets and boots. One of them tips back the hood of their coat and yells out, "Bingo!"

I instantly recognize him as Jimmy from the restaurant. The other marshmallow unmasks herself. "No way. You are so *not* winning this."

It's Siri.

"Couple on the Verge of a Breakup," Jimmy announces, pointing directly at us, as if we're wax statues in a museum.

"You don't even know what they were saying!" Siri argues.

"I didn't have to. I could see their body language through the glass. Just look at them."

"We're not on the verge of a breakup," Xander mutters, still refusing to look at me.

I stare incredulously at him. *That's* the part he chose to refute? "We're not a couple," I correct.

"Could have fooled me," Siri mumbles.

"Whose side are you on?" I ask so sharply, it causes both of us to startle.

It isn't until that very moment—seeing my volatility reflected in Siri's reaction—that I realize how close I am to the edge. How easy it was to just uncork the bottle and let Irrational Ryn fly free. How good it felt in the moment.

But it's the next moment that's the problem. It's *this* moment. When I feel rash and stupid and out of control.

When I vow to rein it all back in and bury it in the ground, where it belongs.

"You guys are just ruining bingo for everyone today, aren't you?" Siri says.

Siri and Jimmy walk farther into the vestibule, continuing to stomp snow from their boots. Siri unzips her jacket. I watch her in fascination. She was *out* there. In the storm. Like it was nothing. Like she was just taking a stroll in the park.

"You went outside?" I ask, focusing on keeping my voice soft and controlled.

Siri lets out a groan. "Yeah. We thought we'd try to get out, but my car is buried under an avalanche, and I just found out from Twitter that they've closed Peña."

"What's Peña?" I ask.

"It's the only road that goes to the airport," Jimmy informs me somberly.

"What does that mean?"

Siri looks at me like I'm extremely dense. "It means no one is getting in or out of this place tonight."

Assembling the Troops

The entire Denver International Airport shrinks to the size of an elevator. And we're all crammed inside. And the solid steel doors slam shut. And the cord breaks.

And we're falling. We're all falling. Plummeting to our deaths.

I scramble for my phone, swipe it on with shaky fingers.

One unread message.

But it doesn't help. Not this time. Not now. I need more. I need to get out of here. I need . . .

What happens when you get trapped in an airport during a snowstorm?

Where does everyone sleep?

If you're stuck outside in a blizzard, how long will you survive?

What are the signs of hypothermia?

How do automatic doors work?

What causes a dashboard clock to stop?

The questions are queuing up in my mind like angry passengers waiting at the customer service desk. They shove each other out of the way, vying for first position. My fingers fly fast over the keys. I'm making so many mistakes, some of the words in my search bar look more like Vulcan than English. But somehow Google manages to translate. Because Google is amazing. And because, obviously, Google speaks Vulcan.

Type question. Hit Search. Click Result. Scan text.

Type question. Hit Search. Click Result. Scan text.

Repeat. Repeat. Repeat.

I'm barely even reading the search results. I'm just trying to answer a single question before ten more show up. Bits and pieces of random information drift aimlessly around in my head like planets kicked out of orbit.

Blankets and water . . .

Two days without shelter . . .

Symptoms include: shivering, confusion, irritability . . .

Sensors triggered by weight . . .

The words might make sense if I stopped long enough to string them together, but sense is not my objective here. Just knowing the answers are out there, just knowing the questions aren't large, gaping unknowns floating around the universe like black holes, is enough.

Seven text messages arrive from my mom during the flurry of question and answer.

Mom: The news says all the flights are canceled!

Mom: And your airline isn't offering hotel vouchers.

Mom: Cheap bastards.

Mom: I tried booking you a hotel myself but the one inside the airport is full.

Mom: And the rest can't get their shuttles to the terminal.

Mom: Because they've closed the roads.

Mom: I should have booked you a room when I had the chance.

I dismiss each text message as soon as it comes in and keep typing. Keep asking. Keep searching.

"Hello?" Siri says, waving a hand in front of my face. A hand I barely even see. A hand that might as well be a gnat for all it does to deter me from my quest. "I'm talking to you. Earth to Mopey Girl."

She may very well be talking to me, but I'm not listening. I turn my back to her and keep tapping.

Tap. Tap. Tap. Tap. Tap. Tap. Tap.

"Uh, what is she doing?" I hear Siri whisper to Xander.

"I have no idea," Xander whispers back.

I hear the sound of a phone ringing, and my index finger pops up, ready to ignore the call, before I realize it's not my phone. It's not my ringer. My phone is on vibrate anyway.

"Sorry," I hear Xander say from what seems like a galaxy away from here, "I have to take this. I'm just going to step away for a minute."

Tap. Tap. Tap. Tap. Tap. Tap. Tap.

"She's not listening to me," Siri complains to someone. Probably Jimmy. "I don't like it when people don't listen to me."

"We know," Jimmy agrees.

"Yeah," Siri says delicately. "I'm just gonna take that now."

Before I can react, she's ripped the phone right out of my fingers. My hands paddle uselessly in the air, like I'm drowning in a pool without water.

"Hey!" I say, trying to sound angry. Trying to muster up any emotion besides shock and numbness. "Give that back!"

"You can have it back when you learn not to abuse it. You went a little cuckoo there for a minute. Scared the shit out of poor Jimmy here."

I look to Jimmy. His expression is blank. Until he realizes he's supposed to play along, and he twists his face into a theatrical grimace.

"See?" Siri says.

My breathing starts to grow ragged. "Please," I beg her. "Please. I have to have it back. You have to give it to me. I really need it." There's desperation in my voice. I can hear it. Siri can hear it. The whole airport can hear it. "GIVE ME THE FUCKING PHONE BACK!!!"

Siri remains impressively calm in the face of my freak-out. "See, *this*," she says, twirling her finger in my face. "Is why I'm *not* giving it back. That's not a normal person's reaction to losing their phone. You clearly are in need of a phonetervention."

"I don't need a phonetervention!" I snap. "I just need my phone back."

Siri looks to Jimmy. "That sounds like an addict to me."

"Mmm hmm," Jimmy agrees with a purse of his lips, and I shoot him a scowl.

I try to reel in my emotion and keep my tone calm and measured. "I'm not an addict. Can I please just have my phone back? I was in the middle of something very important."

Siri glances down at the phone, making my stomach clench.

"Yeah, I can see why Googling how automatic doors work is really pressing stuff." She slides my phone into the pocket of her jacket. "Now, on to the *really* urgent matter of the night. How are we going to celebrate New Year's in less than four hours?"

Jimmy starts to shake his wide hips and pump his fists forward and back, like he's in a rowing crew. "Partay in the airport! Partay in the airport!" he sings.

I stare vacantly at the two of them. We're trapped in this godforsaken place for who knows how long and they're thinking about *parties*?

"Okay," Siri begins, unzipping her jacket. Her voice takes on an official-sounding tone. "Lola from the first-class lounge in the A terminal can score us some good booze. She's got the key to the liquor closet. Marcus has an extra room at the Westin that he said I could use. Arnie from baggage services can get us into Lost and Found. We'll ask Ivanna from Auntie Anne's, Kurt from Hope's Cookies, and Bethany from Dunkin' Donuts to bring the grub."

"Ooh!" Jimmy pipes in excitedly. "Abby at the Hertz counter has awesome playlists on her phone. *And* she slept with Theo from hotel security, so she can boob-flash us out of any problems."

"Good," Siri commends. She digs into her pocket, takes out the phone—*my* phone—and swipes it on. I feel confident that at least it's locked with a passcode now, so she can't actually *use* it.

But then I watch in horror as Siri expertly taps four digits into the keypad, and the screen unlocks. She immediately starts typing a note, mumbling to herself. "Abby, music and boob security. Lola, booze. Ivanna, Kurt, and Bethany, food."

I gasp. "How did you do that?"

She glances at me briefly. "Please," she says. "One-two-three-four? That's the most common passcode in the world."

I wilt in defeat. Of course I would use the most common password in the world. Of course I'm that boring and predictable. And of course Siri would know that.

I try to grab again at the device, but she swings it out of reach.

"And let's see if Gabe can borrow some decent speakers from the Bose kiosk," Jimmy suggests.

She adds this to the list.

"Can I please have my phone back?" I ask again as politely as I can.

Siri shuts off the screen and slides the phone back into her pocket. "Nope. It's got all of our party notes in it. It's an accomplice now. I can't let it out of my sight."

I huff. "I'll e-mail you the note."

"No go. My phone is dead. I need yours." She looks to Jimmy. "Come on. The ball drops in T-minus three hours and fifty-eight minutes, and we have a lot of work to do. I'm tasking you with decorations, food, and music. I'll handle the guest list."

Jimmy and Siri share a nod before striding off into the crowded terminal.

And I have no choice but to follow.

∞

Three months before she died, Lottie got one of her hunches. Hunches were common with Lottie. She was convinced she had "minor" ESP. Not full-blown telepathy, but an inkling of it.

"I can't control it," she once told me. "I don't know when it's going to strike. It just hits me and I have to roll with it."

She'd texted me earlier that morning, providing very little information apart from the following:

Lottie: Wanna hear something crazy?
Me: Always.
Lottie: I'm coming over in 5. Get your mom's keys.

Lottie had her own car. I had to borrow my mom's whenever I wanted to go somewhere. But by the time I texted her back to ask why I was tasked with securing our transportation, Lottie was already at my door.

"Did you get the keys?"

I glanced over her shoulder. Her beautiful, shiny black BMW was parked at the curb. "Why aren't we taking your car?"

"Because he knows my car."

I sighed, the comprehension suddenly sinking in. This was bound to be one of Lottie's revenge rampages. They weren't entirely commonplace, as Lottie was usually the one to lose interest in a guy first, but every once in a while, on a blue moon, a boy broke up with Lottie.

She didn't react as any normal teenage girl would. She didn't cry in her bed and eat junk food and lament about never finding anyone else again.

Lottie was an active dumpee.

She didn't suffer heartbreak.

She avenged it.

"Do we have to?" I asked, whining a little. It was a Saturday afternoon, and I had just started sketching on the back porch.

Lottie glanced down at my clothes. I knew exactly what she was thinking. She was weighing her options. Sweatpants, tank top, and, flip-flops weren't the ideal attire for an accomplice, but waiting for me to change would put too much time and distance between her and her retribution.

Lottie was a right-now kind of girl.

She inevitably decided that my outfit would have to suffice, because instead of making me change, she said, "Yes, we have to. Get the keys. We don't have much time."

"How long are you going to keep my phone?" I ask, trailing behind Siri and Jimmy like a lost puppy. As we go, I keep an eye out for Xander, but I don't see him. I remember him saying he was going somewhere to take a phone call, but this concourse is huge. He could be anywhere.

Siri barely looks back at me. "As long as it takes for you to stop being Mopey Girl and start being Fun Girl."

I sigh. "For the last time, I'm not Mopey Girl."

"Could've fooled me," Jimmy whispers loudly.

"I heard that."

He flashes me a warm smile. "I know."

I'm starting to feel antsy. The idea of my phone in someone else's custody is making my fingers twitch. I make a mental list of my options:

1. Tackle Siri to the ground, pin her down with my knees, while I reach for the phone in her pocket.
2. Report the phone stolen to airport police.
3. Blackmail Siri by threatening to warn the authorities about her party unless she gives the phone back.

I immediately rule out options two and three, because the idea of doing anything that might get me near that airport office again is simply out of the question. And option one is probably a long shot given that I don't have any martial arts skills.

I decide my best bet is to just appeal to the friend.

"So, Jimmy," I say, trying to keep my voice light and conversational. "What was that final bingo square you needed?"

"Couple on the Verge of a Breakup. Why?"

"No reason," I reply with a shrug. "Just that I happen to know of one."

He stops walking and turns to face me, his expression grave. "Where?"

"That's a very good question. How badly do you want to know?"

"Do not play with my heart, Mopey Girl."

I sigh again. "My name is Ryn, okay?"

"Do not play with my heart, Ryn. Stranded Passenger Bingo is a very serious game with very serious consequences." Then he breaks into laughter. "Dang it, I almost made it through that with a straight face. But seriously. Where is this doomed couple you so speak of?"

Siri, having noticed her partner in crime missing, stops and turns back to us with an impatient hip jut. "Guys. What are you doing back there? We have a lot to do. Let's go!"

I beckon Jimmy to come closer. "Get me the phone back and I'll tell you."

"Oh no, you don't." Suddenly, Siri is next to us, yanking Jimmy by the shirtsleeve. "Don't let her sweet-talk you into stealing her phone for her." She points to me like she's scolding one of her children. "And you. Don't even try it. Jimmy may look strong, but he knows I can kick his ass."

Jimmy shrugs. "She's right."

Siri strides off again. Jimmy follows after her, and I follow after Jimmy, quietly cursing both of them.

"So, Marcus gave you the key to his hotel room, huh?" Jimmy is saying to Siri when I catch up with them. He's nudging her playfully with his elbow. "Ooh la *la*."

"No," Siri says gruffly, turning to Jimmy. "No ooh. No la. And definitely no *la*. Nothing is going to happen."

Jimmy ignores this. "You are so getting married and having all of his babies."

Siri turns to scowl at him, and I can just make out the faintest trace of a blush on her dark cheek. "Am not."

"Who's Marcus?" I find myself asking from behind them.

"He's—" Jimmy begins just as Siri blurts out, "He's nobody!"

Jimmy turns and whispers. "He's a millionaire who's in love with Siri."

"Really?" I ask.

"No," Siri responds sternly. "He's not in love with me."

"He's *so* in love with her."

"And he's not a millionaire," Siri says. "He's in the Million Mile Club. There's a difference."

"What's the Million Mile Club?" I ask to their backs.

"It's when someone racks up over a million frequent flyer miles," Jimmy explains, slowing to walk next to me. "The airline inducts them into a special club, and they get all sorts of perks. Marcus flies through Denver like twice a week, and he always stops by the Hub to ask Siri out, but she never says yes."

"Why?" I ask. "What's wrong with him?"

"Yeah," Jimmy prompts her. "What's wrong with him?"

"He's . . ." Siri begins with a huff.

"She can't come up with anything," Jimmy whispers conspiratorially to me.

"He's not my type," she finishes.

Jimmy snorts. "Yeah, right. Rich and powerful is not your type."

"He's not rich," she argues. "And he's only powerful within these walls."

"The airport hotel is entirely sold out, but he got *two* rooms," Jimmy says to me.

"How?"

"When his assistant heard about the storm, she booked him one just in case. And then the airline gave him the other when the flights were canceled. So he's letting Siri throw the party in the second room."

"Does that mean he's *coming* to the party?" I ask.

I notice Siri's pace slow. As if she's just considering this possibility for the first time.

Jimmy claps ecstatically. "Yes! Yes, it does. And you'll have to kiss him at midnight."

"No, I won't," Siri argues.

"Oh, c'mon, you know you want to," Jimmy says.

"No, I don't!"

"You totally like him. You talk about him all the time."

"I mentioned him once," Siri argues.

"Maybe once a *day*."

"You're exaggerating."

"And you're in denial."

"Is he cute?" I ask.

Siri is suspiciously silent, but I swear I see her cheeks color again. I turn to Jimmy for an answer. He nods vehemently and fans himself while mouthing, "HOT!"

"Then, what's the problem?" I ask.

"The problem is she's scared," Jimmy explains. "Because he really likes her. And that's freaking her the fuck out."

I bark out a laugh, immediately regretting it the moment Siri turns around to give me a death stare. The idea of anything scaring Siri is just comical. She seems so tough and fearless.

"I'm not scared," she insists.

"Yeah, and I'm not mopey," I counter.

"Oh! Snap!" Jimmy guffaws and puts his hand up for me to high-five. I do.

And for just that brief moment, I feel like I'm part of something. A member of a club.

"The problem is, he's boring," Siri says, but she sounds incredibly unconvincing.

"He's not boring," Jimmy counters. "He's actually really funny. One time he came to the counter and made this joke about—"

"And old," Siri interrupts.

"Twenty-six is not that old."

"That's seven years older than me!"

"Your father is twelve years older than your mother," Jimmy points out.

"That was an arranged marriage!"

"Well, so is this," Jimmy declares. "I'm arranging your marriage."

"Don't you have decorations and food to secure elsewhere?" Siri snaps, shooing him away like he's a stray cat.

Jimmy flashes me a knowing grin and salutes us both. "See you at the party!" he calls. Then he darts off to tackle his to-do list, leaving me alone with Siri, who now, believe it or not, is in an even fouler mood than when I first met her.

∞

After we got in the car and started driving, it didn't take long for me to realize that Lottie and I were following someone. Lottie kept making snap decisions that she would yell from the passenger seat like, "Turn here!" and "Quick! Get into the left lane!"

But the streets were so crowded, I couldn't figure out which car was our mark. So I just surrendered to my role in Lottie's latest rampage and did as I was told. It wasn't until she directed me to get on the freeway that I recognized the dark sedan two cars ahead of us.

"Wait," I said, squinting at the back of the driver's head. "Isn't that your *dad's* car?"

"Shhh!" Lottie urged, as if he could hear us from three cars away.

"Why are we following your dad?"

Lottie shifted in her seat. If I didn't know any better, I would have said that she looked nervous. But I *did* know better. And Lottie *never* got nervous. It just wasn't in her vocabulary. Plus, I was usually a big enough bundle of nerves for the both of us.

"Move to the right lane or we'll lose him," she directed.

"Lottie. That's not an answer." But I still did as I was told.

"I had a hunch," she said matter-of-factly.

"About your dad?"

"He's cheating on my mom."

I swerved and nearly sideswiped the car in the next lane.

"Ryn!" Lottie screamed.

"Sorry!" I screamed back, then took a deep breath in an effort to calm myself. "What do you mean he's cheating on your mom?"

"I don't think that leaves much room for interpretation."

I was gripping the steering wheel so tightly my knuckles were turning splotchy. "How do you know? Did you see him with another woman?"

The thought of Lottie's parents splitting up made me sick to my stomach. More so than my own parents' separation did. Not because the Valentines were the world's happiest couple or anything. Lottie's dad was hardly around long enough for them to even *count* as a couple. But, as of that moment, they were really the only constant in Lottie's life. I mean, besides me. She changed her mind faster than most people change lanes. Her house, her closet full of expensive clothes, her father returning late at night from his latest business trip—those were the only things that grounded her to the earth.

If her parents got divorced, she might float right off into space.

"I told you," Lottie said, growing slightly impatient with my questions. "I had a hunch."

I glanced at her out of the corner of my eye and instantly knew she was lying. This wasn't a hunch. She looked visibly rattled. She knew something. A secret she wasn't telling me.

I suddenly thought about twelve-year-old Lottie, lying on the floor of her tree house after my parents' divorce. Her red hair fanned out around her face.

"I don't ever want to get married," she'd whispered. "It never ends well."

I glanced over at seventeen-year-old Lottie sitting in the

passenger seat of my mom's Prius. She was staring intently out the windshield, watching the dark sedan in front of us, making sure we didn't lose him.

I wondered what had happened today to propel her into action.

And I also wondered how long Lottie had been keeping this secret buried inside her.

After the third sign for Portland International Airport, Lottie's father's destination was becoming fairly obvious. But, as was so often the case, Lottie refused to see the signs.

"It's not a business trip," she argued after I suggested it for the second time.

"Then why is he going to the airport?"

"It's a ruse." Her answer was so confident. It left little room for argument.

"He's driving all the way to the airport to throw us off his scent?"

Lottie snorted. "Don't be ridiculous, Ryn."

I'm the one being ridiculous?

"He doesn't know that we're onto him."

I scrunched up my face, now totally confused. This was bizarre behavior, even for Lottie.

"Then why is he going to the airport if he's not going on a business trip?"

"Don't you see?" Lottie asked with annoyance.

"Clearly, I don't."

"He's leaving a trail!"

I shook my head. "A trail?"

"He parks at the airport parking lot. He charges the parking to the credit card so that when my mom sees the statement, she has no reason to suspect him."

"And then?" I asked. I didn't want to lead her any further down this path of delusion she was paving in her mind, but I was actually curious.

She sighed, rapidly losing patience with me and my naïveté in matters of the unfaithful heart. "And then he gets picked up. By whoever he's cheating with!"

I exited the freeway, still three cars behind Mr. Valentine's black sedan, and stopped at the light. I peered at Lottie. Her eyes were wide and wild and red-rimmed. Her lips dry and chapped. Her beautiful nails were chewed down to the quick, the remaining red polish frayed and jagged. Everything about her was so *un*-Lottie, it terrified me.

"Lottie," I tried again in a gentle voice. "What happened?"

She was silent for a moment. All I could hear was her strained breathing and the sound of the turn signal *click click clicking* as we waited to turn left. For a moment, I thought she actually might tell me, just to keep the silence from suffocating us both. But then the light turned green and the moment passed.

She pointed at the vehicle three cars ahead of us. "He's turning. Don't lose him."

"I won't," I assured her, easing onto the gas pedal. But I was pretty certain I had already lost Lottie.

∞

Siri spends the next thirty minutes zigzagging across the enormous concourse, recruiting every employee she knows (and some she doesn't) to what she's promising to be the most epic New Year's Eve party this airport has ever seen, making me wonder just how many New Year's Eve parties this airport *has* seen.

Despite the darkness that's fallen outside, the building is extremely well lit. And so vast and open. I stop along the railing of a balcony and take the whole scene in. If this place wasn't my evil nemesis keeping me from getting home, I might find the sight beautiful.

As we pass through a corridor on our way to the baggage claim, I notice a boy standing off to the side, studying one of the large paintings on the wall. I instantly recognize his dark hair and scrawny body.

"Troy?" I slow, keeping one eye on Siri. I can't risk losing her in this massive concourse. Not when she still has my phone.

Troy looks at me with a vacant, almost zombielike expression, as though he doesn't recognize me.

"Ryn," I say, putting a hand to my chest. "Your *sister*."

He blinks twice. "I don't have a sister."

I roll my eyes. "I got you out of the clutches of Simon, the airline employee."

"Ah. Right," he replies woodenly, then turns back to the mural, like I'm not even there.

I glance over at Siri, who has stopped nearby to talk to a baggage handler. For a moment I consider leaving. The kid is weird. And despite what Simon said, he's really not my problem.

But there's something about how small and vulnerable he looks in this vast concourse. It makes me do something I haven't done in a long time.

Care.

"What are you doing?" I ask, following his gaze to the massive painting. But as soon as my eyes register what I'm seeing, I nearly jump back in horror. "Holy crap. What is that?"

The canvas is disturbing, to say the least. It stands at least six feet tall and nine feet wide and it depicts what appears to be a Nazi wearing a gas mask, stabbing a white dove with a giant sword with a demolished city in the foreground.

I gape at it in astonishment. "What is this doing in an airport?"

Troy taps his finger against his teeth, keeping his gaze trained on the troubling mural. "That's what I'm trying to figure out."

"Does this have something to do with the mission you were referring to?"

He nods, still staring pensively at the art. "One of the guys in my master's program swears there's a top secret government conspiracy surrounding this airport. That the Illuminati built it to house an underground lair buried deep within the earth, and that this is where they will go when they bring about their deadly plans for destruction."

I snort. "Sounds like a Dan Brown novel."

"Mmm," Troy says, "I don't read fiction."

"So what does this painting have to do with it?"

"He *said* there are signs confirming the conspiracy, hidden around the airport."

I laugh. "This painting doesn't exactly look hidden. It's huge."

Troy looks at me. "What an astute observation," he says in a robotic tone. "Are you sure you're not an art scholar?"

"Ha. Ha. Very funny. Just because I'm not as smart as you—"

"No one is as smart as me."

"I'm sure *someone* is."

Troy considers this. "Well, very few." He focuses back on the painting. "There's a lot of debate online about what this painting represents."

"Death," I say automatically, without thinking. "It represents death."

Troy looks at me again, but this time there's something different about his gaze. Something inquisitive. As if I've suddenly become the more interesting tableau here.

I keep my eyes trained on the painting, taking in what looks like a river of dead souls emerging from the destroyed city. "And how we're all helpless in its wake."

"Yes, that's what the conspiracy theorists think. But the artist claims he was trying to convey hopefulness."

I snort and point to the middle of the mural, where a young girl and two babies are sleeping on a pile of rubble. "Then he shouldn't have painted three children who can literally do nothing but lie down while their city is being destroyed."

"So you're a conspiracist," Troy states.

"No, I'm a realist."

Troy is silent for a long moment, still studying me. I blink, coming out of what feels like a trance, and that's when I notice

Siri is no longer talking to the baggage handler. I desperately glance around until I spot her heading toward the escalators that lead to the upper level of the concourse. I really don't want to lose track of her as she still has my phone. But I'm also hesitant to let Troy out of my sight. For some reason, I don't like the idea of him wandering around this airport by himself, staring at creepy paintings and searching for apocalyptic clues. Even though he has an IQ of about a million, I feel sort of protective of him.

"Look," I say, "I know you're on some important mission or whatever, but I was thinking maybe you could hang out with me tonight instead."

He looks incredibly dubious. "Doing what?"

I peer over at Siri, who's now stepping onto the escalator. "Well, you see, there's this party."

A look of pure disgust flashes across his face. "A *party*? I'm trying to unravel a conspiracy that may bring about the end of the world, and you want me to go to a party?"

I bow my head, feeling foolish and chastised. "Yeah. You're right. I'm sorry."

But he doesn't walk away. He actually takes a step toward me and cocks his head to the side. "What *kind* of party?"

∞

Troy and I catch up to Siri on the second floor of the concourse. She's making her way to a restaurant called Pour la France! which seems to have the best view in the whole terminal and looks like a Parisian café. The chairs have wicker backs and the coffee drinks are served in cute, French-style white cups with saucers.

Siri walks up to the to-go coffee counter, cutting in front of a huge line of people who all grunt and hiss at her. Obviously, she ignores them. No surprise there. Siri doesn't strike me as the kind of girl who bothers to care what people think of her. It's a personality trait that fascinates me and frightens me at the same time.

The barista is a thin, leggy girl in her late teens or early twenties. She's beautiful, with long, dark hair that's been braided up one side. When Siri approaches, she immediately abandons the coffee order she's working on and gives Siri her undivided attention.

"Listen up, chica," Siri says, sounding stern. "Your mourning period ends tonight. I'm throwing a huge New Year's Eve bash in room 917 of the Westin and you're going."

The girl slouches. "I don't know."

"Nope," Siri replies. "None of that. You're going. There's going to be enough booze there to make you forget about what's his stupid face."

"I don't want to forget about him," the barista whines.

"I don't care what you want," Siri snaps.

"Excuse me!" the customer at the front of the line butts in. "Are you going to finish my drink?"

"In a minute," Siri barks at him. "Can't you see we're in the middle of something?"

The customer looks affronted but backs down, grumbling something to his wife.

"Room 917," Siri repeats. "You better be there or I'll come find you. I know where you hide."

While Troy is distracted reviewing articles about the airport conspiracy on his phone, I let my gaze wander to the dining area of the restaurant. Every table is taken. I don't think it really hit me until now just how many people are going to be spending the night under the same roof. This is going to be one epic slumber party.

Then I spot someone familiar. A tall, beautiful redheaded woman dressed in a flight attendant's uniform. It's the same woman I saw whispering giddily into her phone back at gate A44. The one who reminded me of Lottie. Except now she's not alone.

Sitting across from her is an attractive, thirtysomething gentleman in slacks and a button-down shirt. His red-and-white-striped tie has been loosened to the point where it looks more like a necklace than a tie.

The two are leaned as far forward as they can possibly be, foreheads touching, creating their own little private cocoon. He reaches out and places a hand on her cheek, and she closes her eyes, leaning into his palm.

I wonder if this is the guy she was talking to on the phone when I saw her hours before. If so, how did he get here? Was he already on his way? Did he drive in from somewhere nearby? Through all that snow?

Or is this a completely different guy?

A boy in every port.

I expect Lottie to burst into my head right now and offer her opinion. This is just the kind of romantic interlude that she *loves* to comment on. A quiet, stolen moment between two people who are clearly crazy about each other.

But she's unusually silent.

Come to think of it, I haven't heard from her since I tried to run out into the storm.

"C'mon," a voice breaks into my thoughts. It's Siri. She's nudging me along to our next recruiting destination.

"Where are we going now?"

"We're assembling more troops," she replies as though it's terribly obvious and shame on me for not coming to the same conclusion myself.

"Are you going to war or planning a party?"

Siri links an arm through mine like we're best friends (which we are *not*) and I can't help but notice that she smells like hamburger mixed with what I deduce is some kind of strawberry body spray. As we walk and Troy follows behind us, his face buried in his phone, I glance down at the poofy red jacket Siri is still wearing over her work uniform. My phone is only inches away. I could easily slide my fingers right into her pocket and grab it.

I feel my whole body buoy at the thought of getting it back.

This is when Lottie's shoplifting skills really would have come in handy.

I squeeze tighter against Siri and let my hand sink down against my hip. Then, with the slyness of a cat, I slip two fingers into the soft, downy pocket of her jacket, reaching farther and farther until . . .

"The phone's in the other pocket," Siri says without looking at me or trying to move away from my sticky fingers. "But nice try, Danny Ocean."

Danny Ocean? There's that name again.

My mind immediately flashes to Xander.

Where on earth did he go? I know he left to take a phone call, but that was over thirty minutes ago. He probably used his ringing phone as an opportunity to escape. I certainly wouldn't blame him. He's seen a hint of the crazy that lies beneath. He's glimpsed Irrational Ryn and she's not pretty to look in the face. This is why you don't talk to people. This is why you keep your head down and you don't make eye contact and you don't agree to have burgers with strangers and you do whatever it takes to keep those hidden things hidden.

Because as Lottie always said, *"It never ends well."*

Even so, I can't help but inconspicuously scan the surrounding area for that familiar Animal Muppet shirt. But instead of finding Xander, I notice something else.

Back at the flight attendant's table, her male dining companion has now placed both hands on her face and is leaning in to kiss her. She melts into him, her lips parting seductively. I have to squint to make sure I'm seeing what I think I'm seeing, but there's really no mistaking it.

On his fourth finger, pressed against her flawlessly creamy skin, is a gold wedding band.

∞

I parked three rows away from Mr. Valentine's sedan, and Lottie jumped out before I had even killed the engine. We crept around parked cars like ninjas as we stealthily attempted to follow her father through the long-term parking lot toward the terminal building.

"Lottie," I whispered as she ducked behind an SUV and peered around the edge of the bumper. "I think he's actually *going* to the airport."

She shook her head adamantly. "No, he's not. She's probably meeting him at the passenger pickup."

"Why would he go through all this trouble just to do that?"

"Because that's what cheaters do!" she hissed.

And so the game went on.

We followed Mr. Valentine all the way into the terminal building, hid behind a bank of payphones while he checked in at the ticket kiosk, and skulked after him until he reached the security line.

I grabbed Lottie's arm and pulled her back. "We can't go through there without a ticket," I reminded her.

She turned toward the counter with determination in her eyes. "Then we'll just have to buy a ticket. I have my Visa with me."

"Lottie," I said, running to step in front of her. "I think you need to accept the fact that your father is going on a business trip. Just as he said he was."

She stared at me, but it was as though she was looking right through me. Her eyes couldn't focus. Her mind couldn't accept the words coming out of my mouth.

I grabbed her by the shoulders and gave her a little shake. Her head bounced around like a rag doll. "What *happened*?"

But she still didn't answer me.

I sighed. "I think we should go home."

Lottie turned back briefly, watching her father hand his ticket and ID to the awaiting TSA agent. I could see the confusion creeping across her face. Lottie was never one to admit defeat. At least not easily.

"Okay," she finally relented, facing me. "Let's go home."

But she didn't move. I wrapped my arms around her and pulled her into a hug, squeezing her tighter than I'd ever remembered squeezing her. She seemed to dissolve into me, but she didn't hug me back.

"It'll be okay," I promised her.

She nodded against my shoulder, but I could tell she didn't believe me.

I was just about to pull away when something caught my eye. Lottie's father had bypassed the first security check and was waiting to put his bag through the X-ray scanner. A woman with long dark hair ran up to him and laid a deep, openmouthed kiss on his lips. It was hard to make out clearly through all the other passengers blocking my view, but I was pretty certain she was wearing a black flight attendant's uniform.

I let out a small, pained gasp, and Lottie broke free from my hug. Her back was still to the security line.

"C'mon," I said, trying to keep my tone light and unaffected. "Let's go to Salt & Straw."

I prayed she wouldn't turn around. I prayed if she did, they would already be gone.

"Ryn?" she said, her voice soft, broken.

I kept mine bright and breezy. "Yeah?"

"I'm sorry for dragging you into this."

I let out a laugh, hoping it didn't sound as forced to her as it felt coming out of my mouth. "Don't be. That's what I'm here for."

Lottie smiled a clumsy, crooked smile, making her look like a china doll whose lips had been painted on with an unsteady hand. "You're a good friend. I don't deserve you."

I reached out and squeezed her fingers, noticing how cold and clammy they felt. "Of course you do. You deserve everything, Lottie."

As we made our way back through the airport, I let the word linger on my tongue, feeling its shape, its weight, its significance, before pushing it out again into the world with a single burdened breath. *"Everything."*

∞

I abruptly stop walking. Siri, still attached to my arm, is yanked backward. She turns to shoot me a scowl, but I don't even acknowledge her. My gaze is too focused on the flight attendant and her *married* companion.

Maybe they're married to each other, I think. It's Rational Ryn, trying to rein me in before I even get started.

But I'm trapped inside an airport, twelve hundred miles from my house, thirteen hours away from reexperiencing the worst moment of my life.

Rational Ryn has no place here.

"A flight attendant's life is so glamorous! Think of all the exotic places you get to go. And the people you meet. You could have a boy in every port!"

My breathing grows shallow. I can't seem to keep oxygen in my lungs. I start to feel light-headed as the realization washes over me.

She knew.

About her father. About the flight attendant. About everything.

"Helloooo! Mopey Girl! What. Are. You. Staring. At?"

A hand blurs across my vision, blocking my view of the adulterous couple in the café.

I blink again and tear my gaze away from them. Siri is standing next to me, looking annoyed. Does she *have* any other expressions?

"Sorry," I mutter. "I just . . . I thought I knew them."

"Who? The slutty flight attendant and the two-timing husband?"

My mouth falls open. "How do you know that?"

She brushes this off with a flick of her fingers. "Please. I see those two around here all the time."

"You do?"

"Yeah. They're always coming to the Hub to eat. She flies through here at least once a week. I'm pretty sure he's local and just comes to the airport to meet her."

My mind is reeling. Images flicker through my brain faster than I can keep up.

Lottie. And a black sedan. And tiny liquor bottles. And the tree house.

"A flight attendant's life is so glamorous. You could have a boy in every port!"

"But . . ." I ask. My voice is trembling so badly, I'm barely able to form coherent words. "H-h-how does he get through security if he's not flying anywhere?"

Siri shrugs. "Beats me. I always assumed he just bought a ticket. You know, a paper trail so the wife doesn't get suspicious."

"And then he just goes home?"

"Well, not right away." Siri raises her eyebrows scandalously. "There is a hotel attached to the airport."

I want to hold my hands over my ears in an attempt to block out her words, but it's too late. They're already lodged inside my brain. Rattling around like ghosts with iron chains.

How did you know, Lottie?

I thought I'd kept it from you.

I tried to keep it from you.

I tried to protect you!

How did you find out?

There is no response. The Lottie in my head is stoically silent.

Of course she is. She's not real. She's a figment of my imagination. A cryogenically frozen version of my best friend, trapped in time in my own head. She can't discover new things. She can't have epiphanies. She can't grow up.

She'll never grow up.

She'll be seventeen and foolish forever. Thinking that nothing scares her. Thinking that stealing a tube of lip gloss is the answer to all of life's problems.

But what if the Lottie that I've been living with for the past year is a lie?

What if she knew things—understood things—that she never told me?

What if the real Lottie was a puzzle that I never got to finish? I thought I had the full picture, but there were actually pieces missing. Important pieces. Large chunks of sky and bridges that don't connect.

"This is depressing," Siri's voice smashes into my thoughts, and I blink, dabbing at my eyes. I expect to find moisture underneath, but my fingers come back dry.

Because I can't cry.

Because I'm broken.

Because, according to Dr. Judy, I don't know how to grieve.

Because I'm failing at everything.

Including losing my best friend.

83. I blame Stanford University for giving Dr. Judy a degree.

84. I blame Siri for stealing my phone.

85. I blame Lottie for driving through an intersection on a green light.

86. I blame—

Siri loops her arm through mine again and starts to lead me away. "Let's go. We have more people to recruit."

This time, I leave willingly.

Tiny Bottles

Siri has circled the first and second floor of the main concourse building twice, assembling her New Year's party team. I've managed to amass one troop of my own, and that's Troy. I follow behind Siri, and he follows behind me, like some lame excuse for a processional.

I notice the mayhem has started to die down. The concourse is emptying. Where these people are all going, I have no idea. Perhaps to those blankets and meals that Claudia promised in her announcement.

The airport is vibrating on a different frequency now. The air no longer feels panicked and frenetic. It feels resigned. Everyone has accepted their fate. Everyone has hunkered down for the night.

Well, everyone except me.

Siri is still holding my precious phone hostage, which means she's holding me hostage too.

Siri's next (and I pray final) stop in her party planning mission takes us to the airport's interfaith chapel. I didn't even know airports *had* interfaith chapels.

"It used to just be called a chapel, but the Jews complained that was too Jesus-ish," Siri explains as she pokes her head into the small room, checking to make sure it's empty. "So they changed the name to 'spiritual center,' but the Bible-bangers thought that sounded too hippie."

Satisfied that no one appears to be inside, Siri steps through the doorway and I follow after her.

The room is long and narrow with three rows of chairs all pointed to a vague, nondenominational shrine in the front of the room, lined with various scripture books of different faiths.

"They finally settled on 'interfaith chapel,' until the Muslims complained that there were too many chairs and no room to pray on the floor." Siri points to the door we just came through. "So they built an Islamic masjid next door."

She walks purposefully to a small supply cabinet, yanks open the door, and pulls out a handful of long, tapered candles that she stuffs into my backpack.

"Hey," I protest. "You can't take those. This is a house of worship."

"Actually, it's a room with chairs. I can take them." She zips me up. "Let's go."

We leave the chapel and head to a different set of escalators. These are located across from the bridge that leads back to the A gates. Just as I'm about to step on, out of the corner of my eye, I spot Xander.

He's huddled against a window, speaking tensely but softly into his phone while blocking his mouth with a cupped hand.

My heart unexpectedly lightens as my mind races through the implications.

He's still here.

He didn't leave.

Irrational Ryn didn't send him packing for the hills . . . or the A gates, as it were.

For a brief moment I consider going over there. For an even briefer moment I consider apologizing. But those moments pass just as quickly as they came, and I turn back to Siri, who is already halfway down the escalator. That's when I hear Xander's voice, rising dramatically and echoing off the wall of the emptying concourse building.

"Will you shut up for one second and listen to me, Claire?" he bellows, the easy, laid-back quality of his voice gone. He's at the end of his rope. That bottomless well of patience he seems to have is draining.

"I'm telling you, I didn't say a word to anyone! I swear." He pauses, listening. "I have no idea how they found out!"

Another pause. Xander's whole body clenches like he's a sponge trying desperately to hold on to those few remaining drops of patience. "I'm getting there as fast as I can. You can blame a lot of things on me, but you can't blame me for a snowstorm."

I suddenly have a burning desire to know who he's talking to. His parents? A relative? A girlfriend?

The last option makes my stomach drop to my knees.

Of course he would have a girlfriend.

Strangely, it's the first time I've even thought about it.

Lottie would have figured that out hours ago. Lottie would have found a sly way to sneak the question into the conversation. Lottie wouldn't be standing here like an idiot, eavesdropping on what is clearly some kind of lovers' quarrel.

Lottie wouldn't use the term "lovers' quarrel."

"Who's that?" Troy asks. He must have stopped when I stopped. Except he's not even looking at me, he's still staring down at his phone, presumably searching for more evidence to prove or disprove the Denver airport conspiracy.

I blink out of my trance and focus on him. "He's . . . he's . . ." But I suddenly realize I have no idea who Xander is. He's not really a friend. I've known him for only a few hours. But he's more than just an acquaintance. How much do I really even know about this guy? Hardly anything.

I return my gaze to Xander, huddled in the corner, and think back to the book I saw in the bookstore. The picture of Dr. Max Hale and Dr. Marcia Livingston-Hale with their well dressed, bright eyed son on the back. I know *that's* not the Xander I met in the airport today. The person in that picture looked nothing like the guy in the Muppet shirt standing only ten feet away.

It strikes me then that something is off about this whole situation. About how desperate he was for me *not* to see that book. About the way he's reacted every time I've brought up his parents. About the tense hunch of his shoulders right now as he practically curls around his phone.

It occurs to me that Xander might be hiding someone too. An irrational twin bound, gagged, and stuffed in a closet.

I peer back at Troy. He's scrolling through some Web page on his phone. Without hesitation I snatch the phone right out of his grasp.

"Hey!" he shouts, trying to steal it back, but he's small for his age, and I hold it high, out of his reach. "Give that back."

"In a minute," I say as I attempt to type above my head.

Troy jumps, trying to knock the phone out of my hand. "I'm going to call the authorities," he threatens.

"Good," I say confidently. "Then I'll be able to tell them that I'm not really your sister and you're an unaccompanied minor without a chaperone."

He stops jumping.

I flash him a smug smile. "I just have to ask Google one thing."

With a harrumph, he crosses his arms and, like the rest of the stranded passengers in this airport, reluctantly resigns to his fate.

I lower the phone and type in my first query in almost an hour.

Who is Xander Hale?

∞

The last party I went to was with Lottie. Three months before she died. It was at Poker Guy's house. I'd resorted to calling him Poker Guy, because I didn't want to remember his name. Giving him a name made him real. Giving him a name gave him longevity.

I wanted him to be the shortest of any of Lottie's phases.

I didn't want to go. The idea of hanging out with a skeevy poker player and all of his skeevy friends was not my idea of a good time. But I didn't want Lottie to go alone, either.

I assumed the guy was dangerous. I felt it was a safe assumption given the conditions under which they met. Underground poker games in the bowels of downtown Portland are typically not where great romances are made. I had flashes of the police finding Lottie's body washed up on the shore of the Columbia River three days from now.

In the end, it turned out to be an innocent trip to the mall that killed her. Not a skeevy poker player.

Irony can make you feel like such an idiot sometimes.

The party was nothing like I expected. The house was actually nice. In a suburb. With mowed lawns and barbeques. I tried not to let the surprise show on my face, but Lottie saw it anyway.

"See?" she whispered as Poker Guy took our coats and led us inside. "You need to learn to start trusting me, Ryn."

Trust was a tricky thing with Lottie. You never wanted to give her too much of it. You always wanted to keep some in reserve, just in case.

There were about thirty people packed into Poker Guy's living room and kitchen. They all looked to be in their early twenties. The majority of them were men—clean cut and fairly innocuous looking—but I made a point to size up the few women who mingled among them. They definitely didn't *look* like prostitutes, but I'd learned from watching a lot of television that you could never be too sure.

Poker Guy walked us to the kitchen and handed us each a bottle of beer. Lottie took a long pull from hers while I went to work peeling the label off mine.

"This is my friend Curt," Poker Guy said, grabbing the collar of a well dressed man and spinning him around. He looked annoyed by the rough summoning, but when he saw the two of us, his scowl was instantly forgotten.

"Hello," he said with that curious ring that comes with a less-than-subtle once-over.

"Hi, Curt," Lottie trilled. "I'm Lottie and this is Ryn."

Curt took a swig of his beer. I didn't miss the eyebrow raise he shot to Poker Guy as he drank. A chill crept up my arms.

"Ryn," Poker Guy addressed me, making me immediately want to change my name back to Kathryn. Or to something completely unpronounceable, like Kplxbmwkxv. "You and Curt should get better acquainted."

As soon as the words were out of his mouth, I knew what this was.

This was the getaway scheme. Distract the boring, less attractive friend so I can go make out with the hottie. But before I could protest, Lottie and Poker Guy were already shuffling off somewhere, his hand on the small of her back, her signature giggle trailing in their wake.

"So, what's your story?" Curt asked.

"I'm in high school," I said flatly.

He looked like I'd just slapped him in the face.

Buzzkill Ryn. That's me.

"High school," he repeated hoarsely before clearing his throat. "Like a senior in high school?"

Nice try, buddy.

"Nope. Junior. Seventeen years old. That barely even counts as legal adjacent."

He took another sip of his beer. "Right. Okay." Then he made a show of pulling his phone out of his pocket as though it had just conveniently started to ring. "Sorry, gotta take this."

"Of course," I said, happy to be rid of the pervy friend. The problem was, now I had nothing to do but wait until Lottie either finished her current activity or got pissed about something trivial and stormed off.

As I made myself comfortable on a couch and opened my favorite trivia game on my phone, I silently prayed it would be the latter.

But knowing Lottie, it was really anyone's guess.

∞

Who is Xander Hale?

The question felt different from the thousands I'd asked over the past eleven months and thirty-one days. This wasn't a desperate attempt to ward off the ominous unknown.

This was a genuine curiosity. A genuine yearning to understand.

The search on Troy's phone delivers several results. I scroll through each one, looking for something that would give me a better handle on this train-surfing, rabble-rousing,

Muppet-shirt-wearing boy still hunched around his phone ten feet away.

I click on a Wikipedia entry for his parents first. Xander is listed in the section labeled Personal Life. But there's not much there I haven't already surmised on my own. He was born the same year as me. He lives in Los Angeles with his überfamous psychologist parents, who drew upon their experience raising him—their only child—as inspiration to write the *Kids Come First* book series.

There's not much else.

I click back to the results and continue scrolling. I'm about to return the phone to Troy when I spot a link to a news article. It says it was posted only an hour ago.

The headline reads:

Kids Come First Authors' Son Kicked Out of Prestigious Los Angeles Prep School

My eyes widen and my heart races a little faster as I click the link. It's short. Only a paragraph, but it tells me everything I need to know.

> Xander Hale, only son of renowned child psychologists and bestselling authors Dr. Max Hale and Dr. Marcia Livingston-Hale, has reportedly been expelled from the Archer Academy, an esteemed preparatory school in Malibu, California, known in

the city for educating numerous children of celebrities and important media figures. The information comes from an anonymous source close to the Hale family, although the reasons for his expulsion are still undetermined. Representatives of the Hale family as well as the Archer Academy have yet to provide comment.

Shocked, I lower the phone.

The son of two of the most famous child psychologists got expelled from school? How does that even happen? Dr. Max and Dr. Marcia are supposed to be the end-all, be-all of parenting. If they can't manage to effectively parent their child, how is there any hope for the rest of the parents out there? The poor, clueless souls like my mother, who can't have a single meaningful conversation with her daughter about anything?

How is there any hope for *me*?

It must be some kind of misunderstanding. A mistake. He was framed by a jealous peer. Or unfairly targeted by a vengeful teacher. There's no way he could have been expelled for a legitimate reason. The article said something about an anonymous source. Maybe someone is just spreading vicious rumors about him.

But then I flash back on the conversation I overheard just a minute ago.

"I'm telling you, I didn't say a word to anyone! I swear. I have no idea how they found out!"

I glance up at Xander, who's still crouched in the corner, scowling into his phone.

Is that what he was talking about? The expulsion?

Does that mean it's possible he's *not* on the phone with a girl-friend?

Xander lets out a frustrated sigh as he listens to the voice on the other end of the call and casts his eyes to the ceiling. On their way back down they land right on me, and I feel a strange sensation trickle through me.

His entire demeanor shifts. He stands up a little straighter. His scowl fades.

"Look," he snaps to the person on the other end of the call. "I gotta go. I'm sorry, Claire, but I can't help you." Then he jabs at the screen and returns his phone to the pocket of his bag strap.

"Hey," he says, walking over with a smile that I think is supposed to look casual but ends up just looking painful.

"What was that about?" I ask, even though I know it's not my place. It's not any of my business. If I'm going to attack him for asking me about my text message, I certainly can't expect him to answer questions about his phone call.

Xander glances back at the corner he was just huddled in, as if he already forgot where he was. "Oh, that?" he says, his pitch slightly higher than normal. "Just more people trying to blame me for things I didn't do."

He looks pointedly at me with a look of accusation.

I open my mouth to . . .

To what?

Apologize?

Protest?

Yell again?

I'll never know, because Xander chuckles and adds, "I'm kidding. Chillax. Who's this?" He nods at Troy.

Troy doesn't even bother introducing himself. He swipes the phone out of my hand and chirps, "I'll take that, thank you very much." Then he immediately goes to work, resuming his conspiracy search.

"That's Troy," I explain. "I'm sort of kind of responsible for him."

"Sort of kind of *not*," Troy argues without looking up.

Xander glances between us, clearly wondering what he missed in the time he's been gone. He gives his head a little shake. "Okay, so what's the plan?"

I glance over the railing at Siri, who is back on the ground floor, chatting up some guy. I assume he's another airport employee she's recruiting. "Siri has taken my phone hostage until I agree to go to some stupid New Year's party she's planning."

"A party?" Xander asks, his face brightening. "Cool."

"No. Not cool. I need to get my phone back. I need to—"

"You need to what?" he interrupts, and I notice the subtle edge to his voice. "You need to go home? You need to call a cab? Ryn, you're stuck here. We both are. So why don't you relax and just let go for a minute?"

His words ignite a flare of irritation inside of me. He doesn't know me. He doesn't know anything about me. Who is he to tell me to relax?

"C'mon," he coaxes, his voice lightening again to that playful, easy cadence. "I'm willing to bet all the money I have in my wallet that you've never been to a party before."

He draws his wallet out of his back pocket and holds it up as proof that he's serious about the wager.

I think back to the last party I went to. That horrible night at Poker Guy's house.

I cross my arms. "I'll have you know that I've been to *lots* of parties."

"Fine," Xander allows, his mouth twitching with the hint of a smile. "Then I'm willing to bet all the money I have in this wallet that you've never been to a party you've actually *enjoyed*."

I expect to hear Lottie's buoyant voice telling me once again how easily pegged I am, but she stays silent. I think she might be on strike. For what, I don't know. But I have my theories and most of them revolve around that flight attendant. But I can't deal with that now.

"You can't change the bet," I retort. "The stakes have already been set and you lost."

The smile breaks free, overthrowing his scowl once and for all. "Fair enough," he says, and opens his wallet, pulling out two wrinkled and worn dollar bills. "There you are. All the money in my wallet."

I can't help but laugh.

"Hey! Mopey Girl!" I hear Siri's voice and glance over to see her running back up the escalator. She's waving my phone in the air, and I feel my dread lift. Thank God. She's giving it back. *Finally.*

I practically skip over to meet her. "Your phone's ringing," she announces when I get there. "It's your mom. I'll let you talk to your mom because moms are important, but then the phone goes right back in my pocket."

This is my chance, I immediately think. *I could do it. Take the phone and run in the other direction. Get as far away from these people as possible.*

I look at Xander, who's followed me over here, his eyes pinned intensely on me. I look at Troy, his attention still focused on his Web search. Then, finally, I look at harsh, abrasive, salty Siri who's holding my beloved phone in her hand.

I can see my mom's number flashing on the screen. I still haven't responded to any of her latest texts about me being stuck here overnight. I can only imagine what *that* conversation will sound like. A whole lot of talk that results in absolutely nothing.

A whole lot of words that form sentences but no meaning.

The same dance of avoidance we've been doing for eleven months and thirty-one days.

"Last chance," Siri says, brandishing the phone. "Do you want to answer?"

Ever so subtly, I shake my head and watch the screen change from the incoming caller ID to the pop-up message alerting me of a missed call.

Siri shrugs, returns the phone to her pocket, and spins on her heels. Xander follows after her and Troy follows after him.

I guess I'm going to a party.

∞

I'd been at Poker Guy's house for more than two hours and there was still no word from Lottie.

Is she dead in there?

Did he strangle her and climb out a window?

Is he already halfway to the Canadian border?

These were the questions streaming through my mind as I sat on the supple leather couch and played on my phone. I'd already won twenty-seven trivia games with random strangers across the globe and amassed more than ten trophies. The victories were all empty, though. They felt like placeholders for a life that I should have been living. Every time I started a new game, I told myself this one would be the last. After this, I would get up and talk to people. Make conversation. Ask someone about their day, their interests, their life. It's not hard. Question. Answer. Question. Answer. That's all a conversation is.

I promised myself I would *be* at this party instead of just existing at this party.

And yet every time I won and the little Play Again? bubble appeared on my screen, I always chose Yes.

I always chose wrong.

Occasionally, I would lift my head and watch the various partygoers chitchat and drink and laugh and then rearrange into different group formations and start again. They all made it look so easy to not be me.

Somewhere around eleven o'clock I finally managed to convince myself that this was just not my crowd. That they were all older and more mature and what would I have in common with them anyway? Probably nothing.

I gave myself an out, and I didn't only take it. I leapt on it. I tackled it and wrestled it into submission like a wilderness expert wrestles an unruly crocodile.

The party began to wind down around midnight. Coats were gathered. Hugs were dished out. Sober friends helped stumbling, drunk friends toward the door.

I checked the message app on my phone. Still nothing from Lottie.

I decided to text her.

Me: Hey. Party's almost over. Are you ready to leave?

Minutes passed before I heard back from her.

Lottie: You're still here? I thought you would have left by now.
Me: I wouldn't leave you!
Lottie: I think I'm gonna stay. Why don't you go home? Pete will give me a ride in the morning. I'll tell my mom I'm staying the night with you.

Staying the night?

I didn't like it. I didn't like it at all. Of course, I didn't mind lying for Lottie. I'd done it countless times. But Poker Guy was bad news. Despite the fact that his friends had proved to be harmless, I could feel it in my bones. Lottie may have been blind to it, but that's what she had me for. To be her Seeing Eye dog. To guide her around dangerous obstacles. To make sure she didn't trip and fall.

Me: I think you should come home with me.

Another lifetime passed before she responded.

Lottie: But I'm having fun! I'll text you tomorrow.

Frustrated, I stood up, jamming my phone into my pants pocket. How could I help her if she wouldn't let me? How was I supposed to do my job—keep her safe—if she cut me loose?

Then a disturbing thought struck me. It felt so obvious that I chastised myself for not realizing it sooner.

What if that's not Lottie texting me back?

What if Poker Guy had her bound and gagged in that room and was texting from her phone? Trying to get rid of me so he could finish whatever sadistic plot he had plotted?

The thought made me bold.

I marched down the hallway, knocking firmly on the door that I had seen Lottie disappear behind hours earlier. There was a shuffling on the other side. A repositioning of things.

"Who is it?" called Poker Guy. He sounded guilty. I felt vindicated.

"It's Ryn. I need to talk to Lottie."

More movement. A padding of footsteps. The door opened.

Lottie's face appeared through the crack. She was purposefully hiding the rest of her body.

"What's up, Ryn Ryn?" she asked. She had the loopy smile of Drunk Lottie.

"I . . ." I started the sentence, but I had nothing to finish it with. I hadn't thought this all the way through. I had been so convinced that what I'd find on the other side of this door would warrant a call to the police, I hadn't even considered any other scenario.

But as soon as I saw her face, as soon as I caught a glimpse of half-naked twentysomething Pete through the crack in the door, I knew what I had to do.

"Something happened," I said, forcing the brokenness into my voice.

Lottie's loopiness vanished. Sexy Drunk Lottie was replaced with Concerned Best Friend Lottie. "What?"

I looked down and whispered. "I can't talk about it here. But I really need you to come home with me."

She didn't hesitate. "Give me three seconds," she said. "Don't go anywhere. Stay right by this door."

I nodded, adding a sniffle for effect.

The door closed, and, true to her word, Lottie was back in record time. Her dress was on backward, her hair was a mess, and she was still putting on her shoes when she reappeared. She wrapped one arm around my shoulders and led me toward the front door. We didn't speak the whole way.

I felt guilty for bluffing. For playing the only card I knew would win in a poker game against Lottie. The Ace of Friendship.

But seeing her in the passenger seat of my mom's Prius, safely removed from that place, eased my conscience enough.

I didn't know what I was going to say to her. Once again,

I hadn't thought it all the way through. We drove the first few minutes in respectful silence, but I knew it was only a matter of time before she asked. And I would have to show my true cards. I would have to admit that I bluffed her. I had stolen the pot with a risky bet.

But I didn't care about that.

All that mattered was that I had won.

And this victory felt anything but empty.

It turns out airport parties are a lot like high school parties. Word gets around fast. Within an hour it feels like every single person who was once out there in the concourse is now packed into this tiny hotel room on the ninth floor of the Westin Denver airport hotel.

The decorations scattered throughout the room are suspect. They don't seem to have any apparent theme. In fact, most of them don't even seem to be decorations at all, but rather random items repurposed as decorations. A pendant necklace hangs from the ceiling over the makeshift dance floor, serving as the world's tiniest disco ball. A collection of sparkly purses have been secured to the walls like bizarre modern art installations. A bobblehead of some politician I don't recognize nods away on the desk-turned-refreshment-table. The candles Siri lifted from the chapel are scattered around the room, thankfully unlit. And sitting on one of the beds in the corner is an inflated female blow-up doll wearing a gray blazer, sunglasses, and bangle bracelets, and holding an e-reader.

Xander left to get a drink ten minutes ago and I haven't seen him since. You would think it would be easy to keep track of someone in such a small room, but with this many bodies shoved inside, I can barely keep track of my own thoughts.

For the past twenty minutes Troy has been trying to explain to me the theory of Schrödinger's cat. He doesn't realize that I pretty much stopped listening nineteen minutes ago. I just occasionally nod and purse my lips like he's saying something really fascinating.

"So you see," he says, wheeling his hands in the air. "Until you actually open the box, the cat is *both* dead and alive, proving that multiple dimensions *are* a scientific reality."

"Mmm," I say in response.

"Which means there's a version of this reality in which you aren't even here. In which you were booked on a nonstop flight home and are now sleeping soundly in your bed."

How do I get to that reality? I want to ask, but I'm afraid he might start talking about wormholes or time loops or some other timey-wimey *Doctor Who* stuff.

"I'm gonna get a drink," I announce to Troy and push my way through the people, toward the refreshment table. Troy follows behind me, still talking passionately about the half-dead, half-alive cat.

The drink table has been completely looted. I search for something nonalcoholic. All I need right now is to get Irrational Ryn drunk. I find a half-empty can of Coke and pour the rest into a cup, taking small sips in an effort to make it last longer.

The desk is littered with countless tiny liquor bottles, all empty. It makes me think of the stash Lottie used to have hidden in her tree house. The one my mother still thinks belonged to me. Hundreds of bottles in every variety. Vodka, gin, whiskey, bourbon, rum. Lottie was running her own tiny saloon up in that tree house. She said she would steal them from her dad's briefcase when he got back from business trips, but where did *he* get them?

Did he really buy tiny liquor bottles only to store them in his bag?

Or were they given to him? Perhaps by someone who worked on an airplane?

Lottie? I try. I don't have high hopes that she'll answer me. She hasn't answered me in a while. I'm not sure if she's mad or just running some strategic plot to get me to talk to people other than my dead best friend. I wouldn't put that past her.

"How's my favorite Mopey Girl?" Siri sidles up to me and bumps her hip against mine, spilling some of her drink in the process. I can tell she's already tipsy. After being the only sober one at so many parties that Lottie dragged me to, you start to get a radar for these kinds of things. I'm probably more accurate than a Breathalyzer.

"You have interesting taste in decorations." I motion toward the curiously dressed blow-up doll on the bed.

Siri giggles and I can smell the alcohol on her breath. "Everything you see here Jimmy got from the airport Lost and Found."

I give her a scandalized look. "He stole from the Lost and Found?"

"Not stole. *Borrowed*. We're gonna put it all back when we're done." She picks up a snorkel mask that's been propped up on the refreshment table. "People leave the strangest things at airports." She puts the mask on and then attempts to take a sip of her drink. The liquid runs down her chin, causing her to snort.

"So," she says, holding her hand in front of the mask and miming a fish swimming by. "Are you having fun yet?"

I give her a fake smile. "Absolutely. Troy, tell Siri what you just told me."

Troy's face lights up with pride. He starts from the beginning. "Schrödinger's cat, first proposed by Erwin Schrödinger in 1935, illustrates the quantum theory principle of . . ."

"Whoa, whoa," Siri interrupts, holding her head. For a moment I think she might vomit, and I take a step back. "Nerd Boy. Why don't you go find some *other* drunk chick to talk to about your Dinger?"

Troy does not look amused. "It's *Schrö*dinger and it has nothing to do with the male anatomy."

"Well, at least he understands euphemism," Siri whispers to me through her mask, but it's loud enough for Troy to hear.

"I beg your pardon," he huffs. "I have a physics degree from Stanford. I know a euphemism when I hear one, and I'm afraid *that* was not one. What you did was simply turn something you didn't understand into a bad sex joke."

I bite my lip to stifle a laugh.

"*Bad* sex joke?" Siri retorts, slurring her words slightly. "Okay, brainiac, let's hear you come up with a better one."

Troy rolls his eyes. "My mind is far too occupied pondering worthwhile concepts to waste any time conjuring up lewd jokes. That would be like asking a brilliant surgeon to use his hands to pick up trash on the side of the highway."

"Well . . . ," Siri begins gruffly but then quickly runs out of steam.

Troy is a child prodigy who also happens to be sober. Siri's biting wit is no match.

"Well," she says again as she lifts her mask to take a sip of her drink and then nearly spits it all over me as a thought comes to her. "Aha! Here's a math joke for you, genius boy. What is 6.9?"

Troy flashes me a look. "Um, a rational number."

"Ha! Wrong! It's great sex interrupted by a period."

Troy and I both get it at once, and we let out a simultaneous "Eeeww!"

Siri hoots with laughter. "You should see the look on his face!" she says to me.

"I *can* see the look on his face," I remind her.

Her intoxicated brain catches up. "Oh, right. Well, you should see the look on *your* face!"

"This is a friend of yours?" Troy asks me accusingly.

"Not . . . exactly."

"Hey!" Siri says, scowling again. "Why don't you make yourself useful and go hook up with someone."

For a moment I think she's talking to me, and I'm about to open my mouth to argue, but then I see her gaze is pinned on Troy.

"I don't have time for members of the opposite sex. I'm writing a dissertation on—"

"On how to be a virgin forever?" Siri guesses.

"He's only fourteen," I step in. "Let up a little."

Siri rolls her eyes and scans the crowd through her mask. "So where is that hot boy toy of yours?"

Now I know she's talking to me.

"He's not a boy toy and he's not mine."

"But he *could* be." She taps her head.

"I don't know where he is," I admit. And it's true. I still haven't caught sight of Xander since he left to get a drink.

"There he is!" Siri spots him for me, her face all lit up under the mask. I follow her gaze until I see him by the bathroom, talking to the barista who Siri recruited from the French café. I suddenly feel like someone just punched me in the gut.

He's met someone.

Of course he has.

If Lottie were still talking to me, she would tell me that this was all my fault. That cute boys will only show interest for so long. That the game of hard to get is a delicate one. You have to give them just enough to keep them hanging on, otherwise, they'll give up and try their luck elsewhere.

But it's not like I care. It's not like *I* was even interested. I'm barely emotionally stable enough for a relationship with my imaginary dead best friend. What would *I* do with a real, live boyfriend?

"Oh no," Siri laments dreadfully.

"What?" I turn my attention back to her. She's still watching Xander.

"He's talking to Mylee. That's not good. She just got dumped. And whenever she's emotionally vulnerable, she's trouble."

I feel panic rising up in my throat. I want to ask what kind of trouble she's talking about. Trouble as in she's a serial killer who murders cute boys in Muppet shirts? Or trouble as in she—

"Right now she'll probably sleep with anything that walks."

A thousand-pound stone rolls onto my chest.

"How old is she?" I ask, cringing at the obvious strain in my voice.

"Twenty. But she has a thing for younger guys."

My grip on the cup tightens. This is ridiculous. Why should I care whom Xander hooks up with? It's none of my business. The only thing that should matter to me is getting through this night, surviving 10:05 a.m., and getting home.

That's it.

"You should really do something about that," Siri tells me.

"Do something about what?" I play dumb, sipping the dregs of my soda.

Siri pulls the mask from her face and drops it onto the table. "That!" she says way too loudly, pointing to Xander and Mylee.

"Shhh!" I hiss, grabbing her arm and pulling it back down. Although I'm not sure why I'm worried about her volume. You can't hear anything in this room.

"But you're going to lose him!"

"I never had him!" This comes out way more forcefully than I intended.

"That's not what I saw," Siri insists.

I want so desperately to ask her what she *did* see, but it doesn't matter. It's too late. I can't be here anymore. I've reached my party threshold.

"I need to go." I pick up my backpack from the corner where I dropped it earlier and dart for the door, smacking right into someone walking in.

When I finally overcome the dizziness of the collision, I'm able to focus on her face. That's when all the air gets sucked right out of the room.

It's the redheaded flight attendant. She's changed into different clothes—dark jeans and a low-cut top—and she's let down her hair. It tumbles around her shoulders in long, fiery waves.

She looks more like Lottie than ever.

And following right behind her is the married man.

The Great Popsicle Polarization

It didn't take long for Lottie to figure out that I was lying about what happened at Poker Guy's party. I'm a terrible liar, and after she grilled me in the car on the way home, I eventually caved and told her I had made the whole thing up in order to get her out of there.

She was pissed. She accused me of using her trust to get what I wanted. She accused me of taking advantage of our friendship. She accused me of trying to be her mother.

And I suppose I was guilty of all of that.

But I didn't feel bad. I knew I had done the right thing.

Because what if I *hadn't* stopped it? She probably would have had sex with him. And what if she had gotten pregnant? And what if he decided he wanted nothing to do with the baby? And what if she decided to raise it all on her own because Lottie got it into her head that she could reinvent herself as a teen mom?

Regardless of the catastrophe I prevented, Lottie refused to talk to me for a week. She ignored me at school and wouldn't answer any of my texts or calls. She initiated a full-on Ryn Embargo.

Until one night, seemingly out of the blue, the embargo was lifted.

It was after midnight. I was already in bed, pajamas on, teeth brushed, reading a book for English class when my phone vibrated.

I knew it was Lottie before I even looked at the screen. She was the only one who texted me this late. She was pretty much the only one who texted me, period.

Lottie: Ryn Ryn . . . u awake?

Suddenly, I understood. The nickname gave it away. Lottie was drunk. But whether or not she was good drunk or bad drunk, I had yet to determine. Good drunk meant she wanted to sob on my shoulder and apologize for everything and make us both promise we'd never fight again. Bad drunk meant she wanted to ream me even more for my blatant assault on our friendship.

I debated even responding. I debated giving her time to sober up before having this conversation (whichever version it was.) But then I considered the fallout of that plan. What if this was my only chance to talk to her? What if tomorrow she refused to acknowledge me again?

I texted back.

Ryn: Yes. What's up?

I saw the little bubble appear, indicating she was formulating a response. She seemed to be writing forever, which meant that she was either typing a novel length diatribe or she was having trouble finding the right letters in her inebriated state. The brevity of her response answered my question.

Lottie: Can you please come over? I need you.

Definitely good drunk.

But I still debated whether or not I should go. For a moment, I felt a flash of annoyance. She ignored me for a whole week and then suddenly she *needed* me?

What if I just didn't go? What if I texted back and told her I was tired? What if I just didn't text back?

What would Lottie do if she got a taste of her own medicine?

But then a bigger, scarier question plowed into my mind: What would happen if Lottie *really* did need me and I didn't show up?

I pushed the covers off and stood up. All I was wearing was an oversize sleep shirt. I covered it up with a pair of ratty sweatpants and a hoodie and slipped on my old Converse. I had to tiptoe to the front door to avoid waking my mother and having to answer questions. I didn't think that "Drunk Lottie needs me" would pass for an acceptable explanation.

Despite being only three blocks away, Lottie's neighborhood was decidedly more posh than mine. The houses all had security gates and privacy walls, as if the residents were doing illicit things behind their ornate, hand carved front doors. I knew the code to Lottie's gate and let myself in. As soon as I made it up the driveway, I saw the light was on in the tree house. I crept into the backyard and climbed up the rickety ladder.

I'm not sure anything could have prepared me for the chaotic state that awaited me inside. I froze in the child-size doorway.

Lottie lay on a sleeping bag in the center of the tree house, a shapeless heap of limbs and fabric. Spread out around her, like discarded thoughts, were numerous tiny liquor bottles. Every variety of alcohol was represented. Vodka, rum, whiskey, gin, bourbon. She had drunk them all. The whole stash.

I clambered through the hole and rushed to her side. I thought she was dead. She looked dead. But as soon as I called out her name, she stirred.

"Ryn Ryn?"

"Lottie!" I exclaimed, my body singing in relief. "What happened? What did you do?"

"It's his fault. He did this." Her words were slurred and malformed.

I knew immediately who she was talking about. Poker Guy. She had seen him again. She had gone back over there. Maybe she had even finished what she started.

I knelt beside her and she curled into me, burying her head in my knees and sobbing quietly.

"What happened?" I asked again.

"I saw them together. He's a cheating asshole. He ruined everything!"

"Shh," I cooed. "It's going to be all right." Even as I said the words, anger simmered inside me. I wanted to kill him. I wanted to shove dirty poker chips down his throat until he choked. I knew he was bad news.

I tried to run fingers through her hair but it was tangled and knotted. So I just resorted to petting her head like a dog. She cried harder.

"I knew it all along," she whimpered. "I tried to ignore the signs. I tried to give him the benefit of the doubt. But I was stupid. We both were. So stupid, Ryn!"

"No," I told her. "You're not stupid."

Lottie shivered. It was then I felt the debilitating December chill. And Lottie was dressed in a skimpy peach-colored dress that barely covered anything. I crawled over to the chest in the corner, lifted the lid, and pulled out the thick red-checkered blanket she kept inside. I draped it over her, tucking the corners under her knees and elbows.

"I hate him, Ryn. I hate him so much! I hate him!"

"I hate him too."

She didn't seem to be absorbing anything I was saying. "It was her. It was her all along! She gave him these. I stole them, but she stole him first."

She was talking nonsense now. The alcohol was inhibiting her words. So I just murmured, "I know. It's okay."

"No, Ryn Ryn. You don't know. Not the whole story. Because I never told you. I should have told you. But I never did. I'm sorry. Please forgive me, Ryn Ryn. You have to forgive me."

I bent forward and kissed her wet cheek. "I forgive you, Lottie. I forgive you."

We sat in silence for a long time, Lottie crying into my knee-caps, me stroking her matted hair.

The last thing she said to me before neither of us spoke of this moment ever again was, "Men are stupid. They're selfish, stupid assholes. Don't ever fall in love, Ryn Ryn. It never ends well. Ever."

I knew she wouldn't remember those words tomorrow. I knew it wouldn't be long until she moved on to the next obsession. The next crush. The next Lottie.

She loved giving out advice, but she wasn't exactly one to practice what she preached.

Nonetheless, she never mentioned Poker Guy after that night.

Then again, she was dead two weeks later.

∞

I'm on a carousel and it's spinning too fast. Spinning out of con-trol. Everyone in the room whizzes by me like blurred drawings. Still lifes in motion. Xander laughs at something Mylee says. Siri pours herself another drink. The redheaded flight attendant dances with the man in the suit.

Tiny bottles scattered everywhere. Tiny bottles filling the room. Tiny bottles spread out around Lottie.

"I hate him, Ryn. I hate him so much! I hate him!"

That night in her tree house. It wasn't about Poker Guy at all. It was about her dad. It was about the flight attendant.

"A flight attendant's life is so glamorous! Think of all the exotic places you get to go. And the people you meet. You could have a boy in every port!"

I glare at the dancing flight attendant.

But suddenly, I don't see a stranger. I see only Lottie.

Lottie all grown up.

Lottie how she'll never be.

Lottie living out her last big dream.

The dream that magically manifested two days after the night I found her nearly passed out drunk in her tree house.

Lottie! I scream inside my head. *Talk to me! Please! Tell me what happened that night. Tell me what you saw! Don't leave me like this! Don't leave me without any of the answers!*

No answer.

Wanna hear something crazy? I try again. But not even her signature catchphrase will bring Dead Lottie back to life.

She's given up on me. She's left me alone again. Even though she's nothing more than a construct in my head now. I can't even get Imaginary Lottie to talk to me. That's how pathetic I am.

The music thumps in my ears. It's so loud. So loud. When is someone going to call the cops and shut this stupid party down? The airport police will arrest me for riding round and round on a train, but they won't bust a raging party that so obviously violates fire code?

I focus on the flight attendant who is also Lottie who is also a stranger.

She turns her back to the man in the suit and begins grinding her ass up and down on his crotch. His large hand clamps around her stomach, pulling her closer to him, and all I can see is that bright gold wedding band. It's like there's a spotlight pointed directly on it.

She does a provocative forward bend, flipping her dark red hair on the way back up. Her wild locks fall messily over her face, shrouding her features, distorting her eyes, until she's no longer a stranger.

Until she's all Lottie.

Then something inside me snaps. Irrational Ryn breaks free from her poorly constructed cage with the shoddy broken lock.

How long have you known? I scream into the void in my mind. *Why didn't you tell me that you knew? I could have been there for you! I could have helped you! Is this why you wanted to be a flight attendant? Is this your sick, perverted way of trying to rise above what your father did? Stop lying to me, Lottie! Stop using me in your stupid games! Stop reinventing yourself! Just . . .*

"Stop!" I don't even realize I'm speaking until I'm screaming. I don't even realize I'm collapsing until my hands are covering my ears and my knees are weakening. "Stop! Stop! Stop!"

The music stops, but it's far from quiet. There's a roar in my ears that sounds like I'm trapped outside in the storm. Everyone is staring. Everyone is whispering. The room is spinning again.

I want to hide myself. I want to vanish. I want to evaporate. I want to dissolve into smoke. I want to be anywhere else but here.

I feel an arm wrap around my waist, lifting me up. I don't care whose it is, I'm just grateful to not have to stand on my own anymore. I melt into it. It holds me tighter and keeps me upright.

Then it's leading me away. Out of this room. Into the hallway. Where all is calm and all is bright. I look over at the person half carrying me, half dragging me.

It's Xander.

There are question marks where his eyes should be. There are lines on his forehead that I don't remember seeing before.

We stagger over to the elevator. He jabs at the buttons and jostles me inside. We ride down, down, down. The doors yawn open and we're in the lobby. It's quiet and white and empty.

Xander helps me into one of the chairs and collapses across from me. It's only now I can hear my own breathing. It sounds like I'm wearing Siri's stolen snorkel mask. I try to steady the ragged rise and fall of my chest.

Xander watches me like a wildlife researcher watching a flock of fledgling birds, waiting to see if they'll fly or plummet to their death.

Because apparently those are the only two options in this world.

"Well," he says, finally shattering the silence as he wipes a bead of sweat from his forehead. "That was fun."

∞

Lottie and I met on a sticky summer day in late August. We were eight years old. Her family had just moved to the neighborhood and she went trolling for friends on her bike. I would soon learn this was a very Lottie thing to do: proactively comb the streets for would-be accomplices.

As luck would have it, I was outside, drawing on the sidewalk with chalk.

I always wonder how my life would have turned out if I had chosen to play inside that day. If my mother had run out of chalk.

If it had been raining. If Lottie had turned right out of her driveway instead of left.

Would she have met someone else?

Would she have forced some other shy, introverted girl out of her hermit shell?

And what would have become of me?

I never would have been sucked into her web of intrigue. I never would have seen the kind of things I've seen. Met the kind of people I've met. Played poker with strangers. Spent countless nights in a tree house. Changed my name to Ryn. Almost robbed a drugstore. Become best friends with a girl who would forever alter me.

I probably would have known Lottie the way everyone knew Lottie. As the fierce gust of wind that blew through the hallways at school. As the daughter of rich, absentee parents who didn't care that she threw wild parties (that I probably never would have attended). As the girl with a hundred faces and even more pairs of jeans.

I would have heard about her death from someone at school, and I would have felt a stirring of sadness for the collapse of such a brilliant star. A sun.

But it wouldn't have been *my* sun.

It wouldn't have been *my* light that extinguished forever.

It would have been the star of some far-off, distant solar system. The kind you read about in books. A red giant that ancient people told legends about. A pinprick of light in the sky that had twinkled its last twinkle. There one minute and gone the next.

Noticed, but not missed.

Observed, but not mourned.

I never would have felt the crushing gravity of her absence.

I never would have ended up in therapy.

And I never would have really lived.

But that afternoon in August, the stars were aligned. I went out to draw on the sidewalk. My mother had plenty of chalk. The sun was shining.

And Lottie turned left.

She stopped when she saw me, hopping off her bike and walking it over to where I sat hunched over my latest creation: a purple unicorn.

She asked me if I always drew unicorns, and I told her no, sometimes I drew rainbows *and* unicorns.

She asked if I'd ever seen a unicorn, and I told her I hadn't.

"I have," she swore, crossing her heart.

And that was the beginning of our friendship.

An hour later we sat on my front porch, licking orange sherbet Push-Ups that my mom had brought us. I was always very methodical and meticulous about the way I ate my Push-Up. Applying just the slightest bit of pressure to the stick until a thin layer of sherbet surfaced above the cardboard rim.

Lick.

Push.

Repeat.

But Lottie? She was a rebel. She took her Push-Up and immediately shoved the plastic stick as far up as it would go, until she had a tall orange tower of sherbet balancing precariously on top of the little cardboard cylinder. Then she raced to consume it before the ice cream melted everywhere.

She didn't succeed.

It got on her hands, her face, her fingertips. Some even dripped down onto her knees, which she bent over to lick up.

I was horrified by her process. Or lack thereof. I couldn't understand why she didn't just ease the sherbet out a little at a time, like I did. Why she would risk such a mess and so much loss for no apparent reason.

It was at that moment, in my eight years of life, that I realized there are two kinds of people in this world: those who eat their Push-Up Popsicles a little at a time. And those who try to devour them whole.

Or in other words: There was me and there was Lottie.

And despite how appalled I was at the messiness that resulted from Lottie's method, I would soon come to realize that there's a place for each of our kind.

That the world needs both.

∞

"Sorry," is the first thing out of my mouth. I seem to be doing a lot of apologizing lately. "I guess I'm not much of a party person."

This makes Xander laugh. "I'll say."

I'm almost positive he's going to ask me about what just happened back there. And I'm almost positive I don't even know myself. But instead, he says, "That's okay. We don't have to go to a party to have a rocking New Year's Eve."

"What did you have in mind?" I ask, trying to keep my voice light, despite the heaviness in my heart. "More train surfing?"

"Nah," Xander says. He reaches into his pocket and pulls out a deck of cards, tapping them twice on the coffee table between us. "I was thinking something more like go fish."

My smile is weak but visible. "Where did you get those?"

He studies the deck in his hand. "It's so weird. They were taped to the wall in the hotel room. Like some sort of modern art installation."

I nod, knowingly. "Lost and Found."

Xander gives me a strange look.

"Siri and Jimmy decorated the party using items they 'borrowed' from the Lost and Found."

Xander contemplates this for a moment before saying, "Ahh, that explains the dentures in the bathroom." He removes the cards from the deck and shuffles them once. "So, go fish?"

"No thanks."

"Oh, come on!" he pleads. "I'm really bad at it. You'll definitely win."

"How can you be bad at go fish?"

He shrugs. "I don't know. I ask for all the wrong cards. I have terrible intuition. How about crazy eights?"

I shake my head. "Definitely not."

"Old maid."

I grab the cards from him, give them a quick shuffle, and start to deal. "Poker. Five card draw. Nothing's wild."

Xander looks taken aback for a moment as he watches me deal. "Whoa. You just got like way hotter."

My cheeks turn to red-hot coals.

He thinks I'm hot?

Xander picks up his cards. "So, what are we betting?"

Oh. I feel disappointed as I glance around the empty lobby. There's not even a salt shaker or sugar packet in sight. I start to gather up the cards. "Never mind. It was a stupid idea."

Xander holds his hand protectively to his chest. "Nuh-uh. I'm not giving these up. These are good cards."

"But we have nothing to bet."

"That's not true," he says, cocking an eyebrow. "We have information."

I give him a skeptical look. "What? You mean like state secrets or the true identities of covert operatives?"

He chuckles. "No, I mean like what's up here." He leans across the table and taps my forehead gently with his five cards. He's so much closer than he was a second ago. Than he was an hour ago. Than he's been all night. His gaze latches on to mine, and for a moment my breathing gets all wonky again.

Suddenly, his eyes don't feel like eyes. They feel like microscopes. Nosy, snooping probes searching for things that I don't show. That I've buried deep. For too long.

"I don't follow," I say, casting my eyes to the table and scooping up my cards.

"For every hand I win," he explains. "I get to ask you a question and you have to answer it. Truthfully."

My windpipe starts to close. This is it. He's finally demanding an explanation. For everything. For all the secrets I've never admitted to anyone, including Dr. Judy. *Especially* Dr. Judy.

I swallow, but only dry air chafes my throat. "So that means for every hand *I* win, I get to ask you a question and *you* have to answer?"

He nods. "That's right."

I contemplate all the things I've witnessed today and every question I've asked myself about Xander since we met. How badly do I really want to know?

Is it worth the risk?

If there's one thing I learned from watching Lottie play poker with her life, it's that in order to win, you have to be willing to lose.

And oh, how she did both.

"Okay," I agree before I can second-guess myself. But my whole body turns numb as soon as the word is out of my mouth. As soon as my eyes drop to the five playing cards gripped between my fingers.

I admit, I probably should have looked at them before agreeing to this craziness. This might be the worst starting poker hand in history.

But maybe that's exactly what I need.

Maybe the universe is trying to tell me something.

Maybe it's time I start *answering* questions for a change.

Wagering the Truth

In my hand I hold the two and four of clubs, the seven of spades, the jack of diamonds, and the ace of hearts. My best bet is to keep the ace and try for high pair. I toss the other cards down and announce that I'll be drawing four. Xander draws two. That's not a good sign.

I deal to him, then me, arranging the new cards in my hand.

I still have nothing.

Xander puts down three sixes.

I cringe.

Why didn't I just agree to play go fish? Why did I have to suggest poker?

I show him my garbage hand and he rubs his palms together like a villain in a Bond movie.

"Aha. First question is mine. Okay, I'll go easy on you."

My muscles relax a bit.

"Who is Lottie?"

I nearly choke on my own premature relief. "That's an easy one?"

He looks surprised. "Is that not an easy one?"

"No!"

He twists his mouth thoughtfully. "Okay, fine. I'll try something else. Where are you flying from?"

I exhale loudly. "Atlanta."

"Why?"

"Nuh-uh." I shake my head. "That was a new question. You have to win another hand."

He smirks. "Clever girl."

He deals the next hand. I get stuck with trash again. I try for a straight but fail miserably. Xander lays down a pair of nines. "Why were you in Atlanta?"

I suck in a sharp breath. "My dad lives there."

"So your parents are divorced?"

I press my lips together and raise my eyebrows.

"C'mon!" he whines. "Your answers have to be longer than one sentence."

I cross my arms over my chest. "I don't remember that being part of the rules."

"Well, it is now."

"You can't just change the rules."

He stops to think about that for a second, then gathers up the cards and stuffs them back into the box. "You're right. Let's just go back to the party."

I grab the deck from him and start shuffling. "Fine. Whatever. Yes, my parents are divorced. It happened when I was twelve."

Xander opens his mouth to ask a question. I cut him off. "And

I don't know if it was messy because I wasn't there. They shipped me off to my grandparents' house for the summer. When I got back, my dad had moved out and it was done." I glare at him. "Happy, Dr. Hale?"

This title seems to make him anything but happy. I can almost *see* the way it shuts him down. I really need to win a hand.

I deal the cards. This time, I'm confident I'll win. I have a pair of aces. I keep them and draw three, hoping to secure my victory with a third ace, but no such luck. Xander lays down two pair—jacks and sixes.

My mouth drops when I see them. "What the hell? Is this a trick deck?"

"You shuffled," he points out.

"Did you count the cards to make sure they're all there?"

"Okay, sore loser," he says, his mood seeming to lighten a bit. "Next question. Have you always lived in San Francisco?"

I stare down at my loser aces. "No. We used to live in Portland. We moved ten months ago."

"Why did you—" Xander starts to say, but this time he stops himself. He grabs the deck and shuffles.

I know what question comes next. And I know I'm not ready to answer it.

But I suppose that's not up to me. That's up to the universe. The universe that's never liked me. That's been dealing me shitty hands for the past year. Maybe even the past *eighteen* years.

I pick up my five cards and my throat starts to tighten.

This hand makes my first hand look like solid gold.

Xander draws one card—which means he's either going for a straight, a flush, or a full house—none of which are good news for me. I scrap all five cards and try again.

When he deals me a new hand, I don't even bother to look. Looking won't change them. It'll only draw out the agony longer.

Xander lays down another two pair. I hold my breath and flip my cards.

In my epic, second chance do-over, the universe has dealt me a seven, a four, a nine, a jack, and a king. All hearts.

Xander lets out a low whistle. "Yikes. I guess that means I'm up."

∞

The funeral was one week after the accident. They were going to take my beautiful, bubbly, vivacious friend and bury her in the dirt. It was the most unfitting ending for Lottie that I could ever imagine.

I refused to go.

For three days my mom brought me dress after dress, presumably thinking that my decision to attend was only a matter of finding the right *clothes*. That was so like my mom. Making the whole conversation about a dress. Rather than what it really was.

I hadn't left the house since the accident.

I'd barely left my bedroom.

The shock had worn off and all that was left was the numbness.

To be honest, I missed the shock. It felt like something. It had shape and meaning and definition. The numbness was a vast, infinite void with no entrance and no exit that you could feasibly float around in forever.

The service was scheduled to begin at eleven in the morning. My mom came in at ten fifteen, dressed in a wool, gray pencil dress and matching coat. She had one more contender in her arms. A last-ditch effort to convince me to bear witness to the most horrific sight imaginable: my best friend being lowered into the cold, unforgiving ground.

She held up the dress. This one was navy with a wrap tie.

"How cute is this?" my mom asked.

I rolled over and blinked at her in disbelief. My best friend was dead, and she thought I gave a shit about looking cute?

"Everyone is going to wonder where you are," she prodded.

I shrugged. "So let them."

"Funerals are for the living. For saying good-bye."

"Good for them."

I watched my mom struggle. I watched all the things she wanted to say but couldn't flash across her face.

I needed her to say something real. Something not taken straight out of a textbook for grief. But she couldn't do that. So she stuck to what she knew.

"Lottie would have wanted you there."

I rolled back over and faced the wall. I'd had a lot of time to contemplate that wall, and I wasn't finished.

The truth was, she had no idea what Lottie would have wanted.

None of us did.

Lottie was an enigma. That's what made her Lottie. In fact, if I had to bet, I would say Lottie would have wanted us all to skip the funeral, because funerals are sad and depressing and boring and good lord, why are you putting me in the goddamn ground? I want to fly!

My mom left without another word, and I curled my body around my phone, incessantly turning the screen on and off to check the time. After Googling about funerals the night before, I'd determined that services usually last about one hour before the coffin is lowered into the large, gaping chasm.

I counted the minutes that Lottie was still on this earth, and not buried six feet under it.

When I couldn't bear to count anymore, I stood up and rummaged around in my bottom dresser drawer until I found the birthday gift Lottie had given me only three months earlier.

I slipped the *Doctor Who* case over my phone and turned it round and round in my hand, examining the blue Tardis from all sides. It was a hideous thing. Why would anyone *choose* a bulky blue police box as their phone cover?

But it was the one thing I knew for sure that Lottie would have wanted.

I turned on the phone again and scrolled absently through the pages and pages of apps. How did my phone get to be such a mess? How long had I been haphazardly installing apps without bothering to care where they were? How did I ever find anything in here before?

All of a sudden, I didn't know how I could live like this. I didn't know how I would survive this chaos.

I spent the next thirty minutes Googling phone organization tips, deleting unused apps, and sorting everything else into appropriately named folders. I organized and reorganized and sorted and resorted until everything had a place and a purpose. Productivity, health, social, media, travel, entertainment.

When I was done, my phone was clean, but my life still felt like a mess.

And Lottie was buried in the ground.

I opened the text message app, which I'd placed front and center on the home screen, so it was the first thing I saw when I turned on my phone.

Lottie's last text to me shone bright and vibrant against the white backdrop of the screen.

One unread message.

It had been a week since it arrived. A week since she pushed Send, turned the key in the ignition, and drove right to her death.

10:05 a.m.

10:05 a.m.

10:05 a.m.

My fingers trembled over the screen. Of course, I wanted to read the message. But then I thought of Lottie in the coffin and the coffin in the ground and the dirt filling the hole, filling her mouth until she could no longer speak. Until she could no longer say anything to me ever again.

My trembling hand fell to my side.

I wouldn't read it. I couldn't read it. Because all I could think was:

This is the last thing Lottie will ever say to me. As long as that's alive, she's alive.

And then, right there, sitting alone in my bedroom, while the community of Portland, Oregon, tossed ceremonial dirt on my best friend's grave, Dead Lottie spoke to me for the very first time.

And she said, "That's the craziest thing I've ever heard, Ryn."

∞

I take my time selecting my first question. It needs to be a good one. Because who knows how long it will take for the universe to deal me winning cards again? But the pressure of picking the best question is too much, so I just go with the first one I can think of.

"Who was on the phone before? When I found you in the concourse?"

I watch Xander's body wilt as though this is the subject he was dreading most. That either means I picked the worst possible question or the best one.

"Right," he says, emboldening himself. "Okay." He takes a breath. "That was my parents' publicist."

The answer takes me by surprise. And also relieves me. I just assumed the worst. That he was talking to a girlfriend.

Why would that be the worst?

The question pops into my head immediately, and I immediately dismiss it. It's not my turn to answer the questions anymore. It's my turn to ask them.

It appears Xander is going to stop there, so I give him the same look he gave me. "No one-sentence answers. New rule."

He chuckles. "Karma's a bitch, huh?"

I just smile.

He hesitates, selecting his words carefully. "Something happened. Something that is going to deeply impact the sales of my parents' new book, which just released this week. The one you were holding in the bookstore."

I think about the news article I saw on Troy's phone earlier. "Is this about your expulsion?" I ask.

The shock on his face lasts only a moment before fading away. I wonder if he's used to people knowing more about him than he knows about them. I imagine, with parents like that—who fill their books with every nuance of your childhood—you kind of have to get used to it. "Nuh-uh," he scolds. "That's another question."

I grab for the cards, shuffle hastily, and deal them out.

Just my luck, I get another dud. I swap out three cards, trying for a high pair, but somehow I manage only to make my hand worse.

With a sigh, Xander lays down his cards and says, "Yes, it was about the expulsion."

Confused, I study his hand. It's even worse than mine. He must have assumed as much.

"Claire—the publicist—thinks that it's my fault the press knows about it. She thinks I told someone at school and they sold the story."

"And did you?" I ask.

The silence that follows stretches on for just a beat too long, and Xander won't meet my eyes. "No," he finally says, averting my gaze and fidgeting with the three of spades in front of him. "I didn't tell anyone at school. I mean, it would be good money for anyone who tried to sell the story. The son of the people who literally wrote the book on parenting expelled from school? That's worth a pretty penny, I suppose."

Seemingly anxious to move on, he scoops up all the cards, shuffles, and deals. Xander wins with an ace high, and I brace myself for the inevitable. I remember exactly where his line of questioning left off. He was about to ask me why we moved from Portland. And I will have to tell him the truth. I will have to talk about Lottie.

Of course, I could lie. I could tell him we moved for my mom's work or some other bullshit explanation like that. But that's not how the game works. And something tells me Xander hasn't lied to me once. When he definitely could have.

I guess that's the big difference between real poker and our unique variety.

In this version, you have to have faith in your opponent.

"Why are you always looking at your phone?"

The question takes me by surprise. I'd been steeling myself to talk about the move, already cherry-picking which details to include and exclude. But he didn't ask that. Either because he already forgot about it or decided he had more pressing inquiries on his mind.

My hand instinctively moves to my pocket before I remember with irritation that Siri still has my phone. I really need to figure out a way to get that back. But I have a suspicion that after my little meltdown at the party, it's going to be difficult to convince her that I know how to cut loose.

Xander must interpret my delay as hesitation, because he awkwardly rubs his neck and says, "You don't have to say it. I think I can guess."

Huh?

He can guess that I ask Google questions all day in a vain attempt to keep the one unanswerable question at bay?

I swallow hard. "You can?"

He nods, looking remorseful. "You have a boyfriend, right? He's worried about you stuck here at the airport."

It takes me an unusually long time to digest the words that just came out of his mouth. They're so foreign and *so* off base, I have a hard time even making sense of them.

Once again Xander misinterprets my silence. He sighs. "Yeah. I thought so. I figured it out a while ago. I just kept thinking, or . . . I don't know . . . *hoping* that I was wrong."

What?

I'm assaulted by a barrage of confusing thoughts and emotions. They're overwhelming me, kicking my anxiety up a notch. I'm still trying to process the last inane thing he said. Now he's saying he was *hoping* I didn't have a boyfriend?

Why would he want that? I'm insane. He's seen it for himself. I'm not the datable one. Lottie was the datable one. Lottie was the hot one. If Lottie were alive now, *she'd* be the one he'd be hoping didn't have a boyfriend. I'm just the default choice. Because I'm the only one left.

Xander keeps talking. "I mean, why wouldn't you? You're pretty and funny and cool to hang out with. Even if you do kind of overreact from time to time." He stops talking rather abruptly and then lets out a stutter of a laugh.

Is he nervous?

My mind is still whirling, still trying to keep up.

This is exactly the kind of thing Lottie would know about. She spoke boy fluently. I can barely even read the alphabet.

"Okay, you can say something anytime now," he prompts. "I mean, *please* say something. You're kind of freaking me out. And when I freak out, I have a tendency to ramble."

"Sorry," I say automatically. Because it's the first thing that tumbles out. And, unfortunately, the second thing that tumbles out is, "You think I'm pretty?"

I swear I see splotches of pink bloom on Xander's dark cheeks, but it's impossible to be sure, because he bows his head and starts shuffling the cards. "Yeah. I mean, sure. I mean, obviously anyone would think . . ." He interrupts himself with a throat clear and stops shuffling in the middle of the bridge. The cards fall into a messy, uneven heap. "It's not my deal."

He shoves the jumbled pile at me.

Speechless and more than just a little bewildered, I transfer all my energy into doing the best shuffling job in the history of card shuffling. I split, riffle, bridge, split, riffle, bridge, split, riffle, bridge. Over and over and over until even the universe can't keep track of what card went where.

I can sense Xander watching me the entire time. No, not just watching. Studying. Observing.

I tap the deck twice on the table and deal. It isn't until I pass Xander his fifth card that I realize I never actually answered his last question. He made an assumption about the answer and I didn't correct him.

Is that being dishonest?

Is that breaking the rules of the game?

I never actually *said* I had a boyfriend, so I didn't *technically* lie. But I also didn't pay him his winnings with a truthful answer.

He picks up his five cards and organizes them in his hand. I think about stopping the game right now and admitting my wrongdoing. But if I did, then I would have to tell him the truth. I'd have to tell him that the real reason I look at my phone five thousand times a day is because I'm crazy. So crazy even my therapist doesn't know the extent of my craziness. What would he think of me then?

Would he still think I'm pretty?

Most definitely not. Certifiable trumps pretty every time.

I decide it's much better to just let him go on thinking that I have a boyfriend back home. That he texts me every hour to make sure I'm okay. That I'm in a happy, *healthy*, fulfilling relationship.

It's cleaner that way.

No mixed signals. No eyes locking across the table. No flirtatious smiles.

Nothing can ever happen between us. And it's much easier if we *both* agree on that.

I pick up my cards and nearly let out a gasp when I see that I've dealt myself four shiny aces. One of the best hands a player can get.

I peer up at Xander to make sure he didn't notice my terrible poker face, but his eyes are cast downward at his cards. He looks kind of adorable. With his brow all furrowed in concentration and his perfect white teeth raking over his bottom lip.

He thinks I'm pretty.

And funny.

Despite my attempts to hold it back, a small smile starts to chisel its way across my face. I hide the expression behind my cards. As I focus on my four beautiful aces, a thought comes barreling into my mind that's so terrifying and so unexpected, I don't even know what to do with it.

I think my luck is changing.

A Phone Call from Lord Voldemort

I throw my cards down atop Xander's pathetic two pair. Xander's eyes widen at the sight of them. It's not every day you see a four of a kind. And with aces, no less.

"Whoa," he says, impressed. "I think that warrants *two* questions."

"Two?" I repeat excitedly, but then I think about the repercussions of agreeing to such a thing. If I ask two questions now, what happens if Xander gets four of a kind in the future? Or an even better hand? "That's okay. I'll just take the one."

"Are you sure?"

I nod. "Unlike *some* people, I don't change the rules on a whim."

He crosses his arms in mock offense. "Okay. Fine, Miss Morality. Let's hear your question."

"Why did you get expelled from school?"

His arms fall to his sides and he sits up straighter. Like someone's just jabbed a rod into his spine. He pulls all the cards across the table and begins aligning them into a perfect stack. "Are you sure you want to waste your big four-aces question on *that?*" I can tell he's trying to make his voice sound breezy, but I hear right through it.

"What's wrong with my question?" I challenge.

He shrugs, refusing to meet my eye. "Nothing. It's just, I'm afraid you'll be disappointed by the answer and feel like you wasted such a big win on something so terribly unexciting."

"Why don't you let *me* be the judge of that?"

He clears his throat. "I got expelled because I didn't read the assigned book for English class."

"What? You got expelled for not reading a book? What kind of school is this? Nazi prep academy?"

"That's another question."

"That was a one sentence answer."

He laughs. "Touché." He cuts the deck and looks at the card in the middle. "The book was just the beginning." Then he shuffles and looks at another card. On and on this goes until I'm afraid he's never going to elaborate. When he finally cuts the deck on an ace, he says, "I guess it officially started when Samantha broke up with me. She was my girlfriend. We'd been dating since middle school. We were . . ." He shakes his head and gazes into the empty lobby. "I don't know, we thought we were in love. But what did we know? We were thirteen when we first got together."

I let out a huff of agreement, as if I've been there. As if I actually *had* a relationship in middle school and can relate to the juvenility of it all.

As if I've actually had a relationship . . . ever.

"Anyway," he goes on, his fingers still deftly cutting and restacking the deck. "She cheated on me a few months ago, and I lost it. I just"—he pauses, looking visibly pained to continue—"lost my shit, you know?"

I nod. As if, once again, I can relate.

Although to losing one's shit, I suppose I can.

"I stopped caring about anything. I stopped doing my homework. Stopped studying for tests. Eventually, I stopped showing up to school altogether." When he says this last part, I could be mistaken, but he almost looks *pleased* with himself.

"And your parents let you just ditch school all the time?"

"My parents didn't give a crap because they were never around to give a crap."

"But your parents are—"

"Dr. Max and Dr. Marcia," he says with a dramatic eye roll. "I know. The inventors of the *Kids Come First* method. Well, guess which kid has *never* come first?"

He tilts back on his chair and balances precariously on two legs. In that moment, with his far-off expression and the bitterness weighing down the corners of his mouth, he looks like a little boy.

"I could set the house on fire and they would never know. At least, not until their publicist saw it on Twitter." He lets his chair fall back to the ground with a loud *clack* and deals the cards without another word.

A minute later I lay down a pair of sevens that just edges out his pair of sixes.

"What was the book?" I ask quietly. I almost didn't want to win. This line of questioning has turned him into someone else. Not the Xander I surfed with on the train. And definitely not the Reginald Schwarzenegger I ate burgers with.

Xander looks visibly relieved at my choice of question. He must have thought I was going to delve much deeper. "*A Tale of Two Cities.*"

"You didn't read that?" I blurt without thinking. "But it's so good!"

He squints at me like suddenly I'm out of focus. "Are you on crack? The thing is like five hundred pages of Hemingway droning on and on."

"It's Dickens, actually and I thought you said you didn't read it."

"I started it," he defends.

"Oh, but you *have* to read it. It's such a classic."

"You sound like my English teacher."

That shuts me up.

"My teacher said he might be able to talk the administration out of my expulsion if I just read it and wrote the stupid paper. It's what started my whole downward spiral, so I suppose he thought the book could save me or some symbolic crap like that."

"Hold up," I say. "You mean, you have an *out*—you can make all your problems go away—and you haven't taken it?"

If there was anything in the world that would bring Lottie back, I would do it. I would be lined up, camped out, signed on the dotted line, banging on the doors to let me do it. The idea that Xander has the opportunity to make this all go away and he's choosing *not* to take it suddenly starts my blood boiling.

What does he know about problems? What does know about loss? His loss is reversible. His problems are fixable.

"You think all of my problems revolve around a book?" he fires back, and I hear the hints of irritation in his tone. "If you do, then you clearly haven't listened to a word I've just said."

I shrink down in my chair, suddenly feeling foolish and stupid. *This is why you don't talk, Ryn. This is why you shut up.*

"I don't have a boyfriend!" I blurt out. Because apparently, I just want to make matters worse.

He sets the cards on the table and squints at me. "What?"

I lower my voice. "I didn't technically lie. You made a wrong assumption and I didn't correct you."

He rubs the back of his head, seemingly trying to rewind the conversation and bring my comment back to a context in which it makes sense. "So when I asked why you always look at your phone . . . ," he begins.

"You answered for me. It just wasn't the truth."

I'm not sure how I managed to do it. But somehow his frustration gives way to curiosity. "So what *is* the truth?"

Instinctively, I reach for my phone again and have to remind myself that it's in Siri's custody.

"The truth is I'm insane."

An amused grin cracks the surface of Xander's face. "Well, I knew that."

"No," I tell him in all seriousness. "I'm really insane. Like certifiable. My therapist doesn't even know the half of it."

Therapist.

As soon as the word is out of my mouth, I wish I could take it back.

I just admitted to a cute boy who thinks I'm pretty that I have a therapist? Why don't I just tell him about my menstrual cramps next?

When I brave a glance at him, however, I see that his face is completely neutral. My confession hasn't appeared to shake him at all. Maybe growing up with psychologist parents desensitizes you to the whole therapy thing.

"We're all a little crazy, Ryn," he finally says. "But that doesn't explain why you're obsessed with your phone."

"I ask my phone questions, okay?"

He ponders that for a second. "Like knock knock jokes?"

I roll my eyes. "No. Like every question that ever pops into my head. It makes me feel better to know the answer. Or just to know that an answer exists."

There. I've said it. Aloud. The crazy is out.

Now I just have to sit back and wait for Xander to think up a polite excuse to get the hell out of here.

"Okay," he says with a shrug and starts dealing the next hand. I stare openmouthed at each card that slides across the table.

"That's it?" I ask.

"What's it?"

"That's all you have to say about the phone/question thing?"

He stops dealing after only four cards apiece. His eyebrows knit together. "Was there something else you wanted me to say?"

"I . . ." I stammer. "I don't know. I mean, don't you think that's a little nuts?"

He purses his lips in thought. "No."

"No?"

I don't know why I'm pressing him. I should be grateful that he's brainless enough to not see this for what it really is. But it's suddenly like I need validation. I need him to confirm what I've believed for an entire year. He's the son of two famous psychologists. If anyone should recognize crazy, it's him.

"Actually, I was thinking how impressed I am by you."

I nearly choke on my own spit. "Impressed?"

"Yeah. Most people I know keep their crazy bottled up inside. But not you. You put it out there. You found an outlet. A nondestructive coping mechanism. You figured out a way to deal with all the shit in your head without leaving a huge mess in your wake. Not everyone can do that."

"I . . ." I start to say but don't quite know how to finish.

I've never thought about it that way. Dr. Judy has certainly never analyzed it that way.

But what about the mess in my head?

Maybe my methods aren't as benign as he thinks.

He deals the final card, and I pick up my hand. Without another word I discard one. Xander exchanges three. I lay down a busted straight draw. Xander has a pair of twos.

I lose.

He makes a *tsk* sound with his tongue and gathers up the cards. "Okay," he says, his expression grim. "No more dicking around. It's time for the big one."

I had a feeling this was coming.

I knew I couldn't put it off forever.

I guess I was just hoping that some unexpected act of God would save me. A flood in a city that sits a mile above sea level. A terrorist attack on a closed airport. A hurricane on top of a record breaking blizzard.

"Are you ready?" Xander asks.

I nod. Even though I'm not. Forty-two therapy sessions at two hundred dollars an hour, and I'm still not ready to talk about Lottie.

Will I ever be?

Do you ever actually *feel* ready to talk about something like this?

Or is it just one of those things you eventually have to force yourself to do? Ready or not?

Maybe it's like diving. You can stand on the edge of the board, legs bent, arms above your head, counting to three over and over again, but until you actually make the effort to leap, until you actually *push* off that board, you'll stand there forever. Looking into the water. Wondering how cold it will be. Wondering how hard it will hurt if you do it wrong.

"Are you sure?" Xander asks. There's such tenderness in his voice, such compassion in his eyes as they meet mine, for a split second, I almost *do* feel sure. I can almost make myself believe that the water will be warm.

"Okay, here comes the tough one." He exhales dramatically. "What is your favorite *Doctor Who* episode?"

After a second of disbelief I burst out laughing. I just can't help it. All of that buildup, all of that tension coiled in my legs and arms and throat. I was ready to jump. I was ready to leap off that board and hit the water hard.

"This is not a laughing matter," Xander scolds. "This is a very serious question with very serious repercussions. Your answer could affect the future of our relationship."

"You're right," I say, curbing my amusement. "You're absolutely right. This is a very serious question, and I have a feeling you're not going to like my answer."

He steels himself, bracing against the armrests of his chair. "I knew it. You're going to say 'Midnight.' You're a David Tennant fan, aren't you? All girls are. It's the hair, isn't it? Damn him and his perfect hair!"

"No," I say, shaking my head somberly. "I'm afraid my answer is even worse."

Xander's eyes widen. "What could possibly be worse than admitting your favorite *Doctor Who* episode is 'Midnight'?"

I slouch down in my chair, attempting to make myself as tiny as possible. "Admitting that you actually hate *Doctor Who*."

∞

Xander shoots out of his chair like a rocket and tries to flip the table, only to discover that it's way too heavy. So he grunts, gathers up the cards, and throws them over his head. They rain down around us like giant confetti.

"What are you trying to do to me, woman?" he asks, his voice high and squeaky.

"Honesty was one of the rules, wasn't it?"

"But . . . ," he begins, words failing him. "How can . . ." He tries again. "You . . . That's . . . I . . ." He collapses into his chair, tossing his arms up in frustration. "But the phone case!"

My skin turns to ice.

Of course, that's where this question would eventually go. How could I forget? How could I not think that far ahead? All questions eventually lead back to Lottie. Nothing is safe. Because everything about my stupid, pointless life is somehow connected to her brains splattered across a clock stuck at 10:05 a.m. It's six degrees of separation to a dead girl.

"Lottie gave me the phone case," I whisper, bowing my head. It's the simplest phrase in the world and yet it connects everything. But I can't bring myself to look at him while I say it. While I say her name aloud. "It was her favorite show."

I pray that's enough. I pray that my use of the past tense will be my free pass. My wild card that can be played in place of the real thing.

Xander doesn't say anything for what feels like a lifetime. I brave a glance at him. His head is tilted at a curious angle. His eyes are dark, prying excavators, drilling for precious oil.

He's going to ask. He's going to do it.

Figure it out, Xander! I want to scream.

Your parents are world renowned psychologists, for God's sake! Figure. It. Out.

"*Was* her favorite show?"

My body slams into the water. It's not an elegant dive. My hands don't cleanly slice through the surface, clearing the way for a safe, painless entry. Everything hits at once. My face. My belly. My chest. My legs. Even the tops of my feet. It stings. It burns. It cuts. It bleeds.

It's ice-cold fire.

Who knew water could be so unforgiving?

It's liquid, for crying out loud!

How can it hurt this badly?

The tears pool up, I shove them back. I close my eyes tight. I lock them in.

Keep it together, I tell myself. *It's just a stupid game.*

"I think you have to win another hand to ask that," I say so quietly, I'm certain he couldn't possibly hear. Unless he was one of the X-Men.

But he did hear. Because the next thing he says is like colliding with that wall of freezing water all over again.

"I think maybe you should just answer it."

And beyond all reason, beyond all sense, beyond all meticulously welded armor, the voice of someone who's been shoved under for far too long rises to the surface. It's me. Or some long-ago buried version of me. A version I barely recognize anymore.

"I think maybe you're right."

∞

The call came at 10:52 a.m. It was *my* cell phone that rang. Lottie hadn't listed her mother or father or any family member as the In Case of Emergency contact in her phone. She had listed me. I hadn't even known until the case of emergency presented itself.

I was bent over the toilet, regurgitating the water I'd foolishly tried to keep down, cursing the cook at Pop's Hot Dogs for the millionth time for serving questionable meat, and vowing to become a vegetarian like Lottie.

At first I didn't hear the phone over my retching. By the time I flushed, it was on the last ring. I saw Lottie's name on the caller ID and tried to answer, but it had already gone to voice mail. I called her right back.

"Hello?" came an unfamiliar *male* voice.

My first thought was that I had dialed the wrong number. But then my puked up, malnutritioned brain caught up, and I remembered that I had dialed it straight from the call history. My second thought was that it was a boy Lottie had met at the mall.

I glanced at the clock on my nightstand. It had been less than an hour since she'd left my house after failing to convince me to come with her. There was no way she could have driven to the mall *and* parked *and* met a boy in less than an hour.

Lottie was good but she wasn't *that* good.

"Hello," I said uneasily.

"Are you the emergency contact for Charlotte Valentine?"

The blood congealed in my veins. I froze with my phone pressed against my ear. "I . . ." But I couldn't get anything out.

Was this some kind of joke?

Was Lottie playing one of her pranks on me?

Did she ask some random guy at a mall kiosk to call me and pretend something bad had happened?

"We found your name listed as the In Case of Emergency

contact in her phone," the person on the other end of the call said. It was no longer a friendly male voice. It was now Darth Vader's voice. Lex Luthor's voice. Lord Voldemort and Hannibal Lecter and Gollum. All rolled into one.

I tried for words again, but I barely even managed syllables.

"I'm afraid there's been an accident," the voice of doom continued.

"What?!" I blurted out. I didn't even have to try. The sound just flew out of my mouth.

There was a slight hesitation on the line. Lord Voldemort was stalling. Drawing out my agony like the evil bastard that he is. "I'm afraid Charlotte has been in an accident. I'm calling from St. Vincent's Hospital. Her body was brought in a few minutes ago."

The floor gave out beneath me. I started to fall. Down, down, down. Never hitting the bottom.

Her body.

Not her.

"No," I argued vehemently. "Lottie isn't at the hospital. Lottie is at the mall. She went to the mall. She's at the mall."

I kept repeating it in my mind, knowing beyond all doubt that the repetition would make it true. That it *had* to make it true.

There was no other option. There was no parallel universe in all of the multiverse where Lottie wasn't at the mall. Laughing and flirting and sparkling.

"I'm sorry," Lord Voldemort said.

But he was wrong. He was evil. He was trying to trick me. Because that's what villains do.

They lie.

And I was going to prove him wrong. I *had* to prove him wrong.

I started running. I ran, not because the mall was less than a mile from my house, and not because I didn't have access to a car, but because it was all I could do. It was all my body would allow me to do.

Run.

The man's voice was still on the line, echoing like a psychotic parrot, "Hello? Hello? Hello?" He eventually gave up and disconnected.

I kept running.

She was at the mall. He was mistaken. I would show him he was wrong.

It was cold outside. I was barefoot and dressed in flimsy pajama bottoms and a tank top. No bra. But I felt the chill only on the inside. The ice-cold liquid panic that pumped through my veins, that froze my heart and turned my body to stone.

My stomach threatened to heave the entire way, but miraculously I managed to keep the vomit at bay.

I never actually made it to the mall. I stopped when I saw the intersection that would forever haunt my dreams, awake and asleep. The intersection that would forever divide my existence into two jagged, unequal parts:

Life With Lottie/Life Without Lottie.

I was breathless and agitated and soaked in sweat. My cold, wet tank top was clinging to my body.

A fire truck and three police cars were parked in the middle of the road, their lights whirling and spinning and flashing like a disco. Someone had blocked off the two cross streets with cones. People had already started to gather around the perimeter.

In the center of it all was Lottie's black Beemer.

The car was so demolished, it was hardly recognizable. The entire left side was smashed all the way to the center console. There was no more driver's side door. Just a massive gaping hole where it used to be.

What could have possibly done this?

A giant?

A transformer?

An asteroid?

I got my answer when my gaze drifted a few feet away. The second car—a pickup truck—had spun away from the collision before coming to rest in the middle of the far lane. The hood had been crushed.

My heart pounded wildly in my chest as I searched the damage for Lottie. I ran a few steps closer, feeling a stabbing pain as something sharp—probably shattered glass—wedged into my bare foot.

The car was empty.

My hopes surged.

She got out. She's okay. Maybe she walked the rest of the way to the mall.

Then I remembered what Lord Voldemort had said, and my legs practically gave out.

"I'm calling from St. Vincent's Hospital. Her body was brought in a few minutes ago."

I stepped even closer to the vehicle, close enough that I could see the inside. Close enough that I could make out the drops of blood and shreds of flesh and fragments of brain splattered across the steering wheel and broken dashboard.

Lottie's brain. Lottie's beautiful, vibrant, full-of-life brain. In pieces.

My stomach heaved again, and this time I couldn't hold it back. I vomited air and whatever was left in my stomach.

The clock on the dashboard flashed tauntingly.

A time stamp marking the exact moment the universe decided to give up on me.

10:05 a.m.

10:05 a.m.

10:05 a.m.

And all I could think was,

I'm too late.

I'm too late.

I'm too late.

∞

When I stop talking, Xander is quiet for a long time. I haven't been able to look at him since I started. I do now. His eyes are unfocused and misty. His mouth is slightly ajar. He wets his lips, like he's going to say something, but he doesn't.

Because what do you say to that?

There's nothing.

People try. They've tried for the past year to tell me how sorry they are. To insist that they're here for me. That I can talk to them. But do any of them mean it? Do any of them *really* want to know that I stood barefoot in the street and watched my best friend's brain fragments drip off a dashboard?

Of course they don't.

That's why I've never told that story. Ever. Until right now.

Thousands of dollars in therapy bills, countless parenting books about grief, a year of tapping answerable questions into my phone, and here I am, telling the whole story for the first time to a stranger I met only eight hours ago.

I'm sure Xander is regretting his little poker game of truth right about now.

"I'm sorry," I say. "You probably didn't really want to know all that."

"What?" Xander startles like he forgot I was even there. Then, after he collects himself, he says hastily, "No! I did want to know. I'm glad you told me."

I look away. "No, you're not."

Xander reaches across the table and grabs my hand, stroking his fingers across mine. They're warm. So warm. How can fingers be that warm when they're so far from the heart?

"He was drunk, wasn't he?"

I blink and pull my hand away. "Yeah. He had a blood alcohol level of point-two-five. He ran the red and T-boned her car. Then he walked away without a scratch. That's how much justice there is in the world."

Xander casts his eyes downward to the table. I've made him uncomfortable. This is why you don't tell people things. This is why you don't share. Because they turn away from you. Because they—

"When was this?"

I swallow. "New Year's Day. Last year."

I can see the wheels turning behind his eyes. You don't need to be a prodigy like Troy to do this math. "That's . . . ," he begins to say but loses the courage to finish.

"Yes," I whisper. "At 10:05 a.m. tomorrow morning, she'll have been gone an entire year."

"And that's why you want to get home so badly?"

"I don't do well around people." I let out an empty bark of a laugh. "I guess you've seen that firsthand."

"And the text message? It was from her?"

"I can't bring myself to read it."

He nods, like he gets it. Does he get it? Or is he just nodding the way I nodded when he talked about his girlfriend cheating on him?

"My therapist thinks I'm not grieving her the right way."

Xander snorts. "Your therapist actually said that?"

I shake my head. "She implied it."

"If I learned anything from having shrink parents, it's that there's no wrong way to grieve."

I shrug. "Maybe not. But there's a better way and I'm not doing it."

Silence settles between us once again, and I start to get antsy. I don't like the way Xander is looking at me. Like I'm a lost item that needs to be claimed.

I scoot out of my seat and kneel down beneath the table to

gather the cards Xander tossed in his fit of madness.

"Ryn," I hear him say, and then suddenly he's on the floor with me. Crouched across from me. The table casts a shadow over his dark, chiseled face.

He reaches out and grabs my hand, loosens my grip, removes the playing cards clutched between my sweaty fingers. "You don't have to do that," he whispers.

And there's that look again. I have to get away from that look. I can't be that girl to him. I can't be that girl to anyone. After everything Dr. Judy preached to me about honesty and grieving and letting go of control, I would have thought that telling Xander would have made me feel better somehow. Lightened my load. The truth shall set you free. Isn't that how it goes?

But now all I feel is naked and exposed. An unarmed soldier running through enemy territory with no backup and no escape route.

The truth doesn't set you free. The truth strips you of your armor and leaves you to die alone.

Alone.

Lottie was all alone.

If I had just gone to the mall, if I had just sucked it up and gotten in that car with her, she wouldn't have had to die alone.

Or who knows? Maybe if I had gone with her, the timeline would have been different. I would have taken time to get dressed, washed my face, brushed the vomit stench from my teeth. Maybe she wouldn't have been in that very intersection at that very moment. Maybe she would have lived.

Either way, we both would have been dead or alive *together.*

Either way, it would have been better than this.

"There you guys are!" comes a shriek. Xander and I both startle and peer out from under the table. Siri is stumbling toward us in a zigzag pattern. "What the fuck are you guys doing under there?" She holds her head like it's about to explode. "You know what? I don't even want to know. You can keep your crazy sex stuff to yourself."

Xander gives me a weak smile and crawls out from under the table. He stands and offers his hand, pulling me up.

"We were just taking a little break from all the commotion," Xander explains.

"Well, break's over!" Siri declares. "We're five minutes from midnight, and I need to use you two as a buffer. Marcus just showed up, and he's been trying to get me alone all night."

"Who's Marcus?" Xander asks.

Siri glares at me. "Mopey Girl, fill in your boyfriend. I don't have time for this shit."

I sigh. "He's not my—"

"Less chat. More moving!" Siri attempts to snap her fingers but can't quite manage to line them up right.

Xander looks to me, silently asking if I'm ready to return to the party. I give him a small nod, and we follow behind Siri as she staggers to the elevator. Although I'm terrified about showing my face in that room again, I'm secretly relieved that we don't have to play Xander's game anymore.

Because I'm pretty certain I just lost.

The Return of Cottie

When we get back to the party, Mylee is ranting drunkenly to the blow-up doll on the bed. Someone has replaced the doll's sunglasses with the snorkel mask Siri was wearing earlier.

"I just thought he loved me, you know?" Mylee slurs. The doll stares blankly back. "He told me he loved me. And dumb-ass me, I believed him. Because I believe people when they tell me things. I'm trusting like that. I have a big heart!"

"That girl is kind of wacko," Xander whispers to me as we squeeze into an empty space near the ravaged beverage table. There's absolutely nothing left to drink besides the red goo at the bottom of a jar of maraschino cherries.

"Wait—didn't you almost hook up with her?" I ask, feeling my insides turn.

He gives me the most offended look I've ever seen. "What? No!"

"I saw you with her earlier."

"You saw me trying to get away from her," Xander corrects. "She couldn't stop talking about her ex-boyfriend. It was brutal. I guess she finally found someone willing to listen."

"Don't ever date a high school boy," Mylee advises her oxygen filled friend. "They're all losers. They're all immature asshats who don't understand their own feelings."

"Well, she's got a point there," I tease.

"Hey!" Xander feigns offense. "We are not *all* asshats. Come to think of it, what exactly *is* an asshat?"

"A hat shaped like an ass?"

"An ass shaped like a hat?"

"Derivative," I disapprove.

"Derivative?" Xander raises his eyebrows. "Now you *really* sound like my English teacher. You clearly haven't had enough to drink. Here." He turns to the desk behind us and upon finding nothing but the jar of red sludge, picks it up and hands it to me. "Quick. Shoot this."

"Not a chance."

"It serves me right," Mylee goes on to the doll. "From now on I'm only dating college boys. Nay," she corrects herself, raising her glass and sloshing liquid onto the floor. "College *men*."

"Okay, you guys!" Siri calls out over the music. "Only two minutes left!" The room erupts in cheers, and Xander takes an awkward step toward me.

"Ugh," Siri says, sidling up to us. "I still don't have anyone to kiss at midnight."

"What about your friend Marcus?" I stand on tiptoes in an

effort to spot anyone who looks like the man described to me earlier. It's a lost cause. The place is too crammed full of bodies.

Siri cracks the tiniest smile, but then adamantly shakes her head. "No. No way. I've been trying to escape him all night."

"He did let you completely trash his hotel room. How bad could he be?"

She ignores me and instead gives Xander an interested once-over. I suddenly want to punch her in the face.

"I take it *he's* spoken for?" Siri looks straight at me, and I can feel my cheeks glow red. Good thing this room is so dark.

"Um . . ." I stammer before realizing that Xander is looking at me, too. Like, really looking at me. He's turned his entire body toward me in expectation of an answer. "Um," I repeat lamely.

"Jeez," Siri grumbles. "Will you two figure this shit out already? It's really not that complicated." She turns her evil stare on Xander. "Do you want to kiss her at midnight?"

"Um . . . ," Xander echoes awkwardly before bending down to retie his shoe.

"I'll take that as a yes," Siri asserts before turning back to me, like a pastor at a wedding. "And do *you* want to kiss him?"

I stand speechless in shock. I think something comes out of my mouth, but I'm pretty sure it sounds more like, "huuhanana," than any real word.

"This is ridiculous. I don't have time to play shrink. I have now less than"—she glances at the clock on the desk—"a minute to find someone to kiss!"

"What about Jimmy?" I blurt out, grateful to get the focus off me and Xander.

Siri busts out in a deep belly laugh. "Oh yeah, sure. I'll just tap Rick on the shoulder and ask if I can cut in." She jabs her thumb in the direction of the necklace/disco ball hanging in the center of the room, and I see big Jimmy full-on making out on the "dance floor" with a tiny guy who barely comes up to his neck.

"Oh," I say with sudden realization. Lottie always told me my gaydar was inoperable.

"30, 29, 28, 27!" The room has started to chant.

"Crap!" Siri says, looking desperately around her. "This is hopeless." She catches sight of someone behind her and lets out a yelp. "Hide me!"

I glance up and see a tall man in a suit trying to make his way through the throngs of people. Marcus, I presume. He's good-looking with neatly cropped hair, a strong jaw, and an overall put-together look about him. I really don't know why Siri is so opposed to kissing him. I turn back to Siri, who's slightly cowering between me and the bed that's been shoved against the wall. Maybe she really is scared.

Maybe all of us can be a little scared.

Even someone as brave as Siri.

"Can we leave yet? This party is severely lacking mental stimulation." Troy has suddenly appeared by my side.

Siri peers around me at the little boy genius, sizing him up. I can tell she's weighing her options. At this point it's either tall, suited, and handsome, or annoying, scrawny, and fourteen.

"21, 20, 19!" the collective group counts.

"I've been studying this unique species of stranded airport employees," Troy goes on, motioning to the general population of the room. "And I've deduced that they are entirely unknowable. Their actions make no logical sense whatsoever."

"No," Siri finally decides with a shake of her head. "I'm not that desperate."

"18, 17, 16!"

"Everything changes tonight!" Mylee decrees on our other side. Either she hasn't figured out that her conversation partner is made of inflatable plastic, or she simply doesn't care. "This is my New Year's resolution! Mature, college guys only. With promising futures and smart brains!"

"15, 14, 13!"

I can sense Xander next to me. Is it just me or has he inched closer since this countdown began?

Well, if he did, it's probably just because there are so many people in here.

"What is the point of counting down to midnight?" Troy inquires to no one in particular. "I've never quite understood this social construct. Why not count down every night? The date of January first has no actual significance in the cosmic scheme of things. It's an arbitrary date set by an arbitrary tribe of people thousands of years ago."

"12, 11, 10!"

I feel something warm against my left hand. It's Xander's fingertips. They're brushing my skin, trailing along my palm.

Don't look down, I tell myself.

Looking down—seeing it—will only make it real.

And real things break.

Imaginary things last forever.

"9, 8, 7!"

Xander's fingers interlace with mine.

"Is that really so much to ask?" Mylee shouts over the chanting. "To find a nice college guy who's not obsessed with stupid shit like sports and cars and his ridiculous overly gelled hair?"

"6, 5, 4!"

Xander turns to face me. I can feel his eyes on my cheeks. I can feel his chest brushing against my shoulder. If I turn now, it's all over.

If I meet him in the middle, I can't go back.

This one tiny quarter-turn rotation is suddenly so huge. It's an invitation. It's a question mark.

A question that I can't find the answer to on my phone.

"I just want to hook up with a college guy!" Mylee half shouts/ half screams over the noise.

"Oh, for God's sake!" Siri cries in response. "Do I have to do everything around here?"

She grabs Troy by the shirtsleeve and drags him toward Mylee. He protests the entire way. "What are you doing? Let go of me!"

"Mylee, this is Troy. He's getting his master's at Stanford. So shut up already!"

"3! 2! 1! Happy New Year!" The room breaks into whoops and cheers and applause.

Mylee gives Troy a skeptical look. Then she just shrugs and says, "What the hell?" She grabs Troy by the straps of his backpack, pulls him to her, and plants her open mouth on his. Troy fights back for a moment before finally surrendering to the kiss. He has to stand on his tiptoes to reach her, but somehow they make it work.

Siri glances up at Marcus. He's nearly made it over to us. Panicked, she turns to the blow-up doll, grabs it by the neck, and guides its lips to hers.

Xander squeezes my hand, bringing me back to the moment. To the question that still hangs in the air with a second countdown clock ticking above it.

What would Lottie say if she were here right now?

What would she tell me to do?

I soon realize it doesn't matter. Because she's not here. Not even the imaginary version in my head. Neither one of them can tell me what to do.

Which means I have no choice but to make the decision myself.

I draw in a deep, life-changing breath and slowly turn toward Xander.

∞

I don't know how long I stood in that street, staring into the remains of Lottie's car. Minutes. Hours. Days. Maybe the world ended and began all over again. Maybe the universe contracted and exploded in a bright ball of fiery light, repeating every single instant of time until I was right back here in this very nightmare.

At some point a voice called to me. But it was coming from another planet. In a foreign alien language I couldn't understand.

"Miss? Miss? I need you to move away from the vehicle. Miss?"

I took a step closer to the car. It was like the giant chasm in the driver's side had created a vortex in time and space, and I was a helpless victim in its vacuum.

"MISS!" the voice was louder now but still muffled by a cushion of impenetrable air that had built up around me. "We need to clear this area immediately. It's not safe."

The glass crunched under my bare feet. The shards buried deep into my skin. I didn't cry out in pain. I welcomed them in. I told them to make themselves at home. Stay as long as they like. My skin would heal around them and keep them safe. Hold them there as a reminder that nothing would ever be the same.

"Shit," the voice swore. "I think she's in shock. Look at her feet."

The next thing I knew, I was no longer on the ground. I was being swept up in someone's arms and carried away. My hand gripped tighter around my phone. I let my head drop back so I could see the world upside down. The way it would forever be from this moment on.

Lottie's annihilated car suspended from the ceiling.

Oregon's towering trees growing in reverse.

Flashing red and blue lights hanging like chandeliers from the sky.

"We're gonna need to take you to a hospital," the alien voice explained.

Yes, I thought eagerly. *Take me to the hospital. Pronounce me dead on arrival. Tell everyone I was in that car. Where I was supposed to be.*

"The cuts on your feet are pretty deep. Can we call your parents and tell them where you are?"

I didn't respond. Someone tried to pry my phone from my fingers, but I cried out in protest and hugged it tightly to my chest. It was the first noise I'd made since I arrived.

"Just get her out of here," someone said. "The staff at St. Vincent's will get in touch with her parents."

They carried me to an awaiting ambulance. They secured my arms and legs to a stretcher. Evidently, they thought I was going to fight. They thought I was going to run.

They had no idea I had nowhere left to go.

The ambulance rumbled down the street, carrying me farther and farther away from that flashing clock. Somehow, despite my restraints, I managed to turn on my phone and glance at the screen.

I had one unread text message.

∞

People are singing. People are dancing. People are shouting "Happy New Year" over and over.

The chaos of the impromptu New Year's party surrounds us, but for the first time, I don't even notice it. It's like Xander and I exist in our own little bubble. Counting down on our own clock. Toward our own delayed beginning.

15, 14, 13 . . .

His gaze finds mine and holds it. His eyes are like placid lakes that I slip right into.

12, 11, 10 . . .

His hand reaches for my face. His fingertips trace a line from my cheekbone to my chin. His skin on my skin is like the life raft I've been floundering for.

"Is this okay?" he asks.

9, 8, 7 . . .

My heart pounds along with the seconds ticking by. A steady, commanding rhythm that vibrates in my ears.

I nod.

He takes a step toward me. His hand slides into my hair, holding my head, holding me together, like he's afraid I might shatter.

6, 5, 4 . . .

He leans in, his lips slightly parted. His eyes never leaving mine.

"Is this okay?" he whispers into my mouth.

I nod again. I can feel him close to me. So dangerously close. His breath tickles my chin, sending pulses of electricity through my body.

I let my eyes close.

And that's the exact moment that dormant Dead Lottie decides to resurrect.

"What are you doing!?" she screeches. "Are you falling in love with him? Are you replacing me? Is this how it's going to be now? Bye-bye, Lottie. So sorry you're dead but that's okay, because I've got Muppet Guy now!"

3, 2, 1 . . .

I move my head swiftly to the side. Xander's lips land on my cheek. They linger there for a second. A second that breathes warmth and terror and regret into my skin.

Then that second passes and Xander clears his throat, pulling away. Stepping away. Taking everything away.

I blink the room back into focus. The madness of the party comes charging back at me like a train emerging from a darkened tunnel. And stupid me, I'm standing right in the middle of the tracks.

Behind Xander, Troy and Mylee are still making out like the world is ending and the blending of their saliva is the magic formula that will save us all. Just beyond them, Siri has rejected the blow-up doll in favor of Marcus. She's kissing him wildly. She leaps up and wraps her legs around his waist. He grunts from the impact of her tiny body and falls backward onto the bed, next to the rejected doll.

"Are you okay?" Xander asks.

I wheel on him. "Why do you keep asking me that?" I didn't mean for it to come out quite so forcefully.

This is exactly why I don't tell anyone anything. Why I keep it all to myself. Because it's inevitable. Once you tell someone, they look at you differently. They treat you differently. Normal conversations turn into minefields that they have to tiptoe through. And suddenly every single question that comes out of their mouth is, "Are you okay?"

I shake my head, my voice on the verge of breaking. "Clearly, I'm not okay. I'll never be okay. Okay?"

"I'm sorry!" he tries. "I thought you said it was okay. I thought I was helping."

"Helping?" My voice rises again as frustration blooms in my chest. "Is that what this was? You were going to kiss me to try to make it all better? Because you felt sorry for me?"

"No," Xander replies hastily. "That's not what I meant. I—"

"My best friend is dead. And that's not going to go away just because we have a few laughs in a train car or share a few stories during a game of poker. You can't just kiss me and make it all okay. It doesn't work like that. It's not a scrape on my knee. It's a giant, gaping hole in my heart."

It's happening again. I'm losing control. I need to get out of here. Out of this room. Out of this noise. Away from these people.

"I know that," Xander says, sounding impatient. "But pushing people away isn't going to work either. You can't keep isolating yourself from the world. That's not going to help. It's only going to make things worse."

I turn and shove my way through the people. Xander catches up to me, his hand on mine, pulling me back to him. "Ryn. Wait."

"I don't need your psychoanalysis. I get enough of that from my own shrink." I try to shake his hand free, but he holds on tight.

"I *wanted* to kiss you," he says earnestly. "Not because I was trying to fix you and not because I felt sorry for you. Just because I wanted to kiss you."

"I don't believe you."

He lets go of my hand, looking disappointed. Looking at the ground. "Well, then, there you go."

What the hell is that supposed to mean?

I open my mouth to ask this very question but then decide that I don't even care. I don't want to know. I just want to leave.

I grab my backpack from the corner where I stashed it earlier and push past him, shove my way through the mayhem, through the hallway, into the elevator, jabbing mercilessly at the button for the lobby. When I spill out, I run across the plaza until I'm back in the quiet, well-lit terminal.

I half expect Xander to follow me. But after a few seconds, it's clear that he's not going to.

I'm all alone with my chaotic, rambling thoughts.

Isolated in the middle of this huge airport.

Just like I wanted.

The hospital staff asked me questions.

I lied.

The police took my official statement.

I lied.

My mother squeezed my hand with tears in her eyes and pleaded for answers.

I kept on lying.

"I was in the car," I told her for the twelfth time. "I was right there next to her. I watched her die."

My mother's face clouded with disappointment. She turned away from me. She whispered to a woman in uniform. "Are you sure?" she asked.

The woman nodded. "There was no way she was in that car. She would be dead. The passenger air bag never inflated. Charlotte was driving alone."

She spoke as if I weren't even in the room. As if I no longer existed.

I wished that were true.

"A hospital staff member called your daughter's cell," the woman explained. "She was listed as Charlotte's In Case of Emergency."

My mother faced me again. Her thin, pale lips curved into a weak smile, begging silently for the truth. For words. For communication. For once in her life she was trying. But I wouldn't meet her halfway.

Lottie had been dead for less than two hours, and I was already doing it all wrong. I was already failing.

That was the last time my mother asked me about the car.

We never spoke of it again.

∞

I try to breathe but my lungs don't seem to want to function. I'm choking on air. My heart is fluttering in my chest. Sweat begins to bead on my legs and back. Darkness seeps into my vision.

I stumble over to a nearby bench next to a window and collapse, bending over to stick my head between my knees like I've seen people do in movies.

What does an anxiety attack feel like?

What does a heart attack feel like?

What happens to your brain when you pass out?

I reach for my phone but of course, it's not there, and I am not going back to the party to get it. I don't care how desperate I am.

I glance around the deserted terminal. The sterile white floors. The high, mountainous ceilings. There's a security check-point across from me, but there's no one there apart from a few bored-looking TSA agents.

It's so quiet in here. So empty. Yet, the mayhem in my head makes it feel like I'm back inside that crowded, stuffy hotel room. I can almost feel the storm beating against the window behind me, trying to get in. Trying to reach me.

This is all his fault. Why did he have to suggest we play that stupid game? Why did I have to go along with it? Why couldn't I have just lied? About everything.

87. I blame Siri for stealing my phone and dragging me to that horrible party.
88. I blame the person who left a deck of cards in an airport for not looking after their things more carefully.
89. I blame Lottie for teaching me how to play poker.

"Hey," she growls. "This has nothing to do with me."

Are you kidding? I scream into my head. *This has everything to do with you. If it weren't for you, I would be normal. If it weren't for you, I would be happy. If it weren't for you—*

"If it weren't for me," she interrupts, sounding insulted, "you would be boring."

I laugh aloud. She's right. Of course, she's right. She's always right. If it weren't for her, I would be nothing. I feel like nothing.

I am nothing.

I let out a low whimper and try again to suck in a lungful of air. *Why did you come back?*

"Why?" she asks as though it's obvious. "Because you clearly needed me. You were about to make a huge mistake with that guy."

You were the one who told me to go after him!

"Yeah," she says, "But not to fall in love with him. Not to live happily ever after with him in a two story house with a white picket fence and a golden fucking retriever."

I'm not falling in love with him. I barely know him.

"You can't lie to me, Ryn," Lottie says, sounding amused by my efforts. "I live in your head. I know everything you're thinking. And feeling. You should thank me. I saved you. From pain. And disappointment. And devastating heartache."

I inhale deeply. My lungs finally decide to cooperate, and the beautiful oxygen spreads through my body, chasing the dizziness away, easing the rhythm of my pulse.

You can't save me, Lottie, I say with a sad, emptying realization that hollows out my chest.

And for the first time, I know it's the truth. A truth I've been trying to avoid. A truth that's been following me ever since I was carried away from that intersection. Always two steps behind. Never quite managing to catch up. Until now.

You can't save me, Lottie.

She's quiet for a long moment. And to my surprise I feel a glimmer of relief. That she's gone. That I've outsmarted her. That I've finally managed to win one of these arguments.

But then, true to form, Lottie swoops back in with the grand comeback. The zinger. The final knockout punch.

"I think I just did."

Red-Eyed Demon Horse

After Dead Lottie spoke to me for the first time, I tried desperately to get her to speak again. I didn't know exactly what I'd heard that day of the funeral—a ghost, a figment of my imagination, a sign of my imminent psychotic break—but I knew I wanted it back. Whatever had happened to me, I wanted it to happen to me again.

I craved Lottie's words, Lottie's presence, Lottie's comfort. Even if it meant I was crazy, I didn't care. I vowed I would *be* crazy if that's what it took to have her with me.

I tried everything. Talking to her aloud, talking to her in my head, complimenting her, insulting her, playing her favorite music, reading her favorite books. I even watched *Doctor Who*.

I was beginning to think that it was just a fluke. A onetime occurrence. That I would never hear my best friend's voice again.

But I also knew that there was one thing I still hadn't tried. Because I just couldn't physically bring myself to do it.

I hadn't yet visited the tree house.

The idea of stepping foot in there, of climbing that ladder, crouching through that child-size door, and sitting on those wooden planks, it was too much. There were too many memories trapped in that place. Nine years of friendship seeped into the wood. I knew it would smell of her.

But I was desperate.

And I couldn't shake the feeling that if there were one place Lottie would be hiding, it would be there. It would be within those walls. It was where she hid in life, so why wouldn't she hide there in death, too?

I waited until nightfall. When my mother had gone to bed and the porch lights on our street had all been extinguished. I had barely slept since the phone call from Lord Voldemort, so I was used to being awake while the rest of the world was sleeping.

I put on my raincoat and boots, walked the three blocks to Lottie's house, punched in the gate code, and let myself in. Lottie's house was dark.

I could tell the moment I crawled inside the treehouse that no one had been there. It was exactly as she had left it. Those tiny empty bottles that Lottie had drained on that night she drunk-dialed me were still scattered around the floor. Her stash of unopened, stolen merchandise was still overflowing from a crate in the corner. Her collection of X-rated DVDs was still stacked next to the small TV.

In the blackness of the night I was surrounded by Lottie's dark side.

I crawled to the center of the room and sat cross-legged on the oval shaped rug. Then I closed my eyes and waited.

For a voice. For a creak in the wood. For a hint of breath against my ear.

But Lottie didn't show.

After what felt like hours of frustratingly stubborn silence, I opened my eyes, and my gaze immediately landed on my sketch pad. The one I always kept in here. For those early mornings when I woke up hours before Lottie.

Angrily, I reached for it, removed the black pen I kept stuffed inside the spiral binding, and flipped to the first blank page.

If Lottie wouldn't come to me in death, then I would have to bring her back to life. I would have to create her the way I remembered her. With those beautiful flawless features and untamed hair and fierce eyes overflowing with life. I would do what I always did.

I would draw exactly what I saw.

Except this time it would have to be from memory.

I propped my phone up against the wall so the flashlight shined on the blank page. Then I lay on my stomach, with my pen clutched in my hand, and I started to draw.

It wasn't hard to remember Lottie's face. I knew it better than my own. Every slope and every curve. Every freckle on her skin and every twinkle in her eye.

I could see it in my memory. I could hold it in my mind. It was so clear.

And yet my hand just couldn't replicate it on the page. No

matter what I did, no matter how hard I tried, how many times I started over on a blank page, everything was wrong.

Her chin was misshapen.

Her jaw was off-center.

Her nose was crooked.

Her hair didn't flow.

Her eyes didn't sparkle.

And instead of getting better with each attempt, it only got worse.

Until Lottie was a warped, grotesque monster. A destroyed work of art. A stunning canvas left out in the rain.

I jumped to my knees and scrambled away from the sketch pad, like I was running away from a demon. I was out of breath. My heart was pumping so hard.

That gruesome, twisted face stared at me from across the tree house.

It watched me.

It judged me.

It screamed at me.

And then I heard it. A real scream. From a real voice. Or as real as that voice would become to me over the next eleven months.

"Ryn!" it screeched, completely horrified. "What is the matter with you? Why would you do that to my face? That doesn't look anything like me!"

I collapsed onto my back and closed my eyes, my chest rising and falling in sporadic spasms. I waited for the silence to be broken again.

It didn't take long.

"What happened?" Lottie asked. She sounded far away. Like she was on the other side of the room. I pictured her hovering over that hideous drawing, her pink lips tugged in a disapproving scowl. "You used to be so talented. Your drawings used to look so real."

"I'm sorry, Lottie," I said aloud. "I'm so sorry."

"Don't ever do that to me again," she scolded, and I released a sigh of profound relief. It sounded just like her. It was exactly what she would say. It was exactly how she would react to something so revolting.

It was her. She was back.

"I won't, Lottie," I swore into the darkness. "I promise."

Three hours later, after dawn had broken, Lottie's mother found me asleep in the tree house. She gasped at the chaotic state of the tiny room. The empty liquor bottles. The shoplifted merchandise. Years and years of evidence of Lottie's rebellious spirit.

And my crumpled up, failed attempts to capture it on paper.

"Ryn," Mrs. Valentine said, her voice shaking. "What is all of this?"

I could see it in her eyes. I could see her beautiful, perfect daughter being warped and twisted in her memory until she was just as ugly and misshapen and inaccurate as the faces on those discarded pieces of paper.

I couldn't let it happen. No one was allowed to see her like that. I had made a promise.

"It's mine," I vowed in a clear, unwavering voice. "It's all mine."

∞

It's not Xander who ends up following me out of the party, it's Troy. He has that dreamy, just kissed daze in his eyes and he's walking kind of crooked, like he's drunk, even though I know he hasn't consumed a single drop of alcohol.

He finds me on my bench and staggers over, plopping down beside me. His presence immediately lightens my mood. It's almost as though I feel like I have to put on a show for him. Protect him from my ugly truths.

"Have a good time?" I ask. It feels good to tease someone. To pretend to be normal for someone else's sake. I've been doing it for so long, the disguise slips back on easily. Like a worn-in shoe.

A blush creeps over his cheeks. He clears his throat. "Actually, no. I'm pretty sure I have to get all sorts of vaccinations now. I have no idea where that girl's tongue has been."

"First kiss?" I venture.

He slouches into the bench. "Yeah."

I nod. "I remember mine."

He looks genuinely interested. "When was it?"

"When I was fifteen. My best friend set it up. To this day I have no idea if the guy really wanted to kiss me or not."

He looks like he wants to say something, but I can tell this topic is making him uncomfortable.

"So," I say, changing the subject, "what's it like to be a genius?"

He shoots me a look.

"Sorry," I correct myself. *"Prodigy."*

He leans back on his hands and lets out an overdramatic sigh, like he's about to tell me the sob story of the century. "I'm not gonna lie. It's pretty awesome."

I almost laugh. And it almost feels good. "I can imagine. Being smarter than everyone. Having it all figured out. That's gotta be nice."

He thinks about that for a moment. "Do you know who Albert Einstein is?"

I roll my eyes. "I may not be a *prodigy* but I'm not stupid."

"I don't know," Troy teases. "You didn't know the second law of thermodynamics."

"That's not general knowledge."

"It is to me."

"You're not among the general population."

He nods. "That's true. Well, anyway, Albert Einstein once said, 'Do not worry about your difficulties in mathematics. I can assure you mine are still greater.'"

I squint. "What does that mean?"

"It means everyone's problems are relative. Even mine."

I eye the doors to the plaza between the airport and the hotel. There's still no sign of Xander. I wonder if he decided I wasn't worth the effort after all and found someone else to hang out with.

"What *are* your problems?" I ask Troy.

"Right now my biggest problem is coming to a decisive conclusion about the accuracy of this alleged Denver airport conspiracy."

I grunt. "That must be nice."

"But as soon as I get home," Troy goes on, leaning forward to stare at his shoes again, "my biggest problem will go back to convincing my dad that having a physicist as a son is just as good as having a football player."

"He'd rather have a football player?"

"Have *you* ever met a child prodigy named Troy Benson?"

"You're the first child prodigy I've met."

Troy sighs. "My dad was an all-star at Texas A&M. His *father* was an all-star at Texas A&M. His *grandfather*. And so on and so forth. I'm the disappointment who screwed up a legacy."

"But that's ridiculous. Doesn't he realize how smart you are? What a gift that is?"

"He doesn't understand me. And he can't appreciate anything he doesn't understand."

I bow my head, feeling extremely guilty for belittling him earlier. "I'm sorry."

He shrugs. "Why? You didn't do it."

"I know," I say quietly. "But that doesn't mean I'm not sorry."

"Yeah, well, the feeling is mutual. I don't understand him either. I can't comprehend how he can sit around all day and watch grown men chase around a leather ball. It's one step above Roman gladiators in an arena. And a small step at that. My high school had to shut down the library because there wasn't enough funding, and yet just last year the county got a brand-new three-million-dollar football stadium. It's completely illogical."

I'm not sure what to say to that. So I just agree with him.

"What about you?" he asks. "What's your big problem?"

I glance toward the doors to the hotel plaza again, trying to decide how much to tell him. *What* to tell him. I have so many problems, I can literally pick and choose.

I ball my hands into fists. "I'm obsessed with my phone."

Troy scoffs. "That's not a problem. That's the general state of our society."

"I mean, I constantly ask it questions."

He tilts his head, looking intrigued. "Like what?"

I blow out a breath. "I don't know. Anything that pops in my mind. Like how do revolving doors work and can you get food poisoning from eating stale granola and is it safe to land a plane in a snowstorm?"

"It's not the plane you have to worry about," Troy replies automatically. "It's the ice on the ground."

I snort. That's exactly what Google said.

"But why did you leave the party?" Troy asks.

I think about Xander's lips. So close to mine. I think about his words. *"I thought I was helping."* Then I shake my head. "You probably wouldn't understand."

For a long moment I feel Troy's inquisitive eyes on me. Like he's studying me. Analyzing me the way he would a complex physics theorem. I don't know why, but for some reason I expect him to say something clever or insightful or extremely enlightening. But instead he just rises to his feet and stretches his arms above his head. "Maybe you should focus on *my* problem for a while."

I flash a weak smile. "Which one?"

"Well, since I don't think my father is going to change his mind about football anytime soon, I'll say the first one." He gestures grandly toward the quiet airport. "Care to join me on my crusade to disprove a conspiracy? I could use a research assistant."

"Assistant?" I repeat dubiously.

"Can you describe the fundamental postulate of statistical mechanics?"

"Assistant," I agree glumly.

I glance at the doors one last time. What if Xander comes looking for me? Should I at least tell him where I'm going?

Why? I don't owe him anything. He's not my boyfriend. He's just a stranger I met in an airport, who, after this snowstorm lifts, I'll never see again.

He's nothing to me.

"Okay," I say, standing up and hoisting my backpack onto my back. "Let's go."

$$\infty$$

The months following Lottie's death had no shape or structure. They were infinitely long and, at the same time, astoundingly short. Days would pass that felt like hours. Hours would pass that felt like weeks. I often forgot what day it was. Weekends lost their sparkle. Morning, afternoon, and night were all dark.

I tried to draw other things, harmless things like fruit and animals and park benches. I hoped it would take me away from my pain for a few hours, but it only exemplified it. My warped, crooked lines only reminded me of how straight they used to be.

My worthless, shaking hand only reminded me of the steadiness that I had lost.

When we moved to San Francisco and I started a new school, despite what I told Dr. Judy, I didn't bother to make friends. I didn't see the point. No one would ever live up to Lottie. Anyone I hung out with would just seem like a bland, lackluster replacement to Lottie's sheen.

It would be like driving around on a spare tire. Sure, it can get you from place to place, but it will always feel a little bit off. A little bit flat. Like it was never quite meant to be there long-term.

When my birthday rolled around at the end of October, my mom wanted to do something big. "You only turn eighteen once!" she trilled. "We should celebrate."

I repeatedly told her no. I didn't think it was appropriate to celebrate a landmark that Lottie would never see. But my mother insisted. She told me to invite everyone I knew from school and we would have a big bash. She went all out with the decorations and the theme and the food and the refreshments.

Of course no one came.

I didn't know anyone.

So I didn't invite anyone.

On the day of the party my mom and I sat alone in the living room, staring at the floor in silence. I fiddled with my phone while my mother chain-ate canapés from a nearby serving dish.

"Well," she said, after a huge swallow. "I'm sure it's just because of Halloween. That's the problem with being born on a big holiday. It's hard to compete."

I knew that was the best I was going to get from her. I knew neither us would actually *acknowledge* the truth of the situation. That wasn't our M.O. *This* was our M.O.

"Yeah," I said, rising to my feet and trudging up the stairs to my room. "That's exactly the problem."

I quietly closed my bedroom door and walked over to the sketch pad on my desk. I traced various shapes with my fingertip, not daring to pick up a pen.

"She's trying," Lottie said. "You have to give her that."

I know, I admitted. *I just really wish she wouldn't.*

There was a long silence and then, as usual, Lottie spoke the very words I was too afraid to say aloud. "No, you don't."

I smiled to myself. *You know me too well,* I joked.

She didn't laugh.

I sat down on the floor and crossed my legs, remembering the night, one year ago, when I sat in Lottie's tree house with her head in my lap and her flaming red hair fanned out over my knees. She was wearing that skimpy Twister dress with all the colorful circles.

"What was I thinking with that costume?" she asked, sounding perturbed. "It was so on the nose."

I couldn't help but chuckle.

Lottie? I asked after a moment.

"Yeah?"

I bit my lip, trying to form my random, chaotic thoughts into coherent sentences. *Thanks for being here,* I told her. *I mean, thanks for sticking around. I'm not sure how I would have gotten through this day—or any other day—without you.*

She didn't answer right away, and for a moment, I was terrified I might have scared her off by acknowledging her directly. Like those mythical creatures you're not supposed to look in the eye.

And just when I thought she'd disappeared for the night—crawled back into that dark corner of my mind where she must sleep—I heard her whisper, "Happy Birthday, Ryn."

∞

"What is this one supposed to represent?" I ask Troy.

We're standing in front of another giant, disturbing mural on the ground floor of the concourse building. This one appears to be depicting some kind of funeral. A city burns in the background while children gather around three open caskets.

"What do *you* think it means?" he asks, sounding like a professor challenging one of his students.

I study the painting for a long moment. "Grief, I suppose."

"What makes you think that?"

I point to the burning city. "When someone you love dies, it feels like everything goes up in flames."

He nods. "Well, according to my research, it's another allusion to the end of the world."

"A literal end of the world? Or a metaphorical one?"

"I guess it depends on who you ask. Look." He points to a little girl with dark skin and dark hair, standing just behind the other children. "She's holding a Mayan tablet that supposedly references December twenty-first, 2012, the day the Mayans predicted to be the end of the world."

I lean in closer to the painting and study the tablet clutched in the girl's hands. So many questions race through my mind at once. I choose the one that's been bothering me ever since Troy showed me that first mural of the gas-masked Nazi stabbing the dove. "How exactly do these paintings prove that the Illuminati are going to bring about the apocalypse?"

Troy glances at me out of the corner of his eye. "It's more than just these paintings. These are just the tip of the iceberg. There are many other signs."

"What kind of other signs?" I ask, my curiosity piqued.

"Follow me." Troy spins on his heels and stalks purposefully into the center of the terminal, his gaze cast downward, as though he's counting the floor tiles. "Aha!" he says, skidding to a halt near the exit of the airport train.

I run over to him. "What?"

He points at the floor. "That."

When I look down, I instantly realize what's caught his attention. The tile he's standing in front of is different from the other surrounding tiles. This one has a gold engraving sketched into it in the shape of a cart with wheels. On the side of the cart are the letters *Au Ag*.

"Au Ag?" I say. "Aren't those the periodic symbols for gold and silver?"

He nods, looking only mildly impressed by my knowledge. "Yes, however, some people believe Au Ag is also short for Australia antigen."

"What's that?"

"A deadly strain of hepatitis believed to have been discovered by one of the founders of the airport."

"Seriously?"

"Seriously. Some people claim it's a weapon of biological warfare, intended to wipe out large numbers of the population."

"So that's what you think, then?" I confirm. "That the Illuminati plan to bring about the end of the world with a deadly virus and then hide out in the Denver airport until it's over?"

"I didn't say that," he corrects.

I huff, feeling frustrated by Troy's lack of specificity. "Then what *do* you think this all means?"

"I couldn't possibly say at this point," Troy replies vaguely before turning and striding off again. He heads back in the direction of the bench where we found me after the party. Just a few feet away from it he slows in front of some kind of stone marker that's been erected near the window.

"This marks the location of a time capsule that's been buried beneath the Denver airport," he explains. "See that symbol?" Troy points to a strange diamond shape in the center of the engraving. "That's a Masonic symbol, associated with the Freemasons, who some believe are their own secret society. And look there." Troy bends down and points to an inscription at the bottom of the capstone. "It says, 'New World Airport Commission.'"

"So?" I ask.

"The New World Airport Commission is allegedly the organization that funded the construction of the Denver airport."

"So?" I repeat.

"So, the New World Airport Commission doesn't exist. There's no public record of it."

I squint at the plaque. "Really?"

He nods. "Really. Which makes you wonder, what *is* the New World Airport Commission? Who is actually behind it? The Illuminati? The Freemasons? Some other secret society?"

"But none of this makes any sense," I protest, growing frustrated. "If the Illuminati or whoever are funding airports and developing biological weapons, why would they advertise it all over the airport?"

Troy cocks an eyebrow. "My thoughts exactly."

Next, Troy leads me to the baggage claim area. The carousels are all shut down and empty, and I have no idea what he's going to say about them. That they actually lead through a portal to another dimension?

"Have you heard about the high-tech automated baggage delivery system that runs underneath the airport?"

I think about my own suitcase, probably trapped in the belly of a plane somewhere, and shake my head. "No."

"Well, apparently, it was supposed to be the most advanced baggage system in the country. A series of tunnels and networks underground built to sort and deliver the luggage. It cost a fortune and delayed the opening of the airport for over a year. And now, more than two decades later, it still doesn't work."

I scrunch my forehead. "What?"

"Nope. It was a total disaster. Most of the airlines don't even bother to use the failed system. Which begs the question . . ." He trails off.

"What are the tunnels used for now?"

Troy gives me a proud smile. "Not bad for a lepton."

"A what?"

He laughs. "Oh, that's just what we highly evolved beings call the rest of you. It's an elementary, half-integer particle. Leptons are essential for the makeup of things, but on their own, they're not super useful."

I snort. "Thanks."

He shrugs, clearly not understanding my sarcasm. "You're welcome."

I roll my eyes. "Just get back to the tunnels."

"Right. Well, some theorists believe that the tunnels lead to a secret underground bunker that the president of the United States will use when the apocalypse comes, and that the failed baggage system was just a cover-up."

"The apocalypse depicted in those murals?"

"Yes."

I feel a surge of adrenaline, like the pieces are finally coming together and we're starting to get somewhere. It's the same feeling I get whenever I hit the little Search button on the screen of my phone and the answers begin to appear. "Okay, so the government is planning some kind of apocalyptic attack that the president will survive by hiding out in the Denver airport?"

"Or maybe the Nazis have infiltrated the government and are planning a comeback!"

"Wait, Nazis?" I repeat, confused. "Where did the Nazis come from?"

Troy pulls his phone from his pocket and swipes at the screen. He brings up an image of what looks like a view of the earth from a plane. "Those are the runways of the Denver airport."

I tilt my head to make out the unusual shape in the center of the picture. "Is that a . . . ?"

"Swastika?" he asks. "It sure looks like one. And check out this." He swipes a few more times to the left and shows me the phone again. I nearly gasp at the new image. It's an absolutely terrifying statue of a massive blue mustang horse with illuminated red eyes.

"What's that?"

He takes the phone back and gives it a swipe. "That's the demon horse. It's right outside the airport. The locals call him Blucifer. He's supposed to 'welcome' visitors to Denver. The artist who built the statue was crushed to death when it fell on top of him."

My eyes widen. "Are you serious?"

"*Dead* serious. Some believe the horse is an omen, and the Illuminati erected it to mark the end of humanity."

I press my fingertips into my temples, beginning to feel overwhelmed. "Wait a minute. Now we're back to the Illuminati? Which is it? The Nazis? The Illuminati? The Freemasons? Who's going to bring about the end of the world? Who's behind the conspiracy?"

"I don't know." Troy shrugs, like this doesn't bother him in the slightest. But how could it not bother him? How can he be so calm in the face of all this ambiguity?

"That's it?" I ask, growing agitated. "That's your answer? 'I don't know'?"

"For now, anyways. I mean, it's called a conspiracy *theory* for a reason."

"Maybe we just need more data," I resolve. "Let's go look at the time capsule again." I start to turn, but Troy stops me with a gentle hand on my arm.

"Actually, I think maybe you've had enough. You're getting a little worked up."

I blow out a frustrated breath. "But we can't just stop here. Don't you want to know? You said this was one of your big problems. Don't you want to solve it? Get to the truth? You're a scientist! Aren't scientists obsessed with finding answers?"

And there they are again. Those inquisitive eyes of his. That calm, observing gaze. Except this time, there's something else in there too.

Empathy.

"Yes, we are," Troy says in his usual blunt tone. "But as a scientist, you also need to know when to let go and accept the fact that sometimes there *are* no answers."

His words feel like a punch in the chest. And yet, as soon as he says them, I know he's right.

For the past year I've been searching for answers that I may never find. That may not even exist. No matter how many times I look at all the information, no matter how many times I replay

January 1st, 10:05 a.m., in my head, Lottie's death may never make sense to me.

Troy is still studying me with the same intense gaze. I've suddenly become the more important theory to solve here.

I look to the ground. "I think I'm going to go back to the party."

He nods, like this was his master plan all along. "I think that's a good idea."

"Are you coming?" I ask.

He shakes his head. "No. I've had enough parties for one lifetime. I think I'm going to go find one of those meal vouchers."

Once again I feel that familiar urge to protect him. To go with him. To not let him out of my sight. But I push it away. I'm pretty sure he's not the one who actually needs protecting. The kid can clearly take care of himself. I give his shoulder a quick squeeze. "Good luck, Genius Boy." Then I turn back toward the concourse.

"Hey," he calls a second later, and when I spin around, I swear he's going to reprimand me again for calling him a genius instead of a prodigy.

"Yeah?"

"He *wanted* to kiss you."

I blink in surprise, not sure I heard him correctly. "The guy my friend set me up with for my first kiss?"

He flashes me a smirk. "No."

I bite my lip to stifle the smile that threatens to overtake my face. "How do you know?"

He blushes and stares at his shoes. "I may not be a *normal* guy, but I'm still a guy."

Then, before I can question him further, he turns and walks away.

∞

As I make my way back to the hotel, I'm stopped just short of the doors to the plaza by a strange moaning sound. Convinced that someone must be hurt, I follow the noise to a hidden bench, completely concealed from view by an escalator.

The couple from the train are sprawled out across the entire length of the bench, passionately making out and running their hands all over each other.

Apparently they've made up. *Again.*

I stifle a groan.

Am I the only one *not* kissing someone tonight?

I continue through the automatic doors and walk across the plaza to the hotel. As soon as I enter the lobby, I'm immediately bombarded by Siri's drunk voice calling to me from the bank of elevators.

"Hey! Mopey Girl! Over here!" Then, a little softer, she says. "I know her. That's my friend. Her name is Mopey Girl."

I look over to see her walking with Marcus. Siri is teetering unsteadily and Marcus is holding on to her, struggling to keep her upright.

"We're just going for a little stroll," Siri slurs. "Marcus says I need to walk it off. But I'm totally not drunk." Practically on cue, she stumbles, and his grip around her waist tightens.

"Okay," she admits. "Maybe I'm a little drunk."

"Any chance I can get my phone back now?" I ask her.

She cringes. "Oh! Sorry! I left it in the room."

I breathe out slowly. "Okay. Where in the room?"

She has to think about this. The effort seems to cause her pain. I fight the urge to grab her by the shoulders and shake it out of her.

"Um"—she taps her head—"maybe on the desk. No, on the nightstand. No, I definitely remember having it in the bathroom when I went in there to throw up." This makes her giggle.

I feel sick at the mere thought of Siri's vomit getting anywhere near my precious phone.

"Maybe we should head back upstairs and help her look," Marcus suggests.

Siri swats this idea away with her hand. "No. I remember now. I buried it under the pillows on the bed so it wouldn't get lost."

"Which bed?"

She goes back into her painful thinker stance, twisting her face until she looks like she just swallowed a habanero pepper. "The one by the window?"

"Is that a statement or a question?"

"Um . . ."

I cut her off. "You know what, never mind. I'll find it."

Exasperated, I start toward the elevator. I'll be very glad when I can leave this place and never see that girl again. The elevator is about to close when Marcus's hand cuts through to stop it. He props the doors open with his shoulder. "Hey," he says quietly. "I just wanted to thank you."

I give him a confused look. "Me?"

He releases a heavy breath. "Yeah. I've been trying to get Siri to give me a chance for a really long time, but she always blew me off."

I'm still trying to figure out how *I* fit into this equation.

"Anyway," he goes on, "she said you were the one who convinced her to give me a shot."

"Me?" I say again, like an idiot. "What did I say?"

He shrugs. "I don't know. She just said you convinced her. So whatever it was you said or did to change her mind . . . thanks."

"Oh . . ." I fumble for words. "Um, you're welcome."

He gives me a heartfelt smile and reaches into his pocket, pulling out a black and gold business card. "Here. Take this. If you ever need anything in this airport, just show them this card. It should do the trick."

I take it and slip it into my pocket. Then he backs out of the elevator, letting the doors close.

∞

The party is still going strong when I arrive. I surreptitiously scan the room for Xander, but I don't see him. Not that I care if he's here or not.

I don't.

Jimmy greets me with a beaming smile and a sloppy hug. "For the record, I never thought you were mopey," he says, his words slurring.

"Thanks," I mutter, politely patting his back as I disentangle myself from his large arms.

I push through the crowd and make a beeline for the bed by the window, shoving the blow-up doll aside and searching under all the pillows.

My phone is not there.

I rip the sheets and blanket off, swimming aimlessly in them, my hands feeling every inch, searching for a hard surface.

Nothing.

I make my way to the opposite side of the party to check the other bed, resigning it to the same chaotic fate, but there's still no sign of my phone.

Anxiety tickles the pit of my stomach, and my anger toward Siri comes rushing back.

I search the rest of the room, opening desk drawers, throwing back the shower curtain, crawling on my hands and knees through the mob, my fingers scouring the dirty carpet. I'm getting all sorts of strange looks, and a few people yell things when they trip over me, but I ignore them.

I have to find my phone.

I have to.

The thought of losing it . . .

I can't even go there.

"Has anyone seen a phone?" I shout, but my voice gets swallowed up by the party. I try again a little louder, eliciting a few pathetic headshakes in response.

My anger expands, spreading across the room like a blanket of fire. Why won't these people help me? Why don't they care?

I consider calling the airport police and giving them an

anonymous tip about the disruptive party on the ninth floor of the hotel. I want these people to all to suffer the way I'm suffering right now.

"Maybe you dropped it somewhere in the airport," Jimmy suggests, bending down to talk to me while I'm stretched out on my belly with one hand under the bed. "Why don't you try Lost and Found?"

"I didn't drop it!" I snap, causing him to startle and back away. I immediately feel bad. It's not *his* fault Siri is a stupid, stupid drunk.

Although he does give me an idea.

Maybe Siri *did* lose it. Maybe it fell out of her jacket pocket at some point during the night, and someone turned it in to Lost and Found.

I jump to my feet and sprint out of the room. I remember seeing the Lost and Found office on the opposite side of the concourse while I was following Siri around the airport. It was just next to the international arrivals area.

By the time I get there, I'm completely out of breath. Panting, I pull on the glass door, but it doesn't open. I cup my hands over my eyes and attempt to peer inside. There's no one there.

My heart is pounding in my ears. I bang violently on the door. I'm about to completely lose it. Actually, I think I might have already lost it. I bounce on my toes as I glance around the empty concourse for anyone who looks official. That's when I notice the small sign hanging next to the door.

TO INQUIRE ABOUT LOST ITEMS AFTER BUSINESS HOURS, PLEASE CALL 888-555-2070.

I open my mouth and let out a silent, desperate scream.

How am I supposed to call the fucking number without a fucking phone?

What if it's not even in there? What if someone stole it from the party? What if they sell it on the black market? They'll wipe it clean. They'll erase everything. My apps, my pictures, my messages.

Lottie's words.

Forever unread.

Forever gone.

I drop my bag at my feet, turn my back to the door, and slide all the way down to the cold, hard floor. My butt smacks against the tile as I bury face in my hands.

This is all Siri's fault. If she hadn't stolen my phone, this never would have happened.

No, it's all my fault. I should have stood up for myself. I should have demanded she give me my phone back hours ago. I should have tackled her to the ground and pried it from her skinny fingers.

I should have . . .

"You should have read my message," Lottie finishes in a whisper.

I feel tears welling up in my eyes. I close them tight, shoving fists into the sockets. Then I let out a shuddering sigh that shakes my whole body.

"I should have read your message," I agree aloud.

Between Lost
and Found

I don't know how long I sit there, crouched in a tiny ball outside the Lost and Found office, but at some point, in the darkness of my thoughts, I hear a *click clack*ing sound on the tile.

I pull my heavy eyes open and see a pair of shoes approaching. They slow to a stop right in front of me, and I squint up into the bright fluorescent lights.

"I've been looking everywhere for you," Xander says.

I can't quite explain how it feels to see him there. To know he didn't give up on me. It's like discovering something you never realized was gone.

It's like finding something you never knew you lost.

And then Xander reaches into his pocket and pulls out two identical phones in two identical cases. He holds them side by side, lining them up so perfectly, it almost looks like I'm seeing double.

"I thought you might want this back," he says with a smirk.

I instinctively reach for the one on the right. I don't know how, I just know that it's mine. It's the one with one unread message. It's the one that vibrates with Lottie's energy. Lottie's words.

When my fingers wrap around the familiar case, I expect the very touch of it to bring me comfort. To lighten me. The way it's done for almost a year now.

But the device feels heavy. Daunting. Like it's an anchor. Not a life raft.

I swipe on the phone. I hold my breath. I see the little red number hovering above the app.

One unread message.

I quietly exhale. But for once it's not relief that floods through me. It's dread. It's knowing that something has to be dealt with. An unpleasant task you've put off for almost a year.

Xander lowers to the floor next to me and leans back against the door with a sigh. "Did you ever stop to think what the odds are that two people in this airport would have the exact same phone with the exact same case?"

"I did."

"That's one hell of a coincidence."

I nod. "It is."

But actually, it feels like so much more than just a coincidence.

It feels like a conspiracy.

"Did you also stop to think that if we *hadn't* had the same phone case, we wouldn't be here right now?"

I nod again, but this time, I stay silent. As I stare down at the blue Tardis peeking out between my fingers, I understand exactly what he's saying, and, more important, what he *isn't* saying.

If Lottie hadn't given me that phone case for my birthday, I never would have mistaken his phone for mine when we collided. He never would have texted me to exchange them. He never would have invited me to have burgers with him. I never would have said yes. We never would have surfed in train cars. I never would have been arrested by the airport police. Xander never would have come to rescue me. I never would have tried to run into the snowstorm. We never would have bumped into Siri and Jimmy planning a New Year's Eve party. I never would have seen that redheaded flight attendant and her two-timing *married* boyfriend and run from the party. Xander and I never would have played poker. I never would have told him about Lottie. He never would have told me about his parents and his expulsion. We never would have almost kissed.

A chill runs through me as I turn my head to look at him. He's already there. His eyes are already waiting to catch mine. To hold mine.

His lips say, "I'm sorry."

His powerful, silent gaze says everything else:

"I wanted to kiss you."

"I understand you."

"I need saving just as much as you do."

My breathing has slowed to a calm, even rhythm but my heart is still racing.

"Me too," I whisper.

"Do you wanna go somewhere?" he asks, his eyes never leaving mine.

I nod one more time. "Yes."

He stands and offers his hand to me, pulling me up. He helps me loop my arms through the straps of my backpack. Then he slides his hand into mine, weaving our fingers together, holding on tight.

We start to walk. I don't know where. But I know it doesn't matter.

I think about that night in the tree house when Lottie gave me the phone case. It was the night of my seventeenth birthday. When she dressed up like a Twister board and I dressed up like a hippie. I think about the way she laughed at my reaction when I opened her gift. She was so pleased with herself. So amused by her own lame joke.

I think about the day of her funeral. When I slipped the case on for the first time. When I vowed I would keep it on forever.

To remember her.

To honor her.

To grieve her.

If Lottie hadn't died, I never would have known Xander.

Then You Come and Ease the Pain

"Countries and *R*," I say, taking a sip of soda.

We found a McDonald's that was still open in the A terminal and are sitting in the food court with a tray of fast food.

"Russia," Xander says, taking a bite of his chicken sandwich.

"Romania."

"Rhode Island."

"BZZZZ!" I make a buzzer sound. "Rhode Island is not a country."

"Have you been there?"

"No."

He smirks. "Then how do you know?"

I shoot him a look.

"Fine," he surrenders. "Your point. New category."

Just then we hear a woman's voice yelling from the other side of the food court, and we both look up to see the couple from the train. Apparently, they're on the outs again.

"I'm not eating McDonald's!" the woman is screeching.

"Jesus, Miranda," the man following after her gripes. "One tiny hamburger is not going to kill you."

"Oh, so now you're a doctor?" Miranda asks, throwing up her hands. "First he's a shrink and now he's a doctor."

"You know I hate it when you speak about me in the third person."

"*And* a grammar teacher."

Xander and I turn back to each other and then burst into laughter at the same time.

"You should tell Jimmy that we found his winning bingo square," he says.

I giggle and reach for my phone, before quickly remembering that I don't have his number. Nor Siri's. Nor anyone's from the party.

A shadow of sadness momentarily passes over me.

Is that it? Will I never see those people again?

Despite the fact that Siri pretty much tormented me the entire night. Called me names. Stole my phone. Forced me to go to a stupid party, I think I might actually miss her, believe it or not.

"Your turn to pick the category," Xander reminds me.

I pull a fry from our shared cup on the table and stuff it into my mouth. "Okay. Musical artists and *B*."

"Musical artists like bands or like solo artists?"

I shrug. "Either."

"Bon Jovi."

"The Beatles."

"Billy Idol."

"Bobby Brown."

"Bruce Springsteen."

I take another sip of my Coke. "The B-52s."

"The Bangles!" he says with *way* too much enthusiasm.

I nearly shoot soda through my nose. "Are you a fan?"

Xander nabs a fry. "So what if I am?"

"They're a little girly."

"'Eternal Flame' is a classic."

"You're so full of it."

"You don't believe that I'm a *huge* fan of the Bangles?"

I shake my head. "Nope."

He looks insulted. "I'm the *hugest* fan of the Bangles."

I roll my eyes. "Sure you are."

"How much do you want to bet that I know every single lyric of 'Eternal Flame'?"

"All the money in my wallet."

He regards me suspiciously. "I'm not falling for that."

"What do *you* want to bet, then?" I grab another fry.

"A kiss," he says automatically.

I choke on the fry. "What?"

"You heard me."

"I—" I bumble for words. "You . . . you can't bet something like that."

He shrugs. "I think I just did."

"B-b-but," I stammer, feeling my stomach clench. "That's ridiculous."

Xander bows his head, and I'm pretty sure he's about to shamefully admit that I'm right. That it *is* ridiculous. And he's sorry he even brought it up.

But instead, he opens his mouth and starts singing.

Right smack-dab in the middle of the A terminal food court.

"Close your eyes. Give me your hand . . ." He lifts his head and looks at me with dramatically intense eyes. *"Darling."*

I choke on a nervous laugh.

He stands and grabs my hand, placing it against his chest as he croons, *"Do you feel my heart beating? Do you understand? Do you feel the same?"*

A few tired diners have stopped eating and are looking over at us. My whole body flushes with embarrassment and I bow my head.

Xander tugs on my hand. "Sing with me."

"What?" I cry. "No! You're crazy!"

"C'mon. You surfed in a train. You can sing in an airport food court."

I rip my hand from his grasp. "I *don't* sing."

"Then I'll have to sing loud enough for both of us." Xander steps onto his chair and continues his serenade. *"Am I only dreaming? Is this burning an eternal flame?"*

I glance around anxiously. People are definitely watching now. And smiling. Even some of the employees at the McDonald's are leaning over the counter to get a peek. If I weren't so humiliated right now, I would admit that I'm impressed by Xander's singing voice. It's actually really good.

Xander looks down from atop his "stage," making googly eyes at me. *"I believe, it's meant to be . . ."* He drops his voice a whole octave as he adds, *"Darling."*

"I can't believe how insane you are," I say. "Get down!"

"I watch you when you are sleeping," he sings on in response. Then he turns his gaze on his newfound audience and shouts the next lyric. *"She belongs with me!"*

A few of our fellow diners let out a cheer. I sink farther into my chair.

"Do you feel the same?" he sings passionately, his face scrunching up like he's in a bad music video.

"No," I say. "Definitely *not.*"

"Am I only dreaming?" Xander sings loudly.

"Yes!" I shout back.

The diners "boo" me. Then a few of them actually start singing *with* Xander, obviously grateful to have something else to do besides gripe about being stuck in the airport.

"Or is this burning an eternal flame?"

My whole body has gone numb. I turn in my chair to see at least a third of the diners join in on the next verse.

"Say my name! Sun shines through the rain!" they sing in surprising unison, like they've been practicing this for months. *"A whole life so lonely . . ."*

Xander lowers his gaze back to me. There's something less silly and grandiose about the way he sings the next line. Like he's really *saying* it. Not just making a fool out of himself. *"And then you come and ease the pain."*

I blink up at him, feeling my heart swell. He's so stupid. And crazy. And fearless. And messy. And beautiful.

And I want to kiss him.

We never actually agreed on the bet, but I don't care.

I want to kiss him so badly it hurts to breathe.

"I don't want to lose this feeling," he sings as he steps down from his chair and reaches for my hand. This time I let him take it without a fight. He pulls me to my feet.

"Close your eyes," he croons with his backup singers. *"Give me your hand, darling. Do you feel my heart beating?"*

He places my hand on his chest again. And I actually *can* feel his heart pounding wildly beneath his Muppet shirt. Like it's trying to break right out of its ribbed cage.

Is he nervous?

Or just hopped up on performance adrenaline? He takes a step closer to me. I can feel his breath on my face.

"Do you understand?" he sings, his voice growing quieter. His backup singers follow his lead, winding down to a soft, yet powerful finale. *"Do you feel the same? Am I only dreaming?"*

I glance around the food court again. Outside the windows, snow is still falling like New Year's confetti. Inside, passersby have slowed to watch the impromptu show. The fighting couple is sitting at a nearby table making out again. I turn back to Xander and smile.

"Or is this burning?" he asks quietly.

For the very last line, I let my lips part, and I let the lyrics sigh out of me.

"An eternal flame."

My voice is lost inside the food court choir, but Xander hears it. And it inspires the most adorable, delicious, smug grin I've ever seen.

Then he looks at me. Into me. Through me. He still hasn't let go of my hand on his chest.

His body leans toward me, and at that very moment I want nothing more than to feel his lips against mine. To inhale some of that amazing, infectious energy he seems to take with him every-where. Like a carry-on bag.

His palm rests on my cheek as he steers my mouth to his.

Our lips brush ever so slightly, sending a thousand bolts of lightning through me at once. My kneecaps liquefy. My body shudders.

The entire food court breaks into applause.

And I'm reminded of where we are. What we are. How we ended up here. And every single pair of eyes watching us. My cheeks warm with heat. My stomach tightens with fear. And for the second time that night, I pull away from Xander's searching, questioning kiss.

"Beyoncé," I whisper, stiffening and averting my eyes from his confused expression.

Xander stammers for a moment, obviously trying to figure out what just happened and how my body language changed so quickly. "Huh?"

"Another musical artist that starts with *B*."

He rubs his chin, and I can't tell if it's out of frustration or something else. But then, just when I think he's going to give up on me for good, he says with a chuckle. "Well, there's no way I'm singing any of *her* songs."

∞

"Alligator," I say, covering my yawn as we make our now fifth loop through the A terminal.

"Ape," Xander says immediately. "Are you sure you're not too tired? We can stop."

"Armadillo. No, I'm okay."

It's the third time Xander has offered to stop so we can find a place to sleep for the night. But I've declined all three times. I don't want to stop walking. I don't want to sleep. As long as I'm walking—as long as I'm awake—it's still today. The moment I go to sleep, then it'll be tomorrow. Then it'll be 10:05 a.m. The day Lottie died all over again.

And I'm not ready to live that day all over again.

I'm still trying to survive it the first time around.

So, on we go, walking in countless circles around the A terminal.

"I don't like this category," Xander complains.

I laugh. "Fine, pick a new one."

"Movies. O."

"*Oliver!*" I say immediately.

"You're too good at this game. *Office Space.*"

"*Oklahoma!*"

"Are we doing musicals or movies?"

"They're both musicals that have been made into movies."

Xander shoots me a dubious look but ultimately chooses not to challenge me further. *"Overboard."*

I yawn again. This one is so big, it slurs all my words. *"Ah, tha gray ahn powafuh."*

Xander chuckles. "That's not a movie I'm familiar with."

My yawn keeps going. It has to be the longest yawn in history. When it finally subsides, I repeat myself more clearly, *"Oz the Great and Powerful."*

"Ah, right," Xander acknowledges. *"Outbreak.* And we are totally sitting down now."

I glance around us. There are bodies in nearly every chair of nearly every gate. "No room," I say. "Better keep walking."

"No. Look." Xander points to a small corner next to the security door of gate A22. The way that particular gate is shaped, the space is quiet and relatively secluded.

I scowl. *"Only You.* And I don't want to sit on the floor—" but my words are cut off by another debilitating yawn.

Xander laughs. "C'mon, diva. A little floor sitting won't kill you." He grabs my hand and pulls me toward the alcove. Besides, you still haven't seen *O-cean's Eleven,"* he enunciates the movie title, laying claim to his turn. "And I find that a total travesty."

"Good one," I say.

"Plus, I happen to have it on my iPad."

I allow myself to be led to the corner. "Do you carry the movie around with you at all times on the off chance you meet a girl who hasn't seen it?"

Xander fake-sighs. "Well, now you know *all* my secrets."

He lowers down, props his knees up, and pats the ground beside him. My legs scream for me to sit. My feet are aching. I finally give in and collapse next to him. I admit, it feels amazing. My whole body seems to let out a sigh of relief.

"I'm not sleeping with you," I vow.

Xander slaps a hand to his chest. "Relax. It's just a movie. What kind of guy do you think I am?"

This makes me laugh. "I mean, I'm not falling asleep."

He shrugs. "Good. Because if you fall asleep during *Ocean's Eleven*, I will be terribly offended."

I stretch my legs out of in front of me and lean against the wall, letting my head fall back. Xander pulls his iPad out of his messenger bag and flips open the case. It blinks to life, and he begins tapping at the screen.

"Actually," he says, setting the tablet down to the side, "I'm gonna see if I can find us some blankets."

"Blankets? As in, for *sleeping*?"

He hops up. "Also very handy in preventing one from getting cold."

I screw my mouth to the side. "Hmmm. Sounds suspicious."

He raises his eyebrows coyly. "What can I say? I'm a suspicious guy. Stay right here." I watch him disappear down the corridor, then I pull out my phone and look at the time. My throat constricts. It's 3:05 a.m. exactly. In seven hours, Lottie will have been dead for an entire year.

I stare at the message app on my home screen. The lonely

red circle with the tiny number 1 stares back at me. Taunting me. Baiting me.

One unread message.

"You should probably just read my message," Lottie whispers. She sounds tired too. Tired of trying to convince me to do things I never do. Tired of always being right. Tired of existing within the confines of my head like a genie trapped in a bottle.

I'm afraid, I admit.

And it's the truth. I'm afraid of what it might say. I'm afraid it might be the most significant, groundbreaking, earth-shattering text she's ever sent me.

But mostly, I'm afraid that it won't be.

"I know," she says, and it's probably the gentlest voice she's ever used with me. "You're allowed to be afraid. You're allowed to be sad, too."

I close my eyes, letting her words sink in, trying to make them fit so they don't feel like misshapen clothes that accidentally shrunk in the dryer.

"You're allowed to miss me, Ryn," she says, but her voice suddenly sounds different. As though it's not coming from inside my head, but rather *outside* my head.

When I open my eyes again, Lottie is standing right in front of me. All five foot seven of her.

I know I'm imagining it. I'm not crazy enough to believe she's actually there. But I'm also terrified to blink in fear that she might vanish.

She's exactly as I remember her. Shimmering and radiant. A

star. Her bright red hair falls like silky fire around her shoulders. Her smooth, creamy skin is flawless, without a single blemish. One of her perfectly sculpted eyebrows is raised in a coy question mark.

I do miss you, Lottie, I whisper, but I'm not 100 percent sure I'm still talking silently in my mind, or aloud.

Lottie takes a step closer and sits down next to me. In the very spot Xander occupied. I freeze in place, scared that one move on my part might blow her away like the gust of wind that she is.

She peers over my shoulder at my phone. "Then read the message."

I stare down at the screen. I can still see her out of the corner of my eye, still feel her presence like it never left.

I reach out and hover over the message app, hiding the red circle with my fingertip, trying to imagine what my phone will look like when it disappears.

When there are no unread messages.

When there are no unanswered questions.

When Lottie is really gone.

For good.

I click the message app. Her name glows at me from the screen.

Lottie Valentine (1)

With a trembling hand, I reach toward the message.

"This is good, Ryn," she whispers into my ear, and I swear I can feel her breath on my cheek. "This is progress."

My fingertip lingers millimeters away from the screen. It would be so easy. To just touch it. To just let her words flow over me, embrace me, comfort me. I wouldn't have to erase it. I could keep it on my phone forever. Like a memory that will never fade.

I just have to read it first.

My finger inches closer. I can feel the heat of the screen against my skin. I can feel Lottie reaching out through the phone and pulling me toward her.

I turn and face her with frantic eyes. *What if it's nothing? What if you butt-texted me? What if it's just a string of gibberish?*

"It won't be," Lottie reassures me with a kind smile. But we both know it's a reassurance she can't make. We both know she doesn't really know. She's just as trapped in the dark as I am.

"Just read it," she prompts. "This is no way to live."

She's right.

I know she's right.

And yet I can't do it.

I shut off the screen and toss the phone in front of me like it's on fire. It lies by my feet, helpless and alone on the dirty airport carpet.

"Ryn Ryn," Lottie tries.

No, I snap. *You don't get to do that. You don't get to make this decision for me. You DIED!*

"You can't keep living like this."

Yes! I shout into the depths of my mind. *Yes, I can! I'd rather not know. I'd rather that message be unread forever than be let down by what it says.*

There's silence beside me. Lottie is formulating her perfect power-punch response. Per usual, she doesn't require many words to do it.

"No, you don't."

No, I don't, I echo.

A moment later Xander returns and lowers himself to the ground. I almost scream out for him to stop. Don't move! He's going to crush her. He's going to sit right on top of her. But when I glance over, I see that the space next to me is vacant again.

"I could only find one, so we'll have to share." He inches close to me, our hips touching, and throws the blanket over us, positioning it so it covers our legs.

Then he props his iPad on its stand and rests it between us.

"You're in for a treat, Ryn Gilbert."

I force a smile as I glance around gate A22, searching for Lottie. Did she vanish? Is she gone for good?

Just then, I spot her halfway across the gate, standing next to the counter. She's far enough away that I can't make out every detail, but close enough that I can still see the look of disappointment on her face before she turns and walks away.

One Unread Message

I'm sure *Ocean's Eleven* is an excellent movie. It has an excellent opening. Unfortunately, I fall asleep after five minutes.

∞

When I wake, natural light is streaming into the terminal. My gaze turns hopefully toward the window. The snow is still falling, but there's something more hesitant about it. As though it's just as tired of being here as the rest of us.

Maybe it'll let up.

My head is resting against Xander's shoulder, and his head is tipped back against the wall. He's completely out. His iPad has fallen to the side of his legs. The screen is off.

I wonder how much of the movie he managed to stay awake for.

I carefully ease my head from Xander's shoulder and stretch out my neck. I hear something pop. That can't be good.

Can you get scoliosis from sleeping sitting up?

I instinctively reach for my phone to type in the question before realizing what a ridiculous question it is.

Obviously, I can't get scoliosis from one night in an airport.

Instead, I check the clock.

8:15 a.m.

Less than two hours.

I click back to the home screen.

One unread message.

Careful not to wake Xander, I push myself to my feet and survey the world around us. Even though the sun is barely able to peek through the tempest outside, and even though I was here yesterday, the airport looks different in today's daylight. More hopeful. Less ominous. More familiar. Less hectic. More certain.

There's an end coming.

I can't see it.

But somehow I know it's there.

Finally, my gaze lands back on Xander. On his beautiful dark skin. On his long, curled eyelashes. On the soft sound the air makes leaving his slightly parted lips.

On his Muppet shirt.

Animal, the wildest, most destructive of all the Muppets.

I think about everything that happened yesterday. Pretending to be other people. Surfing the train car. Getting arrested by the airport police. Attending a wild New Year's Eve party. Playing poker in an empty hotel lobby. Singing "Eternal Flame" in the middle of the food court at two in the morning.

Then I think about what my day would have been like if

I hadn't met Xander. If I hadn't crashed into him because I'm incapable of using a moving walkway like a normal person. If we hadn't had the same stupid phone case. If I hadn't said *yes* . . .

I can imagine long hours of staring at my phone and avoiding people and obsessing over the heart wrenching agony that my soul is preparing to endure today.

Yes, today is still today.

But somehow it's not as scary.

Maybe that's because yesterday was hands down one of the craziest, scariest, darkest days I've ever had.

But it was also the most times I've smiled in over a year.

The thought makes me smile now.

Stuffing my phone and my wallet into the pocket of my hoodie, I leave the rest of my stuff with Xander and set off to find something to eat. The food court is already hopping with people looking to get an early start.

An early start at what? I'm not sure.

I get in line at the Caribou Coffee and stare hungrily at the pastries in the display case. When I reach the front, I order two large lattes, one nonfat, and two butter croissants.

"Names?" the girl cashier prompts robotically.

"Uh . . . ," I begin, about to give my real name. Then, I smile and say, "Reginald and Vegina."

She blinks in disbelief and studies me to check if I'm being serious. I turn my face to stone. We square off like that for what feels like an eternity before she finally grabs the two cups and scribbles on them with a black marker.

I tilt my head to see what she's written and am actually pretty surprised that she managed to spell Vegina right.

Then again, I made the name up, so what the hell do I know about how it's spelled?

With the bag of croissants tucked under one arm and a latte in either hand, I head back to gate A22. The route I took to get here is starting to fill with people, so I opt to take the long way around the shopping rotunda.

When I pass by the Tattered Cover bookstore, I spot Xander's parents' book on the front display again. Curiously, I head over to it.

Setting the two lattes down on a nearby stack of books, I pick up the hardcover and turn it around. There's Xander with his parents, dressed in his preppy attire, smiling for the camera. His dark hair is cut way shorter than it is now.

He looks like an entirely different person from the boy I spent the last eighteen hours with.

I think back to all the things he told me during our poker game last night.

His girlfriend breaking up with him. His downward spiral leading to an expulsion from school. How hard it is to live with parents who devote their entire life to *other* people's kids while ignoring their own.

And I suddenly realize that no one was there for him, either.

Even though he had the world's most well equipped parents to deal with hardship, he still faced his alone.

Just like me.

I pull my phone out of my back pocket and google Dr.

Max and Dr. Marcia. I find the same news article that was posted late last night and read it more thoroughly.

> Xander Hale, only son of renowned child psychologists and bestselling authors Dr. Max Hale and Dr. Marcia Livingston-Hale, has reportedly been expelled from the Archer Academy, an esteemed preparatory school in Malibu, California, known in the city for educating numerous children of celebrities and important media figures. The information comes from an anonymous source close to the Hale family, although the reasons for his expulsion are still undetermined.

An anonymous source . . .

I return the phone to my pocket and the book to the table, grab my lattes, and head to the back of the store. I find the title I'm looking for easily and take it to the register to pay. The sales clerk puts it in a green Tattered Cover bag that I tuck under my other arm.

Precariously balancing now *two* bags and two lattes, I make my way back to gate A22.

Xander is still asleep. He stirs when I approach and opens his eyes. I hand him the latte.

"Wow, what service." He smiles up at me and gratefully takes a sip. "Do you need a job? Because I could really use you around the house."

I kick my foot out and jab at his shin. He smirks at me and takes another sip.

"I also got you this," I proffer the pastry bag.

He looks inside and grins. "*Two* croissants! How did you know?"

"Nice try. One's for me."

"Okay, that makes more sense." He pulls one out and takes a large, flaky bite, ignoring the maddening amount of crumbs that stick to his lips.

I bend over and brush them off.

"Thanks," he mumbles with his mouth full, managing to spray even more crumbs down his shirt.

I give up and shake my head. He takes another bite of croissant. I'm about to sit down next to him when he spots the second bag in my hand. "Wha tha?" he garbles.

"Oh," I say, shifting my weight awkwardly. "I don't know. I saw it in the bookstore and thought maybe it would help."

He looks intrigued. "Well, what is it?"

I push the bag into his hands before I can second-guess myself.

Smiling and wiping his fingertips on his jeans, he reaches eagerly inside and pulls out the book I selected. The cover is different from the edition I read in school last year. It features a hand-drawn illustration of a guillotine set up in front of an eighteenth-century building and a man about to lose his head. Across the top, printed in an old-fashioned red script, is the title.

A Tale of Two Cities

Looking confused, he turns it over in his hands a few times, as if he doesn't understand what it is.

"You said last night that your English teacher offered you an out," I explain, feeling my stomach clench the longer he remains quiet. "You know, if you read the book and wrote the paper."

"Yeah," he says with an unsettling edge to his voice, "but I never actually said I wanted to take it."

His response surprises me. "I don't understand. Why *wouldn't* you take it? Why wouldn't you want to fix this?"

But he doesn't answer. He just tosses the book aside and takes another bite of his croissant.

"Wait," I say with sudden realization. "Do you actually *want* to be expelled?"

The pieces are falling into place so fast, I barely have time to process them all. And his continued silence is only confirming the full picture that's rapidly forming in my mind.

"It was you, wasn't it?" I accuse. "You sent the anonymous tip to the press. You wanted the news to get out. You wanted your parents to be exposed for the frauds that you think they are."

Something in Xander's expression—in his whole body— hardens. "I *never* come first," he says tensely.

I pull out my phone and turn it around so he can see the article that's still on the screen. "Their book sales are going to be affected. Their credibility might be ruined. Do you really think that's the best way to deal with this? By making a mess of their career? By ruining their reputation?"

"No offense," he says with a humorless laugh, "but I don't think you can lecture me about the best way of dealing with things."

My eyes narrow. "What is that supposed to mean?"

"I think you know what it means," he replies dryly.

I stare down at the abandoned book on the ground. The solution to his problem. Cast aside. The thought makes me angry. And bold.

"Do you realize how immature you're being?" I point to the book. "You have an out! And you won't even take it! All to spite your parents?"

I watch his expression shift from tense to defensive. "It's really none of your business."

He's right. It's not my business, and yet my frustration is still piloting me. "Do you know what I would give to be able to reverse what happened to me? Anything! *Everything!* But I can't. I will never be able to undo Lottie's death. And here you are with the solution to your problem on a silver platter, and you're *choosing* to ignore it."

"I told you," he snaps. "It's not just about the book."

"No, it's about your parents. And how you refuse to talk to them, so instead you're using your expulsion to get back at them. Like a coward."

That last part does it. Xander jumps to his feet and stares at me, his breathing ragged, his face flushed. "You're calling *me* a coward? You won't even read a stupid text message."

My breath catches in my throat. I glance down at my phone still clutched in my hand, still on. I press the home button, my gaze immediately zeroing in on the messaging app. On the little red circle that's hovered above it for the past year.

One unread message.

"It's not the same thing," I say, my voice low, livid.

"It's a text message!" Xander cries. "That's all it is. It's not a bomb. It's not a loaded gun. It's just a text message."

And then, before I can react, he's reaching out, ripping the phone right out of my hand.

"Give that back," I warn, taking a step toward him. But he takes a step away.

"What are you so afraid of? What it says? Or what it doesn't say?"

"You don't understand," I fire back, my voice dangerously close to cracking. "You'll never be able to understand. Your life—your problems—is a cakewalk compared to mine."

"Just read the message, Ryn. Stop avoiding your feelings and read the damn message! Look, it's easy." His finger plunges toward the screen, and it may as well be a knife plunging into my heart.

"Nooooooo!" I scream, causing a few sleeping passengers around us to stir.

But it's too late.

He's done it. He's clicked it. He's reading it. It's read. It will never be unread again.

After a few moments of stunned silence, I lunge for the device in his hands. He's so startled by my sudden attack, he takes a step back. "I'm sorry," he says quickly, as though coming out of a trance. "I'm so sorry. I don't know what—"

My hand brushes against the surface of the phone as I attempt to tear it from his grasp, but I don't have a firm grip, and it drops to the floor. The case pops off and clatters to the side.

I dive for the phone and pick it up, staring at the screen.

My eyes scour the list of messages, my heart pounding harder with each name that I read.

Mom

Dad

Xander

Cheap-O Airlines

Where's Lottie's name? Where's Lottie's message?

All the while, Xander keeps repeating his pitiful apology over and over. "I'm sorry. I'm so sorry."

But I can barely hear him. My breathing grows shallow. I start to hyperventilate. My heart is racing now. My throat stings. My eyes burn.

"You deleted it," I croak.

"No, I didn't." Xander leans toward me, his brows pinched in concern. "I just read it. I swear I didn't . . ."

"It gone!" I cry. "You deleted it!"

"It must have gotten deleted when you reached for it. Ryn, I swear I wouldn't—"

"It was all I had left of her and now it's gone forever!"

I don't even feel the tears in my eyes until they're rolling down my cheeks like thick, black ink.

I don't even realize I'm crying for the first time in nearly a year, until I'm sobbing.

"There must be a way to get it back." Xander tries to take a step toward me, but I jump away.

"Don't come near me. Don't ever come near me again." The fat tears swallow my words. The sobs shudder my body. If only

Dr. Judy could see me now. Would she be proud? Or would she be sorely disappointed?

Something tells me it's the latter.

"Ryn," he says, his voice barely audible. "I'm really sorry. I—"

"Are you happy now?!" I bellow, waking up every single passenger in this airport. "She's gone forever. And it's all your fault!"

Xander shakes his head, his vibrant blue eyes clouded by something. Moisture? Regret? Pity? "Ryn. It's no one's fault. She—"

"Shut up!" I cry. The tears are coming faster now. A year's worth of anguish streaming down my face. "Now I'll never know what she said to me. I'll never know."

I slide down the wall, collapsing around the phone, cradling it to my chest. I'm weeping and blubbering like a child as I repeat the words over and over. "I'll never know. I'll never know."

Xander kneels in front of me, careful to keep his distance. His face mirrors my pain.

"Ryn," he tries. "I—"

"Just go," I tell him. "Just leave me alone."

He shakes his head. "I can't do that. I'm not going to leave you. Not like this."

I swat at my damp cheeks, trying in vain to brush away the tears, but they're coming faster than I can keep up. "Fine," I huff, scrambling back to my feet. I grab my backpack and toss one strap over my shoulder. "Then I'll go."

The Comfort of Strangers

The A terminal is already awake. People are milling around in search of food and information about the storm.

I run back to the shopping rotunda and up the escalator to the small deserted balcony I found yesterday, but it's completely overrun.

So I keep going.

I cross the bridge over the snowed-in runway, bypassing every moving walkway I encounter. That was how I got into this mess. By taking mechanical sidewalks. By cheating. By trying to move faster than one is supposed to move.

That's how I crashed into Xander and this whole nightmare began.

Along the way, through my haze of snot and tears, I search my phone. I search the whole damn Internet for a solution.

How do you recover a deleted text message?

The answer is, you can't. Not with messages that old.

They're gone forever.

Just like Lottie.

Just like her last words to me.

The interfaith chapel in the concourse building is empty and dark when I burst in. I collapse into a seat in the back row and sob. I haven't cried this hard since I was ten years old and I broke my wrist when Lottie decided she wanted to teach me how to Rollerblade but forgot to teach me how to stop.

The chapel is small but homey. Three rows of upholstered chairs face the front of the room. Books of various faiths are spread out across a single nondenominational altar.

I'm grateful to find a place where I can finally be alone.

I bow my head and weep into my hands, thinking about everything I've lost in the past year. Everything I've lost in the past twenty-four hours. I think about every piece of evidence I've collected that proves life isn't fair. That bad things happen to good people. That the world is a storm that will do anything to suck you in.

Surround you.

Suffocate you.

Until you can't even remember what calm feels like.

Until chaos feels normal.

"Are you okay?" a female voice asks, startling me out of my thoughts and tears.

I could have sworn I was alone in here, but when I lift my head, I see someone—a woman—sitting in the front row. Her back is to me but she looks years older than me. She must have come in while I was crying.

I try to get a look at her face, but her entire body is cast in a strange, eerie shadow. I can't figure out what light source is causing it though. This is a windowless room.

I sniffle and rub my finger under my nose. "Sorry. I didn't know anyone was in here."

The figure remains motionless, facing forward, but she repeats the question. "Are you okay?" Her voice is soft yet strangely familiar. An echo of something so close I can touch it. It wraps a blanket of warmth around me.

I consider lying. Why would I tell a perfect stranger the truth when I've barely admitted it to myself?

Then it hits me that I've already done that.

I've already told Xander things that I haven't told anyone.

"My best friend died," I say woodenly, and I'm awed by how freeing it feels to say that aloud again. "One year ago today. And no, I'm not okay."

When the woman doesn't respond, or even turn around, I keep going. Because it feels good. Because it feels right.

Because it's time.

"And I thought I could hang on to her forever. I thought if I could just keep one tiny piece of her alive, then everything would be fine. She would never really be gone. But now that piece is gone too, and I feel so alone. I feel more alone right now than the day she died. I thought if I could just control the rest of the world, then this one uncontrollable part of it wouldn't matter. Or it wouldn't hurt. But it turns out, I was wrong. Because it hurts like hell."

The tempest of tears is back, dripping down my cheeks like melted snow on a window.

I wait for the silhouetted woman to react the way everyone reacts. With shock. With sorrow. With vows of empty sympathy.

But she doesn't. Instead, in a calm, even tone, she says, "I lost someone too. A long time ago. Someone really close to me. Someone who protected me. Who looked out for me even more than I looked out for myself."

Something about her words hits me deep in my core. Rattles around in my brain. Drifts over my skin, leaving behind a wake of tiny goose bumps.

"Do you miss them?" I ask, my throat thick with fire.

"Every single day."

"Does that ever go away?"

She lets out a sigh. "No."

I suddenly have this vivid memory of sitting in Lottie's tree house the morning after my birthday party, drawing the landscape I saw outside the window. Exactly as I saw it. Exactly as it *was*.

"*You're lucky,*" Lottie said, sitting next to me and staring out that same window. "*That the world looks real to you.*"

But it doesn't anymore. It doesn't look real. It doesn't feel real. It feels like a giant cosmic joke, and I'm the punch line.

"The world just looks messier without her," I whisper so softly, I don't even think it's audible. I'm not even completely sure I said it aloud.

But I must have. Because a few seconds later, the woman

responds. "Grief changes the way you see things forever. Because it changes *you* forever."

More tears well up in my eyes. Will they ever stop now that they've started? I bury my head in my lap and cry for the loss of my friend. For the loss of my real world. For the loss of everything I thought I could hold on to.

"But I think that's okay," the woman says. "Don't you?"

"I don't know," I reply in a shattered voice. "I don't know if I know anything anymore."

"You probably know more than you think you do," she offers kindly.

I lift my head and wipe at my cheeks. "I know that this has been the worst year of my life."

"But the New Year is only a few hours old," she reminds me. "Maybe it will be better."

"Maybe," I admit.

We sit in silence for a long time, listening to the melody of the canned sound track piping in over the speaker system. Some generic meditation music. It doesn't make me feel better, but it doesn't agitate me either. It just is.

"Well," the woman says with a note of finality. "I should probably go. My flight is leaving soon."

She stands, and I crane my neck to try to get a look at her face, but the strange shadow seems to follow her through the chapel.

Where is it coming from?

Then, just as she opens the door, just before she steps through, a sliver of sunlight breaks through the darkness. Cuts through the storm like an omen of things to come. A sign that everything gets better. That tempests don't last forever. It casts a single beam of light across the woman's back and left shoulder, illuminating the familiar dark blue fabric of a flight attendant uniform.

And a single lock of shimmering, golden red hair.

She pauses in front of the doorway, keeping her back to me as she says, "Wanna hear something crazy?"

A shiver travels through my entire body. My heart pounds in my ears. My fingers twitch restlessly. My legs ache.

"Always," I whisper aloud.

I can hear my voice reverberating back at me a million times. An echo in eternity. My entire life—our entire friendship— mirrored in that one single word.

Always.

"It's almost 10:05 a.m.," the woman says. And then she turns to leave.

"Wait!" I call out. Because I don't want her to go. Because she feels like so much more than a stranger. She feels like someone I might have known. Maybe someone I will *always* know.

She stops in the doorway. One foot in and one foot out. A piece of her gone and a piece of her still here.

"This is the last time we'll ever talk, isn't it?" I ask.

There's silence on the other side of the room, and for a minute I think she's not going to answer. That she's just going to leave. I close my eyes and squeeze them tight, steeling myself against the inevitable.

Then, in the faintest of whispers, she says, "Yes, it is."

Moisture forms behind my closed eyelids. But it's a different kind of crying now. There are no choked sobs. No desperate need to breathe. No agony.

It's just quiet sadness.

Sadness that I'll carry around for the rest of my life.

Sadness that I'll eventually learn to live with.

Sadness that will become a part of me. Shape me. Make me stronger.

Because if I can live through this, I can live through anything.

"But that's okay?" I ask.

There's a smile in her voice as she replies. "I think that's okay."

When I open my eyes, the woman is gone, and I'm alone again. I reach for my phone and watch the clock tick over to 10:05 a.m.

∞

For the past year I have been standing still. Too afraid to move forward. Too afraid it would mean leaving my best friend behind.

There is still so much that I fear.

Living another day without her.

Going home and forcing my mother to talk to me like a real person.

Walking into Dr. Judy's office and finally telling her the whole truth.

Basically, everything that comes after this moment.

But I get up. I move. I walk to the door of the chapel. I open it. I step through to the other side.

Because the truth is, I've already left Lottie behind. Everything I've done in the past year, I've done without her. Everything I've done in the past twenty-one *hours*, I've done on my own.

I've always been Lottie's best friend. Lottie's sidekick. Lottie's (reluctant) partner in crime. Squishy, undercooked peas to Lottie's scrumptious, perfectly crisp carrots.

That's been my identity since the day we met.

But what's my identity now? It's a question that's been banging on the door of my subconscious for an entire year. And yet I still can't answer it.

Or perhaps I've just been too terrified to answer it.

Terrified that an answer might actually exist. That the answer might actually make sense. That I might actually *be* someone without her.

I know where to go now. I know what I need to do. And that gives me the strength to move faster. That gives me the courage to run.

I pass Xander along the way. He's coming from the walkway to the A terminal. He's clearly been looking for me.

"Ryn," he tries to say as I sail past. "I'm sorry about—"

"No!" I shout over my shoulder. "No more apologizing. From either of us."

I can hear his footsteps behind me. "What are you doing?" he calls out.

I don't answer. I don't stop. I turn left and head straight for door 612. I barely pause long enough for it to sense my presence and open.

I run through it.

Into the quiet, empty street.

Into the beautiful white chaos.

Into the storm.

The fierce wind whips against my face. The violent snow stings my eyes until the world fades and all I can see is white.

Contrary to what some people think, white isn't the absence of color. It's all colors. It's all things. It's every possibility blended into one blinding light.

I may have stood still for too long. I may have refused to move forward and grieve the death of my best friend. But Lottie wasn't perfect either. She moved too fast. She was always racing to the next thing, trying to be the next person, reinventing herself over and over again.

All this time, I thought it was because she was so full of life, she simply couldn't contain it into one existence. All this time, I thought it was because she was fearless.

That's what she wanted me to believe.

That's what I *did* believe for far too long.

But it was an illusion.

Lottie wasn't fearless. She wasn't running to the next thing. She was running *from* the things that hurt her. The things that frightened her. She moved on so she wouldn't have to face the demons that chased her.

And through it all, I was right there beside her. She needed me just as much as I needed her. I was the planet to her sun. I lit up because I was near her. I spent so many years trying to catch a fragment of her light that I failed to realize I could shine on my own.

And Lottie. She needed someone to orbit around her.

In the end, we both lost. And we both won.

Xander is suddenly behind me. I turn around and grab his shirt and pull him to me. I keep pulling and pulling until I can feel him everywhere.

"Are you crazy?" he yells, wrapping his arms around my waist.

I release a wild, uninhibited laugh. "Yes!" I scream, and then I press my lips to his.

∞

What if life is unpredictable?
What if people leave for no reason?
What if losing is just another part of living?
What if the universe can't be controlled?
What if chaos is good?
What if some questions can never be answered?
What if that's okay?

∞

I think that's okay.

The Clearing
of Things

Kissing Xander is like waking up. Not a blaring, intrusive alarm clock that rips you bitterly from sweet dreams or gratefully from restless nightmares. Not a bucket of ice-cold water thrown in your face. Not even a rough shake from your mother when you're running late for school.

Kissing Xander is like waking up the right way. The natural way.

With the sun.

With light.

It breaks through with slow determination. It eases you out of the darkness gradually. It rouses you with warmth, reminding you that the day is new, and living is good, and anything can happen.

I kiss him harder.

The snow swirls around us like a dance. He wraps his arms tighter around my waist and pulls me in closer, pressing his entire body against me, lifting me right off the ground.

When we break apart, we don't go far. Our lips hover inches

from each other, inhaling and exhaling the same air. The same oxygen. The same universe.

Xander presses his mouth to my cheek. "It's freezing out here," he says into my skin.

"I know."

He leans back to look at me. Really look at me. As though he's finally seeing me for the first time. As though I'm finally letting him. "You *are* fucking crazy."

I nod. "I am fucking crazy."

He laughs as he sets me back down on solid ground. "Should we go inside?" he asks, and I notice a shiver run through his body. Neither of us has jackets or coats. We're both dressed for warmer weather. We're both completely ill prepared for a snowstorm of this proportion.

Maybe that's the whole point.

I shake my head. "I'm not ready to go back inside."

Xander nods, as though he expected this to be my answer. "Okay, then. Wait here. I'll be right back."

He disappears into the building, and I'm alone. So utterly alone in the biggest, messiest blizzard Denver has seen in over a hundred years.

And yet, for the first time in as long as I can remember, I don't *feel* alone.

A billion unique snowflakes keep me company.

The wind whispers reassuringly in my ear.

The soft flurries beneath my feet will cushion me should I fall.

For the first time in as long as I can remember, I know that the universe, in its vast, unpredictable, chaotic wisdom, is watching out for me.

I tip my head back, open my mouth, and let the tiny soft flecks of frozen rain fall in. They taste like tears.

Xander returns a few minutes later. He's carrying one of the airport issued blankets. He smiles and pulls me close to him again. He wraps the blanket around us, cocooning our bodies inside.

Shielding us from the storm.

Shielding us from the cold.

Although, to be honest, I don't really feel it anymore.

∞

"It's called Survivor's guilt," Dr. Judy said to me four months ago. It was right after my mother got a phone call from my school principal to tell her I had spent two hours locked in a supply closet after seeing 10:05 a.m. on a clock.

"It's when someone perceives themselves to have done something wrong by surviving a traumatic event when others did not."

I stared down at my phone, refusing to answer. I knew what she was trying to do. She was trying to put a label on me. She was trying to locate me in one of those giant tomes she kept on her shelf and drop a bookmark at the right page.

Here lies Ryn.

She survived. Her best friend did not.

Case closed.

I didn't want her labels. I didn't want to fit into one of her little boxes. I didn't want to be just another sad case of [insert textbook psychological disorder here].

Because if I were that easy to define, then I would be that easy to fix.

And I didn't want to be fixed.

"You feel like maybe you shouldn't be happy?" Dr. Judy went on, continuing her quest for classification. "You feel like if you were to move on and enjoy your life, it might be a betrayal of Lottie?"

I stroked my phone case, trying to drown out the sound of her voice.

Dr. Judy tried a third time. "You feel like *she* should be the one alive. Not you."

I noticed there was no question mark at the end of that sentence. She wasn't asking me if this were how I felt. She wasn't trying to get me to confirm her expert opinion.

She was reading my mind. She was seeing it scrawled across my forehead. She was pegging me just as easily as Lottie had always pegged me. As easily as Siri had pegged me. As easily as Xander had pegged me.

Because, apparently, I'm not that hard to understand.

Apparently, I'm an open book.

I just couldn't read the pages.

Until now.

Until the guilt melts away with the snow.

∞

I don't know how long Xander and I stand there, warmed by our own heat, strengthened by the touch of each other's lips. But eventually, the snowplow arrives to clear the road, and we're chased back inside.

My cheeks and fingers and toes sting at the rush of heat that crashes into me the moment I cross the threshold. We watch from the window, in silent fascination, as the massive yellow truck drives back and forth over the white sea, clearing snow to the side in giant misshapen mountains, slowly turning the road back into a road.

Slowly turning the Denver airport back into the Denver airport.

Soon cars will drive here again.

Soon passengers will be dropped off.

Soon gates will open, flights will board, and planes will leap into the sky, taking people far, far away.

The snow is falling with less enthusiasm now. Dripping tentatively from the sky instead of heaving down in buckets.

When the job is done and the snowplow moves on, Xander and I step away from the window. We don't talk. We don't smile. We just hold hands and silently think the same thing at the same time.

Soon we'll have no more reason to stay here.

∞

"I'm sorry, entrance is restricted to paying club members only," the woman guarding the first-class lounge says to us as she eyes our messy state with a look of disapproval.

I pull the black and gold card from my pocket and slide it across the counter. "We're friends of Marcus Winslow," I say confidently. "He said it would be all right."

The woman scowls at the Million Mile VIP guest card that Marcus gave me as her shoulders slouch in surrender. "The bathrooms are to the left. And the Wi-Fi password is flydenver. All lowercase."

"Thanks!" I chirp, and grab Xander's hand, pulling him inside the plush, well appointed first-class lounge.

We disappear into our respective restrooms to freshen up. I eye the shower stall and in a split-second decision, start peeling off my clothes. I turn the knob to scalding hot, grab a towel from a nearby shelf, and step inside.

The water and steam feel amazing, washing away all the dust and grime and doubt of the past twenty-four hours. After drying my body and brushing out my hair, I put my clothes back on and leave the bathroom.

I find Xander by the buffet. His hair is wet too, causing me to smile. He's already made us cappuccinos from a fancy coffee machine and is now loading up two tiny plates with fruit and cheese and hard-boiled eggs. We find a seat by the window and stuff ourselves senseless. Once I've had my fill, I turn and stare outside, watching the snowplows work on the tarmac.

Back and forth they go, relentlessly pushing snow aside, clearing an open path.

Setting things right again.

"What did she look like?" I hear Xander ask, and it's only then

I realize he hasn't been sharing my fascination with the snow-plows. He's been watching me instead.

"Who?" I ask, even though I already know. We both do.

But he says it anyway. "Lottie."

I turn back to the window, falling quiet. I've never talked about what Lottie looked like. Not even with Dr. Judy. Obviously, I have pictures on my phone, but I don't dare show them to anyone. I've barely been able to bring myself to look at them. It's almost as though all this time, I've been protecting her memory in my mind. Keeping her to myself. Convinced that no one would ever see her the way I saw her, so why bother trying?

"She . . . ," I begin hesitantly, keeping my eyes trained on one specific snowplow. It's been tasked with freeing the airplane that's currently held captive at gate A4. "She had this amazing red hair. It looked like gold set on fire. And she had this adorable freckle below her left eye that—"

I stop and close my eyes. I conjure up the memory of her face, holding it tight in my mind. Trying to remember exactly where that freckle was. Down to the millimeter.

"I'm sorry," Xander rushes to say. "I shouldn't have asked that."

"No," I tell him. "It's okay. I just . . ." I bite my lip.

How do you explain to someone how important a freckle is?

How do you make them see that it was never just a freckle? That it was a piece of her? That it was a seemingly insignificant fragment that made up a beautiful whole?

You can't.

You don't.

The English language has over one million words in it, and none of them are good enough for Lottie. None of them will capture what I saw when I looked at her. What I see now when I remember her. How she will forever look through my filtered view of the world.

I stare down at my hands. They're empty but no longer shaking. They feel cold but no longer worthless.

They're ready.

I launch out of my seat and run to the bar at the far side of the lounge. I find an abandoned receipt and a pen and dash back over to the table.

I don't say a word to Xander as I slip into my chair and turn over the receipt. I grip the pen tightly in my fingers and start moving it across the page.

But this isn't drawing. At least not like any drawing I've ever done before. This is an outpouring. This is a release. These are all the lines and all the shadows and all the shapes that have been trapped inside me for almost a year. That have been following me around wherever I go. Waiting to be made real.

This is like something moving through me, piloting my hand, emptying my mind until everything around me disappears. The room. The snow. The people.

Even Xander.

This is trying to catch water from a pitcher in a thimble.

This is a year's worth of demons channeled into a fragile piece of paper.

This is me finally breathing life back into Lottie.

When I'm finished, I lean back and look at my creation for the first time. A small gasp escapes my lips.

The left eye is bigger than the right.

The freckle is smeared.

Her chin is too wide.

Her cheeks are too sallow.

Her hair is too flat.

Her smile is crooked.

But it's her. Not perfect. Yet still radiant.

I turn the receipt around so Xander can see. He studies me with fascination for a long time before finally dropping his gaze to my drawing. Then he sucks in a sharp breath.

"Wow," he says, running his fingertip over her face. "She's beautiful."

"Yes," I say quietly. "She was."

And I feel lucky.

That the world finally looks real to me.

A Tale of Two Other Cities

Thirty minutes later, after we've finished another plate of food and another round of free cappuccinos, a news report comes on a nearby TV screen, announcing that the storm is lifting and the first flights out of Denver are scheduled to depart in less than two hours.

I look over at Xander. He's watching the television with pinched eyebrows. Something tells me that he would happily stay in this airport for another week, if he could.

"What are you going to do?" I ask.

He blinks and focuses on me. "I guess I'm going to Miami to talk to my parents. And then I'm going home to L.A. to figure out what comes next."

"What are you going to tell them?"

He sighs wearily. "I'm going to tell them the truth. That it was me who leaked the story of my expulsion to the press. And then I'm going to deal with the aftermath."

I know, as soon as he says it, that it's what I have to do too. I have to tell my mother the truth. That the contraband in Lottie's tree house wasn't mine. That I wasn't in the car with Lottie that day. That the reason no one came to my eighteenth birthday party was because I didn't invite anyone.

And so many other truths that I haven't been able to admit until now.

I have to open that door.

I have to let her in.

I reach out and rub Xander's arm. "Maybe it will be okay."

He cups my cheek and kisses me gently on the lips. "Maybe it will."

∞

When we emerge from the lounge an hour later, the snow has stopped.

Just like that.

Outside the sun is shining, chasing away gray skies, making room for blue.

Everything is white and clean and beautiful.

"Are you ready?" Xander asks, slipping his fingers into mine.

I squeeze his hand and nod. "Yes."

Together, we walk over to the bank of information screens. They're all blank. Dark. Like someone has cut the power.

We look to each other in confusion. Then we wait.

Less than a minute later the monitors blink to life and slowly start to fill. The data repopulates with new flights. New departure times. New gate assignments.

There are no more cancelations. No more delays.

Just leaving.

I feel my phone vibrate in my pocket. I drop Xander's hand and pull it out, swiping on the screen. A new text message has come through. It's from the airline.

I've been given a seat on the next flight to San Francisco. It leaves in an hour.

I check the board for confirmation. There it is. Cheap-O Airlines flight 319 to San Francisco. Gate A28. Departing at 1:32 p.m.

I glance over at Xander and see that he's looking at his phone too.

"What time do you leave?" I ask.

"In an hour," he says, his voice muted and colorless.

"Me too."

"How long is the flight to San Francisco?" he asks.

"Two hours. Miami?"

"A little over three." He pauses, reaches into his messenger bag, and pulls out the copy of *A Tale of Two Cities* that I bought him. "I thought maybe I'd read a book to pass the time. This one is supposed to be good."

"It's very good."

"So which two cities are we talking about here?"

I giggle. "Paris and London."

"Oh." Disappointment flashes over his face. "That's too bad. I really have no interest in those two cities. I'm much more interested in two *other* cities."

"And which cities are those?"

He grins. "Los Angeles and San Francisco."

I nod, playing along, hiding my smile. "Those are two good cities."

"They're not that far apart either."

"No, they're not."

"Less than an hour flight," he adds.

My smile finally breaks free. "I know."

He cocks an eyebrow. "How do you know?"

I shrug. "I may have already asked Google."

∞

Xander and I walk to his gate in silence. A19. Mine is just a short ways down the terminal. We pass gate A5, where Troy Benson sits with a new sign hanging around his neck that says, UNACCOMPANIED MINOR. At least it's spelled correctly this time.

I give him a wave, and he gives me a small salute in response. I wonder if he'll ever come to a finite conclusion about the Denver airport conspiracy. I wonder if anyone will. Probably not. I suppose some theories aren't meant to be proved or disproved.

We pass gate A9, where the kissing couple from the train are sitting, waiting to board their flight. Her head is resting against his shoulder and his hand is on her leg. They look peaceful. I wonder how long that will last. I glance at the screen hanging above the gate. Their destination is Honolulu—a seven hour flight from here.

That doesn't give me a lot of hope.

At gate A11, Siri leaps out at us, scaring the crap out of me.

She pulls me into a long hug. "Mopey Girl! I'm going to miss you so much."

I scowl at the unwelcome nickname. She laughs and musses my still-damp hair. "Relax. It's just a name. It doesn't mean anything. Besides, I already lost at bingo."

"What? Did Jimmy find a Couple on the Verge of a Breakup?" I ask, thinking back to the two people waiting to board their flight to Hawaii.

"No," Jimmy says, appearing next to me, seemingly out of nowhere. His voice shifts to mimic a boisterous sports announcer. "In a dramatic, last-minute, at-the-buzzer upset, I snagged the bottom left corner to complete a momentous diagonal-across victory."

"What was the space?" I ask, glancing between Siri and Jimmy.

Siri rolls her eyes. "When I wrote it on his card, I never, in a million years, thought he would actually find it."

"What was it?" Xander urges.

Jimmy nudges Siri, "Go ahead. Tell them, Lover Girl."

Siri sighs, looking embarrassed. "Someone Making Out with an Inanimate Object."

I think about Siri kissing that blow-up doll at the party and let out a gasp. "That was you!"

She huffs. "Yeah, yeah, I know. It wasn't my finest moment."

Jimmy circles his arms around in an obnoxious victory dance. "Have fun with those ketchup dispensers," he gloats before literally moonwalking away.

Xander and I share a laugh while Siri visibly stews in her defeat.

"Ah, c'mon," I tease. "Don't mope. It's very unbecoming."

Siri scowls, clearly about to tell me off, but just then Marcus approaches from behind her and puts an arm around her shoulder. "Are you ready to go?"

I cock a curious eyebrow in her direction. "And where are you two off to?"

Siri's scowl instantly vanishes. "He's taking me to Greece! First class! How can I say no?"

I smile. "I guess you can't."

She flashes me a wicked grin. "Give me your phone."

"Why?" I ask suspiciously.

She rolls her eyes. "Just give it to me."

I pull my phone out of my backpack and hand it over. Siri unlocks the screen, taps her number into my contacts, and then gives the phone back. "In case you ever have another layover in Denver."

I laugh and give her another hug. "Thanks."

Xander and I keep walking. As we make our way through the terminal, I read the names of all the destinations posted above each gate.

Detroit. Seattle. Chicago. Vancouver. Des Moines. Dallas. Raleigh. Boston.

So many connections between here and there.

So many tales of so many cities.

Until finally we reach Miami.

Gate A19.

Xander's gate.

"Do you realize, this is where we met?" he muses.

I glance around, seeing the familiar moving walkway just behind us. He's right. This is the very spot where I face-planted. It seems like weeks ago. Not a mere twenty-four hours. "You mean, this is where I crashed into you while you were just minding your own business."

"Hey," he says, his tone turning serious. "You can crash into me anytime."

We stand and look at each other for a long moment. Neither of us wants to say it. I'm not sure I even can.

I can't say good-bye to another person today.

"I . . ." I falter.

Xander dives for my lips, stealing my words away with another one of his debilitating kisses. I know I don't have a ton of experience with stuff like this, but damn, the boy is good. I wonder if they teach this in that fancy prep school of his.

I wonder if he'll get back in.

I hope so.

When he reluctantly pulls away, I'm left breathless.

"I . . . ," I try for a second time, but again words fail me.

"Close your eyes," he says. "Give me your hand."

I giggle at the echo of his "Eternal Flame" serenade in the food court, but I do as I'm told. I close my eyes. I reach my hand out for his. He takes it and places it against his chest.

"Do you feel my heart beating?" he asks, and I hear the playful smile in his voice.

I nod. Because I can. Just inches beneath Animal's wild, crazy eyes, Xander's heart is pounding just as wildly. "I understand," I say. "I feel the same."

Then he kisses me again. This time it's light and tender and full of promise. Not even a trace of good-bye.

Yet, it still makes my limbs feel useless.

It isn't until his lips have left mine that I notice he's placed something between my palm and his chest. I withdraw my hand to find a piece of paper, folded several times into a tiny square.

On the front, in red pen, someone has handwritten the number 1 with a circle around it.

One unread message.

"I'm pretty sure I remembered it all," he says quietly. "But you don't have to read it until you're ready. Even if that means you never read it. I just . . ." He hesitates, looking visibly pained as he casts his gaze to the floor. "I just feel better knowing that you have it."

I stare numbly at the note in my hand. Lottie's last words to me. He remembered them. He wrote them down.

He gave them back to me.

Tears spring to my eyes again and start falling down my cheeks. Xander brushes them away with his thumb and smiles, flashing those perfect white teeth. "Good-bye, Vegina Starbucks."

I laugh, which makes me cry harder. "Good-bye, Reginald Schwarzenegger."

Somehow the fake names make it feel a little less real. And a little easier to say.

Nearby, the gate agent announces the final boarding call for

Xander's flight to Miami. He takes a deep, courageous breath. "Well, I guess I can't put this off any longer. Time to face the music."

"It'll be okay," I tell him.

He nods and rakes his teeth over his bottom lip. "Yeah."

He gives me one last kiss. This time, on my cheek. "It's been fun," he whispers into my ear.

"It's been crazy," I whisper back.

His soft lips linger close to my skin, sending shivers over my entire body. "Crazy is good."

He pulls away with a heavy sigh and gets in line to board the plane, keeping his back turned to the door so he can watch me leave.

I inhale a courageous breath of my own and step onto the moving walkway. It will take me to the gate that will take me to the plane that will finally take me Home.

Ironically, it's the same walkway that took me to Xander.

Only in reverse.

I keep my eyes on Muppet Guy until the very last possible moment. Until I can't see him anymore. Until he disappears down the Jetway and the walkway carries me on.

Then I turn around and face everything in front of me.

Epilogue

I hear the distinct scraping sound of the wheels leaving the earth as my plane rises steadily into the air, putting more and more distance between me and my past with each ticking second.

I stare out the window of seat 18A and watch the ground grow smaller beneath me. It looks so peaceful from way up here. So white and sparkling and clean. No footsteps. No tire tracks. No history.

A wonderland.

Completely untouched.

Completely untainted.

Entirely renewed.

I remove the note from my pocket and lay it flat in my open palm. I run my fingertip across the red number 1 written on the front.

One unread message.

But not for long.

With my heart in my throat and my hands shaking, I carefully unfold the paper. Xander's handwriting is rushed and messy, desperately trying to get it all down before his memory fails him.

The message isn't long. A few lines. But I know I will read it countless times. I know I will devour it over and over until the paper crumbles and the ink fades and the words are ingrained in my mind forever. A permanent part of me.

An eternal flame.

But for now, the first sentence is all I need.

Wanna hear something crazy?

The plane shudders as it collides with an unstable current of air. But it keeps the same course. The same path. Ascending relentlessly into the unpredictable atmosphere.

I close my eyes.

I clutch the piece of paper to my chest.

And I whisper into the sky, "Always."

Acknowledgments

It takes a writer to write a story, but it takes a village to turn that story into a book. Thank you to Nicole Ellul—editor, sounding board, Springsteen fan, and the most incredible cheerleader an author can ask for. Seriously, if this book were a football team, we would be undefeated. And to my amazing family at Simon & Schuster and Simon Pulse who work so tirelessly and passionately every day to keep the world reading—Chelsea Morgan, Faye Bi, Jodie Hockensmith, Carolyn Swerdloff, Catherine Hayden, Mara Anastas, Steve Scott, Bara MacNeill, Russell Gordon, Mary Marotta, Liesa Abrams, Jennifer Ung, Jessi Smith, Sarah McCabe, and Mary Nubla (my Instagram buddy). Also a huge, tremendous thanks to Jim McCarthy, my agent, for championing this book from the very beginning and for always knowing just the right thing to say. And to Dana Spector for being everyone's "favorite agent" in Hollywood (including mine).

Thank you to my brilliant friends—Joanne Rendell, Morgan Matson, Jessica Khoury, Marie Lu, and Jennifer Bosworth—who are always just a text or Skype call away whenever I need advice on plot, titles, audio books, life, or Covet Fashion.

Also a *huge* shout out to the fabulous Len Vlahos and Kristen Gilligan (aka Denver's new power couple) at the Tattered Cover, Cathy Berner at Blue Willow Bookshop, as well as all the booksellers, bookstores, teachers, and librarians who have placed my books in the hands of readers. You are the reason I have a job. Your unbridled enthusiasm for books and your boundless support of

Acknowledgments

authors will never go unnoticed or underappreciated. (Courtney Saldana, I'm winking at you right now.)

Also thanks to my remarkably supportive and encouraging parents, Michael and Laura Brody; my talented little sister, Terra Brody; and to my kind and generous aunt, Cathy Brody, M.F.T., for all of your brilliant therapy insight (into my character and me). And as always, to Charlie, for finding order in the chaos on a daily basis.

And no acknowledgements would ever be complete without an exuberant heartfelt thank you to my readers around the world. May you never stand still for too long. May you always live forward.

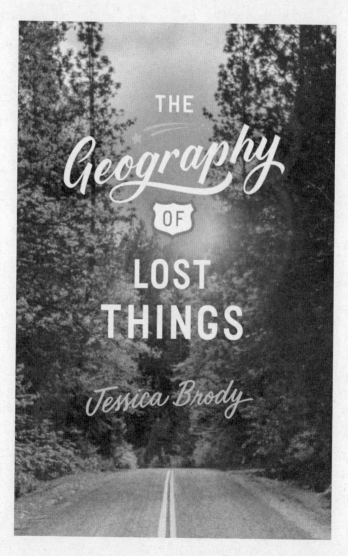

THE ENVELOPE

By the time the messenger arrived at our front door, Jackson had already been dead two weeks. I stared at the large yellow envelope in the man's hand, completely blank apart from my name, scrawled crookedly across the center. I recognized the familiar careless handwriting from years of sporadic birthday cards and notes scribbled on Post-its.

I'm sorry. I have to do this.

I almost closed the door in the messenger's face. I almost told him to go back to wherever he had come from. He was running a fool's errand.

Because I was so convinced there was nothing Jackson could have left me that would ever matter. That would ever erase what he did to me and my mom. Nothing that could possibly change my life. For better or for worse.

As it turned out, I was wrong.

THURSDAY

'Cause in this place,
this holy space,
solace waits
and love negotiates

—"Sleep," from the album
Anarchy in a Cup by Fear Epidemic
Written by Nolan Cook, Slate Miller,
Chris McCaden, and Adam French
Released April 17, 1998

4:05 P.M.

RUSSELLVILLE, CA

INVENTORY: (0)

I stand on the front porch, watching Mom shove her overnight bag into the cluttered back seat of Rosie's sedan. I suppose I could blame Rosie for getting Mom the job in the first place, but that would be petty and childish. We need the money. I know that. Mom knows that. Even Rosie knows that.

It's why Mom is disappearing to Sacramento for a week to serve fancy appetizers to even fancier people, leaving me to finish packing up the house by myself.

> **Graduation is coming up!**
> **How will *you* be spending Senior Week?**
> **A** *Hitting up every party in town.*
> **B** *On a beach in Mexico.*
> **C** *Trying to fit your entire life into a box.*

Not that I really have anything better to do.

Sure, there'll be parties. My best friend, June, already

told me she was having one tomorrow night. But it's definitely *not* what I had planned for the week between the last day of high school and graduation. Although, to be honest, I'm not sure what I had planned.

I just didn't expect *this*.

I didn't expect Mom to give up so easily.

I didn't expect to be the one still fighting.

Mom comes back to the porch to hug me good-bye. She takes in my crossed arms and the permanent scowl that hasn't left my face since she came home last week with what she called "the keys to our new life."

She really should have worked in advertising instead of food service.

"Don't worry," Mom says. "I'll be back in time for the moving truck."

"I could ask Pam for an advance on my paycheck," I tell her.

Still fighting.

Mom sighs. "We've been through this. You know it's not enough."

"Maybe if we sell the car—"

"Ali, give it up. It's over."

"But—" I try to argue.

"But we've been through all the *but*s. A thousand times. There are no more *but*s left."

"There has to be."

Mom brushes a strand of curly brown hair from my face. She's already getting blurry through the tears that are forming in my eyes. I hastily gather up my unruly hair and secure it with the rubber band I always keep around my wrist.

"I think you'll like living in Harvest Grove," Mom says. "They have a pool. And a gym. All the apartments come with new carpeting. No more of that ugly brown shag."

"I like the ugly brown shag."

Mom chuckles. "That's just because you've never seen *nice* carpet before. Plus, you'll have a great place to come home to when you visit me from UC Davis next year."

I swallow down the giant lump that has just formed in my throat.

> **You got a full scholarship to the college of your dreams! What do you do?**
>
> **A** *Start shopping for dorm room furniture.*
>
> **B** *Spend the entire summer obsessing over the course catalog.*
>
> **C** *Hide the letter in your backpack and "accidentally" forget to tell your mother you never accepted the offer.*

"Mom," I say, my voice cracking. "Don't do this. Don't let them take it. We have to fight."

"We've been fighting!" Mom's voice rises and then immediately falls again. "Ali. I'm done. Done fighting. Done trying to get out from under his mistakes. This gives us a fresh start. Please try to understand that I need one."

My gaze falls to the ground. Because I can't look at her when she says stuff like that. Because how do you argue with that? Because she's right.

I know she's right.

And yet, everything about this feels wrong.

"I'll see you in a week." Mom kisses me on the forehead before I can come up with any more useless protests. And then, she's gone. By the time I look up again, Rosie's car is already halfway down the driveway.

I turn and head into the house, navigating through the maze of cardboard boxes. I'm surprised there are so many. I didn't think we had that much stuff. Mom and I share a love of decluttering. We're always finding excuses to throw things away, or donate them to Goodwill.

But I guess everyone accumulates things. Even us.

I walk into the kitchen and put on a pot of coffee. As it brews, I head to the desk in the living room where Mom keeps all the paperwork for the house. Bills, bank statements, legal documents. All meticulously organized in hanging file folders in a drawer. I find the folder I'm looking for and flip it open to the first document inside. I skim over all the fake niceties. The "Dear Ms. Collins, we regret to inform you . . ." Like they're simply writing to tell us that the pillow shams we ordered are out of stock.

I scroll down to the bottom. To the giant black box surrounding the words TOTAL AMOUNT OVERDUE and the deadline FRIDAY, MAY 29.

A week from tomorrow.

I sigh and shut my eyes tight.

She's right. It's not enough. Even if we sold the car and the furniture and Pam was able to give me the biggest advance ever offered to an employee in the history of the pet boarding industry, it wouldn't be enough.

I glance around the living room. At the walls that won't be our walls. At the carpet that won't be our carpet. At the boxes that will be emptied somewhere else. Stuff stuffed into new cabinets. New drawers.

No, not stuffed.

Never stuffed.

Neatly stored. Meticulously organized. Maybe even labeled.

I'm sure most people would look at this house and laugh at my desperation. I know it doesn't look like much from the outside. Or the inside. The drywall has cracks in it. The paint is chipping. The bedrooms are tiny. The kitchen is tinier. The microwave hasn't worked in more than two years. The shower stall in the *one* bathroom that Mom and I share leaks.

But it's ours.

Mom's and mine.

No matter what has happened to us in the past eighteen years—no matter how many times he's let us down—this house has been there for us. A rock beneath the trembling ground. It's been our safe haven—our eye of so many storms. Russellville may be saturated with painful memories, but this house is where all the good ones live. The sights and sounds and smells. Mom singing in the bathroom as she gets ready for work. Rain pooling at the base of the front porch, causing us to have to jump off the last step. Pumpkin bread baking in the oven. Not only in the fall, but year-round, because Mom and I both love pumpkin.

Where does all of that go?

How can the bank possibly repossess things like that? How can they just suck it all up into their vaults and lock it away forever?

The coffeepot beeps, interrupting my thoughts. I shut the folder, slip it into place, and close the drawer. I head back into the kitchen and pull one of the two coffee mugs down from the cabinet. We've never kept a lot of stuff in the house. Just the essentials. Two of everything. Two plates, two sets of silverware, two glasses, two coffee mugs. By the end of next week, it will all be in boxes too.

As I pour the coffee, watching the stream of dark brown liquid fill the mug, I think about holes.

Big, gaping holes cut into the ground.

Holes so deep, you can't see the top once you're inside. And the ground keeps sinking beneath your feet. Like quicksand. Pulling you farther and farther down, until your hope of ever climbing out is gone.

And then, of course, I think about Jackson.

Smiling his disarming smile.

Murmuring his empty reassurances.

Holding a shovel.

Neither of us were all that shocked when we learned that Jackson had died. Mom and I both knew it was coming eventually. Jackson's lifestyle wasn't exactly the kind you'd describe as "sustainable." He had always lived by a code of impermanence. It's why we never had a current address for him. Never knew where he was or when or if he would call. Never knew what kind of condition he would be in when he did.

Mom and I didn't even know Jackson had been sick. Which, of course, was typical. He did everything without telling us or soliciting our opinion on the matter. Apparently, that also included dying.

For the next few hours, I blast the bubbliest music I can find on my phone, drink an obscene amount of coffee, and force myself to pack. I start with my bedroom, opening closet doors and dresser drawers and dumping as much as I can into trash bags. The fewer boxes we have to bring with us, the better.

It feels good to throw things away. Like I'm not only making room in the cabinets, but also making room in my head. Clearing space for better and brighter things. Pushing bad, stale memories out the door.

When the coffeepot is empty and the trash bags are full, I collapse onto the couch, take out my phone, and navigate to my favorite personality quiz website. I scroll through all of the new quizzes that have popped up since yesterday, quickly ruling out the ones for which I already know what result I'll get.

Which Star Wars Episode Best Describes Your Last Relationship?

Episode II: Attack of the Clones.

How Stubborn Are You?

Very.

What Do Your Summer Plans Say About Your Life?

That I have no life.

Finally, I find one that looks interesting—**Which Classic Novel Character Would You Most Likely Have as a BFF?**—and start answering the questions.

I've pretty much taken every personality quiz under the sun. I can tell you who I am in relation to every single television show, movie, book, and one-hit-wonder song. I know what my favorite doughnut flavor says about me (simple and non-fussy); what my dream vacation is (Rome); what Disney villain best represents my dark side (Ursula from *The Little Mermaid*); and what my best quality is based on what pizza toppings I like (selfless).

Personality quizzes have always felt comforting to me. They sum people up, distill the complexities of human beings down to a few digestible sentences.

Just as the quiz spits out my result—Jane Eyre—an alarm goes off on my phone, reminding me that I'm due at Chateau Marmutt, the pet hotel where I work, for my overnight shift in thirty minutes. I basically get paid to sleep in a room surrounded by dogs. It's not a bad gig.

I carry the full trash bags out to the bins at the end of the driveway and turn back to the house, bounding up the porch steps. But I freeze when I see the notice pinned to the door.

Another one?

How many of those things do they need to send us? We get it. You're serious about it. This is not a joke.

The deadline is stamped onto the page like a searing, red-hot brand.

Friday, May 29.

Pay, or else.

Or else . . .

Somehow Mom has come to terms with the "or else." She almost seems to have *chosen* it. But I just can't bring myself to choose that.

I can't bring myself to let them win. To let Jackson win. To let the world win.

June would say it's because I'm too competitive. It's the excuse she always gives when she's losing at a board game, which she almost always does.

And maybe I am. Maybe I can't admit defeat. But this feels like more than defeat. This isn't Monopoly. We're not just turning in all of our little green houses to the bank and forfeiting the game. This is real. A real house. A real family. Real memories steeped into the walls.

> **The bank is foreclosing on your house! How do you react?**
>
> **A** *Keep packing. Can't argue with the almighty bank.*
>
> **B** *Steal all the toilets and fixtures. They can have the walls, but they can't have the towel bars!*
>
> **C** *Refuse to accept the inevitable.*

I rip the notice from the door, crumple it up in my hands, and toss it onto the porch. I slam the front door closed behind me and stand with my back pressed against the wall, breathing hard. My eyes squeeze shut, so I don't have to see the boxes. The furniture. The walls. My nine-year-old self standing by the window, her face glued to the glass, wondering when he was coming back.

Back then, it was always *when*. It was never *if*.

The *if* came later.

"Please," I whisper to the quiet house, as though I'm trying to rally its support. As though I'm begging it to fight back too. Don't let yourself be taken. Stand your ground. Lock your doors. Turn your floors into hot lava. Whatever it takes. Haven't you loved us back? Haven't we been just as much a part of you as you have been of us? Do you really want strangers living in your walls?

I don't expect the house to respond. But somehow it does.

Because just then, there's a knock on the door.